PRAISE FOR *THE BANNED BOOKSHOP OF MAGGIE BANKS*

"A sparkling bookish story about rules just begging to be broken… I couldn't get enough!"

—Abby Jimenez, *New York Times* bestselling author of *Part of Your World* and *The Friend Zone*

"Shauna writes for the girls without dream jobs, the pandemic babies who moved back in with their parents and are just trying to figure it out, and the extroverts who find purpose in bringing people together. This novel is a booklover's dream, with subtle social commentary to boot."

—Iman Hariri-Kia, author of *A Hundred Other Girls*

"*The Banned Bookshop of Maggie Banks* is a charming rom-com about finding your own path and never being scared to break the rules. It's also an uplifting celebration of the power of books to change people's lives. Visit your favorite bookstore, curl up in a comfy chair, and savor every word!"

—Freya Sampson, author of *The Last Chance Library*

"Delightful and deeply felt, *The Banned Bookshop of Maggie Banks* is one woman's instantly compelling search for herself woven into a celebration of how stories enliven and inspire community. It's the perfect book for booklovers."

—Emily Wibberley and Austin Siegemund-Broka, authors of *The Roughest Draft*

"Consider me an official member of the Maggie army! I found myself rooting for every character in this warm, welcoming tale of a woman coming into her own. If you've ever found comfort in a book—or a bookstore—then you'll enjoy watching Maggie discover how powerful the right story in the right hands can be."

—Lucy Gilmore, author of *The Lonely Hearts Book Club*

PRAISE FOR *MUST LOVE BOOKS*

"*Must Love Books* is a heartfelt and exciting debut. With a relatable protagonist in Nora, frank discussions of the millennial experience, and pitch-perfect sweetness, Shauna Robinson puts forth a wise and honest story of how it feels to be a young woman in search of yourself."

—Taylor Jenkins Reid, *New York Times* bestselling author of *The Seven Husbands of Evelyn Hugo* and *Malibu Rising*

"A book for booklovers that takes a hard look at the predatory approach of the corporate world with a heroine who's easy to love and root for. I enjoyed all of the inside look at the publishing industry from the perspective of a young woman scraping together all of her wits just to get by. It's impossible not to root for Nora!"

—Jesse Q. Sutanto, bestselling author of *Dial A for Aunties*

"Honest, relatable, and real, *Must Love Books* is a tender reflection on finding your person while you're still desperately searching for yourself rolled up in a thoughtful novel about the changing work world."

—KJ Dell'Antonia, *New York Times* bestselling
author of *The Chicken Sisters*

"A compelling love story, dishy publishing goss, and a chic urban setting? Yes, yes, yes! But like the works she shepherds through publication, Shauna Robinson's true-to-life story of a struggling editorial assistant is much more than the sum of its parts. Within the pages of *Must Love Books*, the lucky reader will find themselves on an poignant journey of a young booklover with too little support and too many dreams—a place we've all been at one point or another. With emotional honesty and a surprising wit that I found addictive, Robinson's debut is everything a book-about-books fan wants in a novel."

—Kelly Harms, *Washington Post* bestselling
author of *The Overdue Life of Amy Byler*

"Readers will be rooting for Nora from the first page and experiencing her grand highs and heartbreaking lows with their entire heart. Get comfy because you won't be able to put this book down!"

—Sajni Patel, award-winning author
of *The Trouble with Hating You*

The Banned Bookshop of Maggie Banks

a novel

SHAUNA ROBINSON

sourcebooks
landmark

To my parents, who always made me feel like
I could go down any path I wanted

Published by Sourcebooks Landmark, an imprint of Sourcebooks
P.O. Box 4410, Naperville, Illinois 60567-4410
(630) 961-3900
sourcebooks.com

Library of Congress Cataloging-in-Publication Data

Names: Robinson, Shauna, author.
Title: The banned bookshop of Maggie Banks / Shauna Robinson.
Description: Naperville, Illinois : Sourcebooks Landmark, [2022]
Identifiers: LCCN 2022006661 (print) | LCCN 2022006662 (ebook) |
(trade paperback) | (epub)
Classification: LCC PS3618.O3337225 B36 2022 (print) | LCC PS3618.O3337225
(ebook) | DDC 892.8—dc23/eng/20220211
LC record available at https://lccn.loc.gov/2022006661
LC ebook record available at https://lccn.loc.gov/2022006662

Printed and bound in Canada.
MBP 10 9 8 7 6 5 4 3 2 1

CHAPTER ONE

It took three statues to plant doubt in my mind.

The first loomed in the middle of Bell Park as I walked past: a man with his chin held high, one hand on his hip. I didn't think much of it. I only wondered whether his mustache was really that long or if the sculptor just hadn't felt like adding a mouth.

I continued on, passing a sandwich shop, a vintage clothing boutique, and a craft store. The second statue appeared two blocks later, just outside Bell Elementary. A different pose—he had an arm outstretched, palm out, like I owed him money—but the curtain mustache was the same. My gaze fell to the plaque at his feet: *Edward Bell*. I made a mental note to ask Rochelle about it, then checked the map on my phone: five more blocks until Cobblestone Books.

I was crossing the street when I caught a flash of bronze to my right. And even though my mind was set on the bookstore, on air conditioning and freedom from this strange, damp humidity that does not exist in California, curiosity hounded me. I turned and quickened my steps along the uneven brick sidewalk. There, outside the Bell River Post Office, stood that same man with that same mustache hanging past his lips. Again, the plaque thought me more informed than I was, proclaiming *Edward Bell* and nothing more.

Staring up at Edward Bell, I started to wonder if Bell River was more cult than town. Maybe that was the real reason Rochelle invited me here—not because she needed help at her bookstore while she took maternity leave, not because I was unemployed and sick of living with my parents. It may all be a town ploy to get my blood for a sacrifice in the name of Edward Bell.

Only one way to find out. I turned and resumed my path to the bookstore.

Rochelle's invitation had felt a little inauthentic, but I'd thought it was because of the pity behind it. Over the phone a few weeks ago, I'd vented to Rochelle about my sister sending me a listing for an assistant position at her husband's brokerage firm. I'd whined about not wanting to stay in Fremont, not wanting a job that used terms like "fast-paced" and "long hours" and "hustle culture."

My complaint had petered out as I spoke—it's hard to feel justified turning something down when you have no other options. Rochelle had sympathized, then launched into the news that she was planning her maternity leave and looking to hire help at the bookstore so someone could tend to the shop after she gave birth. Planning, hiring, and birthing: three things I'd never been adult enough to do.

"Wow," I'd said, feeling like a kid at show-and-tell who'd brought a uniquely shaped Cheeto and was upstaged by someone with a puppy. "That's great."

I'd tried not to think about myself, sitting on my childhood bed at twenty-eight and applying for jobs in a hometown I didn't want to stay in. Meanwhile, Rochelle left her job at a library last year to take over her father's bookstore when he retired—like a hermit crab effortlessly moving from one shell to another. While I'd spent the past year scuttling around without a shell to my name.

"Do you want to do it?" Rochelle had asked.

"What?"

"Cover the bookstore while I'm out." Her voice became more animated. "From August to December. You could stay with me, get away from your parents, and work at the store. You could use the time to figure out what you want to do next."

She made it sound so rational. So intentional. Ditching my life to work at her bookstore felt like running away, hiding from responsibility. But coming from Rochelle, this idea almost made sense. I wasn't running; I was helping. I wasn't aimless; I was plotting.

"You could take a break from job hunting," she added, and the singsong-y lightness in her voice told me she already knew she'd won me over.

Rochelle's rationale cemented my decision. But that was before I knew about Edward Bell and his blood sacrifice.

I was a few doors down from the bookstore when a familiar figure stepped onto the sidewalk. Dark skin, curly hair, pregnant belly. I broke into a run.

"Rochelle!"

"You made it!" Rochelle pulled me into a hug. And just like that, I didn't care about the blood sacrifice all that much. I wrapped my arms around her and breathed in the coconut-papaya scent of the leave-in conditioner I used to borrow-slash-steal when we lived together in college.

"Get away from me," I said. "Let me see you."

Rochelle obediently turned to the side in the familiar profile view I'd seen her post on Instagram every week. I'd scrolled past pictures like these from other friends documenting growing pregnancy bellies, but I always stopped to read Rochelle's updates. I'd started looking forward to every Sunday afternoon because it meant a new post. Plus, it helped me keep the days straight.

But I ignored the perfectly Instagrammable belly now. I was more interested in the signs of real life. Her twist-out was losing shape, curls loose and stretchy instead of the tightly defined ringlets she wore in her pictures. There was a pimple on her chin, something she might have covered up for social media. But she was the same in every way that counted. She still had the same wide smile, the dimple that appeared on her right cheek but not her left.

"You look great," I said.

Rochelle turned to face me. It was then that I noticed the words *Bell Society* on her black T-shirt in tilted script. I thought back to the statue, but her eyes drifted up to my hair before I could mention it. "What's going on here?" she asked.

I touched a curl, or what used to be a curl but was now a rebellious clump of frizz. "I left my bonnet in a motel somewhere around Utah." I jutted out my lower lip. Rochelle laughed and tried to tuck a frizz clump in with the other curls, laughing again when it sprang back out.

"I got you," she said. "There's a silk pillowcase waiting for you at home. Did you get there okay?"

"I did." Really, I'd parked in her driveway and immediately started walking the dozen blocks to Rochelle's bookstore. After being cooped in a car for the three-day drive, my limbs ached for movement. The suitcases in my car could wait. Everything could wait. I was finally here, in this new place, with four glorious months stretched out before me. Four months when I could make myself useful and dodge the whole career question for a while longer. Four months with Rochelle and...

I eyed the *Bell Society* on Rochelle's shirt. "Who's the Bell guy?"

"Who?" Rochelle lifted her eyebrows a little too innocently.

"Bell Society? Edward Bell? I've seen him a hundred times in the last ten minutes."

"Just a hundred?" She gave me a skeptical look. "You must have missed the billboards."

I studied her expression. She had to be joking, but billboards didn't sound so outrageous now.

"There aren't really billboards," she relented, taking pity on me and my post-driving daze. "He wrote *The First Dollar* right there in the bookstore. He used to work there. He's kind of a big deal."

"So he's an author?"

Rochelle's eyes darted across my face, like she was now the one who couldn't tell if I was joking. "Wait, you've actually never heard of him?"

I held back a laugh. "When would I have? When was the last time I picked up a book? Except for the books you've sent me, which I have totally read," I said quickly, holding up a hand like it could ward off one of her impassioned speeches about how I would love reading if I only gave it a chance.

And Rochelle, whose mouth had already fallen open with a speech at the ready, clamped her lips shut—but her eyes twinkled in amusement. Rochelle was a firm believer that books were the answer to everything—a belief that has never rubbed off on me, no matter how many novels she's gifted me over the years.

I'd always vaguely intended to read them, but I couldn't help that there were a million more fun ways to spend my time than staring at a page. Rochelle had been trying to do just that on the day we met, burying her nose in a book after unpacking in our dorm room freshman year at UC Berkeley. I was the one who broke the silence and asked if she'd like to explore campus with me. She'd lifted her eyes from the page with reluctance, but after wandering around campus and splitting a vat of frozen yogurt topped with mochi and coconut, we were well on our way to becoming best friends. I'm sure reading has its charms, but you can't befriend a book.

"So...this supposedly famous author wrote a book and no one's gotten over it?" I asked.

"*You* may not be impressed, but it's a big draw for tourists. We get a lot of booklovers who come here to see the bookstore, the Bell Museum, his grave site. There's Edward Bell history all over town. It's how a lot of people make a living."

"Will I have to wear a Bell Society shirt?" I asked.

"You will."

"Are matching tattoos involved?"

Her dimple started peeking through. "Yes, but they're very tasteful."

I opened my mouth, but Rochelle was quick to interrupt my thoughts, knowing I could run a bit into the ground just to get a laugh out of her.

"We're done with questions," she said. "Forget the bookstore. Come with me." She linked her arm through mine and started down the street.

I didn't bother to ask where we were going. It put a warm, glow-y feeling in my chest just to be here, joking with Rochelle, when last week I'd been sitting in my childhood bedroom reading a job rejection email to the soundtrack of my parents' bickering. I wanted to soak this all in while I could. After nearly a year being unemployed, after three days driving on a highway and eating crappy road food that had made me greasy inside and out, I'd finally get to take a break.

As we strolled down the sidewalk, I abandoned the statue hunt and looked for the details I'd missed before. The tufts of grass peeking between the cobblestones on the road. The colorful storefronts of the brick buildings. We passed a clothing boutique where a stylish mannequin wore a cute collared dress, a café that smelled like coffee and bread, an ice cream shop with an easel boasting mulberry crumble as the flavor of the day.

Just as the next four months were an endless sprawl of time stretched before me, Bell River felt the same way, a world of possibilities waiting to be explored. This wasn't my parents' suburban neighborhood with manicured lawns and templated homes. It wasn't the bustling electricity of downtown San Francisco where I used to work. Bell River felt unique. Captivating. And, for the next four months, *mine*.

The market came into view when we reached town square. I saw what Rochelle meant about the town being a tourist draw, noticing stalls that displayed tote bags, art prints, and more, all featuring Edward Bell's books, silhouette, or quotes. It was easy to spot the tourists shopping for Bell paraphernalia, but my gaze flitted past them to the people who looked like locals. One vendor abandoned her produce stall to say something to the vendor next to her, who threw her head back with a laugh. A customer leaned against a tentpole, drinking something green and chatting to the person manning the juice dispensers. Something about this swarm of friendly faces made me want to know them, be part of their jokes, be part of something, period.

As if reading my mind, Rochelle led me to the first stall in the lineup, where tables were piled with crates of apples, bottles of cider, and pies. A woman in her fifties was putting apples into a customer's tote bag, eyes animated behind her thick round glasses as she recounted her dog's tense standoff with a bird that morning. When the customer walked off, the woman spotted us and broke into a grin.

"Rochelle!" she exclaimed. "Is this her?"

"It's her!" Rochelle squeezed my arm. "Maggie, this is Ruth."

"It's great to meet you," I said. I extended my hand and Ruth thrust a wet bottle of ice-cold cider into it. "Oh."

"Consider it a welcome gift, honey," she said. That last word sent an appreciative ripple through me. I wasn't used to being called *honey*, but I was a fan now. "Rochelle's told us all about you. I'm so glad you left San Francisco to join us out here."

"Yes, it was very gracious of me," I said with a laugh. She'd spoken as if coming to Bell River was one of many choices at my disposal and not the respite I'd clung to for dear life. I could have corrected her, just like I could have explained that Fremont is not San Francisco, but I preferred her version of events.

"We should make the rounds," Rochelle told her, putting a hand on my shoulder. "Save me a pie?"

Ruth winked and set aside a foil tin. Then Rochelle pulled me to the next stall, where an older Black woman in burgundy overalls smiled at me.

"Rochelle! Is this who I think it is?"

"It must be," I replied, starting to get the hang of things. "I'm Maggie."

"Marcia."

I noticed the handmade clocks behind her, telling time in all sorts of ways. A large circle of unfinished wood with dominoes instead of numbers. Another resembled a dinner plate, a fork and a spoon serving as the minute and hour hands. One clock had a fabric face surrounded by a circle of colorful buttons.

"I didn't know people could make clocks," I marveled. A stupid thing to say now that I thought about it, but I already said it, so.

Marcia laughed, something surprised and infectious. "I know what you mean," she said, turning to look at her handiwork. "I impress myself." Her eyes fell back to me. "If you ever want a custom clock, you just let me know, baby. Maybe something set to California time if you get homesick."

Strange to remember I was in a different time zone now. But the thought didn't make me homesick. It just brought me back to what I'd been thinking before, about all the possibilities this town held for me. New town, new time zone. And maybe, a few months from now: new me.

At the egg booth, a young woman sat on a stool, engrossed in a paperback that, shockingly, wasn't written by Edward Bell. Everything from the concentration in her eyes to the braid she wore her long, dark hair in told me she must be the serious type. She smiled politely and introduced herself as Leena, then dropped her gaze to her book almost immediately. But when I noticed the pictures of chickens adorning her booth and asked their names, Leena set down her book and hopped off the stool.

"This is Sarah McClucklan," she said, pointing at an image

of a speckled brown chicken. "That's Gloria Eggstefan. Pat Henatar. Stevie Chicks."

Leena walked me through the punny names of each and every chicken, ending on Christina Egguilera. I could have stayed behind to squeal over them forever, but then Rochelle whisked me over to Toby, a blond man who sold cloth bags stamped with Edward Bell quotes. I bought one, figuring I may as well lean into the obsession. As he took my credit card, I spotted a clear box of colorful dice at the edge of the table.

"What's with these?" I asked. I picked up a large purple one and turned it over, watching the glitter sparkle in the sun. The numbers, written in gold paint, went all the way up to twenty.

"I've started making my own dice," Toby said with a proud smile. "They don't sell like the Bell stuff, but my D&D group loves them." He eyed me with renewed interest. "Hey, do you play? We're always looking for new members."

"I play a little," I lied, ignoring the amused look Rochelle gave me. I listened while Toby enthused about the Dungeons & Dragons community he founded, now two hundred members strong.

"You play Dungeons & Dragons, do you?" Rochelle teased as we walked off.

I shrugged. "Maybe I'll start."

Today was about possibility, after all. Here, I wasn't a failed experiment in adulthood. This was a place where Ruth gave me free cider and called me *honey*, where Marcia offered to make me a clock, where Leena gushed about her chickens, where Toby invited me to join his D&D group. This was a place where people were openhearted and fun. I'd embrace that fun wherever I could get it.

But not everyone was welcoming. After a whirlwind of new faces and welcome gifts, we circled back to Ruth to pick up Rochelle's pie. While Rochelle paid, I watched an older man in a wrinkled orange button-down hunch over the apple crates. He inspected an apple, then put it back with a frown. The basket in his arm held a carefully chosen selection of groceries: one ear of corn, one head of romaine, one tomato, one pint of strawberries, one half-carton of eggs. He'd been at the egg stall at the same time as me, peering into cartons for cracks while I talked to Leena, but Rochelle had steered me around him without a word.

I watched him inspect and return another apple. On impulse, I selected one from a lower crate and handed it to him. He stared at me, his bushy gray eyebrows almost joining together. Then he cast a suspicious glance at the apple. He turned it half a rotation before he spotted an invisible imperfection and set it on a crate to join the other rejects.

Rochelle and Ruth were reaching the tail end of their conversation, but I couldn't resist another try. I knelt beside a crate and selected an apple that was uniform in color, a pinkish red all over. I handed it to him just as Rochelle turned to me.

"Ready to—oh," she said. "I didn't realize you'd met."

"We haven't," he said in a gruff voice. "She's handing me fruit for some reason." He turned the apple a full rotation.

"Oh," Rochelle said again. "Well. Vernon, this is Maggie." Her tone was strangely upbeat. "She's covering for me at the bookstore for the next few months. Maggie, Vernon lives above the bookstore."

"I guess that makes us neighbors," I said. "If you ever need to borrow a cup of sugar, just say the word."

Vernon grunted, then set the apple on the crate of disappointments. My jaw dropped at the betrayal.

"I should get back to the store." Rochelle caught my eye and cocked her head. I followed her to the edge of the square, where she looked at me with a mixture of amusement and exhaustion. "Leave it to you to approach the grumpiest person in the world," she murmured.

"I didn't know! Everyone else was so friendly." I looked back at the apple stall. Vernon had miraculously found the perfect apple and was handing it to Ruth. I squinted at the apple. It bore an uncanny resemblance to the last one I'd given him.

"Oh my god, don't stare!" Rochelle hissed.

I turned around with a laugh. "What are you afraid of?"

"He's mean!"

"How mean?"

"Once, when I was eight, I was rollerblading down the street, and he yelled at me for going too fast. He said I could have knocked him over. I *barely* brushed past him." She gave me the serious look of a long-held grudge.

I nodded solemnly. "Do you want me to give him a talking-to?"

"Don't you dare."

"Let's go settle this right now," I joked. "Hey, Vernon!"

Rochelle burst into a horrified laugh, even though I'd barely spoken above a whisper. "I can't with you. I'm going back to the store. You go home. You're too dangerous to have around. You know the way back?"

I didn't, fully, but I told her I did. I wouldn't have minded getting lost. There was so much still to explore. More people to meet, more quirks to discover, more reasons to feel like I might be doing something right by coming here.

I retraced my steps in a roundabout way, detouring through side streets when I felt like it. When I reached Rochelle's at last, her husband, Luke, helped me unload my car.

Then we stood in my new room, where my two suitcases sat clumped uncomfortably in the corner. The room bore the markings of a child's playroom—the shelf stacked with board games, the waist-high crayon scribbles on the walls, the rug freckled with polka dots and marker stains. Opposite the game shelf sat a short table and a yellow chair so small it felt like a challenge, daring me to test whether I could fit my hips in it. On the daybed in the corner, I spotted a blanket Rochelle had in college, a soft, purple thing I always gravitated to when I needed comfort. Just seeing it made my heart swell.

"Sorry we've got Dylan's old things in here," Luke said. "We moved some of it to his room, but we didn't have a place for the rest."

"You don't have to apologize for giving me a place to stay," I insisted. "This is only temporary." The word soured on my tongue like a threat, reminding me I couldn't hide in this town's charms forever. By the time I left, I'd need to know what to do next. Suddenly the sprawl of time I'd imagined didn't feel so endless.

I spent the rest of the day in a haze, acclimating to standing still instead of drifting down the highway, the novelty of seeing faces rather than exit signs. I met Dylan, their five-year-old son, who gave a tentative wave before darting back upstairs. He was half-Black like me, hair in springy curls like mine, and I wouldn't read too much into the fact that I compared myself to a child.

In the shower that night, I debated whether I should have come here at all, whether I wasn't just living in denial and postponing the inevitable. I needed to figure out that elusive next step, make a concrete plan, find a job without an end date—whatever that was, wherever it took me. Yet it sounded absurd, the idea that four months from now I'd magically know what to do. I have never been good at knowing what to do.

As I crawled under the fuzzy purple blanket, trying to ignore the steady *tick* of the owl-shaped clock on the wall, I told myself that come December I would have my life figured out.

The ticking sound rang in my mind even as I drifted to sleep.

CHAPTER TWO

I'd had a lot of jobs over the years. Barista. Dog walker. Cashier at Chuck E. Cheese. Office coordinator. It's a zigzag medley that tends to give employers pause. In a job interview last month, the hiring manager took off his glasses in a *let's be frank* sort of way and told me my resume didn't tell a story about my interests, an expectation that felt unfairly impossible. I didn't see why my interests had to involve my job at all.

I thought of that hiring manager now as Rochelle and I stepped inside Cobblestone Books the next morning. He'd definitely approve of Rochelle. He'd see her English degree, her librarian past, her store full of bookshelves, and give her a gold star on the spot, because I guess I'd decided that's a thing hiring managers do.

I shook him out of my head. This bookstore may represent Rochelle's life, her interests, her *story*, but I worked here too now. For the next few months, this was my story, too.

I glanced around the shop, taking in my new workplace. Shelves crammed with books formed narrow aisles. A brown leather armchair sat in the corner near the window. With its cushion cracks and patchy coloring, it looked worn but loved. The haphazard stack of books on a small end table and the plants lining the windowsill made this corner feel intensely cozy.

Beyond the shelves, there was an open space in the back where Edward Bell leered at me from a portrait on the wall. I narrowed my eyes at him.

I ventured into an aisle to get the lay of the land. Something was off about the books here—lots of muted colors and identical spines, many of them black with a stripe in the middle like the books I'd read in English class. Even in the children's section, where I expected splashes of color, the books were oddly dull.

Rochelle found me squinting at a shelf. "What is it?" she asked.

I looked past more muted covers as I tried to pinpoint the issue. "Why is everything old?" I pulled two books from a shelf and held them up: one Shakespeare, one Shaw, neither remotely tempting. The Shaw featured a black-and-white portrait of a lady in a Victorian dress, complete with gloves, ruffles, and a feathered hat.

"We don't sell used books," she said. "Everything's new." I glanced at feathery hat lady with enough side-eye to draw a laugh out of Rochelle. "Okay, okay. We only sell literary classics that were around during Edward Bell's lifetime. He died in 1968, so nothing after that."

I frowned at the cover in my hands. A store that specialized in assigned reading from English classes past didn't seem very appealing. Or profitable. "Why?"

"It was Ralph Bell's idea—Edward Bell's grandson," she said. "He's majority owner of the store."

That explained the portrait. "He's that obsessed with his grandfather?"

"Well." Rochelle tilted her head. "It's more than that. Before Ralph got involved, my dad was struggling to stay in business. This was like...twenty years ago. Then Ralph offered to invest in the bookstore. He runs the Bell Museum, and he had the idea to do something similar here. He brought in the table over there, where Edward Bell wrote his first novel, and made the bookstore more of a tourist attraction. It really turned things around. Ralph decided the store should stick to classics because that's all Edward Bell ever read." She pointed to the portrait, and I noticed the quote written in large script above it.

"'The only books worth reading were written long ago,'" I read. "Ah. We're pro-gatekeeping, got it." I put the books back on the shelves, then looked down at our black Bell Society shirts. "Is there also a snappy Edward Bell quote about conformity?"

"The uniform was Ralph's idea," she grumbled. "Ralph owns the Bell Society, which owns the museum, the bookstore, and...a few other places. I'm losing count."

I gave a hum of acknowledgment. "Are we sure this isn't a cult?"

She laughed. "It's not a cult, but it is time for your initiation."

"Matching tattoo time?" I asked.

Disappointingly, there was no initiation tattoo. Rochelle just launched into an overview of the job. She ran me through the store's hours: closed Mondays, open from ten to six the rest of the week, slightly longer on Saturdays. Having no other hired help made for long hours, she said, but I could always close the store if I needed to run errands, and Luke sometimes helped out on weekends. Then she walked me through the payment process and had me run her card through the payment terminal and print out the tiny receipt strip for her to sign.

"Great job!" She unclicked her pen with a flourish and

beamed at me with pride for my ability to pass the easiest exam I'd ever been given. "That's about it for the books side," she said. "Now there's...the other side."

I followed her gaze to the Edward Bell portrait in the alcove at the back. "I don't have to drop to my knees and say a prayer, do I?"

"Not exactly," she said as we approached the Edward Bell portrait. "Just be prepared to talk to tourists who come in asking about Edward Bell. They'll want to hear about his time working at the bookstore, see his books, see where he wrote his famous novel." She gestured to a wooden chair behind a small round table with spindly legs.

"*Is* it famous?"

"It's famous!" she insisted. "It's on *Time*'s list of 100 greatest novels of all time."

I nodded patiently. "Is it number 100?"

"Shut up and let me give the spiel." I shut my mouth and Rochelle cleared her throat with exaggerated pomp.

"Edward Bell is an exciting part of Cobblestone Books's history. From ages twenty-two to thirty-one, he worked as a bookseller here, dreaming that one day his books would sit on these shelves alongside his favorite novels. He got hardly any writing done until he set up this table. He told his boss it was a place for customers to sit and read, but really Edward used it to write his first novel. He'd come to the bookshop an hour before the store opened, and he'd sit here and write. And after he locked up the store for the day, he'd come back to this table and write for another hour. That's how *The First Dollar* came into existence: a man, a dream, and a table."

I golf-clapped while Rochelle took a bow. "Why didn't he write at home?" I asked.

"He found it too distracting. He and his wife had two young kids."

"I bet his wife loved him being gone all the time," I commented.

"It sounds like you're interested in Edward Bell's home life. May I recommend *Edward Bell: A Biography*?" She pulled it off the shelf and held it up.

"You may not."

Rochelle cracked a smile, breaking the customer service facade. "But you get the idea, right? I wrote out a script for you and some FAQs you can go over."

"Got it, got it. So I should say something like…" I gestured grandly to the table. "Instead of going home and helping his wife, Edward Bell sat here and scribbled all night." I turned to Rochelle. "Like that?"

She gave me a playful shove. "Joke all you want, but tourists coming to nerd out about Edward Bell is the only thing saving me from bankruptcy, so I for one am grateful for Edward and his scribbling." Her tone was light, but I felt the weight of her words. She was looking down now, picking at her nails.

"Is everything okay?" I asked.

"Yeah. Mostly." She rested her hands on the back of the chair, tapping her fingers idly. "Luke's on track to graduate in December and get a job in January, but it's already hard getting by on just my salary. I've been freaking out a little about how we'll make it stretch once the baby comes. But I'm sure it'll be fine?"

"Of course," I said, rushing to her side. I knew things had been tight with Luke leaving his job as a medical technician to enroll in an accelerated nursing program last year, but Rochelle hadn't alluded to any financial troubles. Although, combing through my memory, she had made a few jokes about clipping coupons. "You don't need to worry. I bet the bookstore's going to be busier than ever. You know," I said, snapping my fingers, "I *did* see that list of 100 greatest novels, and you know what? They just reordered it, and *The Finest Dollar*—"

"*The First Dollar.*"

"*The* First *Dollar*, thank you, was number one on the list. Right this second, people are flocking to Bell River to see the table and buy out your entire inventory. I will be here to recite that script and make those sales and sing Edward Bell's praises all day long. And in a few months, Luke will graduate and get a nursing job, and everything will be fine. Okay?"

Rochelle smiled shakily. "Okay."

I let out a sigh of relief. "Good. Should I start memorizing that script?"

"Um. There's one more thing."

"Hmm?" I was so deep in reassurance mode that I'd be willing to agree to whatever she said next. If she needed me to grow a mustache, I'd find a way.

"Ralph Bell wants to meet you. In twenty minutes."

"Oh." I waved it away. "I wanted to meet him anyway. I have so many questions."

"Don't ask him anything weird," she pleaded.

"Only weird questions, got it."

She gave a distracted laugh. "He didn't love that I wanted you to run the store instead of someone from the museum. He'll probably try to feel you out to make sure the store's in good hands."

My stomach flip-flopped the way it does before job interviews. "Right."

In the few minutes we had before we left, I did what little cramming I could. I read through Rochelle's script, read the back of *The First Dollar*, skimmed the titles of the other Edward Bell books on the shelf. When Rochelle slung her purse over her shoulder, I looked up from flipping through a book whose title I'd already forgotten.

"Ready?" she asked.

I put on a bright grin and gave her a thumbs-up for some reason. "Definitely."

Cute, vibrant storefronts lined the streets as we walked, but after a few blocks and a couple of turns, the buildings became more lackluster: a bank, a law office, an interior design firm. We stopped outside another unassuming brick building, where a small sign told us the illustrious Bell Society awaited us on the second floor.

I followed Rochelle inside and up the stairs to a small office space. While Rochelle asked the man behind the front desk for Ralph, I twirled a carousel of pamphlets, taking in spinning glimpses of Edward Bell, the museum, the walking tour of literary attractions.

I plucked out a pamphlet and read through it, learning how the town's name had transformed over the years. In an effort to honor Edward Bell, they had changed the name from Eldham to Bell, then feared that would cause confusion with the neighboring Bell County, then rebranded to Bellville, then worried that sounded too much like Melville, then settled on Bell River despite the fact that there wasn't a river around for miles. The pamphlet glossed over all of this like it was perfectly normal. For the citizens of Bell River, I guessed it was.

I closed the pamphlet when I heard footsteps. A man with gray hair, glasses, and a neatly trimmed mustache that wasn't nearly as colossal as Edward Bell's beamed at Rochelle.

"Rochelle! You're positively glowing!"

"Thank you," Rochelle said evenly. She'd ranted to me a few months ago about how she hated when people said she was glowing. *What am I, ET?* she'd texted. "I know you wanted to meet Maggie, so here she is."

"Of course!" He extended a hand. "Nice and firm," he said. "'A man's character can be judged solely by his handshake.' Do you know who said that?"

I was tempted to play dumb just to see how he'd react, but with Rochelle's worries fresh in my mind, I voiced the only reasonable guess. "Edward Bell?"

"That's right!" He grinned like I'd done something truly remarkable. I love a low bar.

But once he led us to his office in the back room, I started to feel his scrutiny. He sat behind his desk and regarded me thoughtfully, and I tried not to squirm in my stiff wooden chair. I looked around the small room: the window behind him, the bookshelf against one wall, a tall metal cabinet against the other. A familiar portrait of Edward Bell hung behind him.

"What a coincidence; we've got that same portrait at the bookstore," I said. "Really ties a room together, doesn't it?"

Ralph glanced behind him, then slowly turned to face me, his expression pinched. "I wouldn't call it a coincidence. That portrait hangs in all Bell Society businesses."

"Oh, I know, I was just—" I cut myself off when I realized it would be no use uttering *making a joke* under his impenetrable stare. Next to me, Rochelle shifted in her seat. "Nothing," I said. "I like it. I appreciate a mustache." Ralph's eyebrows shot up and my brain short-circuited because Ralph had a mustache too and I couldn't be hitting on my new boss on day one. "On *him*," I corrected myself, feeling my face grow warm. "I meant I appreciate *his* mustache. It's very…"—I gestured to the portrait, racking my brain for a word, any word—"thick."

Ralph made a face. So did I.

"So you wanted to meet Maggie," Rochelle said brightly. "What did you want to talk about?"

"Yes." Ralph blinked out of his stupor. "I want to make sure you're all set for the transition." His piercing gaze settled on me. "Has Rochelle told you about the tourists? They'll have questions about Edward Bell and it will be your job to answer them. Are you prepared for that?"

"Yes," I said. It was only slightly a lie. I *would* be prepared with a little more practice.

"How well do you know Edward Bell?" he asked.

I tossed an uneasy glance at Rochelle, then crossed one leg over the other and turned back to Ralph. "Not as well as you, but Rochelle's been filling in the gaps. She told me about the table today."

"Good, good. And how many of his books have you read?"

I could feel Rochelle's eyes on me, but I didn't break my gaze from Ralph. "None yet, but I'm planning to change that today, starting with *The Finest Dollar*." Rochelle nudged me with her knee. "*The First Dollar*," I blurted out.

Ralph was quiet for a moment, studying me. "You know, we can always move Edward Bell's books and writing table to the museum until you've got a better handle on him. You may not be ready just yet."

"That's not necessary," Rochelle said. "She'll be ready. I've been training her. I'll be working alongside her for the next two weeks before my leave."

"I've got it!" Ralph held up a finger like he'd just had an epiphany that would solve all our problems. "Why don't we have someone from the museum help Maggie out until she's more comfortable? Cynthia's been eager to have a hand at the bookstore for a while now."

"I know," Rochelle said, speaking at a very measured pace. "As I've said before, I don't need Cynthia or anyone else. You said I could choose my replacement, and Maggie is the best person for the job. I know she'll do great."

A beat of silence followed as Ralph and Rochelle stared each other down. My skin prickled with the uncomfortable feeling that this was about more than just me. But a lifetime with arguing parents had taught me how to navigate conflict well. I glanced around the walls for a distraction, then noticed a framed article with Ralph's smiling face in the top right corner. I skimmed the text, which portrayed him as some sort of business genius for his ability to turn around failed Bell River businesses by slapping the Edward Bell name on them. But one line caught my attention: *With a rumored film adaptation of* The First Dollar *in the works, Ralph predicts big things are on the horizon for the Bell Society's future.*

"That's cool," I piped up, pointing at the article. "Is the movie out yet?" Maybe I wouldn't have to read the book after all.

"Hm?" Ralph took a moment to catch on. "Oh, uh." He lifted the frame off the wall and studied the article with an expression I couldn't read, then set it down out of sight. "No. That fell through."

"Oh." I scrunched my lips to the side of my mouth. "Sorry."

Ralph put on a quick smile that didn't reach his eyes. "None of your concern. But it's time to get moving. And if you have any questions," he said, coming around the desk and opening the door, "don't hesitate to ask me or our museum staff. They're all very knowledgeable about Edward Bell." His gaze lingered on me, a pointed message in his eyes.

As soon as we were out on the sidewalk, I let out a long exhale. "I feel so welcome."

"I know, I'm sorry." Rochelle cast an annoyed glance at the Bell Society building. "He's on a power trip lately. He's been dictating the displays we can put in the store. He made us start wearing uniforms. I just had a feeling that if I let him have any more control over the bookstore, he'd find a way to dig his claws in deeper. As if I'm not a part-owner, too. I just hope he doesn't try to take anything out on you."

My throat tightened. An hour ago, I'd been so ready to shower her with reassurances. But now, doubts of my own were creeping through. The bookstore needed to make enough money to cover expenses for Rochelle's growing family. And I needed to become an overnight expert on Edward Bell to keep Ralph from exerting more control over the store.

I tugged down my Bell Society shirt and tucked a curl behind my ear. "I'm sure it'll be fine," I said. But I didn't quite believe myself.

CHAPTER THREE

All morning, Ralph's doubts clung to me like an oily film I couldn't wash off. I did my best to play the part of knowledgeable bookseller—I greeted tourists, showed them the writing table, recited some easy answers from the FAQs. But any time tourists went off-script, I'd turn helplessly to Rochelle. She'd throw on a sunny smile and answer their question in full. And I'd lower my head to read through the FAQs again, hating that I was proving Ralph right.

"Hey," Rochelle said as a customer walked off with an armful of Edward Bell books. "You're doing great."

I looked up from trying to memorize the names of Edward Bell's family members. "I couldn't answer her question about his second book. Or the one about feminist themes in *The First Dollar*."

She waved it off. "It's your first day. You're getting there. Look at that, you even got the title of the book right."

I laughed. "I'm basically an expert."

"Basically," she agreed. "You know what? I have an ob-gyn appointment in a couple hours. Would you feel up to watching the store so Luke can come with me?"

I hesitated. Ralph would probably have a conniption at the idea of me running the bookstore alone on my first day.

"If you don't feel ready, that's fine," Rochelle said quickly. "Luke can watch the store; he'd just have to bring Dylan."

I gave her a grateful smile. It was an easy out, but taking it didn't feel right. I'd come here to help Rochelle. Why did I care what Ralph thought?

"I can watch the store," I said. "I could even watch Dylan too, if he'd rather hang out here than go to the doctor."

My last lingering reservations about managing the store on my own disappeared when Rochelle's whole face brightened. "That would be amazing. Thank you."

For the first time that day, I actually felt helpful. I'd almost forgotten the feeling.

As the afternoon passed, Rochelle took a back seat while I tended to customers, answered questions, and gave the spiel about the writing table. I was getting better at memorizing answers from the FAQs, too. When a man asked where he could find contemporary novels, I told him without a moment's hesitation that there was a Barnes and Noble in Franklin. Someone asked about the history of the building and I showed them a pamphlet, rattling off that Edward Bell eventually bought the building in 1942. By the time Luke and Dylan showed up, I was starting to feel like I really could handle the store on my own, Ralph and his doubts be damned.

"Thanks for doing this, Maggie," Luke said as Rochelle gathered her things. "Dylan hates going to appointments."

"That place smells weird," Dylan said.

"Oh, I bet it does," I agreed. "Doctors' offices always smell like hand sanitizer and...rotten Jell-O." Dylan wrinkled his nose and laughed, sending a rush of joy through me. Ralph may not have appreciated my jokes, but at least Dylan did.

"We'll be back in a couple hours," Rochelle said, ruffling Dylan's curly hair. "Call if anything comes up."

"It'll be fine," I assured her.

It *was*, briefly. But then I noticed Dylan sprawled in the leather chair, sighing in boredom while I spoke with a tourist, and I couldn't not do something. So I asked Dylan to draw me a picture of Edward Bell, and then we got to joking about mustaches, and soon enough we both had paper mustaches taped under our noses as we giggled our way through my dramatic reading of *The First Dollar*.

We were so invested in my reading that the sound of the bell above the door startled us both. I looked up, freezing in place when I saw the startled faces of the group in the entryway, an older couple and, just behind them, a Black man about my age.

I raised a hand to my face, ready to tear my mustache off—but then Dylan exclaimed, "We're Edward Bell!" I knew right then that removing the mustache would have been a grave betrayal.

I eyed the group in the entryway. Then I grinned and put on my deepest voice. "Welcome to Cobblestone Books," I said. "I'm Edward Bell. Have a look around and let me know if you have any questions."

The older couple relaxed into smiles, but the man behind them just furrowed his brow. I ignored him and turned my attention to the couple, now reading the placard by the table.

"Is this where you wrote your book, Edward?" the woman asked.

"Yes," I said. I joined them and launched into the script, albeit from a different perspective. "When I worked here in the early 1930s, I spent two hours a day at this table, writing *The First Dollar*. My wife, who was home with two kids under four, did not appreciate my long hours." This wasn't in the script, but it did make them chuckle. I glanced toward the guy who had come in with them, wondering if I'd won him over. But he jerked his head back, as if my words were a personal affront.

"Did you have any questions for me?" I asked him.

He cleared his throat. "It's speculation to say his wife had a problem with his hours. There's no evidence of that."

I tossed a glance toward the older couple. "The evidence was written all over my wife's face when I got home from work two hours too late."

The couple laughed. The guy in the back frowned, but then the woman made a joke about the long hours her husband spent in his art studio, and I stopped paying that frown any attention.

The couple bought a stack of Edward Bell books, which Dylan helped me ring up. They fawned over Dylan when he handed them their receipt.

"Nice meeting you, Mr. Bell and Mr. Bell," the old man said on their way out. Dylan and I shared a grin, like we'd gotten away with a crime.

Meanwhile, our remaining humorless customer had spent this time strolling the shelves with his hands in his pockets, though his shoulders were too high up and tense for the position to be remotely comfortable. His shirt was buttoned all the way to his throat and his locs were tied in a neat ponytail behind him, ever the picture of order. When the couple left the store, he approached the counter, his watchful brown eyes laser-focused on me.

"Can I help you find one of my books?" I asked in my Edward Bell voice. Dylan giggled next to me.

His expression grew pained. "Uh…" He pulled his hands from his pockets and rested them on the counter. "I'm Malcolm."

"Nice to meet you, Malcolm. I'm Edward Bell."

"So am I," Dylan chimed in.

Malcolm gave an uncomfortable laugh. "Nice to meet you, too. I'm, uh, here on Ralph's behalf. He wanted me to check in and see how onboarding is going."

"Oh," I said, dropping the Edward Bell voice. Just like that, I felt like I was back in Ralph's office being scrutinized. I sat up and squared my shoulders, trying to look as presentable as one can look with a paper mustache taped under their nose. "It's going great. We were just…getting into character."

"Right," Malcolm said, drawing out the word as his eyes fell over me and my newfound facial hair. "This"—he swirled a finger in my general direction—"really isn't what we do at the Bell Society. Ralph takes this kind of stuff very seriously."

"So do I," I insisted. "I was just entertaining him while Rochelle went to a doctor appointment."

The bell above the door rang. I breathed a sigh when I saw Rochelle and Luke. Dylan got up to greet them while Rochelle approached us cautiously.

"What's going on?" she asked. Her eyes traveled down to my mustache. A corner of her mouth perked up, but it drooped just as quickly when she turned to Malcolm.

"Ralph wanted me to stop by and check in on how things were going," he said.

"I'm sure he did," she said, her mouth in a thin line. "And?"

"It's not looking great."

She frowned. "Why?"

"I—" He rubbed his neck. "I don't want to tell people how to do their jobs, but pretending to be Edward Bell and speculating about his marriage isn't how we run things. Ralph's going to want to hear about this."

"This was an unusual situation," Rochelle said. "She was watching my kid. This won't happen again."

"It won't," I agreed, peeling the paper mustache off my face.

She fixed her imploring eyes on Malcolm. "Ralph doesn't need to know."

Malcolm opened his mouth, seemingly at a loss for words. "It's my job," he said at last.

"Do your job another day," she said. "Check in on us again next week, and I promise everything will be in order."

When he hesitated, looking to the wall behind her like he was searching for answers, Rochelle kept speaking. "Look, I just got back from the doctor and I'm supposed to be resting right now. Can you just tell me what you're going to do?"

Malcolm let out a breath. "I'll come back later." He paused like there was more he wanted to say. Then he gave us a grimace of a closed-lipped smile and hurried out of the store.

Rochelle turned to me, her eyebrows raised. I shook my head and shrugged helplessly. "Dylan was bored."

Her laugh was somewhere between disbelieving and delirious. "That sounds about right."

I studied her carefully. "What did you mean when you said you were supposed to be resting?"

Rochelle just laughed again. "Turns out my leave is starting sooner than I thought."

"How much sooner?"

"Today."

My eyebrows shot up. "Why? What happened?"

She lifted and dropped her hand in a halfhearted shrug. "Nothing, exactly. My doctor said she's just being cautious, but she would feel better if I got off my feet and limited my movement until the baby comes. So Luke's going to drive me home, and I guess…you're on your own now. I'm kidding," she added when she saw my face. "I mean, I'm not, but…you can always call me if you have questions."

"You haven't even shown me how to close up yet," I protested.

"Right, you'll need keys." She fished around in her purse, then slipped a key loose and set it on the counter. "Just lock up when you're done. We'll go over the rest at home."

I stared at the key, so small yet so intimidating. "I'm seriously on my own already? I can't do this."

"You can," she insisted. "You'll be great. Just avoid mustaches and Malcolm, and it'll be smooth sailing."

I gave a small laugh. "Wise words to live by."

Rochelle gave my shoulder a reassuring squeeze and Dylan waved at me as they left, but my mind was blank and swirly. From here on out, I'd be manning the store on my own. Ralph had so little faith in my ability to run it that he'd enlisted Malcolm to watch my every move—and I'd put an even bigger target on my back with my mustache antics.

This job might not be the relaxing break from my life I'd thought it would be. Already my mind was searching for ways to do everything at once: get Ralph off my back, win Malcolm over, and keep the store afloat.

The more I dwelled on it, the more impossible it seemed.

CHAPTER FOUR

I wasn't sure what to think as I walked into town for my first full day manning the store on my own. At the farmers' market, I'd been so sure this town was a place where people were friendly, fun, and welcoming. Even meeting Vernon that day—the grumpiest person in the world, according to Rochelle—hadn't fazed me. I'd thought him an anomaly and figured I'd win him over in time.

And then I met Ralph, with his doubts and his scrutinizing stare. Then Malcolm joined the fray, unwaveringly critical in the face of a paper mustache and a harmless joke.

I was beginning to think I'd formed my impression of the Bell River townsfolk too hastily. It might actually be the other way around—maybe those first friendly faces were the anomalies.

I stopped outside the Sunrise Café. People were lined up at the register while others stood to the side waiting for their orders. A woman behind the counter in a Bell Society shirt took order after order with a cheerful smile. I put my hand on the door. This was another chance to meet someone. Another chance to see if my first impression had been way off base. I pulled open the door and stepped inside.

I breathed in the smell of roasted coffee as I took my place in line behind the half-dozen or so people in front of me. I examined the pastries behind the glass counter, spotting an apple cheddar biscuit I recognized from *The First Dollar*, which I'd spent my day off yesterday reading. Likely a marketing ploy Ralph had dreamed up, but I had to admit my mouth was watering.

The customer in front of me ordered a cappuccino without foam, an order that always baffled me when I was a barista—a foamless cappuccino is really just a latte. But the woman at the register didn't bat an eye; she just took the order and wished them a good day.

"What can I get you?" she asked when I stepped up to the counter. Her customer service smile held strong, but up close I could see the shadows of sleepiness under her eyes, the auburn flyaways escaping her messy ponytail.

"Love the outfit," I said, pinching my shirtsleeve and holding it up.

She laughed. A good sign. "I'm still getting used to the uniform. Are you the new girl at the bookstore?"

Word got around fast. I briefly wondered if news had also spread about my close call the other day, but I didn't see any judgment in her friendly face. "Yeah, I'm Maggie."

"Good to meet you. I'm Abigail. What can I get you?"

"An apple cheddar biscuit and a small iced coffee, please." While I inserted my card into the chip reader, I tested the waters a smidge more. "I hope to see you at the bookstore sometime."

She hesitated. Well, that did it. Too much too soon. Time to pack it in.

"Yeah, maybe," she said. "I'm not one for classics, though."

"Oh my god, me neither," I confessed. Abigail laughed, sending a wave of satisfaction over me.

I managed to catch Abigail's eye on my way out. I waved goodbye, and she lifted her hand in return. I made the rest of the way to the bookstore feeling surer of myself. It was decided. People here *were* friendly, and I shouldn't dwell on the exceptions. No use worrying about Malcolm's lack of humor when Abigail and I were basically best friends.

I'd arrived earlier than I needed to, wanting to make sure everything was in order before I subjected myself to customers' questions or Malcolm's scrutiny. I did a lap around the store, straightened the pamphlets by the table, and sank into my seat to enjoy my breakfast. The biscuit was everything I'd hoped for and more: fluffy, buttery, a sharp tang of melty cheddar contrasting against the sweetness from the diced apple studded throughout. The coffee was good too, delicate and almost floral. I would definitely become a regular at the Sunrise Café.

Breakfast over with, I washed my hands in the back—I wasn't going to let Malcolm catch me getting the books greasy—dusted crumbs off my shirt, and patted my mass of curls into order. It was time to open.

The day went as well as I could hope for. People came to see the table and browse the shelves. I recited the table's history and answered questions as usual. Customers came to the register to buy Edward Bell's books and little else. Wash, rinse, repeat.

I stuck to the script for the most part. Answering factual questions about Edward Bell was easy but boring. Most people weren't interested in conversation. They wanted the answer to their question and then they'd nod, look away, and immerse themselves in a book, which I learned was my cue to silently excuse myself to sit behind the register playing Two Dots on my phone. Everyone was here to see Edward Bell and I was just his table's keeper. No one wanted to talk to the keeper.

I did have a few opportunities for conversation, some more entertaining than others. The first was with a man with stringy brown hair who spent nearly half an hour flipping through books in the Edward Bell area before coming to the counter with a stack of them.

"This place is great," he said. "I'm thinking about doing my thesis on the feminist motif in Edward Bell's body of work, and you've got everything I need."

I scanned the books and collected my thoughts. After reading the entirety of *The First Dollar* yesterday, I couldn't understand why customers kept calling Edward Bell a feminist icon. At first, I'd bought into it, cheering on the protagonist, Hazel, in her quest to open a cheese shop and gain financial autonomy. But by the end, when Hazel happily gave up the shop to appease her deadbeat husband, I wondered if Edward Bell knew anything about women.

"*Is* there a feminist motif?" I asked. "I just read *The First Dollar*, and—"

"That's the beauty," he said. "Bell was so ahead of his time. There are layers to it. In one layer, you've got Hazel trying to start her own business so she doesn't have to rely on her husband. That's feminist as hell, right?"

I nodded slowly. "That part I get, but—"

"Then the other layer is Hazel giving up on the shop and going back to being a housewife, which doesn't seem feminist at all, right?" I didn't say anything this time. I was starting to think his questions were rhetorical. "But the *third* layer is what makes him so forward-thinking." He leaned in, his brows arched like he was about to blow my mind. "It was Hazel's choice. She *chose* to leave her business and serve her family, right? Bell's saying women don't *have* to leave their husbands and join the workforce if they want to be seen as equals. It's all about having the freedom to do whatever they want. Some women *want* to assume a traditional gender role."

I considered this as I bagged up his books. "But she says in the beginning that she hates being a housewife."

He nodded, almost smirking. "And *that's* Edward Bell satirizing the stereotype that women are capricious. It's brilliant, right?"

That didn't add up, either. "It doesn't seem like satire."

"Yeah, people miss it if they're not paying attention. Some people like a more heavy-handed message, like Atwood's stuff."

I suspected his comment was meant to be an insult, but the only Atwood I knew was Ryan Atwood, and I didn't think he was talking about *The O.C.* "Right," I said lamely. I handed over his bag.

But he wasn't finished. "Don't tell me you like Atwood," he said. "She's as subtle as a bag of bricks."

I exhaled through my nose. I didn't even know who Atwood was and this guy had me ready to defend their honor. "Well, I love Atwood," I said. "And Marissa Cooper. And Seth Cohen. And Summer Roberts."

His face froze. "Right." He took a step toward the exit. "Have a good one."

I smiled to myself. After that, I spent a while flipping through *The First Dollar* in search of any semblance of satire, but I couldn't find it. The ending still made no sense. I shot off a text to Rochelle, and her reply made me laugh: Short answer, it's a dude's idea of feminism. I've given up on trying to fight it.

The one bright spot came when a woman in pink shorts paused in front of Edward Bell's portrait and posed a question no one had ever asked me.

"What do you think he keeps under that mustache?"

"Probably cocaine," I replied. "Look how wide his eyes are." Emboldened by her laugh, I added, "Or maybe it's not a mustache at all. It could be three eyebrows in a trench coat." She laughed again, and I instantly adored her.

She spent the next few minutes browsing in silence, but she eventually returned to the Edward Bell shrine, running a finger over the spines of his books.

"Are you looking for something?" I asked.

She raised her eyes, expression pensive. "Did he have a mistress?"

"Hmm?"

"I read online that he was rumored to have had an affair, but I haven't been able to find anything about that."

I gave her my best *I'm listening* face, but I snuck a peek at the FAQ sheet in front of me. It was not helpful.

"Well, let's see." I stood and pulled a copy of his biography from the shelf next to the portrait. "This is a long shot, but..." She watched as I flipped to the index and ran down the list of *Ms*. I looked up, feeling both silly and defeated. "No mention of a mistress."

She nodded. "So that's a no?"

I reshelved the book and turned back to her, not wanting the conversation to end. "Never say never," I said. "Let's see what I can dig up."

She followed me to the counter, where I picked up my phone and did a search for Edward Bell's mistress. The top result was a *Guardian* article about secrets of classic authors' personal lives.

"Is this what you read?" I asked, holding it up. She nodded, and I scrolled through it until I reached the section on Edward Bell. I lifted my head. "He was seen kissing another woman in a jazz club?"

"I know! But apparently his rival was the one who said that, so no one knows if it's true."

I looked at the portrait. His face somehow seemed more smug than usual. "I bet it's true," I said. "He's probably got a lot of dirty secrets. I bet he's hiding his mistress under his mustache."

This got another laugh out of her. I basked in it while I could, knowing that as soon as she left the store, it was back to playing Two Dots under the stern stare of Edward Bell's portrait.

"Thanks for trying," she said. "The lady at the museum acted like she had no idea what I was talking about."

"Weird." I busied myself with straightening a pamphlet, but I wondered if I should have shrugged off the question, too. In my defense, *Did Edward Bell have a mistress?* was not in the FAQs.

My curious customer, at least, seemed satisfied that I'd tried. She bought three Edward Bell books and wished me a good day on her way out. The rest of the day passed more slowly. I reshelved books, rang up customers, answered more questions. Occasionally, I'd hear creaks coming from upstairs. I looked to the ceiling, remembering that Vernon lived upstairs and hoping he might come down and make my day more interesting. (He didn't.) By the time I locked up for the day, I was more than ready to leave.

The next day, and the next, and the next, the quiet at the bookstore continued. I could now remember the titles of four of

Edward Bell's ten-ish novels. I had an idea of Vernon's schedule: silence, creaks midafternoon, silence, creaks after five o'clock. I began to stop expecting customers to buy anything other than Edward Bell's novels—with the exception of the few townsfolk who stopped in. Unlike the tourists, who found it a novelty that we carried Edward Bell's lesser-known novels and stocked up accordingly, the locals had no interest in his work. I encountered a man who bought a Virginia Woolf, and another day, a woman who browsed for a while and left with a Thomas Hardy.

But these minor interactions left me wanting more. They weren't outgoing and talkative like the people I'd met at the farmers' market, and I didn't see them daily like my old regulars from my barista days. This bookstore, with its limited offering of classics they'd probably read in high school, wasn't a daily or even biweekly stop for them. There were no new books in stock, nothing that would compel them to come to this store rather than the Barnes and Noble one town over. For the most part, my day revolved around tourists who either browsed in silence or asked me the same questions over and over again.

When Malcolm entered the store first thing Saturday morning, I couldn't help myself from waving enthusiastically. I didn't even care that he was here to "check in" on me. He still counted as a regular. And I was unbelievably bored.

Malcolm, who eyed my waving hand like he feared it had been possessed, did not share my enthusiasm.

"Hi," he said. His fingers absentmindedly tapped the counter. I watched them, then him. There was an uneasy look on his face.

"Do you like the new look?" I asked, gesturing to my face. "I shaved my mustache."

His eyes swept down my face, but he didn't so much as

smile. I supposed the concept of new looks was unfamiliar to him. His locs were still tucked into a ponytail and his button-down was nearly identical to the one I'd seen him in last time, just in a slightly different shade of blue. I imagined Malcolm standing in front of his closet that morning, picking from a row of identical shirts.

He scanned the empty store, then leaned in. "Did you tell a customer that Edward Bell had a mistress?"

The woman in pink shorts came to mind, but it took me a moment to comprehend how Malcolm could have known about her. "Um. She asked me, and I tried looking it up, but I couldn't find anything." I sized Malcolm up and down. "How did *you* know?"

He set his phone on the counter. "Ralph checks the Google reviews of every Bell Society business every morning. This showed up on Cobblestone Books's page today." He tapped his screen. Five yellow stars stared back at me.

I looked up. "Awesome."

Malcolm nudged the phone closer. "No, it's not."

I peered at it again. Under the five stars, a user named Paige F. had written:

Great selection if you're into classics. You can find all of Edward Bell's books here, even the bad ones. Helpful staff, too. The woman working there tried to help me uncover the mystery of Edward Bell's rumored mistress, which has been on my mind since that Guardian article about author drama. She couldn't find anything, but we agreed his mistress must be the dirty little secret hidden in his mustache!

I smiled, but it faltered under Malcolm's serious gaze. "I didn't tell her he had a mistress," I said. "She asked. And I was trying to help. See, she said 'helpful staff.'" I poked the review with my finger, which sent the page into a scroll spiral. "I'm helpful."

Malcolm just stared like he was trying to decide whether to correct me. "Ralph sees it differently," he finally said. "There are some things he doesn't want staff talking about."

"So I should have ignored her?"

"Ralph calls it 'distract and redirect.'"

"Okay," I said. "Now I know for next time."

His face pulled into a barely suppressed wince. "Well."

"What?"

Malcolm sighed. "Ralph has decided to reassign some of your duties to the museum's purview."

I took a moment to parse his words, combing through them for something to counteract the dread washing over me. "Duties like what?"

"Until he feels more comfortable about having you serve as a guardian of Edward Bell's legacy—that's the term he uses for Bell Society staff," he said when my mouth twisted in confusion, "he's going to move Edward Bell's books and writing table to the museum."

The air in my lungs left me. Ralph had floated this idea earlier, in an offer that felt like a threat, and Rochelle had shut him down. Now I didn't have a choice. My first week on the job and I'd let her down. "For how long?"

Malcolm shrugged. "Until you're up to speed. That's all he said."

"Okay." I looked around the store, at the Edward Bell shrine that would soon be empty. "What am I supposed to do until then?"

He gestured to the shelves around the store. "Sell the other books."

"But no one buys them," I protested. "No one likes classics."

"Hey," he said, as if I'd just insulted his mother.

"What? It's true. No one buys anything except the Edward Bell books." My words got quieter as I realized what losing Edward Bell's books would mean. Rochelle had already been worried about whether she could get by on the bookstore's revenue when the baby arrived. My stomach swooped at the thought of what this could mean for her now.

"But it doesn't mean the classics don't matter," he replied.

I blinked away the mental image of an OUT OF BUSINESS sign draped over the store's entrance. "What?"

"I'm just saying classics are underrated."

I raked my fingers over my scalp, trying to think. "How long until we get the books back?"

"You...already asked that," he said. "Just until you're up to speed. It's only temporary."

I laughed. The sound felt faraway. "When I moved in with my parents after I lost my job, I told them it was only temporary. That was ten months ago. Is Ralph going to hold on to the books for ten months?"

"I...I don't know. Probably not." I slumped forward, resting my chin on my arm. Malcolm pursed his lips, his eyes darting around the store as if looking for backup. "Are you...okay?"

"Yep." I nodded for longer than anyone should, but bobbing my head up and down somehow made me feel like I was in control. "I'm great. Super. Stupendous."

"Okay," he said slowly. "If you're sure, then I'll get out of your hair." He leaned forward slightly. "Are you sure?"

"Yeah." I mustered a weak smile.

"All right. Then, um. I'll come by at closing to move the Edward Bell things over to the museum."

"Great," I said. Malcolm waited a beat. When I didn't say anything more, he turned and finally left.

Throughout the day, I paid even closer attention to the purchases customers made, scrutinizing the books they carried to the register, hoping to see an abundance of non-Bell classics in their hands. But nearly all the tourists who came to see the table left with copies of Edward Bell's books—and nothing else. One person, presumably a local, came in, browsed the shelves in silence, and left with nothing. With every Bell book I scanned, every customer who left without making a purchase, I'd sink further down into my chair.

Just before closing, I watched Malcolm and another man quietly pack the stock of Edward Bell books into boxes. They wrapped the table and chair in quilted pads and I held the door while they carried the bookshop's main attraction out of the store.

And then I was left with my classics—and a sinking feeling about how the store would survive the loss.

CHAPTER FIVE

I should have known something like this would happen. Failure is sort of my thing.

I'd never say it aloud, but it's a thought that creeps in whenever my best-laid plans slip through my fingers. A single word whispered in a disappointed sneer, by a voice that wants to be proven wrong but takes so much pleasure in reminding me when it's right. *Failure*.

It all started with Plan A: graduate from college, move in with my parents, get a job as a barista at Peet's, and apply to law school. Not that I'd ever wanted to be a lawyer, but there was something appealing about the fact that it offered a clear, defined path from law school to career. My parents had been satisfied that I was trying for something more, even though I liked it at Peet's. I liked seeing the same people every day: the old man in a yellow cardigan who always said good morning, the woman who came in every day at 8:40 for a small latte and ordered a maple oat scone on Fridays. I poured coffees, studied test prep books, took the LSATs three times, and submitted my applications—and then the rejection letters came streaming in, giving voice to the creeping thought in my head. I'd just spent a year of my life failing.

I changed tactics and moved on to Plans B through F: Find something—or a combination of somethings—that paid enough for me to rent a place of my own. Dog walker, Lyft driver, waitress, cashier, sales specialist at a fancy spa. I drifted from job to job, finding that the fun ones didn't pay enough, and the ones that did pay enough weren't any fun. The spa paid all right, but what was the point if my boss was obsessed with quotas and no one in the break room ever wanted to talk to me? With every job I left, every time I'd come home and tell my parents this one hadn't worked out either, I'd see the word *failure* reflected in their baffled expressions.

And then there was Plan G. I came so close with Plan G. When I got a job as an office coordinator for an online media company, I felt like I'd finally done it. It wasn't just a job; it was an *office* job. I had a desk, steady income, Saturdays and Sundays off. At last, a sure bet that I'd finally fulfilled my parents' wishes, doing something other than serving or retail, using that college degree they'd paid so much for.

Well, *using* is putting it loosely. My main responsibilities included sitting at the front desk, signing for packages, and stocking the office fridge. Still, it was an office job and I'd finally conquered failure and all was right with the world. But even after holding down that job for longer than any other, even after moving into an apartment of my own, my dad still asked me what I wanted to do with my life.

"You don't want to do something related to your degree?" he'd asked, as if I hadn't only majored in political science because I took a course to fulfill a requirement freshman year and decided I liked it okay enough to keep on with it.

I'd just shrugged and sipped my coffee. He still saw me as the girl who used to be his reliable ticket to honor roll breakfast buffets at Golden Corral every semester of high school. But after that, I'd struggled to adapt from the linear path of high school—do well in school and get into a good college—to the more free-form, ambiguous task college gave me: pick a major that will become your career that will become the rest of your life. I'd watched Rochelle major in English with her whole heart, and she saw me skip class and nap through finals week because I didn't know what I was supposed to be working toward. She knew exactly what she was supposed to do, and she did it to the letter: plant her potential, water it every day, and watch her future spring forth. While I spent four years holding an unopened seed packet and staring at an arsenal of terra-cotta pots, realizing I wasn't remotely interested in any path college had to offer.

There was no honor roll I could point to now, no meaningful career I could impress my dad with. My happiness didn't count for anything, I supposed. It didn't matter that I had a group of work friends I'd go out to happy hours with. Or that I founded a club called the Merrymakers, which organized potlucks, cubicle decoration competitions, and birthday parties. Or that my roommate and I had themed movie nights with popcorn and sangria.

My boss had been impressed, though. He'd said in my performance review that he liked the initiative I'd taken with the Merrymakers. And I'd wanted to correct him, that it wasn't about initiative; it was about *fun*. But somehow there was something wrong with that, caring more about potlucks and cupcakes than work.

But even this job, happy as it made me, didn't last. Three years in, the media company was bought by a conglomerate, one that didn't want to pay someone to spend all day monitoring soda levels and remembering birthdays. I held out as long as I could, paying rent from my savings while I tried to find a job. I didn't.

My job at Rochelle's bookstore isn't even a plan—it's an interlude, a reprieve—but somehow I'd failed in this, too. It was only natural. Of course I'd get Rochelle's main source of revenue taken away. Of course I'd send the store spiraling into ruin. I don't know why I expected anything different.

The week that followed my latest failure was an exercise in restraint. Restraint from calling over everyone who passed the window and asking them to come in. Restraint from begging the few people who did enter to please, for the love of god, buy a book. Restraint from audibly sighing every time someone perused the shelves and left without a purchase.

Guilt tugged at me every time the bell over the door rang to announce the departure of yet another person who hadn't bought a book. Rochelle still didn't know the Bell books had been taken away. I'd meant to tell her that day, but I'd come home to find her dozing on the couch, and waking her up to tell her the bookstore was doomed felt cruel.

So I waited. But by the next morning, after a fitful night's sleep, I decided I should have a plan in place. Then I could give her a "bad news, good news" update. So far, though, I hadn't conjured any sort of plan for getting the bookstore's revenue back on track, and sales were falling fast. I needed to act soon.

Like every morning since the Bell books had been removed, time dragged sluggishly on. I'd watched two episodes of *Kim's Convenience* without anyone entering the store. Then, feeling antsy, I walked around the store tidying up shelves and straightening spines. I rearranged some shelves to bring books frontward. Previously, only Edward Bell's books had gotten the front-facing treatment, but that wasn't an option anymore. I stepped back to take in the scene. Austen, Brontë, and Dickens now stared forward, enticing customers to pick them up. They weren't enticing to me, exactly, but maybe some customers might find them interesting. My sister, Tanya, loved *Wuthering Heights* for whatever reason.

I took a picture of the shelf and sent it to my family's group chat, adding the message, Rearranging some shelves at the bookstore!

A picture of a bookshelf wasn't as compelling as the photos of my three-year-old nephew and my one-year-old niece that dominated the thread, but I didn't have much else to contribute. Showing them I was thriving in my new, albeit temporary, job might keep my parents from asking what I was doing with my life.

Mom: Beautiful!
Tanya: Heathcliffffff
Dad: Looks good! Could bookselling be your calling? 😃

I stared at the blinking cursor, not sure how to respond. I could see the high expectations shining through that one little happy face. The distance may spare me from my parents' bickering, but they could still drop hints about their lofty hopes for me. After I'd spent the last year bumming around at home, my dad chose to believe that whatever job I got next was sure to be a calculated move, the career I was destined for rather than another short-term plan doomed to fail. But it didn't mean bookselling was my calling. I wasn't sure why a job needed to be my calling at all.

Thankfully, Tanya then sent a picture of my nephew holding

a book on their last trip to a bookstore, and my dad's question passed unanswered. Tanya protected me from my parents' nudges when she could, even though as the older sister I'm pretty sure it was my job to protect *her*. But maybe role reversals like this started happening when you had your life figured out. I wouldn't know. One second, I was tutoring her in algebra when she was on the verge of flunking; the next, she was enrolled in a Doctor of Physical Therapy program, getting married, and having kids. My scuttling didn't really compare.

In the long gaps between customers, I turned to my phone to conduct more of the searches I'd been doing all week:

bookstore get more customers

bookstore marketing ideas

And then, with my browser in private mode:

Bell River cult

The results were not helpful.

My bookstore-related search results were informative, sort of, but they were constrained by the Bell Society's rules.

Keep a wide, diverse selection of books. (Not an option.)

Collaborate with local vendors and artisans to sell their products in your store. (I texted Rochelle to ask if she'd considered this. She replied that the only non-book items Ralph would allow was the Bell Society–branded merchandise from the museum gift shop.)

Host creative events built around authors, books, themes, or topics. (Not without Ralph's permission, Rochelle texted me. Edward Bell is the only theme he's interested in anyway. Then she sent another text that felt like a punch in the gut: You're so sweet to be thinking outside the box, but no need! I know the store's doing just fine ♥)

When I wasn't brainstorming failed ideas, I was plotting how to get on Ralph's good side. My only recourse while sitting in the empty bookstore was reading more Edward Bell, so I downloaded *No Pen Mightier* on my phone and started reading.

Fifty painful pages later, I was convinced that Edward Bell only wrote this book to put his readers to sleep. In *The First Dollar*, Hazel's quest to start her own business had at least been interesting, but this book, about a man's struggle to write a novel, was mind-numbing. Edward Bell had apparently exhausted his imagination on his first book.

A woman entered the shop as I was struggling to care about the protagonist's lack of inspiration. I lifted my head and greeted her without much hope. When she made a beeline for me, I sat straighter, preparing for the possibility that she, too, was one of Ralph's minions. Even though, in a pair of leggings and an oversized blue cardigan, she didn't look the part. There was something about her expression too, the way she couldn't keep her gaze steady even as she headed for me, that told me she wasn't here on Bell Society business.

"Hi there," she said.

"Hi," I replied, watching her curiously. "How can I help you?"

"I heard you don't carry Edward Bell's books anymore."

Salt on the wound. "Says who?" I asked.

"I heard Cynthia talking about it at the library. She works at Bell Museum," she added.

I groaned. I was town gossip already. "What did she say?"

"She was just talking about how they reconfigured the gift shop to make room for his books. But I wondered if that meant there were any other changes about the books you sell, or if it's still just..." She spotted the shelf I'd rearranged that morning. Austen, Brontë, and Dickens stared back at her.

"Still just classics," I said.

"Oh."

I watched the way her thumb fiddled with the strap of the oversized leather tote on her shoulder. "Why do you ask?"

She looked up, still lost in thought. Finally, she reached inside her bag and pulled out three paperbacks. "I'm an author. I thought that if the rules had changed, maybe you could sell my books here. But I guess that's not the case."

I picked one up. The cover showed a man in a suit looking nobly off in the distance while gripping the shoulders of a woman whose breasts were dangerously close to bursting out of her button-down shirt. The words *Performance Review* hovered over them in italicized letters. Below it was the name *Evelyn Suwan*.

"You wrote this?" I asked.

She nodded. I reached for another book on the counter. *Taste of You* featured a man in a chef's hat staring at a woman whose back was turned to him. *Windswept* had a glowing, pink-tinged cover showing a woman standing on a cliffside in a flowy dress. All the heroines were Asian, like her. It was refreshing to see these colorful, diverse covers in a store filled with musty old classics. I turned to the back of *Taste of You*. Something about a woman hired to save a pretentious chef's failing restaurant, ensuing arguments about cuisine, and long looks from across the kitchen.

"Do you like romance novels?"

I looked up to see Evelyn watching me with interest.

"I don't know." I set the book down. "If I read something, it's usually only because I liked the movie."

This would have elicited a sermon from Rochelle about how

there are so many books beyond the ones that led to movie adaptations. But Evelyn just eyed me like she was trying to figure me out.

"What's your favorite book?" she asked.

Not an answer I had at the ready. I tried to recall the brief list of books I'd read by choice. "I remember liking *The Time Traveler's Wife*?"

An easy smile came over her. "Then you do like romance."

"I guess," I said. "But it was kind of depressing."

"What about rom-coms?"

"I love rom-coms. My favorite movie is *When Harry Met Sally*."

"Rom-com books, I meant," Evelyn said.

I blinked. "There are rom-com books?"

Evelyn's head bobbed quickly up and down, dark hair swishing along with her. "*Taste of You* is a rom-com. You should read it."

"Okay." I glanced down at the books in front of me, remembering her reason for coming in. "You know, we get a lot of questions from people asking where they can find books from this century, and I always direct them to the Barnes and Noble in Franklin. If you have a card or something, I could tell them about your books."

"Yeah, okay." Evelyn dug around in her purse and I went back to staring at *Taste of You*, an idea forming in my mind. Before I'd finished thinking it through, Evelyn dropped a stack of glossy cards on the counter.

"I don't get how it's decided what a classic is," Evelyn said. "Or who gets to make that call. Like, Jane Austen writes romances, and they're considered literary classics, but then you have other romance authors who were around in Edward Bell's time—like Eleanor Alice Burford—and they don't count?"

"Don't look at me. I don't even understand why people like classics."

She stepped closer, leaning her arms on the counter. "And don't get me started on how sex is considered trashy in romance books but so important when it's in something like literary fiction. Why are my books lesser than some guy writing about having sex with a couch?"

"Sex with a couch?"

She nodded emphatically. "There's another literary novel that has a line about a woman being so turned on that her tits double in size... Sorry," she said, looking around.

"That's okay. That's the best and worst thing I've ever heard."

"It truly is." She sighed and dropped her arms to her sides. "I should stop. I didn't come here to complain."

"Right." My gaze went back to the stack of cards on the counter. "Well, I can definitely hand out your card when people ask about contemporary novels."

"Thanks." She paused. "It's too bad you can't sell them. There are a lot of romance readers in town. They buy books online because they don't have a choice. If you carried romance here, it would sell."

I glanced down at the books, which suddenly seemed dangerous and tantalizing. I picked up *Windswept* and flipped through it. The first few pages were all excerpts from readers' glowing reviews. She clearly had a following—just no opportunity to sell to anyone in Bell River. If we sold books like these, we'd corner the market. We'd *be* the market.

"Breaking the classics rule is a risk." My sentence swung up at the end like I was asking a question. Asking for a reason to take this risk. I kept my eyes on Evelyn, hoping for an answer.

A flash of intrigue glittered in her eye. "Did you know romance novels are a billion-dollar industry?"

I broke into a slow smile.

CHAPTER SIX

It's hard to sell books in secret.

I'd been so sure at first. After my encounter with Evelyn, I'd ditched the Bell book to spend the rest of the day reading *Taste of You* and doing more research. The romance market was as large as the mystery, science fiction, and fantasy genres combined. About half of romance readers read a book a week—which I could believe, since I read *Taste of You* in two days. There was something addicting and approachable about romance. And no one in Bell River was selling it.

The next night, after scouring book recommendation websites and compiling a list of buzzy romance novels, I saw an ad for a mystery novel in the sidebar. I examined the cover, dark and intriguing: a woman's profile obscured by shadows. I read the blurb underneath, which called the book "an evocative page-turner," and I asked myself a question that felt practical and devious in equal measure: Why stop at romance?

I expanded my search, reading more recommendations and reviews and synopses, and soon I had a list of more than a dozen books I wanted to carry in the store, in a range of different genres: romance, sci-fi, fantasy, thriller, horror, mystery. And then I was calling sales reps and placing orders in the smallest possible quantities, and before I knew it the storage room was home to a stack of cardboard boxes patiently waiting to fulfill their destiny.

Every time someone entered the shop, I'd look at the storage room door as though I could tell the books inside *This might be the one!* This could be the sale that proved secretly selling modern books under Ralph Bell's nose wasn't absurd. Then I could feel justified for the secrets I'd been keeping from Rochelle—and the lies. The other night, while I was loading the dishwasher after dinner, she'd handed me a plate and asked, "Everything okay at the bookstore? I noticed sales are down."

The plate had almost slipped from my hand. I gripped it tighter and lowered it into the dishwasher. "Yeah, it's great," I said. I rinsed off a stubborn marinara stain, my mind reeling with excuses. "Ralph actually mentioned that all Bell Society sales are down this month. I think he said there are a few big literary conventions going on right now. But things should perk right back up next month." I didn't know why I said that. August was nearly over. *Next month* was quickly approaching.

"Oh." A wrinkle crossed her forehead. "Did he say which ones? I know there's RLA, but that's in September."

I pulled the dish detergent from under the sink and took my time unscrewing the cap. "I don't know. It was such a mess of acronyms that it all went over my head. You know…ABC. BBQ. WTF."

Her forehead crease disappeared. "LOL," she added with a smirk.

I forced a chuckle. "Yeah, that was another one."

It wasn't until she pulled a popsicle from the freezer and headed into the living room that I realized how tightly I'd been gripping the detergent. I set it down, feeling the tension in my muscles relax. But it was hard to feel relieved about lying to my best friend. I could dress it up however I wanted, tell myself I was doing her a favor, letting her concentrate on resting and preparing for her baby rather than worrying about her livelihood. But it still made me a liar.

I'd bought myself some time, but not enough. As *next month* crept ever closer, the need to earn back the revenue I'd lost intensified with each passing day.

I spent days sizing up every customer, assessing whether I could announce my new inventory out of the blue and trust them not to tattle. And every time a browser walked through the store without saying a word, I'd deflate a little.

I even started trying to catch Vernon's eye whenever he passed by the window, as if I could entice him to come in through desperate eye contact alone. He always walked slowly, with a permanent scowl on his face, which gave me plenty of time to try to sell my pleading stare. I think he even noticed once. I caught him glancing through the window for a millisecond, but then he jerked his head forward and continued trudging past. Then I'd hear the familiar sound of him going up the stairwell on the other side of the wall, the jingle of his keys, and the slam of his door, and I'd be left alone with my unseen, unsold books once more.

And so when Malcolm entered Cobblestone Books that afternoon, I couldn't bring myself to panic. Panicking was for people who had something to panic about. Something to hide. With my stock of unsanctioned books in the back room, every one of them unsold and accounted for, I was—not by design—a model citizen.

"Come to repossess something else?" I asked as he approached.

He gave me a weary look. "No. Just checking in."

"On the classics you love so much?"

"Naturally." His gaze fell on the book splayed on the counter in front of me. "What's that?"

I held it up—another one of Evelyn's romances. I'd finished *Taste of You* and moved on to her historical romance *Windswept*. I'd stayed up late last night reading it, eager to reach the moment where Lillian and her reserved neighbor Percy kiss for the first time.

"That's not from Edward Bell's time."

"Good thing I'm not selling it." I eyed Malcolm. "Have you read it?" I asked innocently.

He gave a strangled cough that might have been a laugh or a cry of offense. "I don't read romance," he said.

I stopped myself from rolling my eyes at his pretentious tone. "Why not?"

"It's not my thing." He took a step toward the children's shelf, like that settled the conversation.

"Spoken like a Percy," I said.

Malcolm turned. His brow furrowed ever so slightly. "What?"

"You'd get that reference if you read *Windswept*," I said with a shrug. "You're a total Percy."

He studied me, as if debating whether it was worth his time to argue. "You don't even know me well enough to decide something like that."

"That's totally something Percy would say." I did my best to keep a straight face under Malcolm's stare. Finally, he scoffed and disappeared into an aisle.

Malcolm did the rest of his *checking in*, as he called it, in silence. He walked slowly past the shelves. He stopped every now and then to meticulously align a spine that was one millimeter more indented than the other spines in the row. On one occasion he pulled a book off a shelf and crossed the room.

"This belongs in children's," he said, reshelving it with utmost precision.

"Percy *loves* reshelving books," I said. "It's basically his hobby."

"You know what?" Malcolm turned to me with a considering look. "You're Lydia Bennet." His upper lip curled when he said her name.

"All right, cool. I assume she's awesome." I picked up *Windswept* and started flipping through it. I could feel Malcolm's eyes on me, and I had to bite the inside of my cheek to hide my smile.

"How do you not know who Lydia Bennet is?" he asked.

"The same way you don't know who Percy Northcott is."

Malcolm rolled his eyes. "I'm leaving now."

"Bye, Percy." I winked just as he turned to leave. He paused long enough to toss me a glare before heading out. I laughed and went back to *Windswept*. Not a sale, but just as satisfying.

I didn't have to look up when the bell above the door rang moments later. Malcolm was absolutely the kind of person who needed a few minutes to think up a comeback.

"Yes, Percy?" I said.

"Um."

My head shot up. Leena from the farmers' market stood in the entrance, blinking in confusion.

"Ignore that," I said quickly. "Hi! How are your chickens?"

Leena grinned. "Adorable as always. How are you liking it here?"

No one had asked me that since I'd come to town. I mentally rifled through various interpretations of her question. Here at Cobblestone Books, under Ralph's control? Here in Bell River, where my closest friend after Rochelle was her five-year-old son? Here in this phase of my life, with no discernible plans for the future?

"Great," I told her. It felt like the simplest response. Leena nodded and turned her attention to the shelves, but I was reluctant to let the conversation die. Malcolm I'd teased for entertainment, but Leena had been fun to talk to at the farmers' market. "Who's Lydia Bennet?"

Leena took a moment to think. "She's the annoying little sister in *Pride and Prejudice*, isn't she? The one who runs away with Mr. Wickham?"

I held back a laugh. At least my literary equivalent sounded interesting.

"Why?" she asked.

"No reason." As I watched Leena pick up a book, it dawned on me that she might be open to my new inventory. She'd been reading a modern-looking book that day at the farmers' market. And someone with a posse of punnily named poultry must be my kind of person. I wanted to let her into my world. Show her my chickens, as it were. "Hey, are there any genres you're interested in?"

I'd taken to slipping this question in casually, like I wasn't reading from a script of my own invention. My hope was that the response would give me an opening to steer the conversation to my secret stash. So far, customers had given vague replies or dismissed my question entirely.

Leena shrugged. "I like a lot of genres. Lately I've been reading romance."

My breath hitched. It was like she had a copy of my script. She'd given me the perfect lead-in to my next line: *Do you wish this bookstore sold other genres?*

But before I could open my mouth, she added, "I wish you could find romance here. It would save me a lot of trips to the B&N in Franklin."

I hesitated, my heart pounding. Part of me wondered if this was too good to be true, if she was a Bell Society plant trying to set me up, but the rest of me didn't care. If this was a trap, so be it. At least in the trap I'd finally get to sell an interesting book.

"I've got some romance novels in the back if you're interested," I said. Two lines in and I was already off-script, but I couldn't help it. I pinned my hopes to her and waited for a response.

A stare. Lips curving into a smile. "You do?"

"Just a minute." I raced to the back room, where I did a frantic scan of my stock before finding the cardboard box I'd put together after the genre books arrived. I'd packed one of each book, spines up, a sample platter of genres, but it hadn't ever left the storage room—until now. I hurried back to the counter and set the box in front of her, beaming wildly.

"Oh," she said, perhaps expecting something more sophisticated than a stash of paperbacks swaddled in cardboard. But she began examining the spines anyway, plucking out one book at a time.

The bell over the door signaled the arrival of another customer. A man—midforties with gray scruff—entered the shop. He met my gaze, then immediately averted his eyes, as did most customers who feared I'd try making conversation. I watched him gravitate to a shelf in the corner and hoped he'd stay there. I glanced back at Leena and silently willed her to be discreet.

"Evelyn Suwan," she read, picking up *Windswept*.

"She's a local author," I volunteered. "It's autographed."

She made a murmur of appreciation and flipped through the book. I snuck another look at the man behind her, still pondering the shelf.

"I'll take these two."

I couldn't help the surprised laugh that left my mouth. "You will?" Asking customers if they were sure about their choices was also not in the script.

Watching her sign the receipt, I wanted a way to hold on to her, make sure she came back. The research I'd done on engaging customers came back to me.

"Would you be interested in signing up for our newsletter so we can alert you about new arrivals?" The newsletter didn't exist yet, but that wasn't important.

Already she was unfolding a pair of sunglasses, ready to depart, but she paused at this. "Sure."

For the rest of the day, my eyes kept flitting to her name on my improvised sign-up sheet: *Leena Mahajan*. My shred of proof that someone was interested in my shady venture.

An hour before closing time, I got a text that jolted me out of my thoughts: Rochelle's in labor. Can you close early and come watch Dylan?

CHAPTER SEVEN

Elliot Michael Howard was born on August 29 at 12:47 a.m. He was, I told Rochelle, a very cute baby, though I secretly agreed with Dylan's assessment that, with his pale skin and wrinkly face, he resembled a naked mole rat.

I stopped knowing what to expect when I came home. One evening, Rochelle was upstairs with a screaming Elliot while Dylan sobbed into Luke's shirt on the living room couch and wailed about how Rochelle didn't even see his cartwheel. Another night, Rochelle napped on the couch while Luke fed Elliot a bottle and Dylan played a game on Luke's phone. I kept to the sidelines, not wanting to interrupt. Dylan got into the habit of coming to my room after dinner, pulling a game off the shelf, and setting it up on the rug like we had an unspoken agreement to play. His tactic worked, so I guess we did.

In the meantime, I'd managed to sell a few more books. Leena came back with a friend, who browsed my cardboard box with gusto. I asked a man buying an Agatha Christie if he'd read *The Hunting Party*, he perked up, and he bought two mysteries from my stash.

But selling the occasional book wasn't enough. Sales were still dwindling. Elliot's arrival may have bought me some time, with Rochelle now pouring her energy into feeding and changing him and catching snippets of sleep when she could, but I felt like I'd broken a promise. I'd reassured her that the store would earn enough to support her family, even with Elliot's arrival. Elliot's wails started to ring in my ears like knowing accusations.

I needed a bigger draw than a box of secret books. Most people in town didn't know about my new inventory, and I couldn't advertise it without raising Malcolm's suspicions. I needed to lure more readers to the store—a lot more.

Leena had brought a friend to the bookstore that one time. If only she had as many friends as she did chickens. I mentally flipped through my short catalog of the people I knew in town. Abigail and I were friendly, but she hadn't stepped foot inside the bookstore. Vernon was hell-bent on avoiding me. I cycled through faces I remembered from the farmers' market: Ruth. Marcia. Toby.

Something purple and glittery crossed my mind. Toby, who made his own dice and founded a two-hundred-person D&D group. Maybe I could start a group.

I sat down in the tiny yellow chair at Dylan's coloring table and opened my laptop. A few searches later, I came across a Facebook group called Maryland D&D, founded by one Toby Polk. I clicked through pictures of smiling people sitting around a table, surrounded by drinks, snacks, papers, and dice. I needed something like this, but for book nerds.

I shifted in my tiny chair, which pressed into my spine and my hips all at once. I could invite people to the bookstore for a fun, casual hangout like this. Something clandestine and after-hours, when Malcolm was off the clock and couldn't *check in* on me.

It needed to be something fun. Something they couldn't find in a book. Thinking about the unwanted literary classics that filled the shelves, about the boxes of genre fiction people *did* want, about Malcolm haughtily telling me he didn't read romance, about Evelyn mentioning bad literary sex scenes with couch sex and ballooning breasts, an idea flickered to life.

Suppose I had an author write a funny, ridiculous scene that intertwined a literary classic with an entirely different genre? Characters from a Jane Austen novel with magical powers. Sherlock Holmes looking for love on Tinder. The writer could read their scene aloud at the bookstore. I could charge admission and sell snacks and drinks. Attendees could talk about the reading, the book, the genre, their favorite novels. The author could sign books. People could browse the shelves and buy from my secret inventory. And then, at the next event, I could pick another classic and another genre and do it all over again.

My mind couldn't stop sparking with ideas, bringing me back to my Merrymaker glory days when I organized elaborate murder mystery dinners and costume contests, relishing in the planning, the fun, the inventiveness. I forgot about the sharp pain in my spine and started researching book-related events, looking for a way to find a crowd of booklovers I could advertise this hypothetical event to. What was that convention Rochelle had mentioned when I was spouting off fake acronyms?

More searching. I didn't even care that I couldn't feel my right hip anymore, because I found it. RLA: the Reading and Literacy Association. They were hosting a book festival in DC in two weeks, where librarians, booksellers, publishers, authors, and readers could gather for panels and readings, attend book signings, and buy and sell books. It was too late to register for a booth, but attending at all would let me engage with readers and advertise my event. With any luck, I could have a new swarm of customers.

My event idea was bizarre enough, I hoped, to compel people to come to Bell River. I quickly typed an email to Evelyn, sharing an update on how sales were coming along—exactly three of her books sold—and slipping in that I was thinking of holding an event that involved writing parodies of classic novels with a contemporary, genre-bending twist. I spent a few minutes refreshing my email, wondering if she'd reply right away.

As the minutes ticked closer to midnight, I had to conclude that I might not hear back until morning. After a few false starts, I wedged free from the chair and got ready for bed. But even as I settled under the covers with *Windswept*, my mind kept wandering to my event idea. It felt like something. Something real.

When I woke up the next morning, I noticed a little envelope in my notifications bar. I closed my eyes and reminded myself that it was okay if Evelyn didn't like the idea. Nothing was stopping me from pushing forward on my own. I could pull this off without someone at my side. But the secrets I'd kept from Rochelle coupled with long days spent in a quiet bookstore left me longing for company.

Evelyn's email sent a relieved laugh fizzing out of me.

Yes please I need this to happen now.

A few more emails and she not only promised to serve as guest writer but offered to advertise the event in her newsletter. Our emails progressed to texts as we brainstormed potential themes.

What if we made something a rom-com? I texted while waiting for my order at the Sunrise Café. Something ridiculous?

I vote Moby-Dick just for the dick jokes, she texted back. We could call it Hunting for Dick. I laughed right there in the café.

"What's that?" Abigail slid my coffee across the counter.

I glanced around. The morning rush had mostly died down, and there were just a few others in the store. I moved closer and leaned in.

"If I invited you to an event at the bookstore called 'Hunting for Dick,' how would you react?"

She snickered, then gave me a once-over. "I'd love to see the look on Ralph's face when you suggest that."

I raised my eyebrows once, in the promise of a secret. "He won't know."

I couldn't quite interpret the grin dashing across her face. It could have been interest in the event, but Abigail had also made her discontent with Ralph and his rules quite clear. An eye roll when she recited the latest menu item he'd come up with, prune salad from an Edward Bell book. A curt "No" when a customer asked if she had a favorite Bell novel. It made me feel like a traitor every time I ordered an apple cheddar biscuit, but they were damn good.

Either way, Abigail's eyes had a definite spark when she said, "I would be *very* interested in attending."

I texted Evelyn that we were on.

Even with the high of the event propelling me forward, I couldn't ignore the biggest hurdle in my way: this was another secret I had to keep from Rochelle. She'd complained about Ralph's power trips before, but there was a fear behind it, too. One more toe out of line and Ralph could pull the store from her control and put his museum employees in charge.

But for every day Ralph refused to let me sell Edward Bell's books, the store was suffering, and Rochelle was taking notice. If I advertised this event at the book festival, held it without drawing Malcolm's suspicions, and attracted enough new customers, I could make up for the revenue I'd lost—and maybe even bring in some extra money while I was at it. It couldn't have been easy for Rochelle, being the only breadwinner while Luke was in nursing school, and expenses were piling up. I'd seen the rate at which Elliot was going through diapers. I'd heard Luke and Rochelle exchange worried murmurs about what Elliot's daycare expenses might amount to. If I managed to pull this off, she'd be grateful. I was sure of it.

I could do this. I could go to the book festival, I could drum up attendees, and I could turn the bookstore around. I'd have to close the shop for the day, but business was lacking anyway, and missing a day would be worth it for new customers.

The night before the festival, I went to bed early. And nowhere, not in the ticking clock on the wall or the king of *Candy Land* watching me from his throne on the shelf, did I feel a shred of guilt for what I had planned tomorrow. Foolproof plans have no need of guilt.

CHAPTER EIGHT

The convention center loomed ominously before me, swallowing the street with its shadow. People passed in and out of its doors with purpose while others sat on the steps outside, talking or reading. I stayed where I was, rooted to the sidewalk, gathering my resolve.

I gripped the straps of the tote bag on my shoulder. It held two hundred flyers advertising my bookstore event, which I'd decided to hold at the bookstore in two weeks' time. The words *Hunting for Dick* were shamelessly splashed across the flyer, along with the ten-dollar ticket price that would hopefully add profitability to this whole venture. I'd have to hope interest in the event outweighed any bewilderment about my poor graphic design skills. I didn't know why I added the confetti border.

I tugged on the sleeve of my jean jacket and slowly walked up the stairs. The second I stepped through those doors, I needed to be confident and collected. I needed to sell people on this event, convincingly enough that they'd want to show up. But I couldn't put too much effort into persuading them or they'd notice the desperation hiding in my words. They didn't need to know that the fate of Cobblestone Books, Rochelle's livelihood, our friendship, and my sense of self-worth all hinged on their decision to attend.

Cool air enveloped me when I stepped inside the convention center. I felt like I'd stumbled into something that was half farmers' market, half Scholastic book fair. Booths lined the walls, displaying books propped on tables, on shelves, on carousels. People swarmed around, browsing books and forming lines, their overlapping chatter like white noise at full volume. I walked past displays of striking, vibrant covers with vivid colors and bold fonts, all for books that were obviously published this century. My eyes swept across eager book browsers and abstract covers, hungrily taking in this excitement, this *new*ness, after spending the last month in an empty store with only tired, ancient books for company.

I spotted a booth that sold primarily romance and spent several minutes reading plot summaries and getting lost in rom-com story lines. A pair of exes competing in a baking competition. A woman who discovers her new colleague was a recent one-night stand. A man who returns to his hometown and finds love. I bought three paperbacks on impulse, shoving them into my already full tote, and had to stop myself from buying more.

But there weren't only booksellers here. I passed a woman selling notebooks and purses made from repurposed books. A man selling shirts adorned with literary covers, authors' faces, or quotes. Someone selling muffins. Nothing book-related— just muffins. I was grateful for it, both because I hadn't eaten breakfast and because I wouldn't have to pretend to understand a literary reference when I didn't. My first week at the bookstore, I made the mistake of asking a customer in a block-lettered

Pemberley shirt if that was her alma mater, and she'd stared at me as if I'd spoken gibberish. But there was none of that here. No wistful nostalgia for century-old books. No assumption that one type of books mattered more than another. Only excitement about new stories waiting to be discovered.

I took a bite of my non-literary muffin and kept walking, pondering how to advertise anything without a booth. The answer came when I circled back to the entrance and spotted a table covered in flyers next to the information booth. Not just the professional, glossy materials about the festival, but regular flyers on regular paper with questionable graphic design choices, advertising everything from homemade literary soaps to professional editing services. This was my kind of table.

Keeping an eye on the people behind the booth, still preoccupied with questions and freebies, I pulled the flyers out of my bag. I kept some for myself to pass out and put the rest on the table, wedged between two flyers from bookstores. What a natural fit it was—book sale, dick jokes, book sale. Perfection.

I stepped back, looking over the booths again. Putting flyers on the table was well and good, but I couldn't sit around hoping for people to find them. The number of entrants in the Merrymakers' winter cubicle decoration contest tripled the year I went cubicle to cubicle encouraging people to join.

I did another lap past the booths, this time with an eye toward vendors. Some came from farther away—West Virginia, Pennsylvania—but I homed in on the ones from Maryland or Northern Virginia.

Soon enough, I had a routine down pat: compliment a vendor on their goods, draw a connection by telling them about my store, and hand over the flyer as a sort of afterthought. A

THE BANNED BOOKSHOP OF MAGGIE BANKS   73

woman selling literary candles stared suspiciously at the flyer, as if it were a pamphlet for some new whale-dick religion I was starting, but most vendors at least smiled at the title.

My favorite reaction came from Miranda, a woman at a booth selling chapbooks. She laughed when she saw the flyer. "I can't tell you how much I hated *Moby-Dick*."

Unapologetic disdain for classic literature—my target audience. "Then I'm glad I never read it," I said.

"Wise woman."

Even the people who didn't express enthusiasm weren't the literary snobs I feared. When I presented the flyer to a middle-aged man selling art prints, he gave an uncomfortable chuckle and handed the flyer back to me. "This isn't really my crowd," he said, his cheeks reddening. But there wasn't any judgment in his tone, and his eyes were friendly under the brim of his worn Orioles baseball cap.

I glanced at the posters and prints hung up behind him. A UFO beaming up a slice of pizza. A rocket ship blasting past planets that resembled pepperoni. I wasn't sure why his art focused on the intersection between space and pizza, but someone with his eclectic tastes must appreciate what I was trying to do. I just needed him to see that.

"The theme changes every time," I said. "For the next one, we'd pick a classic novel and reimagine it as...sci-fi."

"Oh, really?" he said. I held the flyer out again. He took it this time.

"It's kind of like a mash-up," I said, watching him read the flyer. "Classic novel crossed with a different genre, with parody on top. You might find that *Moby-Dick* and romance go together just as well as spaceships and pizza."

He laughed. "Good point." I watched with barely suppressed

excitement as he folded the flyer and placed it in his bag. "It sounds fun."

He even agreed to add his name and email to my newsletter list. *Jim Abbott*, I read through his slanted scrawl. Another potential member of the bookstore's growing community.

I didn't know how many of these vendors would make the leap from interest to RSVP—or, I supposed, from RSVP to arrival—but after enough maybes, I began to grow certain that *someone* would RSVP by the end of the day.

I finished making the rounds at the booths a little after noon. I stood at the end of the hall, watching people form lines, talk to vendors, buy books. My duty was done now. I could drive back to Bell River, open the bookstore for the rest of the day, watch a few more episodes of *Kim's Convenience* on my phone while people passed by my quiet, empty store.

Or I could stay here.

I missed feeling like I was part of something. I don't think I've felt it since being with the Merrymakers at my last job. I was still new to reading, but being here, surrounded by people who loved books—all books, not just Edward Bell's dusty words—made me feel like I was part of a club again.

It was decided, then. I'd spent the morning experiencing the festival as a bookseller. I could pass the afternoon seeing it through the eyes of a reader.

I pulled the festival program from my tote and leaned against a pillar. There was a panel on rom-com tropes. A panel on complex female characters in fantasy novels. An interview with a mystery author whose new novel involved solving a murder in an abandoned theme park. Everything looked so interesting and fun and, best of all, had nothing to do with Edward Bell.

I made mental notes of the sessions I wanted to attend, then set off in search of lunch. On my way past the information table, I peered at the flyers and tried to determine whether my stack had shrunk any. I decided it had.

After passing a few restaurants, all crowded with people carrying book festival swag, I picked a falafel truck without much of a line. I placed my order and hopped onto a ledge while I waited.

There were a few tables set up off to the side, in an open area between two office buildings, but they were all occupied. I was considering my odds of scoring a table when I realized there was something familiar about the man sitting closest to me. He was in a gray T-shirt rather than a button-down, but his locs were swept into a tidy ponytail and his posture was rigid, even as he struggled to pick up a taco from his paper plate with one hand. The other hand marked his place in a book. A book that probably only a snob would like.

His name escaped my lips like a reflex.

"Malcolm!"

CHAPTER NINE

I didn't take it personally that Malcolm's response to seeing me was a frown. I wasn't entirely thrilled about seeing him, either. My thoughts raced to the two hundred flyers circulating the festival, whether in the hands of vendors or lying in wait at the information booth. I looked past his furrowed brow to the *DC Book Festival* program on his table. He couldn't see the flyers if he'd already been to the information booth. Unless he'd already seen them and that was what the frown was for, but I've seen this expression a few times now and it looked like a pretty standard dealing-with-Maggie frown.

"What are you doing here?" I asked. He held up the program without a word. "I know, but why? Policing the bookstore isn't enough, you had to take your show on the road?"

"I like books," he called back.

A man at the falafel truck called my number. I collected my lunch, then paused. I could go back to my concrete ledge and pretend Malcolm wasn't sitting nearby, but he had a table. And I should probably find out whether he'd seen the flyers. But mostly: I couldn't pass up a chance to bug him.

I plopped my lunch on his table. He moved his book an inch closer, his head still buried in the pages. I opened my plastic container, and the lid catapulted onto Malcolm's book. He sighed and pulled his book closer.

"How's my favorite broody count?" I asked.

Malcolm finally lifted his head, fixing me with a long stare. "That joke is getting old." He used a finger to push my salad lid out of the way. "And Percy is a viscount, not a count."

I broke into a grin. His expression faltered immediately.

"How do you know Percy's a viscount?" I asked, doing my best to hide the laughter in my voice. "Did you read *Windswept*?"

He gave a dark sigh. "Just enough to determine that you were wrong. I'm nothing like Percy."

"Of course." I stabbed a piece of romaine with my fork, keeping my eyes on him. "How far in did you get? Did you make it to the barn sex?"

Malcolm averted his eyes and cleared his throat. "No," he told the ground.

He definitely reached the barn sex.

Malcolm busied himself with his taco. "Why are you here?" he asked.

"I work in a bookstore."

"I don't see you selling books."

"I'm networking. Shaking hands. Greasing palms." His skeptical look made me want to come up with another synonym just to bug him, but I gave up when my mind went blank. "How's the festival going?" I asked. "See anything interesting?" Like, perhaps, flyers for a dick joke event.

He returned a fallen shred of cabbage to his taco. Apparently he liked his tacos as orderly as the bookshelves he was always organizing. "The usual," he said.

My flyers were far from *the usual*. He must not have seen them after all.

Malcolm looked up and caught me watching him. "What?" he said.

"Nothing." I dug my fork around my salad. He hadn't seen the flyer, but he might come across it after lunch. Unless he was planning to go home soon. I glanced up at him, surprised to find him watching me.

"Yes?"

Malcolm looked away. "I didn't say anything."

"Right." I took a long pull from my water bottle, enjoying the way he couldn't seem to meet my eyes. "What's your plan for today?" I asked.

"I mostly came here to see T. J. Hull. Do you know him?" he asked. I shook my head. "He's an author doing a panel this afternoon. I've read his books since I was a kid."

"Cool." I speared a grape tomato, thinking. So he was staying around the festival. I'd have to find a way to keep him from seeing the flyers. Well, he couldn't come across them as long as he was sitting here talking to me. "What do you like about him?" I asked.

"His books have robots and spaceships and aliens," he said, his eyes growing animated. "I was eight when I read one for the first time. It was the first time I realized books could be fun. I mean, look at this one." He lifted the book he was reading. It showed a cartoon drawing of a kid standing on a planet and looking up at the sky, where several moons shone brightly. *The Many Moons of Evorix*, the title read in large, blocky letters.

I smiled. All his book snobbery and he's sitting here reading a kid's book. "That's not a classic," I said.

"It should be. I've been on a T. J. Hull nostalgia kick all week. His books are addictive. His adult books are good too, but the kids' ones are more fun."

This was the most enthusiasm I'd ever heard from Malcolm. "Too bad we can't sell them at the bookstore," I said, keeping my voice light.

Malcolm just shrugged and took another bite of his taco. I guess I could have been more subtle. He glanced down at his book as he chewed, then slowly back up at me. "What about you?" he asked. "What's on your schedule?"

"I spent a while checking out the booths. Then there's a romance session I want to go to, and maybe a couple after that."

He tilted his head. "No surprise there," he said. He closed his book, and I felt a small thrill. Either he was polite, or he'd rather talk to me than read. "Is that your favorite genre?"

"I..." Yesterday I would have said yes. My interest in Evelyn's books and the romances I'd taken up since then had suggested that, by default, romance was my favorite genre. But seeing the wide selection of books at the festival and reading the session descriptions featuring other genres had me thinking there was more yet to be discovered.

"What?" Malcolm was watching me curiously.

I realized I'd been staring into the distance. I shook my head and speared a piece of cucumber. "I don't know," I said. "I think there's more I might like, and maybe I just haven't given it a chance yet."

Malcolm nodded, a gentle smile on his face. "That's fair. There are a lot of books out there."

I resisted the urge to make another remark about what the bookstore was allowed to sell. Instead, I followed the wispy train of thought forming in my mind. "I guess I hate that I've had to stumble upon it myself. Like, if the books I liked had been assigned in school, I might have actually gotten into reading. Being forced to read *Hamlet* and *The Great Gatsby* and having to analyze everything to death made me hate the concept of literature. Finding meaning in an eyeball and then patting yourself on the back just didn't make sense to me." I set my fork down and looked at Malcolm, who was watching me with interest. And he wasn't frowning. "Do you have any idea what I mean?" I asked.

Malcolm's lips twitched. "Did you ever read the wheelbarrow poem in high school? William Carlos Williams?"

"I think so. It was red, right?"

"Yes. Let me look this up so I can hate it more specifically." Malcolm picked up his phone. I took another bite of salad and watched the concentration on his face as he swiped away. "Okay, I have it," he said. "It's sixteen words. The entire poem is sixteen words. I had an assignment where I had to write a paragraph analyzing what the colors meant. I wrote that I thought it was a reflection of how wheelbarrows are red and chickens are white, and I printed a picture of a red wheelbarrow and a white chicken as evidence." Malcolm grinned proudly. "I got a D."

I gave a surprised laugh. "So you're not a total snob?"

His smile faded into offense. "I've never called myself a snob."

"You don't have to," I said. "It's part of your essence."

He narrowed his eyes at me, but there was something playful about it. "I don't think you know me well enough to know my essence."

I lifted a shoulder in a shrug. "And whose fault is that?"

Malcolm studied me thoughtfully. He looked like he was going to say something, but then his phone buzzed on the table.

"Alarm," he said, checking his phone. "The T. J. Hull session starts in ten minutes." He tucked his book into a backpack at his feet and picked up his plate.

"Right," I said, watching him stand. "I should head back, too." I gathered my picked-over salad and followed Malcolm to the trash can. We'd nearly reached it when I caught sight of a familiar confetti border peeking through the swinging lid. Instinctively I grabbed Malcolm's arm, turning him around before he could see my flyer.

"What?" Malcolm looked from my hand, still gripping his arm, to me. "What happened?"

"Nothing." I grabbed his plate. "Just…let me throw that out for you. Save some time. We don't want to miss that session." I gave him an innocent smile and crossed to the trash can, where I used his plate to cram the flyer fully inside. And hoped this wasn't some sort of symbolic representation of how my event was destined to go.

I brushed my hands on my jacket and met Malcolm at the table. "Ready?" I asked.

He watched me suspiciously as he put on his backpack. "What did you mean, '*We* don't want to miss that session'?"

"I—" I shrugged, like the answer was obvious. "I'm going with you. I have to see what this sci-fi guy's all about."

"Really?" he asked, looking me over.

"Really." I held his gaze, aiming for convincing. It made sense, actually. Better to escort him there in case we came across any other partially discarded flyers.

It may have been my imagination, but I thought I saw the corner of Malcolm's lips move. He quickly covered it up, assuming an impassive expression. "Okay," he said.

"Okay." I slung my bag over my shoulder and motioned for Malcolm to take the lead.

"When does your romance session start?" he asked.

"In an hour."

We reached an intersection. While we waited to cross, Malcolm turned to me. "Maybe I'll join you for that one."

I hesitated. I was tempted to gloat that whether Malcolm admitted it or not, this must mean he enjoyed my company. But calling attention to the delicate truce we'd reached could dissolve it completely.

"Okay," I said, shrugging like I didn't care. "It's only fair."

"It's only fair," he repeated.

I turned my attention to the crosswalk, but in my head I was marveling over what we'd just agreed to. I'd only invited myself to his session in a hurried effort to explain my bizarre behavior, but then it had snowballed somehow. He'd volunteered to attend a romance session. And I couldn't resist the thought that us spending the next two hours together meant I'd get to tease him some more.

The next thing I knew, Malcolm was pointing at the crosswalk sign. "We can cross now."

I redirected my thoughts as we stepped off the curb. "What if you came away from the session with an intense desire to read the nearest romance novel?" I asked.

He glanced at me, then forward again. "Then I guess it's a good thing we're at a book festival."

He was still acting so casual about it, and I wanted to mock him mercilessly, but something stopped me. If he was too shy to admit he wanted to spend the afternoon with me, I may as well let him cling to his illusions.

Did I have illusions? Of course not.

I pressed my lips together, glancing down at my sandals until I had control of whatever my face was doing. "I guess so."

In the convention center I kept my eyes straight ahead as we passed the row of booths. I didn't need a vendor calling me over to ask about my dick joke event, especially when I was trying to stop myself from looking up at Malcolm for signs of what he was thinking.

When we reached the session, people were just starting to take their seats. A man onstage sat in a chair shuffling papers while the chair across from him sat empty.

I paused at a row in the center of the room and started moving into it.

"What are you doing?" he asked.

"Picking a seat?"

"Why would we sit so far away? This is T. J. Hull." Malcolm strode ahead, leaving me behind.

"Why would you let me go first if you wanted to pick the seats?" I called after him. Malcolm, now settling into a seat three rows from the front, ignored me.

"Sorry," I said when I caught up to him, "I forgot you were a fanboy."

"Yeah, well." Malcolm pulled out *The Many Moons of Evorix*. "Don't let it happen again." He began flipping through the pages.

I settled into my seat, trying to get comfortable. My elbow made contact with Malcolm's arm.

"You're on my armrest." He pushed my elbow with his own.

"It's a shared armrest," I said, pushing his elbow right back.

He accepted defeat and went on reading. "Stop fidgeting and read your own book."

I cocked my head. I did have the three books I'd bought this morning. But it would be more fun to just... "I didn't bring one."

"Why not?"

"Why would I bring a *book* to a *book festival*?" I asked. "That's like bringing a roll of toilet paper to a bathroom."

He scoffed, then glanced around as if someone might hear me and take offense. "I suggest not comparing books to toilet paper."

"*I* suggest—"

"Shh," Malcolm said.

"Don't shush—"

"That's T. J. Hull," he whispered. We watched an unassuming man with red hair and a graying beard take the stage. He exchanged a few words with the man shuffling papers, then took the seat opposite him. T. J. Hull scanned the room, absentmindedly picking at his fingernails. I snuck a look at Malcolm, who was watching the nail-picking exploits so intently I half-wondered if he planned to scramble to the stage and sweep up the remnants for his personal collection.

When the session began, Malcolm snapped his book shut and shoved it in his bag. And when T. J. Hull started speaking, Malcolm leaned so far forward that it was a miracle he didn't fall out of his seat.

I wanted to laugh every time T. J. Hull said something completely bizarre as though it were a mundane fact. At one point he mentioned wasp leaders plotting a coup to overthrow the bee empire, and everyone, the interviewer included, nodded and listened with a completely straight face, like *Ah, yes, the political ramifications of the wasp coup are very serious.*

Soon enough, I found myself hanging on to his words, too. Not because I had any idea what he was talking about, but because it was a marvelous thing that there was a book about a bee empire, just as it was a marvelous thing that earlier this morning I'd bought a book about exes entering a baking competition. There must, undoubtedly, be an endless supply of unique and bizarre books to suit every reader's interests. Anyone, it seemed, could be a reader. Eight-year-old Malcolm and his affinity for aliens. Twenty-eight-year-old Maggie and her interest in romance and—apparently, somehow—bee politics. Every moment at this festival opened my world a little wider.

And then another thought floated in there, sneaking in while I was feeling so open to wonders and marvels and possibilities: maybe that means there's a path for me too, a plan that won't fail, and I just haven't found it yet.

The conversation ended with a plug for T. J. Hull's new book, an adult sci-fi novel about an alien colony, and the interviewer mentioned that anyone who had bought his book could start lining up for the signing. Immediately Malcolm pulled that very book out of his backpack and got to his feet.

"You don't have to wait with me," Malcolm said when I joined him in line. He said it suspiciously quickly, and I caught the shiftiness in his eyes.

"No, I'll wait." The opportunity to see Malcolm fawn over someone was too good to pass up. He might get tongue-tied, or ramble, or hyperventilate. Judging by the grunt Malcolm gave in response, he was all too aware of this.

"You're really excited to meet him, aren't you?" I asked. Mostly just to get him to admit it.

"His books changed my life," he said simply. I nodded, holding back my teasing remarks. The concept of idolizing an author this much was beyond me. Even so, it was remarkable that authors could have this sort of impact on the people who read their books. It made me start to understand, a little, why people like Rochelle, Malcolm, and the Edward Bell–loving tourists found such meaning in books.

The line moved steadily forward. An event coordinator onstage motioned to us that it was our turn. We approached the signing table, and then Malcolm opened his book to the title page and presented it to T. J. Hull.

"Hey there! Who should I make this out to?"

Malcolm, now face-to-face with his favorite author, stared at him in silence.

I followed T.J.'s gaze to the name badge hanging on Malcolm's chest. It was showing the blank side. "It's Malcolm," I said. I reached over and flipped it to the correct side. "There we go."

"Yes," Malcolm said. He held up the name badge, stretching it as close to T.J.'s face as possible.

"Normal spelling," he replied. "Got it!" T.J. smiled politely, like the fact that Malcolm was holding a name badge inches from his eyeballs was perfectly normal. I had to look away to keep from laughing.

"How'd you like the interview?" T.J. asked.

Malcolm nodded, like this was a reasonable way to answer an open-ended question. T.J. simply nodded back, a glimpse of amusement slipping through his patient smile. And while the two of them seemed to be having some sort of positive interaction, if synchronized nodding can be seen as positive, I couldn't watch a train wreck and not interfere.

"Malcolm first read one of your books when he was eight," I said. "He said it was the first time he realized reading could be fun."

"That's exactly why I write," T.J. said, glancing from me to Malcolm. "I hated reading when I was a kid, and I wanted to write something that kids could be excited about."

"I definitely was." Both T.J. and I turned to Malcolm, surprised that he'd found his voice. "*The Mysterious Robot on Bexley Street* is still my favorite book to this day."

T.J. grinned. "Thank you, Malcolm. That means a lot." He wrote something under his autograph and handed it to him. "It was great meeting you both."

When we walked off the stage and into the hallway, Malcolm heaved a large sigh.

"Was I awkward?" he asked. "I think I blacked out."

I recalled his excessive nodding but managed to keep a straight face. "No, you were great."

Malcolm opened his book. I crossed the hall to stand next to him, leaning against the wall. T. J. Hull had written *Malcolm, Thanks for coming!* Then, under his scribble of a signature, he'd drawn a robot's head—a square with round eyes, a rectangular mouth, and an antenna.

"What's that?" I asked. I turned to Malcolm, who had a faint, nostalgic smile on his face.

"It's Scrap," he said. "He's the robot in *The Mysterious Robot on Bexley Street*."

I moved closer for a better view, my arm brushing against Malcolm's. "He does look mysterious."

"Oh, he's full of mystery." Malcolm stared at Scrap a bit longer. "You should read it, actually," he said. "I want to know what you'd think."

"Should I be offended that you're recommending a children's book to me?"

"You should be honored that I'm gonna lend you my favorite book in the world."

Put that way, it did feel a little like an honor. "Okay," I conceded.

Malcolm gently closed the book. "I feel like I have you to thank for what happened back there," he said, turning to me.

I glanced from the book to him, feeling my face grow warm. "And what happened, exactly?"

He tilted his head. "I'm not completely sure. But I think it would have gone a lot worse if I'd been alone up there."

Sincere gratitude from Malcolm. I had trouble processing it, this moment, standing so close our arms were touching, his eyes fixated intently on me. "I think you're right," I said at last. Malcolm smiled, something carefree and wide that had his whole face lighting up. I felt my own face doing the same.

We'd never stood this close to one another before. I was almost leaning against him now, drinking in the discoveries. His posture was more relaxed than usual, one foot casually propped against the wall behind him. He was maybe three or four inches taller than me. I once dated a guy who was so tall I had to stand on my tiptoes to kiss him, but Malcolm was at my level, almost. Not that kissing and Malcolm and me had anything to do with one another.

"We should head to the romance panel," he said, snapping me out of my thoughts.

I shifted a step to the side in a nonchalant I-wasn't-leaning-on-you way. "Right."

Since I had no interest in nerding out from the front row like Malcolm, I found us seats in the very back. Beside me, Malcolm unzipped his backpack. I didn't catch on until he positioned *The Many Moons of Evorix* in his lap and started to open it.

I nudged his knee with mine, sending the book clattering to the floor. A few people in the row in front of us turned around and shot us puzzled looks.

"I didn't read during your session," I whispered. I kicked the book under my seat.

"That's because you didn't bring any books."

"And because this is a tit-for-tat kind of thing. If I had to listen to your tit, you have to listen to my tat."

"That is not how that expression works," Malcolm said.

"Shh," I whispered. "The tat is talking."

Malcolm stifled a laugh. I glanced over at him, savoring the victory. He was watching the panel, but the ghost of a smile was still etched on his face.

From mistaken identity to wagers to fake dating, the panel of writers spoke at length about tropes I hadn't even realized were tropes. Twenty minutes into the session, Malcolm had one arm on his armrest, chin sunk in his hands as he listened to an author discuss her twist on the amnesia trope.

I smirked. He couldn't deny that he was wholly entertained. I faced frontward again, but I caught a flash of something familiar. I looked around, stiffening when I spotted it.

In the row in front of us, a woman with bleached blond hair was holding the *Moby-Dick* romance event flyer so that the woman next to her could see it. Even as she bent her head and some of her dark hair swished into view, I could still make out the words *Hunting for Dick*, the image of the whale, and *Cobblestone Books*. I swallowed and turned slightly. Malcolm hadn't noticed. He was still staring ahead, watching the panel. But then he glanced in my direction, almost frowning.

"What?" he said.

"What?" I echoed.

"You're staring."

"No, I'm not. Pay attention." I nodded my head in the direction of the stage. Malcolm's gaze lingered on me, but then he faced the front.

I couldn't keep my eyes from sliding back to the flyer, still in plain sight. The two women were whispering to each other. One of them pointed at *Cobblestone Books*. The other pulled out her phone. Within seconds, they were looking at a bird's-eye view of the bookstore and its surroundings. She tapped *Directions* and the screen zoomed out, showing a solid blue line running from DC to Bell River. I stole a look at Malcolm again, this time without moving my head. He was still engrossed in the panel.

The woman took the flyer and used her phone to scan the QR code. The RSVP page materialized on her phone, with *Hunting for Dick at Cobblestone Books* in large letters at the top. A large RSVP button sat at the bottom of her screen. I suddenly became aware of my breathing, how fast and loud my breaths felt. I closed my mouth and silently sent her contradicting messages set to the loud percussion of my heartbeat: three beats thumped *Do it do it do it*, the next three *Not now not now not now*.

Then the page refreshed, and the words *Thank you!* replaced the text at the top. My phone buzzed in my pocket. She set down the flyer. I let out a breath.

Malcolm turned to me. I held still, staring at the authors onstage, holding my breath because I couldn't trust my breathing. Finally, Malcolm turned frontward. I released a breath as quietly as I could. I spent the rest of the session fantasizing about the event. I had, at least, one confirmed attendee who was interested enough to RSVP. More people would sign up today. Two weeks from now, the bookstore might be thriving with the sort of activity that interested me. Evelyn would read her scene, and we would bond over *Moby-Dick* and dick jokes and romance, and the bookstore could make profits and actually be fun for once.

And Malcolm might find out.

I couldn't stop my mind from leaping to that last part. No matter how much I tried to focus on the event, the scene reading, the laughter, Malcolm was there, too. And it was worse now that we'd spent the last few hours together. Not because Malcolm worked for Ralph, though there was a very real fear in that too, knowing Ralph had the power to take the bookstore from Rochelle's control.

It was more that I knew Malcolm now. This rule-abiding bookworm who floundered into silence upon meeting his favorite author. He'd thanked me with such sincerity after the signing and I couldn't get his grateful smile out of my head. How might that expression change if he knew what I was planning?

"That was really good."

I blinked. The women sitting in front of us were now standing. The room had broken into overlapping conversations. The authors onstage had set their microphones down.

I glanced back at Malcolm. "Really?" I asked. "You liked it?"

"Yeah. I never realized how many modern-day tropes are steeped in Shakespeare."

Of course that's the part he picked up on.

"So you feel like reading romance now?" I asked.

He shrugged. "Maybe. But if I'm reading romance, you have to read a classic."

"But you wanted me to read T. J. Hull's robot book."

"You can read that after. And you can make me read something else, too."

"No." When I saw the surprise on Malcolm's face, like he feared he'd gone a step too far in extending our hypothetical plans, I hurried to say, "I mean, I'm all for continuing this tit-for-tat thing, but books aren't gonna cut it for you. You love reading. I want to make you do something that takes you out of your comfort zone. You're too comfortable."

"Okay." Malcolm leaned back and crossed his arms. "Make me uncomfortable."

An open invitation for so many things. I raised my eyebrows. "How uncomfortable?"

He shrank at my eager expression. "Not whatever you're thinking."

"What do you think I'm thinking?"

"Nothing," he said quickly. "Let me clarify: Take me out of my comfort zone, but not in a weird way."

"That's less fun." I looked around the room, realizing people were streaming in and taking seats. Someone stepped toward the lectern and adjusted the microphone. Another session was starting soon.

Malcolm and I maneuvered to the exit, ending up in the hallway again. I stood directly in front of him, eyeing him as his words ran through my mind. *Make me uncomfortable*.

Ideally, we'd continue this conversation away from the book

festival to avoid my flyers. And if we were going somewhere, it should be somewhere fun. Somewhere I couldn't picture Malcolm at all.

"Know any good bars around here?"

CHAPTER TEN

Another crosswalk, another opportunity to grill Malcolm. I leaned against the pole and fixed my stare on him. "Where are we going?" When I'd asked him if he knew of any bars, he'd simply nodded with a pensive expression and left me to follow. For all I knew, he wasn't taking me to a bar at all. A library was more likely.

As he'd done for four crosswalks now, Malcolm flitted a side-long glance my way before returning his gaze straight ahead. "Patience."

Suspicious. It was definitely a library.

Across the street and down sidewalks we went, until Malcolm stopped in front of a place called Tome. The sign hanging over the door had an image of a martini resting on a book.

"Is this a bar?" I asked.

"A book-themed bar. I've always wanted to come here." He looked up at the sign with something like wonder.

"Big day for you, huh?" I said. "Meeting T. J. Hull, now going to a book bar?"

"I know you're making fun of me, but yes, these are both

firsts." Malcolm pulled out his phone and took a picture of the window, which had a mural of authors sitting around a table talking and drinking. I recognized Edgar Allan Poe, with his dour expression and a raven perched on his shoulder, but I couldn't name any of the others. Edward Bell wasn't in the mural at all. Ralph must hate this place. All the more reason to go in.

When we stepped inside, my eyes had to adjust from bright light to moody darkness. The far-right wall resembled one long bookshelf, except the books seemed too neat and colorful to be real. Malcolm stopped and took a picture of this, too. As soon as we settled into a booth against the wall, I reached out to touch one of the alleged books.

"No touching," Malcolm whispered.

It felt smooth like plastic, and there was an unexpected lightness to it when I wiggled it in place. "I knew it wasn't real," I said.

"I could have told you that."

"But now you don't have to."

Before he could reply, a waiter, a man in his early twenties with large green eyes and piercings lining his ears, came to hand us the menus, two sheets of paper each. He gave me a wary look when he handed me mine.

"Try not to get us kicked out before they've even taken our order," Malcolm said when the waiter walked away.

"No promises." I picked up the drink menu. As could be expected, the drink names were built around literary references. Bloody Mary Shelley. *Jane Eyre* and Tonic. Flaming Doctor Jekyll. I settled on the Tolstoy—a White Russian—while Malcolm ordered a Cachaça-22. I raised my eyebrows at Malcolm.

"Surprised?" he asked when the waiter walked off with our orders.

I considered him carefully. "I guess I figured you for a tap water kind of guy. Seltzer when you really want to let loose."

Malcolm refrained from rolling his eyes, but I could tell he was close. "I'm not a ninety-four-year-old teetotaler."

"Of course not. You don't act a day over seventy-five."

This time, I got the eye roll. I cherished it like the victory it was.

"Do you really think I'm that boring?" he asked.

A pang of guilt dug inside me. I'd seen a different side of Malcolm this afternoon, and there I went dipping back into the well of snap judgments.

"Before today, yeah," I admitted. "I figured you read only classics and worshipped at the altar of Edward Bell and were allergic to wearing your hair down."

I expected another near-eye-roll, but he laughed this time. "Ponytails are easier. And I was just doing my job. That doesn't mean it's my life's passion or anything."

"Why do you do it, then?"

Malcolm took a sip of his drink. "It was a job, and I needed a job."

"That's it?"

He shrugged. "It's not like I wanted to be the town tattletale, but...Bell River has been good to me."

"Meaning?"

"I didn't have the most stable home life. There was a lot of...parents fighting. Things breaking. Police getting involved." He spoke in a monotone voice, like he could pull attention off his words if he made them sound boring enough. "When I was twelve, I got to come live in Bell River with my grandma. As soon as I got there, I felt like I was home." Just saying this made him smile. "It felt like the whole town was looking after me. It was the first time I ever felt safe."

I nodded, looking down. I'd been ready to add my stories about fighting parents, but it never got that bad. They never used more than words.

"So when I graduated from high school, I didn't want to be a burden anymore. I wanted to take care of my grandma. And there was an opening for a job with the Bell Society."

"I can understand that," I said. "I'm only helping Rochelle at the bookstore because I have nothing better to do." I took a drink, my eyes drifting to the rows of plastic books. When I set my drink down, Malcolm was watching me.

"What are you going to do when your time at the bookstore's up?"

Rude of him to ask the question I'd been struggling to answer myself.

"I don't know yet," I admitted. "But I will. Soonish."

This vague answer wasn't good enough for Malcolm. "Do you see yourself staying in town? Going somewhere else?"

Even this felt like a personal attack. I hadn't come here planning to stay, but the more time I spent here getting to know the townsfolk—Abigail at the Sunrise Café, Evelyn and her love of dick jokes, Malcolm and his surprising dry humor, even Vernon and his stubborn refusal to accept my friendship—the more I could see myself staying. But I didn't have the job piece figured out yet, and that was a pretty important part to navigate.

"I don't know," I said. I drained my glass. The syrupy Kahlua taste lingered in the back of my throat. "I feel like I shouldn't be allowed to make my own decisions, honestly. It's like everyone knows what they want to do and where they want to be, and I…don't."

"There's nothing wrong with that."

I tapped my nails against my empty glass. "I know. I don't care, but I feel like I'm supposed to. I'm tired of getting invitations for bridal showers and baby showers, and what's an engagement shower and how is that different from a bridal shower? Why is everyone having so many showers? Shouldn't they be clean by now?"

"I'm a bath man myself," Malcolm said, which we would definitely need to revisit another time.

"I feel like I'm just…the embarrassment of the family. On New Year's last year, I heard my dad telling his friend that he spent Christmas with his daughter and her kids. Not me," I added, pointing to myself. "His daughter, singular, i.e., my sister. And her kids. I was there too, but I'm too pathetic to mention."

"Every family needs an embarrassment," he said. He ignored my subsequent pout.

We ordered another round. Malcolm took his time going through the menu and finding all the literary puns. A smile crossed his face with each one he found, like they were hidden messages from old friends.

"Why haven't you come here before?" I asked.

Malcolm shrugged. "I don't come to DC much. Driving into the city is a nightmare. It's easier to stick to Bell River."

"But you can't get plastic books in Bell River," I said, gesturing to the shelf next to us. "Or a mural of Edgar Allan Poe and… other authors."

"Very true."

"Does anyone ever tell you you should get out more?" I asked.

"My grandma does." He said it so unironically that I snorted.

I thought Malcolm might take offense, but then he started to laugh, too.

"That's pathetic," I said.

"I can't even disagree."

"I could help you get out more," I announced. Malcolm watched me attentively. "You want me to read that T. J. Hull robot book, right? I'll do it if you do something in return. Something outside of Bell River."

Malcolm pondered this. "There *is* a library on Capitol Hill that I—"

"No. I'm picking."

He gave a displeased grunt. "Fine. Then I'm picking another book for you, and you don't get a say in it. I want you to read a classic."

"Fine," I said.

"Fine." He pulled the festival schedule from his backpack and flipped it over. Then he produced a pen and bent his head down.

"What are you writing?" I peered at the paper, but his hand moved to cover it.

"Making a list of all the books I'm gonna make you read."

"That's not fair." I reached into my tote bag for a piece of paper, but I stopped when I realized it was my flyer. I looked across the table at Malcolm—still writing—and pulled out my copy of the festival schedule, along with a pen. I flipped to the back and thought about everything I'd like to see Malcolm do. Before long, I was scribbling just as much as him.

When I set my pen down, my Travels with Whiskey was there, an amber-yellow concoction in a tall glass with a lemon spiral dangling off the edge. I tried a sip. It was like a grown-up soda: tart and bubbly, with an oaky flavor running through. Malcolm was still hunched over his paper, drink untouched. His pen hovered over the list, but he hadn't written anything for a while.

"Tapped out?" I asked.

Malcolm looked up. "I guess so." He took a swig of his Lord Gin and made a face. Probably wishing it were seltzer.

I held up my list. "Trade?"

"Sure."

Before I'd even taken his list, Malcolm was already shaking his head. "No," he said.

"No what? I'm still handing it to you."

"It's too long. This isn't practical."

"There's a back," I added, breaking into a grin when Malcolm flipped it over.

"*No*," he said again. I took another drink and watched the outrage unfold. "I'm not getting a tattoo."

"But that's physical proof that you've gotten out. Your grandma would be thrilled."

"And I'm not going to a wine festival. I don't even like wine."

"But you sure like whining."

His smile ruined the headshaking disappointment he was going for. "You are absurd."

When I tired of gloating, I glanced down at my own list. My grin warped into disgust. "No."

"Hmm?"

"I read *Heart of Darkness* in high school. You'll never be able to convince me it's a good book."

"If I have to get a tattoo, you have to reread *Heart of Darkness*." He held my gaze for several stubborn moments.

"Fine," I said. "No tattoo."

"Good." He crossed it off his list. I sent a long slice through *Heart of Darkness* with a strike of my pen.

"I would like to contest the three Jane Austen books on this list," I said. "You can pick one. I don't share the world's hard-on for Austen."

"Okay." Malcolm rested his chin in his hand and eyed me across the table. "I'll pick *Emma*. Maybe you'll learn something about the follies of deciding what's best for other people."

"If that's a pointed remark, I'm choosing to ignore it." I crossed out *Pride and Prejudice* and *Sense and Sensibility*.

Our negotiations continued like this. We eventually ordered an early dinner, and then we ordered drinks for each other, which was how I came to be nursing a Tequila Sun Also Rises even though I am not a tequila person. It was around this time that our drinks caught up to us. I found myself running a finger along the wall of forbidden fake books, and Malcolm kept writing book titles on shreds of his cocktail napkin and trying to sneak them across the table as addenda.

"And you call me absurd," I said, spotting a jagged napkin corner with *The Crucible* scrawled on it. I plucked it between my fingers, balled it up, and put it in my mouth.

"You just ate Arthur Miller!" Malcolm shrieked, his voice so high-pitched that I burst into laughter. The balled-up bit of napkin in my mouth flew through my lips and landed on Malcolm's forehead. I gasped, met his gaze, and we collapsed into giggles again. When our waiter came to refill our water glasses, I think I heard him sigh.

Eventually we agreed on our lists and put them away—for the sake of everyone involved, we decided. While putting my list in my tote bag, I spotted the remaining flyers I'd distributed that morning, in what felt like a world away. I looked up at Malcolm, now sneaking a fry off my plate.

"What would you do if you were at the bookstore tomorrow and you saw that I was selling something I shouldn't?" I asked. "Something contemporary?" I watched him carefully. Malcolm shoved the fry in his mouth and shrugged.

"I'd have to tell Ralph."

I sagged into my seat. Even in his silly, inebriated state, he was unflappable when duty was concerned. "Why?"

"It's my job," he said.

"You couldn't, you know, let it slide, now that you know me?"

He rested his elbows on the table and folded his arms. "If I miss something and Ralph catches wind of it, I could lose my job. He takes the Bell Society very seriously. As I'm sure you know."

"Okay, but…" I played with the seam on my sleeve, thinking. "What's to stop you from just giving me a warning? Why do you have to tell Ralph?"

Malcolm shrugged. "It's my job. Ralph's my boss."

"So you tattle on your friends?" I asked.

He tipped his head. "I'm not really *friends* with anyone under the Bell Society." This might have gotten a jab out of me at one point, something about his serious nature, his obsession with perfectly aligned books. But after spending the day with him, seeing that beneath the uptight surface was someone capable of giggles and shrieks, I couldn't do it. "But in essence, yes," he said. "I have to report on people even if I know them. It's my job."

"And you like your job?"

He studied me a moment. "I like my town," he said. Like it was the simplest truth in the world.

Remembering the way I felt my first day in Bell River, the warm embrace of friendly faces and kind welcomes, I didn't blame him. I gave up my line of questioning and took a swig of my drink. The tequila and orange juice couldn't counteract the grenadine's sickly sweetness. I ignored the cough-syrup taste and chugged the rest of it.

"Are you suggesting we're friends?" Malcolm asked, stealing another fry.

I grabbed a fry, too. "That or we're holding each other hostage as members of a very controlling book club."

Malcolm chuckled. "They're equally valid."

"I'm starting with *Beloved*, right?" I asked. "I guess I can buy it from myself."

"You can't."

I looked up from my fries. "Hmm?"

"Your store doesn't carry it. It was published after Edward Bell died."

"Really?" I wiped my hands on my napkin, looking him over. "How do you feel about the fact that you and Ralph have different definitions of what makes a classic?"

He took a breath, then closed his mouth like he'd thought better of it. "We should swing by Kramers and get *Beloved*."

"Kramers?"

"Bookstore. Open late. They have pie."

"Sold," I said. "Maybe I'll read *Beloved* and decide I love it so much that Cobblestone Books just has to carry it."

"I wouldn't if I were you," he said with a wry smile.

"That sounds like a threat."

"It is. Don't make me tell Ralph."

I examined his expression—his serious eyes—and shook my head. "You're bluffing."

"Try me."

He didn't look away. I didn't, either. Our waiter came and set the bill somewhere outside my line of vision. Malcolm glanced at it like an amateur.

As I claimed my victory in this staring contest we hadn't entered, a small part of me committed his serious expression to memory—that confidence, his certainty that he wouldn't hesitate to tell Ralph on me if I gave him reason to.

Just a small part. He was bluffing. He had to be bluffing.

But it didn't stop me from feeling sick when I reached for my wallet and saw the *Hunting for Dick* flyers in my tote bag. Tolstoy and tequila were partly to blame, but there was more to the queasiness than my regrettable decision to let dairy and acid mingle in my stomach.

I slapped my credit card on top of Malcolm's. As the waiter took our cards, I leaned back, pretending I was perfectly at ease with this, overspending on a book festival registration, dinner, and too many drinks. That there wasn't a flyer in my bag that could spell out doom if no one showed up, and a whole other kind of doom if too many people did.

That I was perfectly at ease with Malcolm, sitting there, head tilted back, lazily staring me down across the table, all the while possessing the power to end me.

CHAPTER ELEVEN

Fifteen minutes to go.

I moved the last chair into place and arranged the seats into rows as intentional as I could manage. The last two rows were slightly crooked, crammed in front of protruding bookcases, but it might look okay from a distance. I backed up to the front of the room and bumped into the framed portrait of Edward Bell. I'd have to remember to stand still when I addressed the crowd, unless I wanted to send the picture frame crashing down, which would probably set off some sort of legacy guardian failure alarm Ralph had no doubt set up.

I'd decided to hold the event in the only empty space available: the area where the Edward Bell shrine used to be. The table's absence left enough room for a few rows of seating, though Edward Bell would be glaring at us from an awfully close distance. I'd filled the space with chairs from the Sunrise Café. True to her word—and her grudge against Ralph—Abigail had been eager to see the event through, even offering to lend me the café's chairs. Earlier tonight, after the café closed, we'd spent a hurried ten minutes carrying them down the sidewalk, eyes peeled for any stray Bell Society employee who might snitch on our chair heist. Tonight, these chairs belonged to Cobblestone Books.

At least the refreshments by the register didn't seem quite as haphazard. It was nothing special—a card table pilfered from Rochelle's garage—but I'd set out chips, popcorn, wine, and water.

On the corner of this table was a large, shameless tip jar, outfitted with a sign declaring that donations were welcome. I was hesitant to venture into actual illegal activity by selling alcohol without a liquor license, but alcohol felt like a necessity if I was asking strangers to listen to dick jokes. Offering free booze and guilting them into donations with an excessively large jar seemed like the best alternative. The donations, combined with book sales and the ten-dollar-per-person entry fee, just might launch the event into profitability, but that too was an unknown. Thirteen RSVPs didn't mean thirteen people would actually show.

A knock sounded at the door.

I took a deep breath and wrenched the door open, coming face-to-face with two women in their twenties. One had short, bleached blond hair and freckles on her nose. I recognized her as the woman selling chapbooks at the book festival, though I couldn't remember her name. The other, with dark hair and a thin, angular face, held up a flyer. My flyer. They had to be the pair who had sat in front of Malcolm and me at the romance panel. I could hardly remember the panic I'd felt then. Now, standing before them, a surge of gratitude raced through me.

"Is this the *Moby-Dick* romance thing?" she asked.

"Yes! Come in."

She didn't move. "Isn't there supposed to be a password?"

"Yes." I gave her a serious look. "Password?"

"Queefqueg."

"Come in." I held open the door. "You can buy your tickets here at the register." It sounded fake as it left my mouth, that this was a real thing people would pay for. I half-expected them to laugh and push past me to the refreshments.

"Sure," the blond said, reaching into her purse. "Ten each, right?"

This was happening. "Right."

She handed me a twenty, which made it cooler somehow—all cash, no paper trail.

"We've got booze over there," I said. "If you want to partake, I'll need to see your IDs so I can give you a martini stamp for booze." I held up the stamp I'd taken way too much pleasure in picking out at the craft store yesterday.

They opted for the martini stamp. I took their IDs—both DC residents—and stamped away. Going by their IDs, the woman I recognized from the festival was Miranda, while her partner was Cora.

"You're free to head in," I said. "We'll get started at eight."

They nodded and gravitated to the refreshments. Without hesitation they dropped dollar bills into the donations jar and picked up plastic cups. I watched them move to the back, fearing they might see the crooked chairs and cramped space, declare the whole thing a sham, and beg off.

But no. They chose seats and sat down, quickly falling into conversation.

My worst-case scenario was already not a possibility. Someone showed up. Even my second-worst-case scenario was proven wrong, because more than one person showed up. Bell bless this DC couple.

I was better with the next arrival—Jim, the space-pizza artist from the book festival. I remembered to ask for the password, didn't put a question in my voice when I brought up the tickets. Once he paid and got a hand stamp, he asked if he could look around before the reading began.

"It's a little dark in here," he said.

"Sorry about that. The reading's in the back. Our town's weird about lights at night. But a little light's no problem," I told him and myself. I flipped just one switch, casting the entire room in a yellow glow that was hopefully dull enough to go unnoticed.

Before I could dwell on this, another person arrived, then another. I rang up ticket sales, checked IDs, stamped hands. There was a definite chatter happening. People were eating, drinking, and talking. I checked the time—we were due to start in eight minutes. Five people were now sitting in my pilfered café chairs.

Five became seven, then nine. Abigail showed up, wearing an emerald-green jumpsuit with a belted waist. It was my first time seeing her in something other than the black Bell Society shirt. Her reddish-brown hair, usually thrown in a ponytail, was neatly straightened, draping over her shoulders. After she'd helped me move the chairs, I hadn't been sure if she'd show up at all or if I'd tired her out with the manual labor.

"You look great!" I said.

"Yeah, well." She shrugged. "This seemed like a special occasion."

I couldn't stop smiling at that. It was confirmed now: I wasn't an annoying regular. She'd shown up for me, for this.

Leena arrived next. I felt a swell of pride at that—I'd sent an email about the event, disguised as a newsletter, but I hadn't been sure she'd come.

"Hey," I said casually, like I hadn't spent the afternoon scrutinizing her Twitter for signs she might show up. "I'm so glad you made it."

"Yeah. This sounded fun. I invited a friend who didn't RSVP. I hope that's cool."

I tried not to sound too eager when I told her it was perfectly fine. "But they're, um…" I hesitated. Asking *Are they a snitch?* felt rude. "They know this thing tonight has to stay under wraps?"

She waved it off. "She totally gets it."

It was hard to trust strangers with a secret that could threaten Rochelle's store, particularly when some of those strangers lived in town. Leena's friend—a short, Black woman named Dahlia whose ID had a Bell River address—arrived a few minutes later. She seemed friendly enough, exclaiming over the martini stamp and rounding to the refreshments table for a generous pour of wine, but I couldn't help wondering if she had any ties to Ralph.

I watched the door, waiting for Evelyn. The entire event was hinging on her reading her *Moby-Dick* romance scene. Without her, I had a group of people and no dick jokes whatsoever.

At eight o'clock on the dot, as I was glancing at the seated attendees and brainstorming potential jokes—the closest I could think was a play on the word *whalebone*—the sound of a bell made me turn my head. Evelyn closed the door behind her, face flushed.

"Am I late?"

I grinned. "Right on time." I gave her long enough to peruse the snack table and grab a cup of wine, and then we headed to the back. People sat scattered among the rows of chairs. Their conversation, which I'd tuned out while stamping hands and watching the door for Evelyn, was at full volume, the loudest this store had ever been.

I hadn't led a crowd since the last event I'd organized for the Merrymakers—a pumpkin-carving contest, two weeks before I was laid off—and it should have been easy to slip back into this, standing in front of a crowd, introducing the event, telling them what to do. But there was no manager smiling at me from the corner. There was no approved budget, no flyers splashed around for everyone to see. There was only me, doing something I shouldn't, with a group I needed to trust with my secret. My eyes fell on Dahlia, chatting away with Leena. She could probably be trusted. But it couldn't hurt to make sure.

I squeezed into the space between the front row and the Edward Bell portrait behind me. A few people watched me expectantly, but the rest were still talking amongst themselves. I took a breath in. Breath out.

"Hey, everyone!" I said. The voices came to a halt. "Thanks for coming tonight. I know this event might seem a little strange. For anyone who's not from here, Cobblestone Books is supposed to sell only classics." I pointed at the quote above me. "And this might be an unpopular opinion, but I think those classics are boring as hell." That got a smattering of chuckles and a few claps. The wine was a good idea.

"I spent years getting classics like these shoved down my throat, and it made me hate reading. It wasn't until an author in town, Evelyn Suwan, introduced me to a rom-com she wrote that I realized there are so many other genres out there. And for the first time in forever, reading became fun." People were listening and nodding. Confessing in a bookstore that I hated reading felt like sacrilege, but they seemed to understand. I relaxed a little.

"So I thought that's what we could do at these events. Take a classic novel that people think of as required reading. Make it fun by adding romance, or robots, or murder, or another staple of a genre that doesn't get enough credit. And then maybe we can talk about the books we love. If there are people here who love *Moby-Dick*, tell us what you love about it. If there are people who love romance, tell us. I want us to have open minds and come away feeling excited about books we might never have appreciated. How does that sound?"

The crowd was quick to applaud. A giddy laugh floated out of me.

"One more thing before we begin," I said. "Like I said, Cobblestone Books is not supposed to be doing this. We are supposed to be an upstanding pillar of the Bell Society. We're supposed to respect our literary roots. Any events we hold need to be approved by the head of the Bell Society, who is frankly a power-tripping dick." Abigail gave a loud whoop.

"So," I said, assuming a serious expression, "I need to make sure what happens in this room stays in this room. Can we take a quick pledge before we begin?" I raised my right hand. Slowly, they all raised their right hands as well—Dahlia included.

"Please repeat after me: I was never here."

"I was never here," they chorused.

"This event never happened."

"This event never happened."

"And if I speak of this to anyone with ties to the Bell Society, may I be doused in spermaceti," I said. They laughed, but they finished the pledge. I lowered my hand, feeling more at ease. This bookstore was starting to feel like the safe space I wanted it to be. A space that belonged to me. Not Edward Bell, or Ralph, or Malcolm, or even Rochelle.

Next, I introduced Evelyn as our guest writer. She got to her feet and shared how she got started writing romance. She described the simultaneous pride and embarrassment she felt when she handed her mother her first book, knowing her mother would go home, read the steamy scenes she'd written, and possibly never be able to look her in the eye again.

"But there's something freeing in knowing my mom knows exactly who I am," Evelyn continued. "I like writing about sex. Sex scenes let you explore how your characters interact with each other in their most personal moments. I wish more novels had sex in them. I wish novels with sex scenes weren't seen as second-rate literature. So." Evelyn clasped her hands together. "I think we're going to have fun tonight. But I also think this is a good opportunity to set aside any biases you have about romance and give yourself permission to enjoy it, have fun, and see where it can take you."

Her words sent goosebumps along my arms. Like the night was full of possibility.

We went around the room as everyone else introduced themselves. Miranda said she had joined a classics book club a few years ago that spent six months slogging through *Moby-Dick*. "It almost killed the club," she said. "None of us could get through it. But we felt like we were supposed to. Like it said something bad about us if we didn't want to read a classic."

"I had a different experience," volunteered Jim, looking around with a shy smile. "When I read *Moby-Dick*, I was working at a dead-end job in my twenties. All my friends were in college, which I couldn't afford to do, so I read every book I could get my hands on. Reading classics like *Moby-Dick* made me feel like I was still doing something with my life. It kept me sane, weird as it sounds."

Everyone, apparently, had their own reasons for coming. An affinity for comedy, according to a woman who did improv in DC. A love of *Moby-Dick*. A hatred of *Moby-Dick*. A love of romance. Curiosity about this event. With every reason they gave, I started to feel more like we were a united community. Whatever brought us here tonight, we all belonged just the same.

After the introductions, Evelyn produced a few stapled-together pages from her bag and moved to the front of the room. She cleared her throat and began to read, describing Captain Ahab's infatuation with a woman named Bridget, who served as captain of a whaling ship called the *Dick Hunter*.

I surveyed the room while Evelyn read. Every head faced forward, watching Evelyn attentively. There was no whispering, rustling, or wandering. A few people had finished their drinks, but the empty cups sat at their feet while they continued to sit and listen, too captivated for a refill.

A smile slowly came over me. This was working. I could trust the people in this room, and I could trust this event to give everything I'd been missing here: community. Belonging. Not a path, exactly, but who needs paths when you have star-crossed whaling captains and the Dick Hunter?

Just as Captain Ahab caught sight of Bridget's ship for the second time, a loud knock jolted me into reality.

Getting lost in Evelyn's whaling rom-com and the wonder of this event being a success, I'd forgotten, for a moment, how much of a risk this was. I hadn't planned on flipping the other light switch. I hadn't counted on the conversation being this loud.

I waved for Evelyn to continue reading and slowly walked to the door. As if the person behind the door knew I was close, the knock sounded again.

I turned the handle and cracked open the door, crossing my fingers for a lost attendee or a neighbor with a complaint.

Malcolm stood on the sidewalk, his eyes trained on me.

CHAPTER TWELVE

All those fuzzy feelings of trust and belonging quickly drained out of me. I plastered on a smile and stepped outside, quickly shutting the door behind me.

"Hey," I greeted him. "What are you doing here?"

"I was walking Chester and I saw the light on. I figured I'd stop and say hi."

I looked down. A small brown terrier panted at his feet. "You have a dog?" I didn't peg Malcolm as a dog person. In my mind he had a snooty cat, maybe.

"It's my grandma's dog," he said, which explained it. My mental image of Malcolm could remain intact. "Anything going on?" He nodded his head behind me. "This block is usually dead by now."

"At eight-thirty on a Saturday night? You guys really know how to let loose."

Malcolm gave me one of his patient stares. "This block is a bookstore, two antique shops, and a café. There's nothing to let loose with here."

I thought I heard a screech of laughter behind me. "That's

true," I said, speaking louder. "I was just staying late to do some inventory." God help me if he asks follow-up questions about inventory.

I heard it again, that phantom laughter. "How are you so familiar with the hours of every business on this block?" I asked.

"I walk Chester most nights." He gestured down to the dog, who had now given up on the walk and lain down on the pavement. "Plus, you know. It's my job."

"Right. Can't forget your job."

Another patient stare. "Do you want to call me a tattletale some more?"

Remembering him at the book bar, writing book titles on napkin shreds and tossing them my way, I softened. "No."

He glanced behind me. "Are you listening to music in there?"

"Yes." I crossed my arms. "Are you going to tattle on me, tattletale?"

"There it is," Malcolm said, grinning despite himself. "So I finished *The Wedding Date*."

I raised my eyebrows. This was the romance novel I'd picked out for him at Kramers. We'd briefly split up to weave through the aisles, and he'd emerged from the shelves with a copy of *Beloved*, while I'd held up my romance selection for him. I hadn't read *The Wedding Date*, but Evelyn had mentioned it in her newsletter and I'd been wanting to check it out.

We spent two hours at Kramers. I'd wanted to hold on to that tipsy feeling for as long as I could just to prolong the night, browsing books and splitting a slice of something called Goober pie, raving over the delicious combination of chocolate and peanut butter and bickering over who was hogging the mound of whipped cream.

Now, though, standing on the sidewalk in front of a book-store I was desperate to get back into, it was hard to reconcile that feeling with this moment here. Malcolm with his questions and me with my secret that was one too-loud laugh away from being discovered.

"You did?" I asked. "What'd you think?"

"I'm saving my thoughts for our first overly controlling book club meeting. We should schedule that." When he spoke, he kept his eyes on the darkened shop window next door, like he had a sudden need for antiques.

I kept silent, trying to play it as cool as Malcolm was aiming for. "We should," I said. "How's tomorrow?" I realized I was sort of shooting myself in the foot by saying this. I wasn't even halfway through *Beloved*. It had taken a back seat to event preparations, and whenever I settled down to read it, it was written so confusingly that I sometimes had to read the same sentence several times just to understand what was happening. But I liked the idea of seeing Malcolm tomorrow.

His eyes met mine for just a moment, showing a flash of pleased surprise before his cool veneer took over. "Okay."

"Okay," I said. "Well, I'll get off work at six."

"Should I stop by here to pick you up?"

"Yes. No," I corrected myself. "I don't know. Maybe. It depends." On how much post-event evidence I'd have left to hide.

"On what?" he asked. His voice was tinged with a hint of uncertainty, like he feared I was having second thoughts.

"On nothing," I said quickly. "Just...my schedule. Errands. Sunday things. It's the lord's day, you know. I should clear it first with the big man upstairs."

After a moment of wary silence, Malcolm asked, "You're going to...ask god...about having dinner with me?"

"No," I said. "That would be weird." Another suspicious look from Malcolm. "Sometimes I just say things," I explained.

"So I'm gathering." There was a slight smile turning up his lips. I wasn't completely flubbing it. "Why don't I just text you the restaurant?" he said.

"That works."

Malcolm stared. I stared back.

"You don't have my number," he said.

"Yes," I remembered. "That is true." Malcolm watched me, as if waiting for something, and I realized that was my cue to get his number. "Yes," I said again, pulling my phone out of my back pocket. "Enter it in."

The second I handed him my phone I regretted it, fearing he might accidentally come across the event page I'd been obsessively monitoring all week. But all he did was enter his number, send off a text to himself, and hand the phone back to me.

"Thanks," I said, trying not to sound too relieved.

"I'll see you tomorrow."

"See you tomorrow."

While Malcolm and Chester walked down the block, I stayed in place, staring at his name and number. Wondering what it meant, our plan for tomorrow and his number in my phone. If it was a date. If that was allowed.

Another peal of laughter sounded through the door. I peered forward, watching Malcolm and Chester stroll along the sidewalk, now a full block away. No chance of him overhearing it now. I let out a sigh of relief and stepped back inside.

I quietly closed the door behind me, hearing Evelyn recite

something about eating chowder by candlelight. I turned to start making my way to my seat, then startled at the sight of a figure standing by the register. Gray hair, heavyset frame, permanent scowl. Vernon had finally come to my bookstore. At the worst possible time.

I stood there, motionless, watching Vernon watch Evelyn read her scene. Ahab and Bridget were exchanging lustful looks over soup. That wasn't too bad. But then Bridget set her spoon down and declared that clam chowder wasn't the only viscous white liquid she planned to swallow tonight.

People laughed. Vernon frowned. My face burned.

Evelyn looked around, her thumb pressed against her lip as she drank in the reactions, oblivious to Vernon overhearing her every dirty word.

"I was worried about that one," she confessed. "I have a gross sense of humor."

"Ten out of ten pickup line," said Dahlia. "I might use it myself one day."

Evelyn went back to reading, blissfully unaware. I stared at the floorboard while Evelyn's words swirled around me, sounding farther and farther away. I thought I'd prepared for every contingency, but I hadn't prepared for Vernon showing up out of the blue. When I'd been out on the sidewalk just minutes ago, I'd been worried about Malcolm hearing the laughter through the door. But I hadn't considered what Vernon could overhear from upstairs. I'd heard every floorboard creak he made; I should have known that went both ways.

Vernon didn't know me at all. And going by Rochelle and her childhood roller-skating grudge, he felt no goodwill for Rochelle, either. He could tell Ralph everything I'd done here tonight, and he wouldn't even consider what it would mean for us. I wouldn't get the Bell books back now. Tonight was supposed to be the turning point, the moment when the store became profitable again, when I began to make up for what I'd cost Rochelle. And now I'd been found out.

Another wave of laughter rolled through the room. Evelyn was now describing how Ahab licked chunky drips of chowder off Bridget's breasts. Vernon made a guttural sound, like a snort mixed with a scoff. I watched him, desperately searching for a sign, some context, some tell about whether it was a weird laugh or a disapproving jeer. He wasn't smiling. But he wasn't frowning, either. All I could tell, from the way his eyes remained on Evelyn, was that he was listening.

I spent the next painful few minutes searching for clues. At some point Vernon turned to completely face the reading so that all I could see was his back, and then I had to search for signs in more imperceptible cues: tilts of his head, changes in his stance. My findings were inconclusive.

The scene came to a rousing conclusion when Ahab dropped down on one knee and proposed that they give up hunting Moby-Dick and get married. Evelyn lifted her eyes from the page with a smile, then read Bridget's response: "You've got all the dick I need."

Amid laughter and applause, Evelyn let her pages flutter to the floor and took a bow. I clapped along with the others, sneaking another glance at Vernon. He wasn't clapping.

After the reading, people stood to mingle and share book recommendations. Cora and Dahlia discovered they shared a love for horror and raved about someone named Carmen Maria Machado. Jim gave Miranda some suggestions for classics her book club might find more approachable. Evelyn raved to Jim about a romance he might like.

I tiptoed through the crowd, hiding behind a bookshelf to peek at Vernon. He surveyed the refreshments table like he was gathering evidence.

"Do you still have that noir novel?" Leena asked, making me jump. "It was purple, with a lady in sunglasses on the cover? I want to show Abigail something."

Right, my secret books. My primary reason for luring everyone here tonight. I nodded and forced a smile, then dipped into the storage room for my box of hidden inventory. I set it on the counter, then stepped back. I wanted to find my way to Vernon, but he was busy talking to Evelyn, and then I had to get behind the register when people started lining up with their purchases, and why hadn't I ever learned to lip-read?

I rang up more sales than I'd made all week. Leena and a few others bought copies of *Moby-Dick*. Miranda bought the classics Jim recommended. Dahlia bought an Edith Wharton and a few books from my secret stash. I wrote down some titles I'd heard people recommend to one another, deciding to add them to my inventory.

"Do you have any mysteries?"

I looked up. Vernon stood before me, peering into the cardboard box.

"That's all I've got so far," I said. "Is there anything you'd like me to start carrying?"

He said something about Sue Grafton, which led Miranda, standing nearby, to gush about a mystery she'd read recently. I added it to the list. Then Miranda went off to talk to Leena, leaving me alone with Vernon. I watched him sift through the books with all the same care he'd used to choose an apple that day in the farmers' market.

"It was nice of you to join us tonight," I said. He gave a noncommittal grunt, still rifling. I tried again. "I hope the noise didn't disturb you."

He plucked out a book and examined the cover. "Of course it disturbed me. That's why I came down." He held up *Windswept*. "Is this by that woman who did that reading? I'd like to buy something of hers."

I gave a dazed laugh. "You liked it?"

"I wouldn't have stayed if I didn't," Vernon said, frowning at me.

"Of course." I laughed again, and he kept frowning like I'd lost my mind, and what a beautiful frown it was, all wrinkles and confusion wrapped in a shroud of judgment, and *Vernon liked the reading*.

He huffed and waved *Windswept* in my face. "Well?"

I blinked, remembering his question. "Yes, Evelyn wrote that. But you might like a rom-com more, if you liked what you heard tonight. Any interest in reading *Taste of You*?" I held it up. Vernon took it from me, read the back cover for several long moments, and handed it back to me. "Sure."

I smiled. It wasn't often that I had the knowledge to recommend a book to someone. I scanned it and ran my own card through the reader. "Consider it a gift. An apology for the disturbance."

"Fine," he said curtly, like I'd made an enemy. Then he dug a bill out of his wallet and shoved it in the donations jar. "Will you be doing more of these?"

"That's the plan. But I'll let you know ahead of time so we don't bother you."

He scoffed. "*Bother*," he repeated. "The only way you'd *bother* me is if I don't get an invitation."

"Okay," I agreed. "I can do that. And, um, Ralph doesn't know about these events, so if you can..." I paused, not sure how to word it. I couldn't ask him to raise his hand and recite the silly pledge. Then again, he might be receptive to it. He was full of surprises.

"Ralph is my landlord," he said. "I am well versed in keeping things from him. If he asks, I don't have any pets." He fixed me with a meaningful look until I got the hint and somberly nodded in agreement. Then he took his rom-com and exited through the back door to the stairwell, and I was left with the delightful satisfaction of finally winning over Vernon.

I glanced at my phone. I wanted to text Rochelle to brag about making friends with her nemesis, but I couldn't. She couldn't know what I'd done here tonight, not if I wanted any chance of making sure these events continued.

While some attendees started trickling out the door, others stayed behind to browse and keep talking. I went through the receipts from tonight's book purchases, adding in what I'd earned from ticket sales and a rough guess at what the donations jar held. This was undoubtedly more than I'd made in the last couple of weeks. But I'd told Rochelle business would bounce back to normal in September, and one night of great sales wasn't enough to get the store on track for the entire month.

"Is this all you have?" Jim asked.

I followed his gaze to the picked-over box on the counter. "Unless you want classics, yeah," I admitted. "But I'm planning to restock and add some new ones, too." I held up the list of titles I'd jotted down.

He was quiet for several long seconds. "I don't want to be rude."

"We all just listened to a clam chowder sex scene together," I reminded him. "You can be rude. We're there."

Jim laughed. "I was just going to say that the little free library outside my house has more books than you do. I know you've got the older books," he added, waving a hand at the shelves behind him. "But..."

"You want newer ones," I finished. "No offense taken. I've just...got a lot of constraints."

He nodded, turning thoughtful. "Do you have an online store?" I shook my head. "Really?" he said. "In this day and age, a bookstore's got to have an online presence."

"Well." I cocked my head. "Officially, we're not allowed to sell books published after 1968, so we're not really living in this day and age."

"Officially," Jim repeated. He tapped a finger on the box of secret inventory. "But you're selling newer books unofficially, aren't you? Why not set up an unofficial online store?"

He may as well have been speaking another language. "Um... how would that even work?"

Jim, it turned out, knew exactly how. He explained that his sister ran a bookstore in Baltimore, and that he'd set up the website for her. He told me about how she partnered with a company that handled her online sales. She could sell any book the partner company carried in their warehouse. They managed the packing, shipping, and inventory. And she got a fair percentage of profits.

"Why don't you give her a call," he said, writing down her phone number. "I'm sure she can answer any questions I can't. But let me know if I can help with the website." He handed me a card. He'd written a phone number and the name *Susan Abbott* on one side. I flipped it over. The other side showed Jim's business card, advertising his services as a web designer.

"Okay," I said, my head spinning. "Thank you."

"Sure." Jim returned the pen to the cup on the counter. "I'll see you at the next one."

His words rang in my ears like a promise. *The next one.*

After he left, I went back to studying the card, twirling it between my fingers, reading between the lines for the possibility it held. With Jim's help and Susan's advice, I might keep our profits up after all.

This felt like the missing piece, the justification I needed to keep my secret going. The events would provide a burst of profits and fun, and the online store might bring in enough sustained revenue to keep us going. I didn't love the idea of lying to my best friend, but I needed this. She already had the career, the path, the husband, the kids. She was exactly where she was supposed to be. And I was lost, adrift, without even a white whale to chase. I still didn't have a path. I didn't have a plan for what I'd do once my temporary job at the bookstore was up. I'd meant to look for jobs, but I hadn't since coming to town.

But I did have the people I'd brought together at the bookstore tonight. And that felt worth protecting.

CHAPTER THIRTEEN

Just out of view from the restaurant's window, I stood on the sidewalk and shook my hands low at my sides, then wiggled my shoulders. Better to get all my weirdness out now.

There was nothing to be nervous about, really. This wasn't a date. We'd said at the book bar that we were either friends or book club members. Malcolm had framed this dinner as a book club meeting. But that didn't change the fact that I'd changed out of the jeans I'd worn to work today in favor of a purple midi dress that left my shoulders bare. Or that I'd spent ten minutes deciding which lip color made my mouth the most kissable.

I pursed my lips, now a lovely shade of Crushed Velvet, and pulled open the door to Wok House.

The red-accented walls and lamps that glowed a soft golden yellow gave off date vibes to me. Malcolm had suggested the restaurant. That could be telling. Or I was projecting.

I spotted Malcolm at a secluded booth toward the back, talking to a woman with graying hair. His locs weren't tucked into a ponytail for once; they spilled down his shoulders, framing his face in a way that suited him. He'd also ditched the plain button-down for a checkered green shirt that actually allowed me to catch a glimpse of his neck. I wasn't the only one who'd changed out of my work clothes for tonight. That had to mean something.

When he saw me approaching, he grinned at me but continued nodding and listening. The woman caught on and turned just as I reached the booth.

"Is this Maggie?" she asked, drawing out my name like it held all sorts of meaning.

Malcolm's lips nearly disappeared into his mouth. "Mmhmm," he uttered in a tone that at least tried for casual.

I stifled a laugh as I slid into the booth. Two big signs for date, right off the bat.

"Malcolm's told us about you," the woman said, beaming down at me.

"Has he?" I raised a brow at Malcolm, who shrank into his seat.

"I told my *grandmother* I was having dinner with you," he said with great composure. "Ellen and my grandma are close. Too close," he added, shooting her a glare.

"So, you're obsessed with me," I said once Ellen left us alone.

"I've never been so betrayed before," he muttered, running a hand over his locs.

"I like the hair," I said.

He broke into a knowing smile. "I thought you might."

I held his gaze until my face got warm, and then I pretended to study the menu. Wearing his hair differently just for me had *date* written all over it.

"So," I said after we placed our orders. "*The Wedding Date*."

"Am I going first?"

"You are."

"Okay." He cast his eyes upward, thinking his verdict through. "I thought it was well written."

Too diplomatic to be the truth. "Would you read more from her?" I pressed.

"Um." Malcolm scratched his neck. "I think if I didn't have a book on me, and her book was there—"

"And if you didn't have a choice, you'd read a romance?" I finished. "Reading this changed nothing for you, then? You still look down on it?"

"No, I just..." Malcolm squirmed. "I'm not into romance. Or...fake dating setups. But I'm impressed that *despite* that, it kept me pretty captivated."

"What a rave."

He steadied his gaze on me. "Now you."

I straightened, suddenly self-conscious. "Me?"

"What did you think of *Beloved*?"

"Depressing as hell."

"Yep."

"I get why you like it," I said. "It's beautiful. Hard to read sometimes, but beautiful. I don't know why this was never assigned reading for me in school."

He nodded emphatically like that was exactly what he'd hoped I'd say. "I've had that same thought with a lot of books I've come across. I learned pretty early on that if I wanted to read Black literature, I couldn't rely on school to assign it to me."

I nodded. "Can I read something a little happier next time?"

A gentle smile crossed his face. "We can do that," he said.

"Good." And now, while Malcolm was still looking at me like that, I couldn't help slipping in a question. "You said before that the bookstore doesn't carry *Beloved* because it was published after Edward Bell died. Do you think it should be allowed to?"

Malcolm's eyes narrowed slightly, like he knew exactly what I was doing. But then he sighed. "Yes."

"You do?"

"Of course. There wasn't a Black author on the *New York Times* bestseller list until 1970. By running the bookstore the way he does, Ralph is keeping it very, very white."

I hadn't considered this. Going by the stony expression on Malcolm's face, he clearly had. A lot. "Have you told him this?" I asked.

He shrugged. "Ralph just points to the Black authors we do carry."

"So the 'I have Black friends' defense," I said.

Malcolm gave a dark laugh. "Pretty much. Who needs Maya Angelou or Toni Morrison when you have slave narratives?" He took a drink of water. I was going to ask another question to keep him talking, but Malcolm leaned back and continued, "There are a lot of things I wonder about when it comes to Ralph and Edward Bell."

I stayed silent, waiting for him to keep going. But no, now he decides to clam up. "Like?" I prompted.

Again he gave me that *I know what you're doing* look. I stared him down.

"Like the fact that Ralph has a cabinet of Edward Bell's private letters in his office. Letters that were never published, never made it into his biography, have never been seen outside the Bell family. I have to wonder what's in them. Are they private letters, or are they…*private* letters?" He lifted his eyebrows for added emphasis.

My jaw dropped. "Are you gossiping about Edward Bell? What would Ralph say?"

Malcolm smirked over the rim of his water glass. "Ralph would never believe you if you told him."

"Fair enough." I thought back to the tourist whose review had upset Ralph so much. "What if they were letters from a mistress?"

"Could be."

"Oh my god. What if they were dirty?" Already I was thinking of the people who came to last night's event. They'd surely appreciate a dirty letter.

"I guess we'll never know," he said. "Ralph would never tell."

"Can I ask why you work for Ralph if you don't agree with everything he's doing?" I asked.

"Because..." His eyes grew serious and focused. "I think there's room for change. We should be more honest about who Edward Bell was instead of glossing over the stuff we don't like. Like, his biography alludes to a couple of racist remarks he's made. I don't know what those are, or the context behind them, but that would be interesting to know. Tourists don't come to Bell River because they worship him; they come because they like his books and they want to learn more about him. The good and the bad. Knowing more about his life could change the way we interpret his books, which I would love to explore. If I move up in the Bell Society, maybe I could convince Ralph to let people see a more nuanced side of Edward Bell."

God, he was so certain. I've never been sure about any of my plans, and here Malcolm had been chasing the same goal for a decade. "That is a very long con," I said.

"As opposed to what?" he asked. I looked down. Of course

the long con was all he knew. He hadn't started and ended a million plans that went nowhere.

"Well, what's stopping you from breaking into Ralph's office, reading the letters, and starting a revolution?" I asked.

"Common decency."

"Overrated," I scoffed. "What if you do all of this and nothing changes?"

Malcolm shrugged. "At least I'll have tried."

"And you think this is the only way?"

"Can you think of a better way?" he asked.

I glanced down at the tablecloth. "If I could, I wouldn't tell you," I mumbled.

"You wouldn't have to. I'd figure it out."

This cocky bastard. "Right," I said, meeting his eyes. "And then you'd tattle on me, right? Because you're fine tattling on friends?"

Malcolm frowned a little, like I'd misspoken. "We're not friends. We're colleagues."

I stifled a laugh. "We're colleagues?"

"Yeah. Well." He ran a finger along the underside of his jaw, thinking. "I mean, there is a power imbalance because I'm Ralph's eyes and ears for the bookstore. But that just means we shouldn't be friends. Which we're not."

"Right," I said. "This is a work dinner. I'm sure you're submitting your receipts to Ralph." I fought off a smile as Malcolm thought this through, a crease forming in his brow.

"We're colleagues," Malcolm said again. His gaze wandered before settling on me.

I kept a straight face, aiming for disinterested. I might have been offended if I believed him.

Although a small part of me couldn't help wondering: If he didn't even see us as friends, was this confirmation that there was no potential for more-than-friends? Had I been imagining something that wasn't there, back when we were being giggly and silly over drinks at the book bar? When we shared a slice of pie at Kramers as we waited for our buzz to wear off? Was it only delusion that had me coloring my lips a kissable shade of Crushed Velvet tonight?

"Figures," I said lightly. "Rochelle said you have no friends."

When I'd told Rochelle I was going on a maybe-date with Malcolm tonight, she'd given me a knowing look and said something about worlds colliding. Rochelle had never had any preconceived notions of whomever I dated in the past. It had been simpler, me showing her a few pictures from a dating profile, introducing them in person during our college days or, after college, texting her a very detailed post-date recap. I think she liked having the vicarious glimpse into dating apps, the hit-or-miss experience of making conversation with near strangers. Aside from someone I'd dated for a year and a few casual encounters since then, it was mostly misses.

But getting to know someone Rochelle had known since middle school was a different experience. She became the one divulging information, plopping next to me on the couch and telling a story about the time Malcolm argued with their biology teacher about the definition of *mitosis* in eighth grade.

When I'd asked if she had any other stories about middle-school Malcolm, she'd shrugged and said, "I don't know. He hung out at the library a lot."

But I realized now, playing back my words, that telling Malcolm he didn't have friends came across more rudely than I meant for it to. "She was joking," I added hastily.

"No, she's right. I'm not a big people person, I guess you could say."

I could. I have. "Why?"

"I prefer to be left to my own devices."

"You mean books?"

"Books are my primary devices, yes," he said.

"But you started a book club with me," I reminded him.

"I like certain people." His eyes locked on mine with enough significance to make something inside me flutter.

"I'm certain people?" I asked.

"You are."

My gaze fell to my hands in my lap, letting his words wash over me. "That's good to know." I looked up and caught him watching me with a pleased smile, satisfied with his effect on me. *Colleagues*, I reminded myself.

Our food arrived then. I leaned back as a large plate of cashew chicken was placed before me.

"Can I ask why you work at a bookstore?" Malcolm asked.

I plucked a cashew off my plate and ate it. "Because it's better than living with my parents?"

"But this is Rochelle's bookstore, right?"

"Yeah. So?"

It wasn't enough of an answer for Malcolm. He gave me a patient look a teacher might give a student who'd said the wrong answer. "But why you?"

"We're best friends," I said, starting to feel defensive.

"I was just thinking about how it doesn't seem like your thing. I wondered what was."

I stopped hunting for cashews and set my fork down. "I don't think I have one."

"Well, what do you like to do?"

I shrugged. "My favorite thing to do is nothing, but no one's going to pay me to do that."

"Nothing?"

"I don't know. I'm good at distracting myself from what I'm supposed to be doing."

"What do you mean?" he asked.

I tipped my head back, thinking. "Well...at my last job, I got so into organizing a scavenger hunt that I forgot to restock the kitchen and everyone had to survive on coconut water for a week."

"Disgusting," Malcolm joked.

I gave a small laugh and examined my thumbnail. "Once, in college, I didn't study for my poli-sci midterm because I was too busy bulk-buying spoons for my bad movie club's showing of *The Room*. Or, another time, I had an assignment in my media studies class to identify film techniques in a movie of my choice. I picked a Mary Kate and Ashley movie because I thought it would be funny...and then I got sidetracked for the rest of the semester because I started a blog dedicated to rewatching Mary Kate and Ashley movies. I may or may not have almost missed my final because I was livestreaming *Passport to Paris* to forty of my followers." I glanced up, expecting Malcolm's usual stoicism. But he was watching me with fond amusement in his eyes, a soft smile coming over him.

"What?" I said.

"Nothing, I just...I think there's something there."

"About being doomed to repeat myself for the rest of eternity?" I offered. "Or are you saying I should restart my Mary Kate and Ashley blog?" I kept my voice light, but I couldn't help dwelling on this unfortunate pattern of mine, how much it must have set me back. What if I'd tried harder in that class? What if I'd contributed more at work, beyond parties and potlucks? Until I broke that pattern, my life might always be a cycle of well-intentioned plans and the distractions that made them fail. Even now, I was still finding ways to get sidetracked, putting all my energy into bookstore events when I should be figuring out my next plan.

"No and *no*," he said. "I just meant that I don't think you're doomed at all." He spoke with such sincerity that it chased away my cynicism.

I couldn't think of a retort. All I could do was smile back, a little bit speechless and a little bit touched. "Thank you." *Colleagues*.

As we ate, taking bites from one another's plates every so often, we discussed what our exclusive book club would do next.

"You're reading *The Mysterious Robot on Bexley Street*," Malcolm said.

"Okay," I said, spotting another cashew. "And you..." I fixed him with a devious grin. "There are so many possibilities."

"We said no tattoo," he warned.

"I know."

I delighted in the increasingly apprehensive way he was looking at me, how he leaned back slightly more with each passing second. There *were* so many possibilities that had made it onto the list that night—I didn't know how he missed *Take a cooking class and fall in love with the instructor*, a plot from a rom-com I'd bought at the book festival, but it was on there. But I truly didn't want to torture him (mostly). Thinking over what I knew about Malcolm sticking to his own book-devices and hardly ever leaving Bell River, about Rochelle recounting how he always hung around the library at school, I wanted to push him a little. Make him uncomfortable but in a way that was, possibly, good for him.

"There's a showing of *Jurassic Park* in Adams Morgan in a couple weeks and you're gonna go to it," I said.

"I have to watch a movie in public?" He spoke with such disgust that I may as well have suggested he strip naked and go streaking. Come to think of it—well, it was too late to add it now.

"*Jurassic Park* is based on a book, isn't it? There you go. You still get to be left to your devices. Just in a different format."

Malcolm harrumphed. "I don't even know where Adams Morgan is."

"Oh my god, it's a neighborhood in DC. It's sad that you don't know that," I said, omitting the fact that I also hadn't known about Adams Morgan until I'd come across it this morning while researching activities for Malcolm to do. But I wasn't from here. "That's exactly why you need to get out more."

Malcolm sighed but didn't argue any further. "Then you need to finish the robot book by the Saturday after next, and we'll meet that Sunday to report back." He said it stubbornly, like he was exacting revenge on me somehow by requiring that I read a book and see him again.

"Sure," I said, a smile sneaking across my face. It was hard to dislike the prospect of another homework assignment when I'd get to see Malcolm afterward.

After fortune cookies, another visit from Ellen that had us both laughing, and a reapplication of Crushed Velvet in the bathroom, Malcolm and I started for the exit. My mind buzzed with what could happen next. Nothing, if we were colleagues. We'd go our separate ways and that would be that. But my quickening pulse didn't seem to believe me.

"Well, look who it is!"

I turned. Ralph stood at the pickup counter, scribbling on a receipt. When he noticed Malcolm behind me, he did a double-take. I stopped in my tracks, dread rising inside me. Malcolm's insistence that we were colleagues took new meaning now that I was staring at Ralph's surprised face. Malcolm bumped into me from behind, sending me stumbling forward, but he put a hand on my arm to steady me.

"Why are you—oh. Ralph. Hi," Malcolm said. He cleared his throat and took his hand off my arm. I instantly missed the warmth from his touch.

I stepped to the side so that I was no longer directly in front of Malcolm. No one said a word. The woman behind the register returned from the kitchen with a large paper bag, which she deposited in front of Ralph.

"Getting dinner, huh?" I said.

Ralph tore his gaze from Malcolm and noticed the paper bag. "Uh, yes." He went back to staring at us. "You two had dinner here as well, did you?"

I glanced at Malcolm, who was blinking a lot. "Yes," I said. "I guess we all had the same idea. This seems like a good place for colleagues to hang out. Since that's what we all are." When no one said anything, I kept going. "Would you ever do a work happy hour here?"

After a pause, Ralph said, "Good idea. I'll think about it." He went back to staring between us. "How's the bookstore?"

"It misses Edward Bell," I quipped. Rudely, no one

laughed. "I mean…it's good," I continued. "You should stop by sometime." I clamped my lips together, instantly regretting the offer.

"I think I should," Ralph said. Of course this would be the one time he listened to me. I held still, scanning his face for clues as to whether it was a passing remark or a threat. But then Ralph turned and picked up his paper bag. "Have a good night. I'll see you tomorrow, Malcolm." He gave Malcolm a look with a touch too much significance on his way out.

We stood in still silence for a few moments. A waiter maneuvered past us with a steaming tray of dumplings and crab Rangoon. Malcolm let out a sigh.

"Nothing to worry about, right, colleague?" I said on our way out.

"I guess we'll see."

We stood outside Wok House, neither one of us making a move to go anywhere. It had rained briefly, giving the air a damp, earthy smell. The road and sidewalks were shiny from rain—and yet the air was still warm on my shoulders. The concept of rain in warm weather was still something I had to get used to.

Malcolm turned to me, his expression distant but not the blinking panic I'd seen before. "Can I walk you home?" he asked.

I was quick to agree. I couldn't remember the last time anyone walked me home. There was something old-fashioned and quaint about the concept. On the way, I asked Malcolm if he remembered getting into an argument with his biology teacher in eighth grade, and he dove into an impassioned explanation about her misunderstanding of *mitosis*. I respectfully kept my laughter to a minimum, mostly.

When we reached Rochelle's, the porch light was still on, beckoning me inside. I lingered.

"I had fun tonight," I said.

"Me, too."

"You feeling okay about Ralph?" I asked.

He nodded, though he still looked like his mind was elsewhere. "Yeah. It'll be fine."

"Good." Still, I didn't leave. "Malcolm?"

"Yeah?"

"Do you want to sneak into Ralph's office and find Edward Bell's dirty letters?"

He laughed. "Not a chance."

"Coward."

"Snoop."

"I'll find a way to get those letters if I have to con Ralph myself," I said.

"I believe you."

I studied him, surprised to hear him deviate from our usual banter. He was gazing at me with an odd, mystified expression on his face. "What?" I asked.

Malcolm shook his head. "I just...I don't think I could tell on you after all."

"Is it because you're impressed by my nosiness?" I asked. My smile waned under the seriousness in his eyes.

"No," he said quietly. "It's more that..." He leaned in and kissed me before I knew what was happening, leaving a trace of soft lips on mine. I caught him before he could pull back too far, returned the kiss with another that was slower, longer. He tasted like sesame oil and fortune-cookie vanilla.

"Damn it," Malcolm murmured. He said it like he'd lost a

bet, except there was a smile blooming across his face. He took a step back. "Have a good night."

"You, too." I watched him walk away. He walked slowly, head down, shoulders hunched, probably thinking about what he'd just done and what it meant for his job.

I smirked. So was I.

CHAPTER FOURTEEN

I spent my day off alternating between leisure and anxiety. I started reading *The Wedding Date*, did a load of dishes while Rochelle and Elliot were napping, and checked my phone for a response from Malcolm. His confidence that we were nothing but colleagues had seemed to shatter when we ran into Ralph the night before. And maybe it was the good kind of shattering, I thought, remembering how he'd kissed me afterward. But he'd still seemed distracted, like consequences might be coming. I kept thinking about Ralph mentioning that he would drop by the bookstore and wondered what might be in store for me tomorrow.

That morning, I'd texted Malcolm, Everything okay with Ralph? He didn't respond.

At a few minutes past noon, though, when I got to a deliciously dirty part of *The Wedding Date*, my phone buzzed.

All good, he replied.

Another text followed: a screencap of an email confirming his ticket purchase for an outdoor movie in Adams Morgan.

Guess I'm ready for Jurassic Park in the park, he texted. Doesn't sound redundant at all.

I thought—perhaps naively—that was that. That Ralph had seen we were getting along and didn't think anything of it. That Malcolm taking steps to fulfill his book club assignment was proof that we could go on as normal, with Malcolm checking on me at the bookstore but us being more than that when we were off duty.

And so I didn't think any more of it. I read for a bit longer, then pulled out Jim's card and called his sister. She shared her experience setting up an online bookstore with BookBin, telling me that the partnership enabled her to reach a wider audience and sell a broader selection of books without having to prepare and ship the online orders herself. I didn't go into the Bell Society rules I was skirting; I just told her I was looking for a way to grow my customer base by selling books I couldn't physically carry in the store. And Susan said she thought BookBin could help me do just that.

That very evening, I submitted an application through the BookBin website. I spent the night checking my phone every time it buzzed, hoping for a response.

I picked up my phone while I sat in the bookstore the following morning. Still no reply. I sighed and leaned back to survey the store. No customers, as usual. I swiped out of my inbox and opened up Netflix. I'd finished *Kim's Convenience* last week and was now working my way through *Schitt's Creek*.

I was twenty minutes into an episode when the door swung open. I straightened my posture and tapped the Mute button, then looked up to find Dahlia standing in front of me.

"Hi," I said, pasting on a smile to hide my surprise. "Do you...need something?"

She held up the strap of the laptop bag on her shoulder. "Is it cool if I work here for a couple hours? I'm drowning in spread-sheets. Usually, I go to the café, but I thought that chair looked pretty comfy when I was here the other night."

I followed her gaze to the leather armchair in the corner. It had gone unused since Dylan last sat there the day of the paper mustache incident. "Sure," I said. "Go for it."

She settled into the armchair, and soon the store's usual silence was filled with mouse clicks and typing. It was soothing, like I was back in my office job.

My phone vibrated, and I pounced on it. A new email. I scrolled through it in disbelief.

"Oh my god," I said.

Dahlia stopped typing. "What?"

"I have an online bookstore." I looked back down at the email informing me that my application had been approved. "I mean, I still have to set up the website, but I'll be able to sell...pretty much every book out there."

"That's huge!" Dahlia said.

"It is," I agreed. I felt a pang of guilt to know this was some-thing else I was keeping from Rochelle, but when I thought about what this could mean for her finances, I knew it would be worth it.

I sent off an email to Jim. Throughout the day, as Jim and I swapped emails about website specifications, the store continued to see more activity. Evelyn came by to get my opinion on a couple of cover options she was considering for her new book. Dahlia weighed in too, and then they wandered over to the café to show Abigail. They returned with sandwiches, even one for me. I set up the refreshments table from the other night, placing it in the alcove where the Bell books used to be. After dragging over the two chairs from behind the register, we had a make-shift lunch table. While Dahlia sat in the armchair by the window and worked on her spreadsheets, Evelyn walked me through the changes she planned to make to the cover, and I showed her the website layout Jim and I had decided on. Evelyn, still chewing, peered at the layout on my screen, then nodded enthusiastically.

The rest of the week passed in much the same way, with familiar faces coming by to talk, browse, read, work. Marcia from the farmers' market stopped by, dropping her voice and saying she heard I carried thrillers from this century. I gladly rang her up, and she winked at me on her way out. Vernon came by for another rom-com and to check on the status of the mystery I'd ordered for him. As I rang him up, he noticed the table where Evelyn and I had eaten lunch. He commented that it looked pathetic without more chairs, and not long after heading upstairs with his purchase, he came right back down with a chair in tow— then another, and another, until four wooden chairs sat around the table. Evelyn sat there one day to work on novel revisions; later that afternoon, Leena joined her, using the space to stuff envelopes for her sister's wedding invitations. Abigail brought by samples of a chai cookie recipe she was testing, and we sat around the table taking bites and weighing in. I brought a cookie upstairs to Vernon, who sniffed it suspiciously before taking a bite. When I mentioned that Abigail was downstairs hoping for feedback, he shut the door on me. Abigail commented that at least he hadn't thrown the cookie back in my face. Others' expec-tations for Vernon, I was learning, were very low.

Even when Vernon wasn't in the store, hearing his creaks upstairs was a comforting sign that I had another friend nearby. When he wasn't spending a few days a week working at a locksmith shop he owned on the other side of town, he was at home, creaking around with his cats.

Jim finished the website, refusing to accept any payment except for a discount on his first online order. I sent out an email to my small but growing newsletter list, sharing the link to my new online shop. As an extra precaution against Ralph, who I knew liked to scour the internet for reviews and mentions of Bell Society businesses, Jim had hidden my website from search engines.

Overnight, I had a modest stream of online orders. Nearly everyone on my list had submitted an order, and I knew it couldn't be because they all had an urgent need for books. My heart swelled when I thought about them submitting orders just to support me.

"I guess that August slump is over," Rochelle said one night, peeking her head in my room. "It's wild how well things are going this month. It's like night and day."

I looked up from the rom-com Leena had lent me. "Yeah. Thank god those literary conferences are over with."

"Thank god for *you*." She took a seat on the edge of my bed. "We're on track to do better this month than we did last September. And Luke said you haven't even needed him to help out at the store?"

"Yeah, no need," I said with a shrug. "You need him more." Luke had texted me a few times, offering to cover the store on Saturdays or Sundays when he didn't have class. I'd probably sounded capable when I'd turned him down, breezily responding that I had it under control and suggesting he stay home with Rochelle. I didn't need him coming to the bookstore and discovering everything I was hiding.

"You're a wonder," Rochelle said.

I gave her a tentative smile. "I barely know what I'm doing."

She squinted playfully at me. "I refuse to accept that. You're a brilliant businesswoman and there'll be a statue of you in the park by the end of the year, mustache and all."

She wouldn't be singing my praises if she knew the risks I was taking, but I let the warmth of her words curl around me anyway. I did feel like a brilliant businesswoman. I may have lost the store's main revenue drivers, but I'd plotted and planned and brought in a new source of funds. I had to think she'd be at least somewhat impressed if she knew everything I'd done. She'd also be surprised, disappointed, and upset after she learned about the lies and the risks. But I liked imagining there was pride in there, too.

The following week, I sat in the store reading *The Mysterious Robot on Bexley Street* while Abigail read in the armchair, as she now liked to do during her breaks, and Dahlia worked on her laptop at the table.

I looked around the store, reveling in the fact that I had company now, then went back to my book. I'd never been drawn to science fiction, but T. J. Hull's writing had hooked me immediately from page one, in which a young boy heard a knock on his door long past bedtime, crept out of bed to answer it, and came face-to-face with a robot in an apron asking to borrow two sticks of butter and a cup of brown sugar. Of course I had to know what happened next.

When the bell above the door rang, I glanced up, expecting Evelyn. I almost dropped my book when I saw Ralph. He strode into the store, then paused when he noticed Abigail.

"Shouldn't you be at the café?"

She lifted her head from her book. "I'm on break."

Then he turned his attention on me, coming up to the register. "Good afternoon," he said. He eyed the Sunrise Café coffee cup on the counter. "I ask staff to keep their personal items out of reach from customers."

"Oh." I set it out of sight. "I must have put it there when I was reshelving. Sorry. Sorry, customers," I joked to Abigail and Dahlia. My smile wilted under Ralph's serious expression.

"How's the store doing?" he asked.

"Good. Great," I corrected, deciding a little embellishment never hurt anyone. Then, thinking it might be better to downgrade lest he think I didn't want Edward Bell's books back in the store, I settled on "Good" again. I'm sure I was very convincing.

"Hm," Ralph said, evidently unconvinced. "Why is there a table over there?"

"People like having a space to sit and work," I said. "Kind of in the tradition of Edward Bell." A total fabrication, but it sounded like something Ralph would say.

"I wouldn't want to confuse tourists into thinking *that* was his writing table." He cast a discerning eye toward it.

"Then it's good there are no tourists here," I said brightly.

Before Ralph could respond, the door swung open and Marcia came walking in. "Can I get the sequel to—" She stopped when she saw Ralph.

Ralph snapped into customer service mode, giving her a genial smile. "The sequel to what?" His gaze fell on the book in her hand, the psychological thriller I'd sold her last week. "We obviously don't carry that. I'm afraid we don't have the sequel here." A puzzled expression came over him. "Why would you think Maggie would have it?"

"My break's over," Abigail announced. "Time to get back to work." She raised her eyebrows at me over Ralph's shoulder on her way out the door.

Noticing the stony way Marcia was looking at Ralph, I said, "I don't think she thought I had the sequel. I think she was just asking if I knew whether it was out yet. Right?" I caught her eye.

"Right," Marcia said slowly. "I wouldn't want to waste a trip to Barnes and Noble."

"Ah." Still he studied her with suspicion. "I don't see why you'd feel the need to go to Barnes and Noble at all when you've got a bookstore right here."

"I like reading books I haven't read yet," Marcia deadpanned. "I'm weird like that."

"So weird," I echoed. "I tell her that all the time. Anyway, Marcia, I happen to know the sequel is out and available for purchase wherever you buy books. Not here, obviously. But maybe... online somewhere."

"Good to know," Marcia said, catching on. "Thank you for your help, Maggie." She shot Ralph an annoyed look on her way out.

"Some people have poor taste in literature," Ralph said, leaning in like he was divulging a secret.

I remembered the middle-grade sci-fi T. J. Hull book in front of me and pushed it from view. "Right."

"I don't understand the direction this store is taking," Ralph said, turning to glance at Dahlia at the table. "I'm not sure I like the idea of people coming here to...loaf around."

I was finally starting to find day-to-day life at the bookstore appealing; I shouldn't have been surprised that Ralph wanted to take that away.

"I'm sure if you brought back the Bell books and the writing

table, that would change," I said. I regretted my words immediately. I knew I should want the Bell items back, want to undo
the mess I'd gotten Rochelle's store into, but then where would
Dahlia work on her spreadsheets? Where would Abigail take her
breaks, or Evelyn do her writing? How could I enjoy the store's
atmosphere when it was crawling with tourists asking questions
about Edward Bell?

"In time," Ralph said vaguely. His shrewd eyes scanned the
store again. "I noticed sales are up this month. Any big sellers?"

"Oh. Yes. Um." My gaze darted around at the shelves. "It's
been a mix. A little of this, little of that. I know we got an influx
of people attending literary conferences." Apparently, I believed
my literary conference lie could get me out of anything.

"Interesting. The sales report has been showing a lot of sales
attributed to 'miscellaneous' recently. Why isn't it reflecting the
correct titles?"

I looked away, as if he could discern the truth through eye
contact. "Yeah, good point." I held up a finger. "Actually, I think
I was updating it wrong. I'll fix that."

He gave a disapproving hum. "Make sure you do."

Ralph gave the store one more once-over, and then he left,
the bell over the door ringing cheerfully to celebrate his exit.

I opened a drawer and pulled out the clunky laptop Rochelle
used for bookstore business. She'd shown me how to update the
sales report Ralph checked every week. I *had* been updating it—I
just hadn't known where to put the revenue from my secret stash.
Throwing it all under *Miscellaneous* was apparently too obvious
an approach.

My fingers hovered over the keyboard. I was already being
deceitful, between the events and the secret inventory and the

online store. No harm in sprinkling more dishonesty on top, in theory. But lying on an official Bell Society spreadsheet felt more black-and-white. It was one thing to hide the truth; it was another to write down a lie and sign my name to it.

But this was what I needed to do to keep the store profitable. Rochelle needed the money. She had said it was a relief knowing the store was in my hands. I couldn't let her down. Nor could I let down the group of—dare I call them my friends?—who were slowly making themselves at home here. And Jim had put so much work into designing my website.

It was a lie, but it was a necessary lie. I could make the sales report believable. With some help.

"Hey, Dahlia?" I said. She lifted her head and pulled out an earbud. "You're good with spreadsheets, right?"

After reviewing the sales report, Dahlia suggested I stop by her house after work. That evening, I locked up the bookstore and followed the path on my phone to the address she'd texted me, a two-bedroom cottage at the end of a gravel road. There in her kitchen, painted a sunny shade of yellow, we sat at the table and walked through the report. Using the bookstore's previous reports, Dahlia ran a query to identify the store's top sellers in the last few years, Bell books excluded. Then, with some formulas that flew over my head, she outputted scenarios for different combinations of classics that added up to the sales I'd made so far.

"This one matches the sales you have right now," she said, clicking on a sheet. "And if that looks good to you, I've automated it in this next sheet. Going forward, all you'll need to do is enter your sales revenue here, and it'll populate the quantities for the classics you've theoretically sold to match that figure."

I rested my chin in my hands, staring at her dreamily. "I barely understood that, but you're amazing."

Dahlia laughed and slid the laptop toward me. "I'll take the compliment."

I bought Dahlia dinner as a small thanks. We ordered delivery from a Thai place she recommended and sat at the kitchen table sipping Thai iced tea and eating a rich, spicy green curry that put warmth in my belly. She told me about spending years at an accounting firm before deciding she'd rather strike out on her own. Now, as a self-employed accountant, she'd built a growing base of loyal clients, and she enjoyed working on her own schedule.

I'd mostly listened and asked questions, reluctant to share my own meandering job history. I was more talkative when the conversation turned to books and TV shows, and we fell into a lively discussion of Molly from *Insecure*.

I left feeling more at ease with the idea of submitting my false sales report. I wasn't alone with my bookstore lies anymore. I had people around me, helping me, cheering me on. I'd do what it took to hold on to that.

The next morning, I submitted the fake sales report to Ralph. Dahlia had been confident that it was credible. I just needed Ralph to feel the same way.

CHAPTER FIFTEEN

Looks good, Maggie. More soon.

I received Ralph's response to my fake sales report within an hour. I sat in the bookstore staring at the five words on my phone. Relief had flooded through me at first—*looks good* was an excellent sign that he hadn't spotted anything fishy.

More soon was an ominous sign-off, though. There was no telling what that *more* meant. It could be related to the report, or he might have something else up his sleeve.

But I wouldn't dwell on that. He didn't spot any issues, so I was in the clear.

I picked up *The Mysterious Robot on Bexley Street*. I was only about thirty pages from the end. It had been a fast read, filled with silly plotlines and amusing misunderstandings. As I'd read, I couldn't help thinking that T. J. Hull would love my event at the bookstore.

Maybe even as a guest writer.

I flipped to the end of the book, then stopped when I found the *About the Author* page. A thrill ran through me when I read the last sentence of his bio.

T. J. Hull technically lives in Baltimore, though he spends most of his time on a spaceship, touring the galaxy with creatures from planet Zepharo.

He was local.

Before I knew what I was doing, I took out my phone and did a search for T. J. Hull. I found his website, then navigated to the *Contact* page.

Dear T.J.,

You were kind enough to sign a book for my tongue-tied friend Malcolm at the DC Book Festival. He really appreciated your drawing of Scrap! He's got me reading *The Mysterious Robot on Bexley Street* now, and I'm loving it. I'd have actually liked reading if I'd been handed this in third grade!

Which brings me to my question. I work at Cobblestone Books in Bell River, Maryland. I've been putting on underground events that celebrate the joys of genre fiction and put a funny spin on a literary classic. At our last event, our guest author Evelyn Suwan wrote a hilarious scene reimagining *Moby-Dick* as a romance. The lighthearted tone you struck in *The Mysterious Robot on Bexley Street* is exactly what we go for.

Would you be interested in being a guest author? You would write a scene that puts a science-fiction spin on a classic novel of your choice. Our attendees would love to hear your take and buy your new book.

Let me know your thoughts!

Maggie Banks

When I hit the Send button, I felt like anything was possible. It was a long shot that he would agree, but I had a nonzero chance. He was a local author. I could tell that his brand of humor was exactly what these events were supposed to be: utterly absurd and unabashedly genuine.

The day carried on as normal. Dahlia was working from her home office because she had calls to make, but Evelyn came in at noon to do some writing in the armchair. I'd finished the T. J. Hull book and moved on to the thriller Marcia had enjoyed so much, which hooked me immediately. When my phone buzzed, I picked it up—then did a double-take when I saw the screen. T. J. Hull had emailed me back.

Dear Maggie,

I do remember you two coming to my signing! Your idea is an interesting one. I'm certainly intrigued.

I'll have to check my calendar before I can commit, but I've already got some ideas rolling around in my head. There are so many classics I'd love to put a sci-fi twist on. *The Great Gatsby* is the first that comes to mind. I've always thought there was more to that green light than meets the eye...

Stay tuned!

T.J.

I reread his words, letting the notion wash over me. T. J. Hull was thinking about coming to my event. T. J. Hull had replied to my email. T. J. Hull and I were basically best friends.

Malcolm would freak out if he knew. He'd bring a stack of books for T.J. to sign and stare creepily at him in starstruck silence. I'd have to translate for him again, and T.J. would understand. We were best friends, after all.

Except I couldn't tell Malcolm. He'd have to do his duty and inform Ralph. It was tiring, hiding things from the people I cared about.

But I knew one person I could tell. I called Evelyn over and showed her the email.

"That's huge!" she said, handing the phone back to me. "You'd have a line out the door."

My smile fell. Somehow I hadn't considered that. I remembered the enraptured audience in T.J.'s session at the book festival, the long line of people who waited for a signature and a chance to say hello. Surely they'd be eager to attend an informal event, listen to him read a new piece, and talk to him afterward.

I thought it through as the day passed. Yes, I would have to prepare for all sorts of possibilities. I would need to think of a way to prevent people from making a scene outside the bookstore. I'd enforce a limit on attendees if I had to.

But I wouldn't back out. This was too good an opportunity to pass up. I'd find a way to make it work.

And when T. J. Hull emailed me the next day with the dates he was free, I was ready to charge ahead at full speed. This event would be my biggest yet. Which wasn't saying much given that I only had one under my belt, but that didn't make it any less true.

I was drafting the event page that afternoon when I saw

Vernon walk past the window. I waved, but he either didn't see me or had gone back to ignoring me. I tried waving both arms, but he disappeared past the window, and I soon heard his steps going up the stairwell behind me.

Well. Now was as good a time as any to tell him about the next event. He'd refused to give me his email address the night of the last one, muttering about spam when I asked if he wanted to join my newsletter list. In-person invitation it was.

I opened the door to the stairwell, then treaded up the creaking wooden steps and knocked on his door.

After a long pause, a low voice called out, "Who is it?"

"It's Maggie."

When Vernon opened the door, he raised his eyebrows expectantly, and I realized that was all the greeting I was going to get.

"I'm holding another event," I said. "It's on October 13, and you're welcome to come. It might be more crowded than the last one. The author is pretty well known." I launched into an explanation of how T. J. Hull had come to agree to it, and then, since he didn't seem to recognize the name, I talked about the books T. J. Hull was most known for. And when Vernon still didn't say a word, I meandered into a plot summary of *The Mysterious Robot on Bexley Street* for reasons I wasn't sure of.

"That's about it," I finished lamely, willing myself to stop talking but not sure how with the silence still hanging between us. "T.J.'s going to do a sci-fi retelling of *The Great Gatsby*. I'd love to have you there. But like I said, it'll be more crowded, so I understand if that's not your thing." I cut myself off and waited for Vernon to respond.

"How much more crowded?" he asked, squinting in thought.

Evelyn's words about having a line out the door came back to me. "If I have to put a cap on it, it'll be a max of twenty. If some people don't mind standing."

He turned around and surveyed his apartment. "I feel like I could fit thirty people up here."

I laughed in sheer disbelief. "What?"

"You have all those shelves in the way, right? I've got an open floor plan." Vernon ventured farther into his apartment, leaving the door to nearly close on me. I pushed it open and stepped inside. He had a large living room with two worn fabric couches, one of which sagged in the middle. Two cats were curled up in the sagging center, sleeping. Past the living room was a dining room, though it held only a small, round wooden table with one chair.

"People could sit on the couches," Vernon said, stepping through the apartment. "Four people at that table, once I get my chairs back," he muttered under his breath, as though bringing his chairs down to the bookstore hadn't been his idea. "You could put more chairs over here and over there." He gestured to the dining room, then to the space between the couch and the window overlooking the street. "No bookshelves in the way. What do you think?"

I was still glancing around the room, feeling like I was five steps behind him. "You'd do that?"

"If you help me set up and clean up, sure. What do I need this space for?" Vernon frowned, like he was almost mad at me for asking. Vernon, I was learning, had a way of looking his grumpiest when he was being his kindest.

I let the idea take shape in my head. I wouldn't have to worry about Ralph or Malcolm coming by the bookstore and noticing the noise, because this would all be upstairs, out of the Bell Society's purview. This wasn't even a forbidden event, then—it was just a party. People wouldn't be lining up at the bookstore; they'd be entering through Vernon's separate entrance. I could bring my box of forbidden books upstairs and make in-person sales that way.

"Okay," I said. I grinned and met Vernon's eyes. He nodded once, his expression still unwaveringly stern, but I knew some part of him had to be excited, too.

That afternoon, I set the date and published the event page. I was co-hosting a party with the curmudgeon upstairs, and T. J. Hull was coming. Since T. J. Hull was a big name, I bumped the ticket price from ten dollars to twenty. I watched the RSVPs start to come in: first one, then two, then eight by the end of the night. It was so strange and wonderful that this was happening at all, but I felt a pang to know I couldn't tell Rochelle or Malcolm. The people I wanted to tell most.

———

Talking to Malcolm while sitting on a secret was a precarious balance.

When we met for dinner at an Italian restaurant and he asked how I liked *The Mysterious Robot on Bexley Street*, I had to stop short to keep from revealing something I shouldn't.

"I loved it," I said at last. "It was funny and weird, but also profound."

Malcolm smiled. "Right? It's so good. I started his new book yesterday. You can borrow it when I'm done if you want."

I took a drink of water, thinking about the copies I'd ordered for T. J. Hull's event, scheduled for two weeks from Saturday. "Maybe," I said. I wiped my upper lip and changed the subject. "How was the movie?"

A look of distaste swept over him. "Terrible."

"Really?" I gave him a long, disbelieving stare.

"Yes!" He began to list the many ways I'd wronged him on his fingers. "I had to drive in DC, which is a nightmare. This guy in front of me kept laughing too loud during the movie. And it almost rained."

I frowned. "Almost? So you're saying it didn't rain?"

"No, but I kept looking at the sky and thinking it would, and working on my contingency plan for what I'd do if it rained."

I bit back a smile. "What was your contingency plan?"

He started arranging our silverware like an obstacle course. "I was going to step around the dude in front of me so I could accidentally drop my fries in his lap." He weaved the saltshaker past a fork, stopping once to tilt some salt onto it. "And then I'd step around the lady with the plaid blanket, maneuver past the family by the tree, stop by the food truck for more fries, and then go back to my car." He set the saltshaker next to the drink menu, then looked up at me like all of this was perfectly reasonable.

"I see," I said as seriously as I could manage. "I'm deeply sorry for the inconvenience. Was there anything remotely good about this terrible outing I forced you to endure?"

"You're mocking me," he observed.

"Yes."

He grunted his disapproval. "Well, I had to drive around to find parking, but I ended up parking by a vintage store that had some interesting stuff. I bought a lamp that was kind of cool," he grumbled. "And then I guess I found a bookstore that sold out-of-print books, and I spent a while there, too. So *maybe* I had fun after all."

I tried not to rub it in too much. By his own admission,

Malcolm didn't get out much. And when he did, it was carefully planned: a book festival he had registered for, a book bar he had long read about on Yelp. I liked expanding his comfort zone, getting him to start seeing what the cities around him had to offer besides museums and bookstores.

"You're welcome," I said. Going by the way Malcolm's eyes narrowed, he seemed to hear the *I told you so* in my voice.

After we'd discussed our next assignments—a soapmaking class in Franklin for him, *Emma* for me—we walked around town. I'd braced for another chance encounter with Ralph on our way out, but all that greeted me was a cheerful hostess and a bowl of mints that wouldn't undo the pungent effects of the three slices of garlic bread I'd eaten. I took one anyway.

As if Malcolm was also recalling our surprise encounter with Ralph, he brought him up when we neared Bell Park. "I heard Ralph came by the store," he said. "He said you cultivate a lively atmosphere. I don't think he meant it as a good thing."

I popped the mint in my mouth and stuffed the wrapper into my jacket pocket. My fingers crinkled the cellophane as we walked. "I'm choosing to take it as a compliment."

I was quiet for the rest of the walk, thinking about Ralph stumbling upon the T. J. Hull event in a couple of weeks, how much more I had left to do. T.J.'s books should arrive in time, but it couldn't hurt to check on them in the morning. The event page had already reached its cap of thirty RSVPs. I had to check in with Vernon about setup and logistics. And I had to figure out what I'd do next when my time at the bookstore came to an end. The thought of hunting for a job I didn't care about stole the air from my lungs.

It occurred to me that even if I didn't know what I wanted

to do next, I had a feeling about the where. I was making friends here. And more. I glanced at Malcolm.

"What are you thinking about?" he asked.

I took in a deep breath. "I think I want to stay in the area after my time is up at the bookstore. Get a job, get an apartment." I paused. "Do you think that would be a good idea?"

Malcolm's eyes hung on me even after I'd finished speaking. A smile started in the corner of his mouth and spread slowly across his face. "I think that's possibly the best idea you've ever had," he said.

"Possibly?" I teased.

"Definitely."

I bit my lip, taking in the moment. His contentment, the glow of the streetlamp above us, the nervous hope thrumming in me at the prospect of making a decision once and for all. The reluctance I'd felt at the prospect of job hunting felt less real now, replaced by that same buzzy feeling I had when I first emailed T. J. Hull. There was something magical about possibility. It makes everything fluttery and light and so wonderfully *possible*.

This was going to work. The T. J. Hull event, my plans to stay, even Ralph and his watchful eye. It would all work out. Anything—and everything—was possible.

CHAPTER SIXTEEN

It was easy to see how T. J. Hull got his start writing funny books for kids.

The T. J. Hull who showed up twenty minutes early on Saturday evening was different from the one who participated in the Q&A at the book festival last month. That one listened carefully, spoke thoughtfully, and made the occasional joke. This T. J. Hull took one step inside Vernon's apartment and cackled as soon as he saw a framed photo in the living room.

"Catward Bell!" he exclaimed. I followed his gaze to a picture of a cat that bore a striking resemblance to the Edward Bell portrait downstairs. There was a black stripe of fur under its nose in lieu of a mustache, and it stared at the camera with a glare not unlike Edward Bell's.

Vernon popped his head out from the kitchen. "I liked the idea of hanging it near the door to piss my landlord off," he said. "He's an Edward Bell fan." Which was a mild way of putting it. "You the hotshot author?" he asked T.J., giving him a once-over.

"Yes," T.J. said. "You can call me 'hotshot' for short."

Vernon grunted and went back into the kitchen, but a couple

of early arrivals on the couch laughed. T.J. glanced in their direction, a boyish grin coming over him. They were both first-time attendees from out of town, and they'd been watching him from afar since he arrived. Now that he was looking right at them, they both averted their eyes.

"You guys been here before?" he asked, crossing the room. One of them, a balding man in a leather jacket, lit up as T.J. approached. Like he was a celebrity. I supposed that for some readers—like Malcolm—he was.

A twinge took root in my gut. Malcolm. He'd have loved to see T. J. Hull in a more relaxed setting, no signing line rush, no self-imposed pressure to say the perfect thing in one brief moment. If all of this got out, I wasn't sure what would upset him more: that I'd sneakily run a series of unpermitted events under his nose, or that I'd kept him from another chance at talking to T. J. Hull.

But this would never get out. I trusted T.J. and the two fans he was speaking to now. All three of them were from out of town and would have no reason to go blabbing to Ralph. As the night wore on, with each door I opened and each hand I stamped, I confirmed that yes, I trusted this person, too. The T. J. Hull fans and the familiar faces, too: Evelyn, Dahlia, Leena, Marcia, and Abigail, who came bearing a box of pastries from the café. I trusted them all.

I led them through the pledge, looking on as they all vowed with complete solemnity that if they ever spoke of this event to anyone with ties to the Bell Society, may they be exiled to the valley of ashes. I caught Vernon's eye as even he recited along. No one here would tattle.

After running through my spiel, I gave the floor to T.J. and made my way to the kitchen, where I could keep an eye on the refreshments. I leaned against the counter and brought a cup of wine to my lips.

"You know," T.J. began, "over the decades, my books have been banned for the weirdest reasons. Dialogue with mild cursing. Violence. Queer characters. Taking the lord's name in vain." He said this last part in a stage whisper, then turned around as if checking to see if anyone overheard. He startled exaggeratedly at the Catward Bell portrait behind him. This got several laughs, loudest of all from Bell River locals.

"Not to toot my own horn, but banned books are inherently seen as more interesting. Am I right?" I joined the audience in clapping and whooping. "Which isn't to say that the classics that have been around forever *aren't* interesting. I was obsessed with Mark Twain when I was growing up, though funnily enough his books were banned once upon a time, too. But if you put some books to one side and say, 'You can only read these,' and if you shove some other books in a corner and say, 'Don't, under any circumstances, read those,' well, that corner's going to look mighty appealing, isn't it?

"From what I understand, Maggie here at Cobblestone Books can *only* sell classics. So I like to think that what we're doing here tonight is our way of putting together a corner of our own. She's carrying a small but mighty selection of science fiction—including my new book, if anyone was wondering," he added out of the side of his mouth. "And in this corner of ours, we celebrate our favorites, but we have fun with them, too. Because if you can't have fun with what you love, then what's the point?" After the audience applauded, he took a seat and began to read from a sheaf of papers, describing how a group of aliens beamed to life from the green light at the end of Daisy's dock and tried to take in their baffling surroundings.

T. J. Hull, I was learning, went all-out for readings. As he described the aliens trying to blend in at Gatsby's party, he pulled faces and read dialogue in distinct voices, evoking loud laughs at almost every line. He must be used to it given that most of his books were for kids. His website had shown pictures of him doing readings at schools and libraries. But this didn't seem like an act he put on for just kids. I suspected this was T.J.'s personality, and he did these readings with his silly voices and strange faces because it was fun. He got to do what he loved. Why couldn't I do that, just type *fun* into a search bar and find the job I was suited for?

Jim came by the kitchen for water and popcorn, pulling me from my thoughts. "How's the online store doing?" he asked.

"It's great, thanks to you," I said. "The website's amazing." I'd put a link to the store's website on the event registration page, and some online orders had trickled in as people registered.

Jim shrugged off the compliment. "You outdid yourself with this one."

My lungs and probably my ego swelled when I took a breath and tried not to beam. "Thank you."

I noticed the cups of wine were nearly gone and set about pouring some more while T.J. dropped the revelation that Gatsby was also an alien whose family was imploring him to return to his home planet.

A knock came from behind me. While T. J. Hull kept reading, I left the kitchen to let in the late straggler.

It was hard to tell who was more surprised when I opened the door: me or Ralph. I halted, at a loss for words, acutely aware of my thudding heart.

"Maggie?" Ralph frowned, then peered behind me. "Where's Vernon?"

I turned around. T.J. was still reading, but the Bell River locals—particularly Abigail, who watched from the couch with wide eyes—knew something was going on.

"Outside," Vernon said, appearing beside me. He ushered us into the hall and shut the door. The three of us stood at the top of the stairs, Ralph glancing from Vernon to me. "Can I help you?" Vernon prodded.

"I was on my way home when I heard the commotion from your apartment," Ralph said. "Which is…unusual for you. Is everything okay?"

"Just a party," Vernon grunted. "We'll keep it down. Thanks for stopping by."

Ralph laughed. "Party? I've known you my entire life and you've never had a party. Does Maggie have something to do with it?" His eyes—and Vernon's—settled on me.

I pulled on the sleeve of my sweater, twisting my finger around the fabric. "Well," I began, "this is a meeting of a book club I started. We read classics and talk about their influence on Edward Bell."

Ralph crossed his arms. "And Vernon is a member of this Edward Bell book club?"

I waited for Vernon to respond, but he didn't. The tension in the air thickened as the silence stretched on.

"Yes," I said at last. But that was apparently the wrong thing to say, because then Ralph's expression hardened.

"Vernon has never had a kind word to say about my grandfather," Ralph said. "That cat poster is Exhibit A in a long list of disrespect. What's really going on?"

I kept silent this time, wringing my hands to keep from talking.

"None of your business, Ralph," Vernon said, a warning in his tone.

"It *is* my business," Ralph retorted. "It's absolutely my business that my tenant is mocking Edward Bell and pulling my employees into it. Why do you even live here, if you hate Edward Bell that much?"

"I never said I hated him," Vernon said.

Ralph shook his head. "You know, I'd expect more from you. Especially after everything he's done for your family."

"You have no idea what he's done for my family," Vernon growled.

I looked between the two of them, trying to decipher the subtext. Vernon's family had a history with Edward Bell?

Ralph sighed and ran his hand down his face. "I don't want to get into this. I'm under a lot of pressure right now and I can't have whatever this is"—he gestured at the closed door—"happening on top of everything else. The Bell Society has some big changes coming down the pike. Anyone who can't get on board will have to be the first to go. Maybe it's time to put an end date on that lease, Vernon."

Vernon glowered at him in response, jaw set, eyes murderous.

"I'll be in touch," Ralph said. He turned to me. "Whatever Vernon's doing in there, I advise you don't take part."

I shook my head, not sure how this could have escalated so quickly. "It's really not what you think," I said. "We were just—"

"Good night, Ralph," Vernon said.

I let out a breath once Ralph disappeared out the door. "What just happened?" I asked, turning to Vernon. "What were you talking about? What changes does he mean?"

He only rolled his eyes and stalked inside. I followed him, my head swimming with questions.

We came in at the tail end of T.J.'s reading. T.J. described Gatsby telling his alien family that he had decided to stay on Earth indefinitely with Daisy. In the bizarre but moving conclusion, Gatsby showed up at Daisy's house to profess his love, only to learn Daisy had run off with the oversized pair of glasses from the optometrist's billboard. Despondent, Gatsby stepped into the green light to return to his home planet.

T.J. finished his reading to a round of thunderous applause. People began forming a crowd around him, talking about his piece, asking questions, requesting signatures. Others browsed the box of books I'd brought and took their purchases to me. I quickly sold out of the stock I'd ordered of T. J. Hull's newest book, but some bought the other science fiction books I'd stocked, or copies of *The Great Gatsby*.

After the buying died down, I stepped away when Abigail waved me over. She was standing near the children's section with a woman I hadn't seen here before, who had a round face and wore winged eyeliner applied with an expertise I'd never been able to master. I learned her name was Kat, and that she worked for a Bell Society bed and breakfast two blocks over.

"I didn't know there was a Bell Society B&B," I said.

Kat gave a dry laugh. "We're Ralph's secret shame."

"What do you mean?"

"He bought the B&B a couple years ago. He had all these plans for renovating and expanding and capitalizing on the surge in tourism we were gonna get when the movie came out..." She raised her eyebrows with a meaningful look.

"And then the movie deal fell through," I finished, remembering the framed article in Ralph's office.

"Exactly. So, no renovations, no new tourists. And last year our HVAC system stopped working. Ralph paid for the repairs, but then he let some staff go to cut costs. Which made us too understaffed to do a good job, which led to bad reviews, and now tourists would rather stay at an Airbnb instead. But, you know…" Her top lip pulled upward. "At least we got matching T-shirts out of it."

I groaned. "That sucks. I'm sorry."

"That's Ralph for you."

I nodded, stepping closer. "Ralph said something about big changes coming," I said, lowering my voice. "Do you know what that means?"

Kat grew thoughtful. "He did come by last week and talk to my boss for like an hour. And that was weird, because he never comes by. I heard them say something about the bookstore."

I frowned. "What about the bookstore?"

"I don't know," Kat said with a shrug. "That's all I overheard."

I turned to Abigail. "Have you heard anything? About plans, or…evictions?"

"No." She studied me. "Why? Did he say something to you?"

I stared into my cup. "He said he has plans. I don't know what that means. But it sounded big."

"I'm sure it's minor," Abigail said. "He exaggerates. He made me sit through an hour-long PowerPoint presentation last year just to tell me he was adding a yule log to the café's winter menu."

"Yeah, I'm sure," I said. I took a sip of wine, tried to make myself believe it.

"Tonight was awesome," Kat said. "I'm amazed you pulled this off. When's the next one?"

The thought of holding another event put a knot in my stomach after my encounter with Ralph. "I don't know. We'll see."

Abigail and Kat continued talking, but I looked around the room while Ralph and Vernon's argument played over again in my mind. I glanced at Vernon, now standing among the group crowded around T. J. Hull. I watched Abigail and Kat and wondered if Ralph had seen them here, if they too would face consequences as part of whatever he was planning. None of this would have happened if I hadn't kept roping people into my risky ventures at the bookstore.

I needed to find a way to protect them—all of us—from whatever Ralph had planned. But I couldn't do that until I knew what it was.

CHAPTER SEVENTEEN

The days that followed saw a steady uptick in customers. A couple who had attended the T. J. Hull event came back, this time curious to explore the literary attractions. They stopped by the store on their way to the museum and greeted me like we were old friends, then leaned in and asked to buy from my sci-fi stash.

A few locals came by too, also to ask what books I had stashed away. My collection was growing now. In addition to stocking up on more sci-fi titles for last week's event, I'd also updated my entire inventory to keep the selection fresh. Sales from my hidden inventory had never been better, and the online store was doing well, too. But this all counted for nothing if Ralph's mysterious plans were going to throw a wrench in things.

I'd asked Vernon about it, to no avail. Asking what he knew of Ralph's plans got me a shrug, and probing about his family's past with Edward Bell earned a gruff "None of your business." I tried asking Malcolm too, when we met for lunch on my day off, but his eyes got shifty and he said something about classified information.

And so when Ralph entered the store that week with a woman

in a Bell Society shirt, I was already on edge. Dread snaked through me, even more so when he caught sight of Dahlia at the table in the back and said, "Would you mind leaving us? We need to have a quick Bell Society huddle."

Dahlia stood to pack up her laptop, tossing me a meaningful look. I'd babbled to her yesterday about my worries for so long that she'd taken me out for drinks to help get my mind off things. It had, briefly. But it would take a lot more than two cranberry vodkas to keep me from worrying about whatever Ralph had in store.

When Dahlia left, I faced Ralph, feeling my shoulders tense up. "What did you need to talk to me about?" I asked.

He broke into a cheerful smile that looked unnatural on him. "I've decided to return Edward Bell's books and writing table to the bookstore."

I hesitated, waiting for more. "Really?"

"Really. We've enjoyed having them at the museum, but their home is here. They're not selling as well at the museum. I know you've done well selling the classics here." I averted my gaze, thinking of the falsified sales reports I'd been sending him. "I'm sure that with a little more time and practice you'll be able to sell the Bell books even better."

My shoulders relaxed. No bad news yet. "Great!" I glanced at the person next to him, wondering if she was going to start hauling in the books.

"And I wanted to introduce you to someone," Ralph said. "This is Cynthia. She's a transfer from the museum." The word *transfer* put a cold feeling in my chest.

"Hi," I said slowly.

Cynthia, a woman in her fifties with brown hair in a sharp,

polished bob, smiled and extended a hand. "I'm looking forward to working with you."

My face froze. I turned to Ralph.

"I know there's a learning curve as you get up to speed on Edward Bell," Ralph said. "Having Cynthia here will help ease you into things."

"But I've been at the bookstore for two months now," I said. "I'm eased."

Ralph and Cynthia chuckled. "Cynthia will help keep the store's ambiance in check, too. She'll see to it that there won't be any more loiterers." He nodded his head to where Dahlia had been sitting. That empty chair had never looked sadder.

"Cynthia is a fantastic resource if you have any questions," Ralph continued. "She's read every Edward Bell book several times."

Cynthia beamed. "I'm a bookworm," she said with a modest shrug.

"Me too," I countered, because it felt like the only way to compete. Ralph's gaze dropped to the book sitting on the counter, a rom-com Evelyn had lent me: *At First Swipe*. On the cover was a colorful cartoon image of a phone in a woman's hand, her thumb ready to swipe on a dating profile. Definitely not a book by Edward Bell or his contemporaries. I don't know why I keep leaving things on the counter. I picked it up and set it on my desk.

"I also have some news," Ralph said. He and Cynthia shared a look so secretive that I thought they might join hands and tell me they were expecting. "I've been in talks with an investment group, ByGone, about an idea that could take tourism to the next level." He waited a beat. I think he was going for a dramatic pause, or maybe he expected me to prod him along, but all I could do was wait for the news to hit.

"I've done some research into writing retreats," he continued. "They can be very lucrative, especially if there's a big name attached. Some go for two to three thousand dollars per person. I've been putting together a proposal for what I've tentatively called the Edward Bell Writers Retreat." He lifted his chin proudly. "It will be a three-day retreat, held weekly, where writers can come together for an immersive experience. They would stay in town, do some writing, share critiques of their work, attend writing workshops, and have one-on-one time with experienced authors. There will be group dinners, recreational activities, guided tours of Bell River, lessons about how they can apply Edward Bell's writing process to their own lives. Exciting, right?" He looked at me expectantly.

I chewed on my lip, trying to process his words. "Yeah," I said. "Definitely. But...what does this mean for the bookstore? Or the other Bell Society businesses?"

He laughed. "That's the question, isn't it? There are a lot of moving pieces. I'm still working it out. We'll need a place for guests to stay. Space for the group workshop. Space for people to do their writing. Catered meals for breakfast, lunch, and dinner. A facilitator who can lead the workshops and offer feedback. Options for recreational activities. I'll need to think about how the Bell Society businesses will factor in."

"How?" I pressed. "How would you factor in the bookstore?"

His eyes glinted, like he'd been hoping I'd ask. "I was thinking that for an extra fee, a writer on the retreat could be the store's writer in residence for the day. They could sit at the table where Edward Bell did his writing, right here in the store, and get the true immersive experience of writing like Edward Bell. Tourists would love it too, right? Coming to the bookstore and seeing a real, live writer at Edward Bell's desk, hard at work. To really sell the immersion, we could limit the books we carry to just the ones that were available during the years Edward Bell worked here. And Edward Bell's books, obviously."

"So…" I scratched my head, trying to keep up. "You'd put even more limits on the books we can sell?"

"Not too much more. Just no books published after 1935. Which should be fine considering the top sellers have been older classics anyway, right? Wasn't *Pride and Prejudice* the biggest seller last week?"

"Yes," I said, inwardly cursing myself for not anticipating that my fake reports could have consequences. I shook the thought aside. "What about Vernon's apartment?"

He tilted his head, his face clouding over. "It would make a great suite for a writer or even a couple of writers. Or it could be the facilitator's apartment."

"Or it could be Vernon's apartment," I insisted.

Ralph shook his head. "For this proposal to work, I've got to use every investment I have. Every building, every business, every person. I've got to think about what purpose they're serving now, and what purpose they'll serve to the retreat. If someone can't—or won't—be useful, I've got no place for them."

A chill crept over my skin. I thought of Ralph sitting in his office, staring at a spreadsheet with the names of everyone connected to the Bell Society, categorizing us as either *Useful* or *Not useful* with a simple click without any regard for how that decision would impact us.

"But for the people I do have a place for," Ralph continued,

"this would be big. It would boost tourism, bring in more revenue. Who knows where we could go from here. One of the investors at ByGone has a connection at the University of Maryland. If all goes well, who knows. Imagine an Edward Bell MFA program. A Bell River campus!" He gave an excited laugh.

I smiled weakly. "When will we know?" I croaked. "About who's useful?"

"I wouldn't worry about that now," he said. "We can talk more once the proposal is approved. For now, enjoy having the books back. Cynthia can help you move the...other table." He cast a dubious glance toward the card table in the alcove.

Ralph took advantage of my silence to tell me this was all still just an idea, that he appreciated my discretion, and that the Bell books and table would be brought over this evening. Then he left me to contend with my new colleague.

Cynthia clasped her hands together. "I love bookstores. I used to work at one right out of college."

"Yeah, it's fun," I tried. Or, rather, it *was*.

I started folding up the refreshments table, mentally eulogizing the alcove and its brief span as a hangout spot. I looked around the empty space one last time before I picked up the table.

"Let me get the door," Cynthia offered. My stomach dropped when I remembered my secret inventory in the other room.

"No," I choked out. "I've got it." I shifted the table to one hand and grabbed the door, grinning maniacally at Cynthia as if my ability to use both hands was a marvel.

In the safety of the storage room, I began hiding the evidence of my illicit bookselling. I'd placed some of the books on a cart, but I made quick work putting them back into boxes, keeping one eye on the door. I moved the boxes to a low shelf in the corner, then rolled an empty cart in front of it.

When I returned, Cynthia was roaming the shelves not unlike the way Malcolm used to. Except she didn't stop to straighten any books like Malcolm would, which annoyed me somehow. She reached the end of a shelf and noticed me watching, and I quickly smiled.

"I figured I should reacquaint myself with the layout," she said with a laugh. "I don't actually come here much. I'm more of a library person."

Probably because the library didn't carry such a limited selection, I thought to myself, but I forced a laugh right back. I sank into my seat while Cynthia continued examining the shelves.

She was more than a Bell Society crony. Cynthia was a babysitter and Ralph was a dictator, and I'd never felt more powerless.

CHAPTER EIGHTEEN

Cynthia is a leg-jiggler.

When she's not standing by the Edward Bell shrine giving the same rehearsed speech to our new influx of tourists, and when she's not hovering by a shelf ambushing customers with book recommendations, she's sitting at the register next to me, jiggling her leg up and down. It doesn't make a sound, but I can see it out of the corner of my eye. It gives me an unsettling feeling, like I forgot to turn off the stove.

The leg-jiggling felt like the final insult. After Ralph dropped the news of his writing retreat master plan, I texted Rochelle the update. She responded with a string of angry emojis and insults directed at Ralph. Then, after a long pause, she texted, Ralph can't keep doing shit like this.

Vernon's reaction was more muted.

"He can do what he wants," he said when I showed up at his door. "He owns the building."

"But you've lived here for years," I said.

Vernon simply shrugged. "If there's one thing Ralph loves, it's power. I'm not giving him the satisfaction of reminding me how much power he has. He owns the building. That's all there is to it."

I shook my head. "But if I hadn't thrown the T. J. Hull event at your apartment, he wouldn't have overheard it, and he wouldn't have assumed you were mocking Edward Bell—"

"Stop right there," Vernon said. "This is not your fault. Ralph would have evicted me no matter what. God knows he looks for any reason to milk that man for all he's worth. You couldn't stop him unless Edward Bell himself crawled out of his grave to give Ralph a talking-to." He stared me down. When I didn't respond, he said, "Let me know when you set a date for the next event. I'm game if you are." He started to close the door on me.

"Wait," I said. "What if I got Ralph to change his mind?"

"What if hell freezes over?" he retorted. He shut the door, leaving me standing in the dim hallway without an answer.

When I got home, Rochelle and I explored what avenues we could. We looked up the organization Ralph was partnering with, ByGone, and learned that they were a woman-owned group that primarily funded educational ventures in the literary arts.

"What the hell is Ralph telling them to make them think his money grab is a good idea?" Rochelle said. She scrolled down another page on ByGone's website, as though the answer would appear there.

"The usual, probably," I said. "You know, Edward Bell's the best writer there ever was. He invented feminism, mustaches, et cetera."

She gave a dry laugh. "Well, when you put it like that." She closed the laptop and sank back against the couch. "I guess all we can do is wait."

But waiting wasn't good enough. I thought about Vernon

saying the only person who could stop Ralph was Edward Bell himself. My thoughts drifted to that file cabinet in Ralph's office. If I could somehow get in and find something incriminating on Edward Bell—evidence of a mistress, racist remarks, anything— ByGone might decide not to partner with Ralph. They wouldn't want to invest in a venture built around an author who wasn't the perfect feminist icon Ralph claimed him to be. And Ralph, with no funding, might back off the idea altogether. But once I thought through the practicalities—sneaking into the Bell Society, in the dead of night, like a burglar—I pushed it aside.

But now, sitting next to Cynthia in all her leg-jiggling glory, I was starting to compile a mental list of the annoyances she caused.

In addition to her penchant for movement, her mere exis-tence meant locals could no longer come into the store to browse and buy forbidden books. When Leena came in that Friday afternoon, she stopped when she saw Cynthia sitting next to me, enthusiastically scanning a customer's books. Leena turned to me, a question in her eyes. I grimaced and shook my head. She silently left the store.

When Abigail came in the next day during her break, she'd been sitting in the armchair for all of twenty seconds before Cynthia approached.

"I'm sorry, but would you mind taking your break elsewhere?" she asked. "Ralph says this chair is for customers only."

Abigail shot her a steely glare but obeyed and headed for the door, giving me a sympathetic look as she left. I wanted to call out to her, ask her to come back, but there wasn't anything I could say with Ralph's loyal watchdog around.

The bookstore was no longer a place for people to read, relax, write, or work. It was back to being filled with snobs and tourists who asked the same questions about Edward Bell and made me feel stupid for asking if this Miss Havisham they name-dropped was a friend of theirs.

Maybe I shouldn't have minded it as much as I did. I had, after all, only started selling the forbidden books and holding the events to make up for the revenue I'd cost when the Bell books were removed from the store. Now that they were back and business was returning to normal, I should have been fine to let my extracurricular activities slip away.

But it felt so much bigger now. Selling forbidden books wasn't about making extra money anymore; it was providing a necessary service. People here were desperate for books to read—books they didn't have to drive to the next town over to buy. And they wanted a place to gather and talk and be excited about books that had nothing to do with Edward Bell.

The more I sat there, hostage to Cynthia and her jiggling leg, the more compelled I felt to find a way around this. I couldn't let everything return to the boring, dissatisfying status quo. I wanted more for my new friends. I wanted more for Rochelle, for myself. I couldn't leave the bookstore a worse place than when I'd gotten here.

I needed to find a way to change Ralph's mind.

Even if it wasn't entirely legal.

CHAPTER NINETEEN

I looked up just long enough to thank the waiter handing me a menu before returning to my book. I was four pages from the end of *Emma* and Malcolm hadn't shown up yet. I'd meant to finish it during lulls at the bookstore, but we were getting more customers now that the Edward Bell shrine was restored, and Cynthia had tut-tutted under her breath when she saw me reading on the job. Which left me with no choice but to finish *Emma* while waiting for Malcolm in a Greek restaurant.

"Really?"

I didn't bother glancing up. I read to the end of the page, then turned to the next. "Hey."

The table moved slightly as Malcolm took a seat. "You told me you finished it."

"I did finish it. Five minutes from now, if you'll let me."

He sighed but waited quietly while I speed-read my way through a summary of weddings. Finally, after reaching the last line, I closed the book. Malcolm, chin in hand, watched me with half-lidded eyes.

"Oh, hello," I said. "Nice to see you."

"Wish I could say the same."

"Would you rather I didn't finish it and pretended I did?"

Malcolm's brows arched, unimpressed. "Presenting me with a worse alternative doesn't magically improve the present situation," he said.

"Would you rather I was lying dead in a ditch somewhere?"

He tried to maintain the pretense of his exasperated stare, but a smile broke through. "Are you saying that's an option?"

"Don't act like you wouldn't be devastated over my corpse."

Malcolm burst into an easy laugh that made his shoulders shake. I sipped my water and looked him over. His green sweater hung nicely on his frame, shirt collar peeking out from underneath. Half his locs were pulled into a bun while the rest hung down on his shoulders.

"How was the soapmaking class?" I asked.

He sighed the sigh of the deeply burdened. "You didn't tell me I'd have to work with a partner."

I laughed. "I didn't know. Tell me about your partner."

"His name is Hal. He has six siblings, he spent twenty years as a sales rep for a pharmaceutical company, his best friend is a guy named Jackson who makes his own bread, he likes green tea but not the way it smells, he has eczema on his hands and needs a soap for sensitive skin, he—"

"All right, I'm good on Hal. What else?"

"If I had to listen to Hal, you have to listen to me talk about Hal."

I sighed and listened to Malcolm rattle off more minutiae—including the fact that their instructor referred to them as *Hal and Mal*, a name I'd have to pocket for later.

"What about the soapmaking part?" I asked once Malcolm exhausted the both of us with Hal trivia.

Malcolm produced a paper bag and slapped it on the table. I peered inside, finding six rectangular bars of soap encased in individual paper sleeves. I pulled one out. It was pale orange and pink, and it smelled sweet, bright, and citrus-y. "Is this orange?"

Malcolm smiled. "Orange essence."

"I love orange." I brought it to my nose again.

"I know."

I looked up. "What do you mean?"

"I wanted to make something you'd like, and sometimes you smell like oranges," he said with a shrug.

A grin teased at my lips. "You know what I smell like? And you made me a soap?"

Malcolm remained straight-faced, though now he was playing with his fork. "I mean, it's not necessarily a compliment to know what someone smells like. My coworker Brent smells like an Axe body spray factory, and that's not a good thing."

I was full-on beaming by this point. "Do you think it's a good thing that I smell like oranges?"

He pretended to think it over. "It could mean you're overdoing it on Vitamin C. Don't people pee out the nutrients they don't absorb?" He frowned and cocked his head. "Or is that a myth?"

"I don't know, but I love it when you talk about pee at the dinner table. And I'm not overdosing on oranges; it's from my lotion. But I appreciate the concern." I went back to examining the soap. It was mostly orange, but there were some splotches of pink throughout. "What's with the pink?" I asked.

"Um." He straightened the sleeve of his sweater. "Well, our instructor was showing us the things we could do with layering and designs, and since I was doing orange, I thought maybe I'd add some pink and go for a sunset kind of effect, but...it didn't turn out right."

I held the bar of soap to my chest. "I love my splotchy sunset."

"You definitely can't find it in stores." He ran his finger along the edge of the bar in my hand. "You see how the edges are beveled? That makes it fancier for some reason."

I raised my eyebrows. "You beveled my edges?"

"How do you make everything sound dirty?"

"It's a gift." I gave the soap one last sniff and placed it in the bag. "Thank you for the soap. And I'm sorry about Hal."

"He wasn't so bad," he admitted. "Your turn." He tapped a finger on the book between us. "How'd you like *Emma?*"

"Is it bad that I imagined all the characters as the people in *Clueless?*"

"Nope."

"Then good. It was decent. I liked it more than *Pride and Prejudice*." Or what I'd read of *Pride and Prejudice*, anyway.

Malcolm nodded, squinting a little. "I guess that's something."

After dinner, we walked around town. The sky dimmed blue-black and the streetlamps glowed a hazy yellow. I caught sight of the bronze statue that had baffled me my first day in town. Edward Bell stood nobly between the slide and the swing set. I didn't have the energy to glare.

"How is Ralph getting ByGone to bankroll his vanity projects?" I asked.

"Ah, so you've heard. It's the usual way, I think. He would have given the typical spiel about how the Bell Society brings in tourism and revenue and promotes interest in American literature, and how the writers retreat would...I don't know, inspire the next generation of authors or something."

"And that makes it okay for him to do whatever he wants to people he doesn't find useful? That makes it okay for him to evict Vernon?"

"I never said I was on board," Malcolm said.

When we reached Oak Street, I noticed we were drawing closer to my home. "You live in the other direction, right?" I asked. "Can I walk you home this time?"

Malcolm glanced at me, surprised yet pleased. "Sure." He turned us around, and we walked in silence. There weren't many cars on the road. Not much went on here past eight on a Sunday night.

"How did you even meet Vernon?" Malcolm asked.

I shoved my hands in my jacket pockets. "He comes by the bookstore sometimes," I mumbled.

"Are you friends?"

"Are you jealous?"

He laughed. "Just surprised. Vernon doesn't really make friends."

"Well, I do." I went back to the topic on my mind. "How long have you known about this writers retreat plan?"

Malcolm studied me, as if reading the unspoken accusation in my eyes. "I didn't know the details until a couple of weeks ago. Before that, Ralph just talked vaguely about big plans."

"So you've known for the last two weeks and you didn't tell me?"

"Maggie, it was my job."

"Your job sucks," I burst out. When Malcolm's face went slack, I took a breath and tried to backpedal. "I just meant...you don't always have to do everything Ralph tells you to."

Malcolm was quiet for a few moments. Finally, he sighed. "I don't take commitments lightly," he said.

I considered his profile in the soft glow of the streetlamp behind him. Malcolm, who attended the soapmaking class I signed him up for because it wouldn't occur to him to back out of the drunken agreement we'd made in the book bar. Malcolm, who made me orange-scented soap because he remembered small details about me like the smell of my citrus lotion.

"I know you don't," I said.

He reached for my hand and squeezed it. I squeezed back, feeling something like understanding pass between us. We walked on, still holding hands.

"Your hand's cold," he said.

"Yeah, this jacket's more cute than warm."

"Well, as long as it's cute."

Malcolm lived in a narrow townhouse with a porch swing out front. The porch light was on, I suppose left on for him.

"Thanks for the walk," he said, turning to face me.

I took a seat on the porch swing, not wanting to end the night just yet. "I'm chivalrous like that."

"Is that so?" Malcolm sat next to me, his leg flush against mine.

"But not so chivalrous that I'd turn down a good-night kiss."

He chuckled and took the hint, dropping his gaze to my lips and leaning in. There was a certainty to it, that one kiss would lead to the next, and the next.

"Can we go inside?" I murmured.

"If we're quiet. Is that okay?" He pulled back, meeting my eyes. I nodded and followed him inside, where we crept past the dark kitchen to his bedroom. Sneaking around felt very high school, but I wouldn't have wanted to take him to Rochelle's with kids around. It was almost comforting that, in some ways,

Malcolm was no more adult than I was. It made me feel like I wasn't alone in this messy, uncertain stage of my life.

Sex isn't especially sexy when you're trying to stifle every sound. We couldn't quite lose ourselves completely or fall into every impulse and desire, but I liked being in the moment with Malcolm. At one point the headboard slammed into the wall so loudly that we froze, eyes locked. When a few seconds passed and we didn't hear anything beyond the murmurs of whatever show his grandmother must have been watching in the other room, we carried on. But when the headboard slammed again, the volume of the TV murmurs quickly increased tenfold—evidently his grandmother trying to drown out our noise with what sounded like *NCIS*. Malcolm and I immediately burst into mortified giggles. I whispered a dumb joke about *NCIS* being an aphrodisiac and he laughed again, dropping his head into the crook of my neck.

We eventually moved the bed away from the wall and continued with no further headboard incidents, but the peaceful relaxation that swam through me afterward was caused more by the laughter than the orgasm. I'd never laughed like that during sex before. Being with Malcolm made me feel so delightfully myself, giggles and goofiness and all.

When we lay curled together under the warmth of his blankets, Malcolm propped himself on his elbow with a contented smile. He opened his mouth and hesitated just long enough for me to know something serious was coming.

"Can I ask you something?"

Every relaxed nerve in my body tensed. "Sure."

"What are your plans for when Rochelle goes back to work at the bookstore?" he asked. "You said once that you were thinking about staying in the area, and I just wondered if…" He met my eyes, then looked away, tracing a finger along the seam on his bedspread. "If you're still planning on that," he said at last.

I found his hand and threaded our fingers together. "I'm definitely planning to stay," I said. He broke into a thousand-watt smile that made his eyes crinkle. "I've been applying for jobs and everything." I held back that the last job I'd applied for was for an executive assistant position that sounded like a chore. It was still an avenue that would let me stay here. Even if that meant leaving the bookstore behind while Ralph pursued world domination.

Malcolm planted an obnoxious kiss on my cheek with a loud smacking sound that made me laugh. "That's great!"

"It is," I agreed.

If I thought about everything except the job itself, it *was* great. If I didn't compare the job to how much fun I had running events at the bookstore, it was downright wonderful. I thought about Malcolm saying he didn't take commitments lightly. My string of failed plans must have meant the opposite: that I'd commit to anything and back out when it was convenient. But that was never how I'd meant for it to go.

I wanted to do things differently this time. The more time I spent in Bell River, the more I wanted to carve out a place for myself here, but I couldn't ignore the practicalities that required. My time at the bookstore would be up in two months, and I would need a job, and the executive assistant position was a job. I could grin and bear and *commit*, just like Malcolm. And if it felt like turning my back on the people I'd come to care about, leaving them at Ralph's mercy, then so be it.

I set the thought aside like that was that, decision made. But it still weighed so heavily on me that I turned down Malcolm's offer to walk me home. I figured I could use the time alone to clear my head and make myself see reason. But as I walked, warm in the hoodie Malcolm insisted I take, breathing in the clean-cotton-and-pine scent that reminded me of him, I still struggled to come to terms with the idea of going all in on a job I didn't care about. Particularly when there were a great many people I *did* care about who would fall victim to Ralph and his master plan.

My phone vibrated in the front pocket of Malcolm's hoodie. I reached inside, feeling my phone and then something thinner, with hard edges. I pulled it out.

It was a white plastic card with Malcolm's smiling face on it. Above it were the words *Bell Society*. I turned it over once, then twice. It was an access card. I stopped in my tracks.

My phone vibrated again, pulling me out of the bad idea forming in my mind. I checked my phone, seeing two texts from Malcolm.

> Let me know when you get home okay.
> Also it's still not too late for me to walk you home.

I turned the card over in my other hand. This could get me into the Bell Society's office. Where Ralph's file cabinet might hold something on Edward Bell that could hinder the deal with ByGone.

I put the card in my pocket, then typed out a quick text to Malcolm.

> Thanks, but no need! I'm almost home 😃

I turned around. I had one stop to make first.

CHAPTER TWENTY

Standing in front of the dark Bell Society building, I fiddled with the access card in my pocket, just as I'd done for the entire walk over.

It wasn't too late to turn back now. But I knew I'd made up my mind as soon as I'd changed course for the Bell Society.

I eyed the glass door, then the square badge reader next to it. A small dot in the center glowed red, like it was warning me to stop, turn around, and go home.

I jumped when my phone buzzed in my pocket. I pulled it out.

Home yet?

Just Malcolm being considerate and unknowingly making a liar out of me.

I typed out, Safe and sound! Then, as an afterthought, I added a kissy emoji. I'd used it as a joke once and it had shut the conversation right down. Malcolm did not take well to affection by way of emoji.

I glanced behind me. The sidewalk was empty. The buildings across the street—a bank, a sandwich shop, and a home decor store—were dark and empty. I turned back to the badge reader and held Malcolm's key card to it. It gave a soft beep, flashed green, and the door quietly clicked. I grabbed the handle and pulled, bracing myself for an alarm. But the door opened easily. I slipped inside.

I paused just inside the door to gather my bearings. There was no front desk. No security guard roaming the floor. I looked up. No cameras I could see, though I didn't know what I would have done if I'd seen any. I wasn't a particularly inconspicuous figure, especially with my poofy hair. I brought a hand to my curls, then wrestled them into a loose bun. This felt slightly stealthier.

I followed the path I remembered to the Bell Society office—up the stairs, down the hall, then left—and stopped when I reached its glass doors. Next to them was another badge scanner, warning me with another red light. I ignored it and held up the key card. The doors clicked again.

The office was eerily quiet. I'd been in empty offices before— usually when cleaning up after a party that went on into the evening—but being here in this one, so neat and tidy and *not mine*, felt unnerving.

My phone vibrated in my pocket. Malcolm was undeterred by the emoji.

Good. Now get back here.
Kidding.
Sort of.

His words tugged at my heart. Going back to the warmth and comfort of his arms was tempting. But I'd come this far.

Too late, I replied. But next time, definitely.

He replied with a heart, something so uncharacteristic and endearing that I sent back five hearts and five kissy emojis. Not to be obnoxious but because I wanted him to know I felt this too, that I knew what we'd done tonight was a big deal, that I wanted so much more time with him.

I put my phone away and crept past the reception desk, then past a desk I realized was Malcolm's, going by the jacket on the back of the chair and his neat handwriting on the Post-It stuck to his monitor: *Run report Monday at 10*. This too felt like a warning, this comforting presence from a familiar person in an unfamiliar place, hinting that anything else I came across here might not be as friendly.

I pressed on until I came to Ralph's office. The door was ajar. I slipped inside and closed the door behind me. The window behind his desk had its blinds open, providing the brick wall next door an excellent view of the intruder within. I crossed the room and pulled the cord, fumbling until the blinds slumped unceremoniously to the windowsill. Then I turned around, settling my gaze on what I'd come here for: the cabinet in the corner. Ralph's private archives.

I took slow, careful steps toward it and flipped the light switch. Squinting in the bright light, I ran my fingers under the cold metal of the top drawer handle and pulled. It stayed shut. I pulled again, harder, but it wouldn't budge. I examined the cabinet, spotting a keyhole in the top left corner.

I tried the middle and bottom drawers too, but they didn't move. I sighed and stepped behind Ralph's desk. Inside his top drawer, I found a mess of unopened tea bags, paperclips, and errant pens. I ran my fingers along the bottom, feeling for something key-shaped, but all I kept finding were Post-It pads.

The next drawer was neater, folders and papers. I pulled out the whole stack and hefted it onto Ralph's desk, then began rifling. Meeting agendas. Tax forms. Emails with Bell Society employees. A letter from First Trust Bank. I scanned through it, looking for anything to do with Bell Society plans. My eyes fell upon the first paragraph: *This letter is a formal notification that you are in default of your obligation to make payments on your business loan.*

I checked the date on the letter: June. Ralph's enthusiasm for the writing retreat plan was starting to make sense, especially when I remembered what Kat had said about how Ralph hadn't been able to make good on his B&B renovation promises when the movie deal fell through. But pursuing a venture that could cost people their livelihoods couldn't be the only way to set his finances back on track.

I set the letter aside and kept rifling through the drawer, stopping when my fingers touched something small with a jagged edge. I pulled it out and slowly opened my hand. There in my palm sat a small, silvery key, holding more power than it knew.

I went back to the file cabinet, gripping the key tightly. Holding my breath, I inserted the key into the lock. It slid right in, making a satisfying click when it turned into place. When I tried the top drawer again, it rolled open slowly, heavy from the weight of the dark green hanging folders inside, each one labeled with a tab in cursive scrawl. *Letters from JB. Letters to WB. Letters from CE. Letters from JL.* On and on and on. The folders in the next two drawers were thicker, labeled with the titles of his novels.

I hefted out a few folders from the top drawer and sat cross-legged on the carpet. With no better approach in mind, I picked the folder closest to me and started sifting through the letters, all of them thin and yellowing and giving off a faint musty smell.

I began skimming a few letters in each folder, searching for something that might be useful: proof of the racism Malcolm had alluded to, or revealing letters with his alleged mistress. Something that might call Edward Bell's character into question and give ByGone second thoughts about funding a project in his honor. Thanks to the Edward Bell FAQs I'd memorized for the bookstore, it was easy to identify his family members by their initials—JB was his wife, Josephine; WB his son, William. At last, my Edward Bell knowledge was useful for something besides answering tourists' questions. I identified the rest of the initials using context clues and the index of the Edward Bell biography in Ralph's office: CE, his editor; JL, his friend and fellow writer. If I weren't desperately trying to stop one of Ralph's business ventures, I might have enjoyed dropping these names the next time I saw him, just to impress him and finally hear him deem me a worthy guardian.

I yawned and rubbed my eyes. I'd lost all sense of time here, but it was long enough to make my foot fall asleep. I stretched my legs out in front of me and arched my back, feeling my bones crack. Then I checked my phone. Rochelle had texted me asking if I was all right. I replied that I was at Malcolm's, then added several eggplant, droplet, and eye emojis. My emoji usage is, perhaps, excessive. But Rochelle, who fired off a string of eye emojis in response, hadn't found any of this unusual. I could stay here for as long as I needed and no one would suspect a thing.

I straightened up again and reached for the last folder. It

didn't have a label at all. I guessed it was empty, but I checked anyway. When I opened it, several papers fluttered at me.

I picked up the first page. The signature at the bottom indicated it was from a name I hadn't yet come across tonight: Louise. After a description of the weather, she wrote, *I enjoyed seeing you at the luncheon, too. As to your question, I'd be happy to see you again. Perhaps we could meet for lunch the next time you're in town?*

In the next letter, Louise wrote something that halted my breath. *I had a wonderful time with you, but this cannot continue. We must think of Josephine.*

I sat back on my heels, letter still in hand.

Edward Bell had a mistress after all.

These last few months, I'd been suffering the consequences of trying to answer a tourist's question about Edward Bell's love affair, and the evidence had been sitting in Ralph's office this entire time.

I flipped through the rest of the letters in the folder, checking to see if they were all from Louise. The same blue-inked, loopy scrawl persisted on every page. One of the pages I flipped past gave me a strange sense of déjà vu. I turned back to it.

When Hazel got fed up with the world, she liked to look out the window and imagine the passersby as her companions in misery.

I stared at the page until the words blurred and cleared again. Then, all at once, something clicked into place. I set the letter down and walked to Ralph's bookshelf. I pulled out *The First Dollar* and flipped to the first page.

When Hazel got fed up with the world, she liked to look out the window and imagine the passersby as her companions in misery.

Edward Bell wasn't just an adulterer. He was a plagiarist.

CHAPTER TWENTY-ONE

With every rustling page Vernon turned, I leaned forward a little more. By this point I was now perched on the edge of the couch, practically hovering over his coffee table.

He turned another page. His brow remained furrowed in concentration, but he still didn't say a word. Finally, I couldn't keep quiet anymore.

"What do you think?" I said. "They wouldn't partner with Ralph to fund a writing retreat built around a man who stole his most famous book—from a woman at that."

Vernon lifted his head, and his expression gave me pause. It was thoughtful and distant, not the victorious glee I'd imagined. Last night, as I'd stood in the dark Bell Society office feeding Louise's letters into a copier, those pages had been a momentous boon, the shining answer to everything. But now, in the light of day, looking from the thin stack of letters in Vernon's lap to his reserved expression, the discovery didn't feel as impactful as I'd imagined.

"What?" I prodded.

"I'm not sure this would do what you're hoping for," he said.

"Why wouldn't it?"

"You have evidence of an affair, which isn't earth-shattering. And you have a partial manuscript. Ralph can spin this however he wants. He could say Louise was his secretary, and Edward dictated the manuscript to her."

I bristled. "But Louise says in her letters that the story is her idea," I said.

"I know," he said. "I believe it. But I don't know that Ralph would. He could say these letters are fakes."

"But—"

"Suppose these investors do believe you. Suppose word gets out that Edward Bell stole his book. What would that do to the people who rely on tourists to stay in business?"

I slumped against the couch, stunned into silence. I'd been so eager to derail Ralph's plans and save the day, but Vernon was right. This revelation would do more than thwart Ralph's deal. By exposing Edward Bell as a fraud, I was putting all Bell Society businesses—and Bell River—in jeopardy. Would tourists still want to visit the Bell Museum to see the childhood home of the man who only pretended to write the book he was most famous for? Would they still come to the bookstore to see the table where he didn't actually write the book they loved? Would Rochelle lose her job if business at the bookstore suffered enough? Would Ralph have to downsize Bell Society staff and let Malcolm go in the process?

Thinking of Malcolm raised another complication, I realized. If I presented the evidence to Ralph, he might suspect Malcolm had something to do with my discovery, knowingly or not. I'd done what I could to cover my tracks last night—on my way out, I'd placed Malcolm's key card on the floor next to his desk, figuring he'd assume it must have simply slipped from his pocket. But Malcolm would probably be Ralph's prime suspect if I made my discovery public. Malcolm might very well pay the price for my snooping.

All of this added up to an equation I couldn't solve.

"What do I do?" I asked helplessly.

Vernon looked me over. "You look like you could use some sleep."

I forced an empty laugh. Thanks to my late-night letter reading, I was running on four hours of sleep. I hadn't even had any coffee yet. I'd been so eager to show Vernon what I'd learned that I'd barreled upstairs as soon as I'd set foot in the bookstore this morning. I'd thought Vernon would have relished learning Bell was a fraud. Now, in the face of his disappointing practicalities, my droopy eyelids whispered that maybe I should have stopped for coffee.

The sound of movement downstairs pulled me from my thoughts. Cynthia was here.

"I should go," I said. Vernon tapped the letters against the coffee table, then tucked them back into the Spider-Man folder I'd pilfered from Dylan. "I'm still thinking of a way to stop this," I said, tucking the folder into my backpack.

"I'm sure you are," he said with a grim smile.

I slung my bag over my shoulder and trudged downstairs, taking the exit that led to the sidewalk. I stopped in at Sunrise Café, where I exchanged distracted pleasantries with Abigail while I waited for my coffee. It was no use letting her in on the secret when, as Vernon said, it could send the town's economy into ruin.

I sipped my coffee in the bookstore, watching Cynthia stand

in front of the writing table and tell an attentive tourist how Edward Bell wrote *The First Dollar* there. I eyed the table with disdain. The only writing he did at that table was probably love letters to his mistress Louise.

I pulled out my phone, scrolling through my inbox while Cynthia was occupied.

> We would love to interview you for the executive assistant position. Would you be available to speak with us Monday at 9am?

I suppressed a groan. I remembered this posting well. In this assistant role for a finance executive, one of my duties would be to "maximize accountability among key stakeholders." I wasn't sure what that even meant, but I'd pasted it into the skills section of my resume and my blatant plagiarism somehow worked. A good lesson from Edward Bell: plagiarism gets you everywhere.

I felt like I was being cornered by things I didn't want. Working at the bookstore with Cynthia shackled to my side. Ralph and his plans to ruin the bookstore and the livelihoods of everyone he didn't deem useful. The overwhelming secret I'd uncovered about Edward Bell and the disastrous implications it brought. And now this job had come to join the fray, this position at a boring financial investment firm that I couldn't muster any interest for.

But this job would give me a reason to stay. I replied to their email with a shower of fake enthusiasm and scheduled the interview.

The day passed slowly. I concentrated on ringing up books and avoiding Cynthia's watchful gaze. She'd seen me yawn ten times too many today, and when I came back from my break with my second cup of coffee, she lifted an eyebrow. And, of course, when she returned to her seat after speaking with a group of tourists, she happened to glance at me right when I'd tilted my neck back to drain my cup of the last dregs of coffee. I tried to gracefully return my neck to a normal angle.

"You seem tired today," she said.

I picked up a rogue pen in front of me and returned it to its cup. Cynthia commenting on my obvious sleepiness didn't mean she had security footage of me rifling through Ralph's office, but I couldn't look her in the eye anyway.

"Yeah, I didn't get enough sleep last night."

"That's too bad. Do you want to go home now and get some rest?"

I turned to Cynthia, who was watching me like a concerned mother. There was something kind about her, when I wasn't being annoyed by her leg-jiggling or her brown-nosing or what her very presence meant for the bookstore. I considered her offer, thought longingly about stumbling home and crashing in bed for a glorious late afternoon nap. But Rochelle, who hated the fact that Cynthia had been foisted upon the bookstore, wouldn't want me leaving early and giving Cynthia any ideas about taking over the store completely.

"No, I'm fine," I said, even though my tired eyes urged me to reconsider.

"Are you sure? I have that meeting with Ralph tomorrow, so I won't be in until one. It's only fair that you leave early today."

I nodded without really listening. But once I played her words back, I turned to her. "What meeting with Ralph?"

"You weren't on the email? I'm helping him prepare for

ByGone's visit. We need to set the itinerary and plan the tour. The bookstore will be a stop, of course," she said with a laugh.

The laugh I gave in return was awkwardly delayed. I was too busy processing the news of ByGone's visit. "Why are they visiting?"

"They're meeting with Ralph to hear his formal proposal for the writing retreat. Ralph's going to show them the Bell Society locations so they can get a feel for what we do here."

I nodded again, probably for too long. ByGone visiting posed an opportunity. I could get them to change their minds about the proposal without having to reveal Edward Bell's secret or how I'd gotten it. Kat and Abigail were already unhappy with Ralph. Assembling a group of Bell Society employees who could convince the ByGone representatives to reject Ralph's proposal just might save us.

"I'm sure he's going to involve you, too," Cynthia said quickly, taking my silence to mean I was offended. "I'm just helping with some of the planning."

"Right." I stood, covering my mouth when I yawned. "I think I will take you up on that offer and go home early."

"Sure thing. I bet you're ready to pass right out."

I pulled on my jacket and hoisted my purse over my shoulder. "Can you forward me that email about ByGone's visit?"

When Cynthia agreed, I set off for home. On my way past the Sunrise Café, I saw Abigail through the window, wiping down a table. I wanted to run in and tell her what I was thinking, but the idea was still only half-formed. I needed to think it through before I tried to convince people to agree to something that might put their jobs in jeopardy. Ralph wouldn't take kindly to seeing his employees sabotage a deal right in front of him. I needed logic, nuance. But my brain was too foggy for that right now.

Rochelle was upstairs when I came home. I paused at the bottom of the stairs. I still hadn't talked to her about my date with Malcolm last night. In college, I used to come home from dates and recap them on the couch over ice cream. But this situation—a date followed by illegally trespassing in my date's workplace—couldn't be given the same analytical recap as the others.

I also needed to figure out how to tell Rochelle what I'd learned about Edward Bell—if I told her at all. It pained me to keep yet another secret from her, but in my sleep-deprived state I couldn't think of a way to tell her this without spilling everything else: the Bell books being removed and then returned, my secret inventory, the events. I'd find a way to explain it. But not today.

I turned and went to my room, quietly closing the door behind me. I flopped onto my bed. My last thought before sleep came to me, heavy and all-encompassing, was that I would fix it. I remember feeling confused about what this *it* was, because there were so many *it*s I needed to fix. Leaving Rochelle in the dark about so much lately. Stealing Malcolm's key card and lying to him the night we slept together. Vernon losing his apartment. Sitting on the truth about who really wrote Edward Bell's novel. Ralph's impending deal with ByGone. My hazy plan to involve Abigail and Kat in a stand against Ralph. What it could mean for their jobs. The question mark that punctuated every thought about what I'd do when my time at the bookstore was up.

They swirled around me, waiting for an acknowledgment. But by then I was hopelessly, gloriously asleep.

CHAPTER TWENTY-TWO

Sitting in the bookstore without Cynthia felt like a return to normalcy. It was fleeting—she'd be coming in later today after her meeting with Ralph—but I savored the silence.

I took my seat behind the counter, sipping my coffee as I scrolled through my phone. I'd managed to wrestle some pieces into place. I wouldn't call it a plan, exactly, but it was starting to form the outline of one.

I'd texted Abigail and Kat to ask about meeting up. I didn't give a reason but hinted that time was of the essence. We made plans to meet at Abigail's café at closing time. Adding Rochelle brought our group's total to four. Four Bell Society employees who were unhappy with Ralph's changes. We must be able to come up with something.

As morning bled into afternoon, I entertained tourists, sharing the fabricated tale of Bell's writing habits. I held back from saying more. I didn't roll my eyes when one man leaned in and shared that he was "really into feminism" like that basic fact made him a unicorn. Simply put, I perpetuated the lies like a true guardian of Edward Bell's legacy would. Ralph would be thrilled.

Evelyn stopped by later, lingering by a shelf while I rang up

Bell books for a customer. When they headed out with their stack of hardcovers, Evelyn sprang up to the counter.

"Have you checked your email?" she asked.

"Not in the last hour."

She lowered her eyes to my phone. "Check your email."

I eyed her suspiciously but did as asked. A slew of unread emails, all from people I hadn't heard of, peppered my inbox. I tapped one at random.

I'd like to come to your next event, but I don't see any information on your website. When is the next one?

I went back to my inbox, spotting an email from Evelyn.

You're famous! See below 😃

She'd forwarded a newsletter from T. J. Hull. In addition to sharing the cover of his forthcoming book, he gave a summary of other updates—including his evening with Cobblestone Books. I scrolled past a picture of T.J. with his arm around a fan on the night of the *Gatsby* event. I could even see a corner of Vernon's Catward Bell poster in the background.

I highly recommend attending Cobblestone Books's next event if you're looking for a night of fun!

He'd included a link to my website, along with a note that our online store carried copies of his new book. Puzzled but curious, I logged on to the dashboard for my online store. Sales were pouring in.

"How's your inbox?"

I looked up. Evelyn was watching me with a knowing smile. I gave a disbelieving laugh and held up my inbox with its mountain of unread emails. "T. J. Hull is an agent of chaos."

"I guess he had a good time." She rested her elbows on the counter and leaned forward, peering at my screen. "Cathy Larson emailed you?"

"Um." I checked my phone. "I guess. Who's that?"

"She's a mystery author. A pretty big one. One of her books is being made into a Hulu series."

I opened the email from Cathy and skimmed through it. "She said she knows T.J. She wants to be a guest author at my next event. What?" I asked, seeing Evelyn's eyes grow wide.

"You have to do it."

"But I'm not doing any more events." It wasn't something I'd officially decided, but it felt like the only suitable course of action now that I had the Bell books back, not to mention Cynthia's presence in the store.

Evelyn's face fell. "That's it? The *Gatsby* night was the last one? And now they're done forever?"

"Yeah, I guess so," I said wistfully. It did make me feel incomplete, knowing my last event had come and gone without me even knowing it. If I'd known, I would have savored every moment. I would have seen it off right.

"What are you thinking?"

"Nothing."

I think she could tell I was entertaining the idea, because she watched me closely, waiting for me to say more. But at that moment, the door opened and a group burst through, filling the store with chatter. At first, I feared they too might have been sent by T. J. Hull, whose newsletter list seemed to include every human with a pulse—but hopefully not Malcolm, I thought, my throat going dry at the thought.

Thankfully, these were typical Edward Bell tourists, as they immediately gravitated to the shrine in the back. When they immersed themselves in reading the placard and sifting through his books, I glanced back at Evelyn.

"Are you gonna do it?" she asked. She started to smile, as if she already knew the answer.

I felt myself smiling too, enticed by the thought of gathering my fun-loving group of attendees one last time. It could be my last hurrah. One final chance to have fun before everything changed: my job, Ralph's writing retreat plans, the employment of all other Bell Society staff.

I checked my phone, scrolling through emails and texts. No word from Malcolm. If he'd gotten T. J. Hull's newsletter, I would have heard from him by now. Cynthia and all her hovering posed a threat, too—but I always held events after closing anyway. I could pull this off.

"I'll do it," I said. Evelyn squealed, then stepped aside as the group brought their purchases to the counter. Another stack of novels from literature's fabled feminist.

I scanned the books, sneaking glances at Evelyn every so often, unable to keep from smiling. The last couple of weeks had felt like one snafu after the other. The thought of holding another event felt like a comfort. Even if it was starting to feel like the last comfort I had left.

CHAPTER TWENTY-THREE

A warm light shone through the window of the Sunrise Café in the distance, lighting up the dark street. As Rochelle and I drew closer, I tried to assemble my thoughts, focus them on the clandestine meeting we had planned, but they kept circling back to a comment Rochelle had made a few minutes ago.

After zipping me into a puffy, navy-blue coat she dug out of her closet—because, as she insisted, my light jacket was no match for forty-degree weather—Rochelle had stepped back in satisfaction and said, "As soon as you get that job, I'm taking you shopping for a winter wardrobe."

The reminder had made my chest deflate. I'd almost forgotten about my upcoming interview for the executive assistant position. I'd told Rochelle, Malcolm, and my family about it, wanting to prove that I was doing something, moving forward, finding a path, not getting caught up in my distractions. They'd all responded with an enthusiasm I couldn't match.

I spent the walk to the Sunrise Café dwelling on this job I couldn't bring myself to care about. I wished I were capable of being excited about a job, but that's never been the case for me. I have to scrounge for something to like, something that has nothing to do with the job itself. It always makes me feel broken, because I don't think it's like that for everyone. Other people have some fundamental calling or purpose. Rochelle has had her ups and downs about working at the library and then the bookstore, but she was always anchored by her passion for books. And if the worst-case scenario happened and she lost her job in our efforts to convince ByGone to pull out of the deal, she would surely find another book-adjacent job.

Malcolm wasn't passionate about Edward Bell, but he liked order. A job enforcing rules, in a town where he'd always felt safe, made sense to him. Abigail loved crafting new recipes. Evelyn loved writing and marketing her books. Dahlia liked the organization of her spreadsheets, the autonomy her freelance job provided. Everyone had something leading them on some sort of path. And I had a scattered trail of happenstance.

When we reached the Sunrise Café, a sign on the door read CLOSED, but I knew Abigail had left the store unlocked for us. We wrenched open the door and stepped inside. I spotted Abigail and Kat sitting at a table in the far back corner, out of view from the window.

I could feel their eyes on me once Rochelle and I sat down across from them. Only Rochelle knew what I'd come here to say. Abigail and Kat were going off the vague text I'd sent asking if we could meet about the Bell Society changes Ralph was planning. But vague information can be powerful when paired with trust, and I felt fairly certain that I had the trust of each woman at this table. The prospect of what I could do with that trust, for better or for worse, had me feeling jittery as I took my seat. I took a breath and folded my hands in my lap.

"Ralph submitted a proposal to ByGone to get the funds to start a writing retreat in town," I began. "He's planning a lot of changes. He said anyone he doesn't have a use for will be first to go."

"Who does he have a use for?" Abigail asked.

"I don't know. So far, I know it's not Vernon. Ralph's evicting him and turning the space above the bookstore into a guest suite. We won't know what else he has planned until the deal goes through. *If* it goes through." I looked around the table. "Cynthia told me ByGone is coming here in late November. They'll be hearing his presentation and touring the Bell Society attractions, including the café and the B&B. I was thinking we could let ByGone know how we feel about everything Ralph's doing. If they knew his employees weren't on board with the changes, maybe they'd back out."

I watched their faces carefully. Abigail had a distant look in her eyes, like she was thinking it through. Kat was nodding, but her expression was unreadable.

"Or Ralph could fire us," Kat said.

"Or he could fire you," I repeated.

"It's definitely a risk," Rochelle said. "We'd understand if you're not up for it."

"But you want us to, don't you, Maggie?"

Abigail was watching me. Rochelle glanced between Abigail and me. My fingers found the zipper at the bottom of my coat and twisted it back and forth.

"I think the message is more effective coming from all of us," I said. "If it's just Rochelle and me, Ralph could easily fire us to make sure the deal goes through. But if it comes from other Bell Society businesses too, it might have more of an impact.

Otherwise, what's to stop them from doing even more? Ralph was even talking about an MFA program later on down the line. How many other people will that impact? Where does it end?"

A heavy silence fell over us. I looked down at my lap. I'd gone all in on trust. I shouldn't have pushed.

"I'll do it," Abigail said.

My head shot up. "You will?"

"Me too," Kat said.

I stared at them, lost for words. Knowing they trusted me made it scarier, the fact that they were willing to follow me on a gamble of a mission. Next to me, Rochelle was still watching us all curiously.

"We should get more people," Kat said. "I can ask around at the B&B."

"I'll talk to people at the café," Abigail chimed in.

"I'll ask around, too," Rochelle offered.

"Great," I said. "I can also try to scrounge up support." All three of them stared at me. "What?"

"You'll scrounge?" Rochelle repeated skeptically.

"What?" I asked, feeling defensive.

"I think she means you won't need to do any scrounging," Abigail said. "I'm pretty sure you can convince anyone to do anything. Vernon hates everyone and somehow you've become his best friend."

Rochelle laughed and turned to me, her mouth open. "Vernon? My nemesis?"

I forced a chuckle. I'd asked Abigail and Kat to refrain from mentioning the events in front of Rochelle. Discussing my unlikely friendship with Vernon was harmless enough, but given that my event was what first drew Vernon into the store, we were uncomfortably close to one of the many secrets I'd kept from her.

"Fine," I relented. "I'll *drum up* support. Better?"

Abigail grinned. "Much."

I promised to keep them posted on any new information I heard from Cynthia about preparations for the upcoming visit. We decided we would meet again soon, after we each did our part to spread the word. As Rochelle and I said our goodbyes and headed home, I felt like the hazy plan I'd dreamed up was slowly becoming more real.

"They love you," Rochelle commented.

"Hm?"

"Abigail and Kat. I've lived here all my life and I barely know them. You're here for three months and you've built yourself an army."

"I don't have an army," I scoffed.

"You've got three people who would do anything you say. Four including Vernon, which I have questions about. Actually, five. Malcolm."

"Malcolm doesn't know what we're up to. He can't."

Rochelle shrugged. "He's still part of the Maggie army at heart."

"Maggie army's a terrible name."

"I'll think on it." She let out a sigh, creating a visible puff of air in front of her. "I've always been impressed at how you can float through life, drawing people to you wherever you go. You're like a magnet. Ooh, maybe that's the name. Magnet army."

I gave her a small shove, making her laugh. "I don't float through life," I said. "Not at all. *You* float through life."

"Me?" Rochelle laughed again. "I have no idea what I'm doing."

I shook my head. Comparing Rochelle's path to my jagged trail was absurd. "I have less of an idea," I said quietly.

Rochelle eyed me. "Okay, I'll allow it. But I bet you have more of an idea than you think."

I glanced at Rochelle, feeling my eyes well up just a little. "I bet you do, too," I said.

Rochelle smiled and looked down. There is an enveloping warmth caused by knowing your best friend believes in you. No number of winter coats could possibly match that feeling. We walked the rest of the way home in silence, both of us, I think, holding on to that feeling.

Tonight I'd roped Abigail and Kat into something I probably shouldn't have, and it might not bode well for any of us. But if I saw myself the way Rochelle saw me—and maybe, just for tonight, I would—I could choose to believe this would work out. I could trust, just as Abigail, Kat, and Rochelle did, that I knew what I was doing. And for the brief sense of security that thought gave me, I almost didn't care if it wasn't true.

CHAPTER TWENTY-FOUR

My day off normally had a lazy start. I'd gotten into a routine of reading in bed with a steaming mug of coffee next to me, setting a relaxing tone for the day ahead. But this morning, I flung the covers aside as soon as I woke up. I had a mission today. I mentally went over my agenda while I cleaned my teeth.

First up, breakfast with Dahlia and Evelyn. I was going to tell them what Abigail, Kat, Rochelle, and I were planning. They'd been with me every step of the way so far. I hoped they might be able to spread the word in their networks. Many of Dahlia's clients were business owners in town, and Evelyn belonged to a circle of local writers.

Next, lunch with Leena and Marcia. As farmers' market vendors, they knew everyone who had a booth in the town square on Saturdays. Leena and Marcia might be able to persuade them to join the fray.

Later tonight, I was going to set up the registration page for my next event. After T. J. Hull's newsletter ambush, I'd exchanged emails with Cathy Larson, the mystery author who had asked to participate. She'd already decided on *Pride and Prejudice*. I'd run the date past Vernon, who confirmed he was game to host it in his apartment again. I bumped the attendance cap to forty, thinking it hadn't seemed *all* that crowded at the *Gatsby* event, and if this was going to be my last hurrah, I may as well go out with a bang. Not everyone who registered would show up anyway. I was looking forward to making the page live, alerting my newsletter list—which had grown considerably thanks to T. J. Hull's email—and watching the RSVPs climb.

I rinsed off my toothbrush and got in the shower. I tossed my loofah between my hands, thinking through what I'd say to Dahlia and Evelyn. I wasn't used to having to prepare my words for them. I missed our casual hangouts at the bookstore, sitting in comfortable quiet, free to speak about whatever we were doing: a line I read that made me laugh, an email Dahlia wasn't sure how to interpret, a plotline Evelyn was struggling with.

I was still thinking as I got dressed. My phone buzzed on the small coloring table I used as a nightstand. I picked it up, expecting a text from Evelyn or Dahlia. I frowned when I saw the calendar notification: Interview at Portfolio Advantage—9 a.m.

My heart thudded into panic. I had a job interview in half an hour.

Franklin was a twenty-minute drive without traffic and I was still only half-dressed. I looked down at the sweater I'd pulled on, featuring a dinosaur traipsing through a garden. Less than half-dressed, then.

I rifled through my closet until I found the few interview-appropriate shirts I'd brought with me, which hadn't seen the light of day since I'd come here. I pulled a white blouse off the hanger, giving it a quick sniff as I slipped it over my head. Old suitcase wasn't a terrible thing to smell like. I opened a drawer, tossing aside jeans and leggings until my fingers touched the stiff fabric of my dress pants, folded into a square. A square it didn't want to forget, going by the deep wrinkles running down the legs. But there was no time to iron.

I texted Dahlia and Evelyn on the way to my car, asking if we could push our breakfast date by an hour or two. Then I checked the route to Portfolio Advantage: twenty-seven minutes away. The interview started in twenty-four. I clicked my seatbelt in place and took off.

After a stressful drive marked by speeding and almost missing my exit, I pulled into a complex with one minute to spare and hurried into the stark, gray office building looming ahead.

I spilled out of the elevator and gave my name to the receptionist, then fell into a stiff chair in the waiting area. In the quiet of the office, I became acutely aware of how out of breath I was.

I peered at the one magazine on the coffee table: *Financial Planning*. I picked it up and idly flipped through it, passing glossy page after glossy page without absorbing a word. I thought about Evelyn and Dahlia, who had agreed to meet after my interview. I made a mental note to ask Abigail if she had any menu ideas for the *Pride and Prejudice* event. I wanted to go all-out for this one, not just chips and popcorn but something in keeping with the theme.

I googled *Pride and Prejudice food* and scrolled through the results, frowning at the mention of something called white soup.

"Maggie?"

I looked up to see a tall, slim man in a crisp suit. I slipped my phone into my purse and stood to greet him. He had a brief handshake that Ralph probably wouldn't approve of. He shepherded me past a row of gray cubicles and into a small room at the end of the hall. On the way, I noticed people at their desks taking calls in low voices, a water cooler next to a window, and a kitchenette with a fridge devoid of magnets. Everything I saw suggested that this office was sparse. Focused. Disinterested in fun.

My interviewer and prospective boss—Robert Colvin, vice president and CFO—led me straight to the meeting room, shut the door behind us, and launched into the interview questions while I was still taking my seat.

"Tell me about yourself."

That question was a trap. He didn't want to hear about *me*. He wanted to hear about the value I could bring as an employee, not the fun I'd had recently getting into thrillers and how I liked green olives but not black olives. He was asking why he should hire me. Really, every interview question ever could be rephrased as *Why should we hire you?*

And honestly, sitting here in wrinkly pants and my head swimming with Bell River and *Pride and Prejudice* and white soup, I wasn't sure I had an answer.

Still, I did my best to go through the motions, reciting my usual answer about my administrative experience. Robert ran through the rest of his questions, all focused on my admin work. I elaborated on it in full, but it felt like a lie when it was the least important part of my job. It would be like saying all I did at the bookstore was sell books. That may have been the case on paper, but there was so much more I was proud of: bringing people together. Cultivating an atmosphere of laughter and silliness. Giving people access to the books they actually wanted.

"Do you have any questions for me?"

I snapped out of my train of thought. "Yes," I said, partly

stalling to buy time. "I was wondering…" Well, I had my *Pride and Prejudice* event on the brain anyway; I may as well come out with the only thing I cared about. "As far as things like office parties or company picnics, is there anything like that I should expect?"

Robert studied me with an inscrutable expression, then gave a hearty chuckle. "A fellow introvert, are you? Don't worry. When you're at work, you're here to work. I never go to those office functions, and I make sure my assistants aren't needed there, either. Let somebody else hang balloons and play Secret Santa, huh? We've got real work to do!"

I joined in on his laughter while sirens went off in my head. He thought I was an introvert? I couldn't go to office functions? He was so unfamiliar with the concept of Secret Santa that he thought *play Secret Santa* was a phrase people used?

This misunderstanding somehow convinced Robert that we were two peas in a pod. He set down my resume and started walking me through the particulars of the job, interjecting anecdotes and asides. He told me about the CEO's executive assistant, who took suspiciously long lunches and was always trying to get them to hire her nephew. He talked about the system I would be expected to use to manage his calendar. He told an anecdote about a time when an assistant misinterpreted a client's coffee order, then brought up my barista experience as another reason I was an asset.

"We'll still need to check your references, but I think you'll be a great fit," Robert said. "Would you be able to start by the twenty-third?"

"Um." The *Pride and Prejudice* event was scheduled for the end of the month. I couldn't leave the bookstore before that. "I'll be out of town that week," I said.

"Okay. November 30?"

I hesitated. The prospect of leaving the bookstore before my time was officially up felt wrong. Like I'd be giving up on it. Suppose the protest didn't go according to plan? Rochelle might need me.

"I don't think I can make that work. How about...December 30?"

A pause. "That's over a month out," he said. "Is there a reason you won't be available until then?"

Nothing I could say aloud. "I've got some projects to finish up," I said.

Another pause. I bit my lip.

"You had said in your cover letter that you'd be available to start immediately," he said slowly. "We need to get someone onboarded this month."

"I'm sorry. I guess I wasn't thinking."

Robert was polite despite his disappointment. He wished me luck in my job search and walked me back to the lobby.

I walked to my car feeling like I'd bungled everything. I'd be out of a job soon, and I'd been given an opportunity, but I was too invested in the bookstore and Bell River to commit.

I knew Rochelle, Malcolm, and my parents would be confused, all in different ways. Rochelle would put a positive spin on it and tell me it was all part of my float-through-life plan. Malcolm would start to think I wasn't serious about staying in the area—or about him. My parents would decide that it must be because my calling was something else, something I was sure to find next time, if I only applied myself and stopped giving in to distraction.

But when I parked on Oak Street and rounded the corner on Sunrise Café, seeing a glimpse of Evelyn and Dahlia through the window, I felt like I was coming home. Dahlia caught my eye and perked up, Evelyn lifted her hand in a wave, and even that empty chair sitting between them seemed especially friendly. This felt right.

Which didn't mean anything. It didn't pay rent. But after the stress and disappointment of this morning, I'd let myself indulge in this. Sinking into a chair beside my friends. Breathing in the roasted coffee smell of the Sunrise Café. Forgetting about jobs and reality and next steps and the future. For this morning, I could give in to distraction.

CHAPTER TWENTY-FIVE

I kept my eyes glued to the door on Saturday afternoon. Tourists streamed in and out, but I was leaving early today, just as soon as Malcolm stopped by to pick me up. Now that my days at the bookstore were back to tourists and tedium, I was looking for any chance to escape it.

I'd already cleared my afternoon off with Cynthia. I was sure the news would reach Ralph, make him doubt my abilities even more, but I didn't care what he thought. A week from today, the ByGone folks would be touring the town, and when they came to the bookstore, they'd find a group of people ready to protest the deal. Over the last week, Abigail and Kat had gotten some employees interested in joining us, and Dahlia mentioned recruiting a few people, too. Leena and Marcia were still gathering support from farmers' market vendors. If Ralph had a problem with me cutting out of work early today, he'd be in for a rude awakening next week.

At last, I spotted Malcolm approaching through the window. I leapt up and waved a wordless goodbye to Cynthia on my way out the door. Outside, the air felt less suffocating.

No Cynthia or tourists to tiptoe around, just Malcolm and his endearing complaints.

"I hope you're ready for disappointment," he said. "It's not what you're thinking."

"It's a pumpkin festival!" I said. "How could that be disappointing?" I'd seen the flyer while we were grabbing lunch and I'd insisted Malcolm attend as another book club assignment. When objecting didn't work, he'd made me join him.

"It's the 10th Annual Riverside Dental Pumpkin Festival and Charity Drive," he reminded me.

"I don't see anything wrong with that."

"It takes place in a parking lot."

I shrugged. "I love parking lots."

"They're just trying to get new business and lure people in for teeth cleanings."

"Well, I'm like two years overdue, so they can sign me up."

Malcolm sighed. "I already have a dentist. What if someone from Plaza Dental sees me there? They'll think I'm a traitor."

"Then maybe Plaza Dental should have thought about hosting a 10th annual dentist…pumpkin festival charity thing."

"You have to admit the name is ridiculous."

"It's descriptive," I said. Malcolm laughed.

When we reached the festival, I had to admit it was smaller than I'd expected. Riverside Dental stood on a strip lot between a donut shop and a grocer. Their shared parking lot amounted to about twenty spaces, but they'd made the best of it. We approached the table nearest us, where a young man sat next to a pile of goody bags. After we paid the suggested entrance fee, which we were told would help them provide free dental work to underserved populations, we were handed a small plastic bag each.

I peered into mine as we walked farther into the parking lot, pulling out a pumpkin eraser, a pumpkin-shaped stress ball, and a toothbrush. "Free toothbrush!" I said.

"It's not free if you paid a ten-dollar entry fee."

"It was a suggested donation," I corrected him. "I'm very charitable."

Tables and booths were scattered across the parking lot. I breathed in the smell of sugar and popcorn wafting from a booth selling pumpkin-spiced kettle corn. At another table, a woman from the neighboring donut shop sold donuts and pumpkin spice tea. One table held a large pumpkin, with a sign inviting us to guess its weight for a chance to win a free teeth whitening. At another table, with a banner advertising Greg's Groceries, a man sold pumpkin soup, cornbread, and chili-spiced pumpkin seeds. Some people milled around the tables while others stood around eating popcorn or playing cornhole.

"What do you think?" Malcolm said.

"It's the best dental pumpkin charity thing I've ever been to."

Malcolm laughed and surveyed the parking lot. "The kettle corn does smell pretty good," he admitted.

While we waited in line for the kettle corn, I thought I saw the young woman behind the booth watching me. I didn't think much of it, but when I got to the front, she smiled brightly. "Are you Maggie?"

I gave a surprised laugh. "I am."

"I'm Amy. I'm in a writing group with Evelyn." She cast a furtive glance at Malcolm, like there was more she was holding back from saying.

"Oh, cool," I said. "Evelyn's great."

She waited until Malcolm was preoccupied with paying.

Then, leaning in closely as she handed me a paper bag of warm, cinnamon-smelling popcorn, she said, "Evelyn told me about the thing you're planning. I'm in."

I pulled back, taking in her expression. There was a determined look in her eyes. I nodded, feeling jittery but sure. "Good to know."

Malcolm and I stepped aside, walking the perimeter of the parking lot and eating popcorn by the handful. I couldn't help marveling over what had just happened. Evelyn had gotten Amy on board and she didn't even know me. Maybe Rochelle had a point about my army.

Malcolm went off for pumpkin spice tea just as I spotted a sign by the cornhole display advertising a pumpkin hockey race.

When Malcolm found me a few minutes later, I had to press my lips together to keep from smiling.

"This is pretty good," he said, handing me the tea.

I took it, eyeing him over the cup. Pumpkin-and-clove-scented steam wafted up my nostrils when I took a sip. "It's good."

He studied me suspiciously. "Why are you smiling?"

"I've decided on your next assignment."

His mouth fell open. "You said *this* was my assignment."

"I know. But you were saying this was just a meeting in a parking lot, and you were so convincing that I felt like I should really make sure you got something out of it."

"Like what?" he said reluctantly.

I glanced around the parking lot in a show of wide-eyed innocence, coming to rest my gaze on a man handing out hockey sticks to the people clustered around him.

"Maggie," Malcolm intoned. The man, with one hockey stick left, looked around, then lifted the stick when he spotted me. "Why is he staring at us?"

"I signed you up for a pumpkin hockey race. It starts in five minutes." His eyes went round, but then the man behind him clapped him on the shoulder.

"There you are. Malcolm Green, right? Why don't I know you?"

His mouth set in a line of grim tolerance, Malcolm said, "I go to Plaza Dental."

He chuckled. "Plaza, huh? We'll make a Riverside man out of you yet." He motioned for Malcolm to follow him. Even as Malcolm followed, he turned to me and mouthed, *No he won't.*

While Malcolm awkwardly held a hockey stick and learned the rules of the race, I spotted Marcia at the weight-guessing table.

"Hey," I said, sidling up next to her. "Fancy running into you."

"Hey, baby." She jotted something down onto a square of orange construction paper and dropped it in the jar of guesses. "I don't know why I bother. I was off by forty pounds last year."

I watched Malcolm, who was being handed a miniature pumpkin, then took a step closer to Marcia. "Have you heard from any of the farmers' market vendors?"

She cocked her head. "Maybe."

"What did they say?"

"Seven yeses and counting," she said, breaking into a grin.

"Seven?" It was hard to keep track of our numbers now. Abigail told me she had two coworkers lined up. Kat had three. Dahlia mentioned a few clients who were interested. I hadn't heard from Evelyn yet, but Amy was proof that she'd been gathering support. Leena and Marcia had told me they would talk to the farmers' market vendors they worked with, but I'd taken their silence this week to mean it wasn't going well.

"Had to wait for Saturday to roll around so we could talk to them in person," she said.

"Wow. Thank you."

"I invited a few of them to the *Pride and Prejudice* thing. I hope you don't mind."

"That's fine," I said. I did wonder how we'd fit everyone in Vernon's apartment. When I posted the registration page earlier this week and emailed my newsletter list about it, all forty slots filled up in less than a day. But a few extra spots would be fine. Marcia deserved to invite who she wanted after all the support she'd gathered for me.

The man running the pumpkin hockey race—who Marcia informed me was Jack Birch, a dentist at Riverside Dental—announced that it was about to begin. He explained that the first contestant to push their miniature pumpkin from one end of the parking lot to the other and back while keeping their pumpkin intact would be crowned winner. Malcolm, standing at the starting line with the others, caught my eye and shook his head again, but there was a smile turning up his lips.

At the sound of a bullhorn, the contestants were off—all except Malcolm, who jumped at the noise and took several seconds to notice everyone had started without him. I could almost hear his sigh as he began pushing his pumpkin ahead of him, walking as leisurely as if he were using a metal detector at the beach. Then, as his competitors reached the end of the parking lot and began turning around, Malcolm gave up on the race entirely and cut through the parking lot to me, pushing his pumpkin along.

"Contestant six is disqualified," Jack announced as Malcolm gently pushed his pumpkin onto my shoe.

"How'd I do?" he asked.

"Beautifully."

"I needed him to know he would never make a Riverside man out of me."

I laughed. "I'm very sorry for not realizing how seriously you take your dentistry."

He spun the hockey stick in place. "Apology accepted. Fair warning, if you ever step foot inside Riverside Dental, I won't be able to talk to you again."

"I completely understand."

After Malcolm returned the hockey stick to a disappointed Jack Birch, we picked up the makings of an early dinner—pumpkin soup, cornbread, and a pumpkin pie—and started walking to his place. The sun was setting, casting a warm, orange light on the houses we passed.

"How are you liking *The Grapes of Wrath*?" he asked.

My gaze dropped to my feet. My book club with Malcolm had taken a back seat to planning the protest and the *Pride and Prejudice* event. "I haven't started it yet."

"Okay. Don't leave me hanging for too long. After your thing last week, and now the festival, you owe me two books."

My "thing" last week was a group painting lesson at a studio in DC, where students followed a painting tutorial while drinking wine. Malcolm had texted me a stream of complaints the entire time, from the group of loud, drunk women in front of him to the instructor's vague instructions.

She said to draw trees in the color I vibe with, he'd texted. I DON'T KNOW WHAT COLOR I VIBE WITH.

Yet afterward, the finished picture he texted me appeared to be a perfect depiction of a pond with trees and mountains in the distance. (The color he vibed with, apparently, was dark green.)

And then, he'd admitted, he'd gone to a bar with the couple next to him, who he'd bonded with over murmured jokes about the drunk women in the front row.

"I'll read it," I said. "I've just been busy."

"It's okay." Malcolm glanced at me. "Did anything ever pan out with that job?"

"Um." I took a breath and turned to him. "They were interested. And I turned it down," I said before the smile crossing Malcolm's face could fully take shape. "I just...it was soulsucking and boring, and I couldn't do it. He hates office parties! Who hates office parties? If I have to work somewhere, I need it to be a place I can stand. I do want to get a job so I can stay here. This just...wasn't it." I paused in place when I realized Malcolm had stopped walking. I braced myself for a speech on misguided priorities.

"If it's not for you, it's not for you. That's okay."

"It is?" I asked in a small voice.

"Of course."

I swallowed past the lump in my throat. "I didn't want you to think it meant that I wasn't serious about staying, because I am."

"I know."

I shook my head, smiling in disbelief. "How can you freak out about the color of your trees and what your dentist thinks about you and be so sure about this?"

"Priorities." Malcolm kissed me, then pulled back, his eyes curious and searching. "I had a feeling something was up with you," he said. "You've seemed a little distant lately."

My smile began to feel strained. It was a fair assessment. "I've just been dealing with a lot. Changes at the bookstore, job hunting, figuring out housing."

Malcolm gently rubbed my arm. "You know you can talk to me about that stuff, right?"

I nodded distractedly. The words were nice, but the reality was disconcerting. If I told him about the protest, he'd feel obligated to inform Ralph. If I told him about Edward Bell's secret—and what I'd done to uncover it—he'd be upset that I'd put his job at risk to follow a hunch.

"Is there anything you want to talk about now?" he asked.

I shook my head, afraid that if I uttered a single word, it would all come spilling out. "I'm good. But thank you." I leaned in and kissed him before he could say anything else.

For the rest of the walk to his house, his thumb stroked the palm of my hand. Even though he didn't know the half of what was really on my mind, the gesture was reassuring all the same.

When we reached his house and he opened the front door, my heart skipped at the sound of a woman's voice inside. I stepped inside to see a Black woman sitting at the kitchen table talking to Ellen, who I remembered as the woman who fawned over me at the Chinese restaurant.

"Maggie," Ellen said, once again drawing out my name with embellishment. "Good to see you again. Is this your first time here? In the light of day, anyway?"

"Ellen!" Malcolm squeaked. Ellen, meanwhile, snickered and shared a look with Malcolm's grandmother.

"It's nice to meet you, Maggie," his grandmother stopped laughing long enough to say. "I'm Yvonne." Her warm smile almost washed away the mortification of her and Ellen laughing over our apparently public-knowledge sex life. From everything Malcolm had told me, I'd expected a frail old woman, but she was tall, sturdy. A green-and-yellow silk scarf tied in an intricate knot covered her hair, and she watched Malcolm with sharp eyes as he began setting bowls, plates, and spoons around the table.

"What's all this?" she said.

"Maggie dragged me to the dentist's pumpkin festival." He set the food in the middle of the table, then nodded his head for me to sit down.

She raised her eyebrows, glancing from me to him. "After all that fuss you made the one time we went?" She turned to me. "He was *convinced* our dentist was going to find out and disown him on sight."

"That's what he said to me!" I exclaimed. Malcolm sighed, then lifted the lid from the soup. I leaned toward Yvonne. "He got disqualified from the pumpkin hockey race and I think he's still upset about it."

While Yvonne and Ellen cackled, Malcolm shook his head and started eating his soup. They spent the rest of the dinner finding ways to tease Malcolm. Ellen brought up the time he reorganized her silverware drawer because the clutter bothered him, and Yvonne told me about the rock collection he used to have. Malcolm sat through the meal with much headshaking and grumbling, but he smiled at every memory, and he laughed right along with them when Yvonne described his obsession with geodes.

Once Ellen headed out after dinner, Malcolm reached for Yvonne's bowl. When I picked up my bowl and began to stand, he took it from me and told me to sit back down.

"No use bothering," his grandmother told me. "He likes to be helpful."

"I am helpful," Malcolm said from the sink.

She sighed and glanced at me from across the table. "He *needs* to be helpful."

"You need my help," he called over his shoulder.

"That's his excuse for why he can't move out," she told me wryly.

"It's almost winter!" Malcolm protested. He began clearing the leftovers off the table. "Who's gonna shovel the walk if I'm not here?"

"Plenty of people. I'm a very popular person."

"I do it for free." Malcolm put the rest of the soup in the fridge. "Your best option is the kid across the street, and he'd expect money."

"I have money."

"Money you should be saving."

I stayed silent during the back and forth between Malcolm and Yvonne—no doubt a conversation they'd had many times before, an ongoing disagreement they'd treaded over and over again. Neither one of them seemed to mind trotting this out in front of me. They let me see them with their guard down like I was already part of the family, a thought that sent a longing ache through me.

He'd let me into his life, and I was plotting to sabotage his boss's business deal. When I held the protest, he'd find out that I'd concocted a plan and shared it with everyone I trusted, and that that list didn't include him.

I hoped I'd find a way to make him understand that the mistrust was only in a professional capacity, only because I knew he took his job seriously.

I'd have to hope he'd see it that way, too.

CHAPTER TWENTY-SIX

Do you want to do something tonight?
I can't stop thinking about the protest tomorrow.

I got Rochelle's text while I was taking a long lunch at the vintage clothing shop down the street. Cathy Larson had posted on the event page that she'd be coming in full *Pride and Prejudice* regalia, and the idea rippled through the attendees. Abigail posted that she had a renaissance faire outfit she was modifying to pass as a costume, and Evelyn posted a picture of the flowy dress she planned to wear. And so I stood in Recycled Threads flipping through a rack of period gowns, looking for something passable.

I stopped perusing long enough to text Rochelle that I had plans I couldn't get out of. But Rochelle stayed on my mind, even as the saleswoman was showing me dresses that might fit the bill. Rochelle would spend tonight worrying at home and I'd be having fun at the bookstore, throwing my largest event ever. Made larger by the fact that I invited the saleswoman when she said she loved *Pride and Prejudice*.

Even that night, standing in my room slipping the dress over my head, I still thought about Rochelle, now sitting on the couch watching TV to distract herself from her jumble of nerves.

I smoothed down the fabric and studied myself in the mirror. The simple embroidered white dress reached just past my calves, with buttons down the front and capped sleeves that went to my elbows. I'd put on leggings underneath for warmth, but even so, the regency look—as Harriet the saleswoman had called it, which sounded more accurate than my vague description of "old-timey"—was still there. I'd swept my hair into a messy bun, letting a few curls loose to frame my face. But as excited as I was to dress up tonight and see my events off right, a small part of me wanted to change into pajamas and join Rochelle on the couch, clinging to normalcy before the big protest tomorrow.

I eyed my coat on the bed. I'd meant to put it on and tuck my dress into my leggings so Rochelle didn't see my outfit and start asking questions. Instead, I slung it over my arm and walked out into the living room.

Dylan, sitting between Luke and Rochelle on the couch, was first to spot me. "You look like a princess."

Rochelle looked me over. "You do," she said with a laugh. "Where are you off to?"

I hesitated for just long enough to make up my mind. "I'm going to Vernon's," I said. "Do you want to come with me?"

"What?"

"It's a party, kind of. You'll see when you get there."

She frowned, regarding me suspiciously. "Vernon doesn't throw parties."

"You should come and see. If you hate it, you can leave."

"I—" Rochelle exchanged glances with Luke and Dylan. "I guess I'll be back." She stood, then looked down at her pajama bottoms. "I need to change first. Do I have to be a princess, too?"

"Yes!" Dylan said.

"No," I said. "Jeans would be fine. Whatever you want to wear is fine."

I waited at the bottom of the stairs while Rochelle got changed, aware of the curious glances Dylan and Luke were sending my way. Rochelle came down in jeans and a sweater, and I ushered her out the door before she could ask me anything. As we walked in the cold night air, I dodged her questions, refusing to answer until she could see it for herself. She gave me confused looks even as we walked up the creaking stairs to Vernon's apartment.

"About time," he said when he answered the door. "What's-her-name is already here."

"Cathy," said a voice behind him. I looked past Vernon to see a Black woman with short, tightly coiled hair. She wore a purple dress with capped sleeves and matching gloves that reached her elbows. "Is one of you Maggie?" she asked us.

"I am," I said. "This is Rochelle, who actually runs the bookstore. I'm just helping out. Rochelle, this is Cathy Larson."

Rochelle's eyebrows shot up. "As in the author of *The Gravedigger's Code*?" She turned from Cathy to me, eyes brimming with questions.

"That's right," Cathy said with a laugh. "Tell me about your bookstore. I didn't get a chance to see it."

Rochelle cut a disbelieving glance at me before turning to Cathy and launching into her family's history with Cobblestone Books. I knew Rochelle would have questions for me when she

THE BANNED BOOKSHOP OF MAGGIE BANKS

finished talking, but I still had to help Vernon set up. I left them to talk and excused myself to the kitchen.

I began unloading the snacks I'd brought over yesterday: boxes of madeleines, crackers, and shortbread cookies. My research on *Pride and Prejudice*–themed foods brought me no conclusive results, so I'd decided a boozy tea party would be on brand enough.

Abigail was first to arrive, brandishing a large Tupperware of homemade currant scones. Next came Leena, holding up a platter of deviled eggs. I greeted them with hugs and exclamations, but I was eager to meet the new faces, too. A nervous-looking man with gelled dark hair, who held up the event page on his phone and asked if he'd come to the right place. A woman in navy-blue coattails who examined the martini stamp on her hand with delight. I showed them inside, offered them drinks, and introduced them around.

I tried not to memorialize the night in my head too much, but the thoughts would sneak their way in. This was the last time I'd stamp hands and greet attendees. This was the last time I'd see out-of-towners, like Jim and Miranda. But at least it wouldn't be the last time I'd see others, like Dahlia, who arrived bearing miniature cucumber sandwiches. Or Marcia, or the gaggle of farmers' market vendors behind her. I recognized Ruth, holding a jug of cider, and Toby, who handed me a large bottle of whiskey. I could hardly see Vernon's kitchen counter under all the offerings.

People continued to stream through the door at a steady rate. Evelyn came with Amy, the woman I'd met at the pumpkin festival, and a few others from her writing group. Harriet, the saleswoman who had sold me my dress earlier today, showed up too, wearing a pale blue dress and gloves. I tried doing the math to determine just how many people had been invited unofficially instead of signing up through the registration page, but I lost count. As the room filled up, it became clear that we'd well surpassed my cap of forty. People stood all around the room, talking and mingling, enjoying snacks and drinks.

"Are we ready to get started?" Cathy asked. She stood at the front of the living room, pages in hand.

"Yes," I said. I stole another glance at Rochelle—still puzzled, a faraway expression on her face like she was doing long division in her head—and made my way to the front. I kept looking at Rochelle as I gave my introduction. When I led the crowd through a pledge dooming them all to spinsterhood if they ever said a word about what took place this evening, I noticed Rochelle also raised her hand and recited along, smiling a little. A small flutter rose in my chest.

I introduced Cathy, then stood off to the side as she took her place. Cathy talked about never connecting to *Pride and Prejudice*, feeling too removed from the problems of high-society white people to give the book the same reverence so many other readers did.

"It's a good story," she said. "I mean no disrespect to Jane Austen. It's not easy for women to make their voices heard, especially back in the day. I mean, if you're white, it's not *impossible*, but I'll give Jane Austen credit for getting her words out there. But her books have never been my favorite. I was excited to come here tonight for a chance to reimagine a book I've never found interesting. Full disclosure, my books have a lot of murder in them." She glanced down at the pages in her lap, then lifted her head to eye the crowd one more time. "Darcy fans, don't come for me.

"*Fitzwilliam Darcy's body was found in the stables*," Cathy read. A few surprised laughs rang through the room. Cathy described a string of mysterious murders that ensued, each victim's body scrawled with a sin, such as *pride* in Darcy's case or *greed* in another victim's. The story was told from the perspective of a Black woman named Janet. As Janet worked with Elizabeth Bennet to try to solve the string of murders that followed Darcy's, she sometimes had to endure Elizabeth's well-meaning but borderline racist questions and comments.

I slipped into the kitchen and continued to listen as I manned the drinks. As Cathy read, people found ways to get comfortable despite the limited seating: a few perched on the arm of a couch, some leaned against walls, and others, like Dahlia and Leena in the corner, sat on the floor like children during story time. It was strange to think how this had all started just two short months ago: an idea, a dick joke text from Evelyn, and a pile of poorly designed flyers with an inexplicable confetti border. How bizarre and fortuitous that it had turned into this, a standing-room-only event with a notable author in a grumpy old man's living room.

I could have been more comfortable, though. My legs were getting tired from standing, and the room was so hot and crowded that sweat was quickly forming on my back. I longed to take my leggings off. I plucked a couple of ice cubes from the freezer and poured myself a whiskey. Then, knowing I still had to explain myself to Rochelle after the reading was over, I added another healthy glug and chugged it down.

Cathy described how the murderer ran out of sins to write on victims' bodies and moved on to virtues, like *charity* or even simple facets of the human condition, like *sleepiness*. Eventually, Janet and Elizabeth discovered Mr. Collins was behind the killings and had him arrested. The scene ended with Elizabeth showing up at Janet's door, holding up a newspaper with news of a murder in a nearby town, and Cathy read: "*It is a truth universally acknowledged, that a single woman in possession of a thirst for adventure, must be in want of a good murder.*"

The room burst into applause. I looked around the living room to gauge Rochelle's reaction, but then I noticed Abigail moving to the front of the living room.

"Can I say a few words?" she asked. The room quieted down. "For those of you who don't know, this might be the last event from Cobblestone Books. I know," she said when disappointed mutters rang through the audience. "It's because Maggie's time at the bookstore is up in December, and our boss plans to implement some changes. He's going to start an Edward Bell–themed writing retreat here in Bell River. He wants to evict our host, Vernon, from his apartment, and put even more restrictions on what the bookstore can sell. No more events, no more secret books from Maggie. And those of us who work in his other businesses don't know if our jobs are safe. He might fire us and repurpose our businesses into something he can use for the writing retreat. He's bringing some investors to town tomorrow to convince them to fund his idea. What he doesn't know is that we'll be gathering to protest the changes. If you want to join us tomorrow, come see me."

Abigail's determination sent goosebumps along my skin. I hadn't thought about using tonight to get people invested in our cause against Ralph. But it made sense, I realized, hearing the murmurs spreading through the room. Over the last couple of months, the bookstore had become a hub of activity, a place for people to gather and have fun. I shouldn't have been surprised that they would care about the pending changes.

"All that aside," Abigail continued, glancing at me, "I want to make a toast to Maggie for putting these events together and giving us all a reason to meet up and laugh about books. And to Vernon, for inviting us into your home." She raised her plastic cup and the rest of the room followed suit, echoing our names. I glanced at Vernon, who gave Abigail a somber nod. I blinked back tears and ran across the living room to throw my arms around Abigail.

"Thank you," I said into her hair.

"Thank *you*." She pulled back, her hands on my shoulders. "You did all this."

A crowd began to form around us, some people telling Abigail they wanted to join in on the protest, others talking to me about how much they had enjoyed the events. I basked in it, listening, nodding, delighting in the fact that it wasn't just me memorializing tonight anymore. They loved these events just as much as I did, and I loved them fiercely for seeing the magic I saw in nights like these.

As Abigail was sharing details about tomorrow's protest, I spotted Rochelle standing on the outskirts of the crowd around me, watching us with wonder in her eyes. I weaved past people to reach her.

"So," I said tentatively. It's hard to think of anything to say after fifty people have raised a toast in your honor. "We should talk." When Rochelle nodded, I led us past the crowd and downstairs to the dark bookstore, where the air was deliciously cool on my skin.

I stepped inside the storage room and turned on the light. Then, leaning against the door, nerves jostling inside me, I finally told her the truth: the Bell books being taken away, the first

Moby-Dick event, the online bookstore, the *Gatsby* event, Cynthia, T. J. Hull's newsletter, all culminating in tonight's grand finale. Rochelle listened silently, her dark eyes steeped in concentration.

"You know," she said, "I was finally able to put money in savings last month—for the first time since Luke started nursing school. Is this why the store's been doing so well lately?"

I nodded. "I didn't tell you because you had enough to worry about, and I thought..."

"I know," she said. "I don't love being kept in the dark, but..." She shook her head, dazed and disbelieving. "Tonight was really cool. I guess I shouldn't be surprised. Your army is just bigger than I thought."

I breathed a sigh of relief. "It's not usually this crowded," I said. "Things just sort of snowballed." I could even hear them now, talking and laughing, louder than ever. I doubted there'd be any booze left over tonight.

"Maybe tomorrow when we talk to Ralph we can get him to agree to letting the store throw events like these," she said.

"Yes!" I pulled Rochelle into a hug. "That would be so much fun." I stepped back, seeing Rochelle's smile, and my jumbly nerves melted into nothing. "I usually sell books around now," I said. "Do you want to see my secret stash?"

"That sounds like a bad pickup line, but sure."

I led her to my hidden cardboard boxes in the corner, then brought out the box of Cathy's books I'd ordered in.

"How did you sell all these without Ralph catching on?" she asked. "He's so obsessive about the sales reports."

"Dahlia helped me fake them. She's good with spreadsheets."

"Wow." Rochelle shook her head. "How do you think of every detail for this, but forget to pay the electric bill for three months?"

"I thought I'd set up direct deposit!" I insisted. "I was also nineteen."

She laughed. "I know. I just like giving you shit. But this is amazing, really. I can't believe you pulled this off."

I was quiet a beat too long, savoring the pride swelling in me. I willed myself to remember these words, this moment, trot them out the next time I felt like a failure. Then I patted the box of Cathy's books.

"Should we go upstairs and sell some books?" I patted the box of Cathy's books.

Rochelle grinned. "Sure."

I hefted the box into my arms and Rochelle opened the door, but I didn't move. I only stared.

All the bookstore's lights were on, and at least half the crowd was now down here, clutching drinks and talking. Someone had brought a stack of cups and a bottle of wine from the kitchen and set them on the counter.

"You're all supposed to be upstairs," I said.

"Oh, you don't mind, do you, sweetie?" Ruth said. "It was so crowded up there. Marcia was getting light-headed." She rubbed Marcia's arm and looked down at her with concern.

Marcia, sitting in the chair behind the register, smiled sheepishly. "I'll be fine. But I could use a few more minutes."

"Of course," Rochelle said. "I'll get you some water."

While Rochelle disappeared upstairs, I placed the box of Cathy's books on the counter. Cathy noticed and offered to sign them, and soon people were forming a line for signed copies. I grabbed the card reader from upstairs and began processing sales, keeping an eye on the window. As soon as this line came to an end, I'd dim the lights and usher everyone except Ruth and Marcia back upstairs.

But people kept coming down the stairs, and I was too busy scanning books and printing receipts to ask them to return to Vernon's apartment. I peered at the line ahead of me. Just a few customers remaining.

Except some people who had just come from upstairs were now joining the line, and Cathy was taking her sweet time making conversation, asking their names, asking how they liked the reading, writing a personal greeting for each attendee. I took a steadying breath and continued scanning books.

Between Cathy making conversation, the chatter from the rest of the attendees, and Ruth, Rochelle, and Marcia quietly talking next to me, I didn't quite register the sound of the bell ringing. It wasn't until I heard Cynthia's voice that I realized what that sound meant.

"Maggie. What's going on?"

My heart thudded in my throat. Cynthia stood just inside the doorway, looking around incredulously. I frantically darted my gaze around the room, seeing it through Cynthia's eyes. The wine bottle on the counter. The people standing around and talking like they were at a party. The plate sitting on Edward Bell's historic writing table, bearing one lonely deviled egg and a half-eaten scone. The author beside me signing books. Me, scanning novels the store wasn't allowed to carry.

The room fell silent. Even the first-timer from out of town seemed to know it was an ominous sign when someone walked into a room and took Cynthia's tone.

"It's not what you think," I said. "Vernon was having a party upstairs, and it was getting hot, and Marcia wasn't feeling well, so we came down to cool off, and—"

"And you're selling books you're not supposed to be selling," she said. "I don't know what this is, but I know that can't be the full story."

"But—"

Cynthia held up a hand. "Look, I'm not your boss. I'm sure Ralph will get to the bottom of this. But you need to shut this down right now. Ralph and the ByGone investors are three blocks away, having dinner at Fig Leaf. They can't walk by and see this."

I gaped. "They're here tonight? The itinerary said they were coming tomorrow."

"No, they're *touring the town* tomorrow," she said, her voice low and serious. "But they arrived tonight."

I brought a hand to my temple, trying to focus. I needed to shut down the event before Ralph came upon it, or he'd fire me before I had a chance to do the protest. My brain, sloshy from the whiskey, took a moment to catch up.

"The investors?" Cathy said. She turned to me. "Are those the people you were planning that thing for?"

"Fig Leaf is just down the street," someone said. "We should go talk to them now."

"No," I said. "We're leaving." I stood and crossed the room to the door. "Thank you for coming, but the store is closed. You can head back up to Vernon's or you can go home, but the bookstore is off limits." I held the door open. A few people went upstairs, but the rest spilled into the street.

When the store was empty save for Rochelle and Cynthia, I began cleaning up the cups and plates they had left behind.

"Why aren't they leaving?" Cynthia said.

I turned around. The crowd hadn't dispersed at all. In fact, it had grown. I moved closer saw that people were streaming out of

Vernon's apartment, using the street entrance to join the group on the sidewalk.

I poked my head out the door. "What are you doing?"

"We're going to Fig Leaf to protest," Dahlia said.

"No!" I squeaked. "The protest is tomorrow!"

"Let's give them a piece of our minds!" shouted an out-of-towner. I recognized him as the dark-haired man who had been so nervous when he first arrived. I'd clearly made him feel too welcome. The crowd cheered.

"You're not even from here!" I said. "We're waiting until tomorrow."

"Let's go!" he shouted.

I watched in horror as the crowd began moving. Not dispersing in different directions like I'd asked. But marching, unified. Right toward Fig Leaf.

I exchanged harried glances with Rochelle. Then, with no other recourse, I flung open the door and ran after the crowd.

CHAPTER TWENTY-SEVEN

Whiskey, scones, and deviled eggs sloshed uncomfortably in my stomach on the walk to Fig Leaf. The talkative crowd ahead was workshopping potential chants—they seemed particularly fond of rhyming *Bell* and *hell*—but their energy didn't reach our cluster at the back. Abigail and Kat were murmuring about how Ralph might react, while Evelyn, Leena, Dahlia, Vernon, Rochelle, and I walked in silence. Cynthia hovered at my side, every so often shooting me pointed looks that made my skin prickle. I ignored her and turned to Rochelle at my other side, who watched the crowd ahead of us with worried eyes.

"This is fine," I decided. "We're having our protest as planned. It's just…happening early."

"And in costume," Vernon reminded me.

"Yes," I said, looking down at my dress. "And in costume." I rubbed my arm, wishing I'd brought my coat. "Maybe we can pretend this was part of the plan. We can work the outfits into our speech. We could say we're making a statement about how Ralph is stuck in the past."

Abigail made a sound that seemed like a cross between a laugh and a groan. "Perfect."

"Do you have those talking points we were working on?" I asked Rochelle.

"No. They're on my computer."

"Okay. That's fine. I'll…improvise." I tried to remember what Abigail had told the crowd earlier tonight, but the words jumbled together in my head. Then the crowd added to the jumble by practicing their chant, and soon intones of *To hell with Bell* filled my head.

My pulse accelerated when I saw Fig Leaf in the distance. A small group stood outside the restaurant. My first thought was that they were part of our crowd, maybe just the fast walkers. But as we drew closer, I recognized a familiar profile. Slim build, rigid posture, locs falling to his shoulders: Malcolm. Next to him, eyeing our approaching crowd with a frown, was Ralph.

I stopped walking, but Rochelle put a hand on my back and nudged me along. "No turning back now," she said.

We walked with the crowd, their chants of *To hell with Bell* growing louder, and came to a stop when we reached Ralph. I held my breath, waiting.

"What do we have here?" Ralph said.

Just as I was taking comfort in my position at the back of the group, I heard my name rumbling through the crowd.

"Where's Maggie?"

"Get Maggie."

"Maggie?" Ralph echoed. "What about Maggie?"

The crowd parted, leaving me exposed. I locked eyes with Malcolm, who watched me with a questioning gaze. Reluctantly, I stepped forward to face Ralph.

Ralph cleared his throat and turned to the people next to him. "This is Maggie," he said. "She's an employee at Cobblestone

Books. I see she couldn't wait her turn to meet you!" He gave a forced, high-pitched laugh.

The others with him—two women in their sixties, along with another woman who seemed to be in her early fifties, all bundled up in scarves and wool coats—laughed, too. Ralph ran through a quick but terse round of introductions: the older pair were Paula and Edith, and the other woman was named Sandra. We exchanged polite smiles. Then they stared at the large crowd behind me, a sea of flowy dresses, ruffled shirts, and cravats.

"Thank you for stopping by, Maggie," Ralph said. "You and your...friends...can continue on your way now."

"Are you going to a costume party?" asked Sandra.

"No," I said as politely as I could. I'd have liked to follow it up with a reasonable explanation, but my mind drew a blank.

"Have a good evening," Ralph said, a warning in his voice.

This was my out. I could wish them all a good night and turn around. But I knew the crowd behind me wouldn't stand for it, and maybe for good reason. I'd wanted a crowd for my protest, and I had one. Yes, some of us were dressed strangely, I was tipsy, and I couldn't feel the tips of my fingers, but the ByGone group was here and this was as good a time as any to air our grievances.

I summoned my courage and opened my mouth, suddenly aware of how dry it was. "We actually have something to say to you," I said.

In an instant, Ralph's expression transformed from cordiality to suspicion. "Is that so?"

"Not me," Cynthia said from somewhere behind me.

"Not Cynthia," I agreed. "But the rest of us."

"And what do you have to say?" It may have been phrased as

a question, but he spoke it like a reprimand. Like consequences lurked just underneath his words.

I squared my shoulders. "We'd like you to reconsider your proposal for the writing retreat. It's not in the town's best interests."

Ralph studied me for several quiet seconds, and then he put on an unsettling farce of a smile. "She's been in town for a few months and now she's an expert on what's best for everyone," he said to the group with a chuckle. Paula and Sandra laughed along with him, but Edith watched me curiously.

"Why would you like us to reconsider?" Edith asked.

"Edith, you don't have to—"

"I'd like to hear her," said Edith.

Ralph shut up. He turned to me, his stare so intense I felt like it held a threat. "Go ahead, Maggie."

Edith nodded for me to speak. I trained my eyes on her kind smile, and my shaky nerves stilled.

"For starters," I began, "it's not in the best interest of Vernon, who has lived upstairs for the last twenty years. He'll be evicted if this plan goes through." I gestured behind me to Vernon, who raised his hand.

"He would have several months to secure new housing," Ralph told his group.

"It's not in the best interest of Rochelle," I continued, "whose family has managed the bookstore on their own for decades. It's also not fair to put more restrictions on what the bookstore is allowed to sell. People here already have to go out of town when they want to buy books because this bookstore doesn't offer the stories they need."

"Our sales of classics have skyrocketed in the last few months," Ralph told his associates. "There's definitely interest there."

Goddamn my fake sales reports. Telling him the truth wouldn't reflect well on me. But if I needed to lay my cards on the table to show him how misguided his classics rule was, so be it.

"That's not true," I said. "I've actually been selling modern books and marking them down as classics."

Ralph jerked his head back. "But the sales reports—"

"I faked them." His nostrils flared, but I pressed on. "It's not in the best interest of Abigail, who has worked at the café for seven years, or Kat, who's been at the B&B for five, or any Bell Society employee. It's not fair to tell them that if you don't find them 'useful,' they're going to lose their jobs. You said you invested in these businesses because they were struggling and you wanted to help them."

"I *did* help them," he insisted, gesturing an arm out toward everyone behind me.

"You did," I allowed. "You helped them stay in business. You gave tourists a reason to visit. But letting staff go just to prop up this writing retreat idea doesn't do them any good. Who's going to serve the people who live here? We want you to think about the real impact your proposal will have on the people of Bell River."

Speech finished, my breath left me. I clasped my cold hands together and tried to hold my ground under the stares from Ralph and the ByGone group.

"Do you all feel this way?" Ralph asked.

A chorus of yeses—and one firm denial from Cynthia—came from behind me.

"The menu items you've made us add to the café are very hit-or-miss," Abigail said, coming forward. "No one wants a salad made from prunes, gelatin, and mayonnaise. And you made us take tuna salad off the menu to make room for it."

"But now they can try a meal from their favorite books," Ralph said. "You'd be hard-pressed to find prune salad anywhere else in the country."

"Wonder why," Vernon muttered.

"And it's like you don't care about the B&B at all," Kat said. "There's more to investing in a business than putting your name on it. We've been a skeleton crew since you cut our staff, and it just keeps getting worse. Two more people quit last year and you haven't even replaced them."

"I do care," Ralph insisted. "I just haven't been able to—" He glanced at the ByGone group, then thought better of what he was going to say. He straightened his posture and turned to Kat. "The ByGone proposal includes earmarked funding for the B&B so we can turn it into a space for the writers retreat."

"But we don't want that," Kat shot back. "That wasn't the plan when you bought the B&B."

Ralph took a deep breath, then checked his watch. "I hear your concerns, but we should get going. Why don't we find a time to discuss them in private?"

"Okay," I said. "Do we have your word that you won't move forward with the writing retreat proposal?"

Ralph's brow wrinkled. "No." He turned back to the group with a strained smile. "Maggie is a temporary employee. Her time is up next month, and then this will all die down."

"As part-owner of Cobblestone Books, I can say with complete certainty that I'm just as unhappy as Maggie about these changes," Rochelle said.

Ralph gaped at Rochelle, then shook his head. "I see." He leaned in to the ByGone group and said quietly, "We can always make changes in management."

A chorus of boos sounded from the crowd behind me. I turned to Rochelle, who darted a worried glance at me.

"Thank you for voicing your opinions," Ralph said, speaking louder, "but it's time for you all to leave."

Several long seconds passed. No one moved.

"That's an order," Ralph said. "I would advise all Bell Society employees to listen to me."

I took a moment to look around. Everyone was still standing firm, eyes locked on Ralph, collectively telling him, *Your move*. My wobbly uncertainty left me. I had an army of fifty behind me and we weren't backing down. I turned back to Ralph, feeling the corner of my mouth turn up. He may have power, but we had numbers.

Paula leaned in to Ralph. "Perhaps we should—"

"You're fired."

I let out a shallow breath. "Who?"

"All Bell Society employees standing here, except for Cynthia and Malcolm, are fired," Ralph said. "Effective immediately."

My stomach lurched. Protests and boos rang through the crowd.

"That's a low move, Ralph," Marcia said.

I glanced around, catching Rochelle's dumbfounded stare and Abigail's wide eyes, then turned to Ralph, my mouth hanging open. "You can't do that," I said.

Ralph leaned in to mutter something to the ByGone group. They nodded and whispered among themselves. Like we were invisible.

I tugged on my sleeve, wishing it were long enough to cover my freezing arm, wishing I could shape my scattered thoughts into a response, wishing I had any idea what to do next. I'd known losing our jobs was a possibility, but I hadn't really expected Ralph to fire us all. I'd thought he might fire me, the orchestrator of this whole protest, and I wouldn't mind because my time was up next month anyway and what was one more short-lived job on my resume?

But now I'd cost my friends their jobs and we were no closer to stopping the ByGone deal. Ralph would smooth this all over and go on with the itinerary as planned, they'd agree to the proposal, and then Ralph would go back to controlling everything he could get his hands on. He controlled the books we could sell, his employees, and the narrative of the author who once lived here.

The thing about having nothing left to lose is that it frees your options considerably. There was another tactic I could employ. All my underground activities at the bookstore started when Ralph punished me for having the gall to entertain a tourist's suggestion that Edward Bell had a mistress. Poking holes in Ralph's perfect image of Edward Bell just might convince ByGone to reconsider, or at least get them wondering what else he could be keeping from them.

My nerves turned to cold, hard steel. "You should know that Edward Bell had a mistress," I told the ByGone group. "He's not a feminist icon. His legacy is built on deceiving women."

Ralph stiffened, glaring my way. "And you think you know more about Edward Bell than his own grandson?" He turned back to the investors. "Those rumors are completely unfounded, I assure you."

My nails dug into my palms. "No, they're not! You know I'm telling the truth."

"Maggie," Ralph said, his voice dangerously measured, "I don't know what you're talking about."

I barked out a laugh. The investors were looking at me like I'd gone insane. I buried my hands in my hair. "You're really gonna stand there and tell me you don't know what I'm talking about? I bet this is exactly what Edward did to Louise, isn't it? He stole her book and passed it off as his own, and then he probably tried to tell her she was wrong when she confronted him. I know what I saw. I'm telling the truth and you know it."

Ralph went completely still. Next to him, the investors exchanged puzzled looks. Malcolm watched me, his gaze focused yet distant at the same time, like he was piecing something together.

"Who's Louise?" Paula asked.

I went back over my words, realizing too late what I'd said. I shrank back, searching helplessly for what to do next. I caught Vernon's eye. As if reading my mind, he shook his head.

But taking my words back felt wrong. Just an hour or two earlier, Cathy had said it hadn't been easy for women to make their voices heard in Austen's time. Over two hundred years later, Louise was still paying the price. She wrote a novel and Edward Bell stole her words and silenced her voice.

Ralph was doing the same thing now, wasn't he? He'd done his stealing the legal way, buying his way into businesses under the guise of making investments. But now, snatching away these businesses and doing with them as he pleased, he was using his privilege and power to get his way.

The cycle needed to end. It may have been the whiskey, or the cold, but I felt sure that the truth needed to come out. The Bells needed to be stopped. Louise's voice needed to be heard.

"She's the author who really wrote *The First Dollar*," I said. "Edward Bell stole her book and published it as his own." Murmurs went through the crowd. Ralph's eyes went wide. "The evidence is hidden in Ralph's office," I continued. Malcolm was frowning now, but I tore my gaze from him and looked at the ByGone group. "The entire Bell Society is based on a lie. Do you really want to fund a lie?"

"Now you're just grasping at straws," Ralph said with a frantic laugh, shooting glances at Paula and the others. "That's quite a story you've fabricated."

"I'll prove it." I pulled my phone from my back pocket. I had a PDF of the letters I'd scanned the night I was in Ralph's office. I also had the email addresses of the ByGone employees, thanks to the itinerary I'd snagged from Cynthia. I opened a new email addressed to the ByGone staff and all Bell Society employees, then attached the PDF. I lifted my chin and looked Ralph dead in the eye when I pressed Send.

Ralph's mouth twisted like he'd tasted something sour. "What are you doing?" he asked.

I ignored him. "Check your email," I told the ByGone group.

Sandra went first, pulling out her phone and peering at her screen. "There's nothing there."

"It might take a bit," I said, starting to feel awkward. "It had a large attachment." Standing around waiting for an email to send wasn't quite the dramatic reveal I'd anticipated. Then again, none of tonight had gone according to plan.

At last, a lone chirp broke through the silence. Edith checked her phone, then Paula and Sandra. The Bell Society employees followed suit, soon getting lost in their screens. People began crowding around the Bell Society employees, reading their phones over their shoulders.

"I can't believe this," Rochelle muttered.

Ralph turned to Paula. "Let's take this back inside," he suggested.

Paula lifted her head. "Why don't we talk tomorrow?" she said. "We should look into this." The ByGone group exchanged glances, then took off down the street.

A few out-of-towners let out halfhearted cheers at the ByGone team's departure, but Ralph's firing outburst had dampened the mood. The Bell River locals remained silent.

I released a shaky breath and looked around. Abigail and Kat were staring at me blankly. Rochelle looked up from her phone, her forehead wrinkling. She stared right through me.

"Do you have any idea what you just did?" Ralph said, his voice low and serious. "What this means for the Bell Society? For Bell River?"

I scratched the back of my neck. "I-I was trying to—I didn't think..." The words died in my throat.

He shook his head. "Malcolm, come with me." Ralph cut his way through the crowd, which parted to make room. Malcolm seemed to freeze in place, his eyes searching me. I stared numbly back. At last, he followed Ralph down the sidewalk.

I turned to face the crowd. The Bell River folks only gaped at me.

"What will this mean for the farmers' market?" asked Ruth.

"Or any of the shops downtown?" said Harriet.

"Or the museum?" Cynthia said, her face scrunched in worry. "Who'll come now?"

Bile burned the back of my throat as the reality of what I'd just done came crashing down around me. I'd convinced everyone here to join me in this protest and then I'd lost them their jobs. I'd put the livelihoods of the entire town in jeopardy. For all of Ralph's grandstanding, he really had once saved the businesses he had invested in. Rochelle had told me how her father struggled with the bookstore until Ralph bought into it. With the secret I'd just revealed, the bookstore didn't stand a chance of recovering—nor did any other business in town that depended on tourists. There was no Bell legacy to fall back on now that I'd shattered the illusion.

I glanced around at the people who, up until this moment, had considered me friends. I didn't see kinship in their eyes anymore. Only confusion and mistrust. Like they were looking at a stranger.

"I'm sorry," I choked out. "I didn't think this would happen."

A sea of blank faces stared back at me.

I couldn't think of anything more to say. And if I did, I doubted they would listen. Helpless, I turned and walked away. I'd thought, maybe naively, that someone might chase after me. Maybe Rochelle, Abigail, Evelyn, or Vernon.

No one did.

CHAPTER TWENTY-EIGHT

Wok House was as good a hideout as any.

I hadn't meant to come here. I'd trudged along, head down, eyes stinging in the cold. I passed shops that had closed for the night, empty and dark, and I felt like I was glimpsing into Bell River's future: a town run out of business by the outsider who exposed the lie they needed to survive.

And then I passed Wok House, with its lights still glowing through the window, a hopeful suggestion that maybe I hadn't destroyed everything just yet. The sign in the door told me they'd be open for another forty minutes. I walked through the door, letting the warmth envelop me. At the hostess stand, a woman I hadn't met before led me to a booth in the back. I settled into my temporary hideout and ordered a cup of oolong tea. When it arrived, my frozen fingers grasped it gratefully.

Ellen, spotting me on her way to another table, paused next to me. "Maggie! Malcolm didn't say you were coming."

I forced a chuckle. "Just felt like some tea."

She lingered beside me, as if there were more she wanted to say. I avoided her gaze and picked up my tea with more concentration than it required. I blew on its steaming surface like it was my life's mission to cool it down.

"Enjoy your tea," Ellen said, her smile a fraction dimmer than it had been just seconds ago.

"Thanks." I watched her leave, knowing I'd killed a conversation with rudeness. I blew on my tea and took a sip that burned my tongue.

I ordered a bowl of hot and sour soup. It gave me something else to focus on, more curls of steam to lose myself in, another hot surface to blow cool and try my luck on.

As I was trying to scoop a single mushroom into my spoon—no tofu, no pork, just a sad mushroom, alone like me—someone slid into my booth. I jumped, my spoon clattered on the table, and Malcolm was sitting across from me.

Part of me wanted to crawl under the table and hide from reality. The rest wanted to crawl in his lap and hear him tell me everything was going to be okay.

I bit the inside of my lip and met his steady gaze. "How'd you know I was here?" I asked.

"Ellen called and asked what I did to make you so sad."

I exhaled, which was the closest thing to a laugh I was capable of. "I guess there's no hiding in Bell River."

"What's with the outfit?"

I looked down at my dress. "I was hosting a secret *Pride and Prejudice*–themed event at the bookstore." When he didn't say anything, I kept talking. "I've done a few now. They're sort of genre-twisted parodies of classic novels, which I know sounds weird, but Malcolm, they were so fun," I insisted. "Vernon liked them, of all people. He came to the first one, and then he let me hold the rest in his apartment. I think you would have liked them, too. T. J. Hull did one."

His brow wrinkled. "Wait, what? T. J. Hull came to the bookstore?"

More guilt flooded through me. "I'm sorry I didn't tell you," I said. "I knew you'd have to tell Ralph, and I didn't want to put you in the middle of it."

"But you *did* put me in the middle of it. Ralph fired me."

"What?"

Malcolm drew in a long breath, his jaw set. "He checked the security log. Apparently my key card was used to access the building one night." He paused, his gaze lingering on me like a question. When I didn't deny anything, his mouth formed a line of grim acceptance. "He knows we're close. It's easy for him to assume I could have used my card to get into his file cabinet and give you the letters."

My stomach sank. "Malcolm, I'm so sorry."

"Did you steal the card from me?"

"No! It was in your hoodie the night we…"

"The first night we had sex?" he finished, giving a disbelieving laugh. "Is that why you left that night? You couldn't wait to use the card as soon as you found it?"

"No, I didn't know until I already left. And then I thought… it was worth a try. I was just looking for something I could use to thwart the deal, but then I found…" I sighed. "I was hoping I didn't have to use it, so I planned the protest, but then Ralph fired everyone, and everything just kind of happened from there." I averted my eyes, now stinging with tears.

Malcolm sighed. "And you didn't think about how it would impact me?"

"I did! Of course I did. It was why I was hoping I wouldn't have to reveal it, but…the protest didn't go according to plan."

"And you decided I was an acceptable casualty."

"It's not something I decided; it just happened. But now that you mention it, would it really be the worst thing if—" I caught myself and stopped.

"If what?" Malcolm narrowed his eyes. "If I lost my job?"

"I didn't mean it like that, but...you don't even care about Edward Bell. And you said you were hoping to get Ralph to change the rules, but is that ever gonna happen? I tried and I got a bunch of people fired."

"Well, you don't exactly think things through, do you?"

I jerked my head back. "At least I tried to do something."

He nodded slowly, his mouth in a grimace of a smile. "And you're saying I don't try?"

"I..." I shrugged, at a loss. "You've had the same job for ten years. You've lived with your grandmother for fifteen."

"And what does that have to do with anything?"

"You say you can't move out because she needs you, but you're using her as an excuse to put your life on hold. She knows it. She said as much at dinner last week."

"She is the only real family I have," Malcolm said, his voice quiet but steady.

"And that'll always be the case if you don't ever try to start a life of your own. I know you said you don't take your commitments lightly, but it's okay to change your mind."

"Believe me, I'm rethinking all sorts of things."

From the steely way he was looking at me, I knew exactly what—or rather, *who*—he was rethinking. A lump formed in my throat.

"And maybe you're not the best person to talk about taking things lightly," Malcolm continued. "I don't know if you take anything seriously. You keep saying you're going to find a job and stay in town past December, but have you done anything to make that happen? You turned down the only job that was interested in you, and it seems like you've been too busy with these secret events and this protest to do anything else."

"Too busy with distractions, you mean?" I said quietly. "I've heard that before."

Malcolm's gaze lingered on me, searchingly. "I should go," he said. "Not that I have a job to get back to anymore, but." I think he meant to be funny—he even tried for a chuckle—but all he managed was a breath. He slid out of the booth.

"I'm sorry," I said. "I really didn't mean to involve you in this. I just liked being with you."

Malcolm nodded. "So did I." He smiled sadly and turned around. I watched him walk down the aisle, leave through the door we'd once walked through together, and disappear down the sidewalk.

CHAPTER TWENTY-NINE

My next hideout was a place I'd heard a lot about but had never been to: the Barnes and Noble in Franklin.

I'd left Wok House right after Malcolm, too uncomfortable to sit there in my sadness with Ellen watching from the sidelines. I walked to Rochelle's and stood in the driveway, building myself up to the idea of going inside and coming clean about yet another secret I'd kept from her. But I felt too empty for another emotional conversation about my failures.

So I got in my car and left.

Now I sat by the magazine rack in a corner, surveying Barnes and Noble. So many books, of all genres and time periods, curated and displayed in a way that had nothing to do with Edward Bell. I watched a woman pick up a book from a display table. She examined the back cover, read the first few pages, then pinned it under her arm and sank into a fabric armchair. She drew her feet up underneath her the way Abigail did when she read in the bookstore's armchair on her breaks.

The thought of Abigail made my heart twist. All that time, building a friendship, building a community, and I'd wrecked it in one fell swoop. And now I had nothing to show for my time here. I'd just been supposed to work quietly at the bookstore for a few months, enjoy a reprieve from living with my parents, and use the time to figure out my next steps. Instead, I'd founded a secret community, incited a rebellion, and gotten people fired. I'd gotten distracted—again.

Someone brushed past a standing rack of book lights, sending one falling to the floor with a clatter. The woman reading in her chair was so engrossed in her book that she didn't look up at the noise.

Just past her, I spotted a sign: Now Hiring.

I rested my chin in my hand and let the idea turn over in my mind. I wouldn't have to put up with Ralph here, or any of his rules. People here were free to browse and read the books they wanted. I could be part of that, part of this place that served as a literary escape for Bell River townsfolk. And yet the thought of working here made me feel hollow inside.

It didn't make sense. I should be glad to work here. I'd get to be around customers and recommend books, and—well, I had a very limited list of books I could recommend, considering I'd only started getting into reading in the last few months. But still, the idea of it was logical when I thought about it.

But I was missing a crucial component of myself that everyone else possessed. In some way or another, I've felt apathetic about every job I've ever had. Even with my last job at the media company, I hadn't been excited when my boss had called to offer the job. I'd just politely accepted, because I needed money and health insurance and a roof over my head, and a job would provide me with all those things. Over time, I'd carved out a place for myself there, filled it with the things I knew would make me happy, and made it a better place for everyone.

Maybe I could have done the same thing at the financial investment firm. But I'd been so determined to not repeat my past mistakes, so sure that if I didn't get a flutter in my chest at the prospect of working there, it must mean it wasn't the job for me. But that couldn't be a feasible approach either, holding out hope for a flutter I might never get. Every job might always feel hollow. Which had to mean the problem was me.

An announcement rang over the speakers that the store was closing in fifteen minutes. I dutifully stood and plodded to my car, where I sat behind the wheel staring at nothing. I could have driven somewhere else, found another excuse to hide, but I owed Rochelle the explanation she deserved. Then she could give me the lecture I was overdue, and I'd go to my room and stop procrastinating on where to go from here. It might be the Barnes and Noble in Franklin. Or, a small voice said, it might be back at my parents' house in Fremont. I could try to find a job in this area, but my plans never turned out the way I wanted them to. Today was a prime example of that.

I came home to find Luke on the living room couch immersed in a textbook. He looked up with a polite smile. "Rochelle's upstairs."

I nodded. I was sure Rochelle had told him about tonight. He probably knew a showdown was coming. I gathered my resolve and started up the stairs.

Rochelle sat on her bed sorting through a pile of clean laundry. She glanced up when she saw me in the doorway, then went back to the laundry. "I'm looking for a matching sock," she said, holding up a tiny white sock that could only belong to Elliot.

I gingerly perched on the bed and started sifting through the pile. Finally, I found it, a small white sock clinging to one of Dylan's shirts. I plucked it free and held it up.

"Thanks." Rochelle eyed me as she rolled the socks together. "Where have you been?"

"Hiding." I picked up a hand towel and began folding it, thinking through what I wanted to say. "Tonight was unexpected."

"To put it mildly." She folded a shirt and ran her finger along its sleeve to smooth out a wrinkle. "All night, I've been wondering why you didn't tell me about anything. The events, the secret inventory, the online bookstore, now the thing you discovered about Edward Bell. I understand why you did it. But I don't get why you didn't tell me."

I looked down at the hand towel in my lap. "I guess...I was afraid you'd make me stop. I felt like I was helping people at the bookstore and I didn't want to give that up. The store meant too much to me."

"Why?" she asked.

"Why what?"

"Why did it mean so much?"

I twisted a corner of the towel between my fingers, trying to put words to a feeling. "It felt like the only thing that was real. The only thing that was mine. Everyone else has careers, and families, and I—I had the bookstore. I know it wasn't really mine. I just wanted to hold on to it while I could. It felt like...when I was there, I could do anything—and whatever I did, people would want to be part of it with me." I gave an embarrassed laugh. It sounded so trivial spoken aloud.

She watched me with a puzzled expression. "And...you think that's not possible now? You think the bookstore did all of that for you?"

"Well...it was an important part of it. I didn't really know how passionate people were about books, or how much power books have, until I started working there."

"Maggie." Rochelle set down the shirt she was folding and scooted closer. She lowered her head to catch my gaze. "It's not the bookstore. It's you."

I frowned, trying to make sense of it. "What do you mean?"

Her eyebrow arched. "You think all this happened because of the power of books?" She was almost smirking, but not unkindly. "Maggie, if I worked in a back-alley dumpster and asked you to take over for four months, you would have made that dumpster the most beloved spot in town. You'd have people lining up for trash."

I squinted at her. "I still don't know what you mean."

"Okay. How many Mary Kate and Ashley movies did we watch together in college?"

"Um." I thought back. "Like ten? Twelve?"

"Do you think I gave a single shit about those rich white girls?"

My jaw dropped. "But the nostalgia!"

"I didn't grow up watching their movies! I did it because of *you*. You had that blog, and you made that drinking game for the rewatches, and you hosted live rewatch parties, and you had that weird conspiracy theory that they were feuding with Robert DeNiro, which I still don't understand—"

I laughed. "I just thought it was funny."

"Exactly!" she said. "You brought us all into this ridiculous world that you made up. And you do that with everything. That's what I meant when I said you float through life. You do what you want, and it's amazing."

I sat there processing this, my mouth still open. "But I don't know what I'm doing," I said.

"Who says you have to?"

"Everyone else seems to know."

"Do you think *I* know?" she challenged.

I scoffed. "Of course you know."

"So…getting pregnant at twenty-three? Working at a library, leaving because I hated it, taking over my dad's bookstore right when my husband quits his job and starts nursing school? Getting fired? That was all planned?"

I darted a glance at her. "I got you fired."

"No, *I* got me fired," she said. "I knew what I was doing. But my life isn't planned, and it's not perfect. It's okay that yours isn't, either. You don't need to compare yourself to anyone."

I nodded, feeling the bridge of my nose tingle. "Okay," I said. I wiped my nose and pulled her into a hug, getting a whiff of her familiar coconut-papaya leave-in conditioner when she wrapped her arms around me. I pulled back and rested my head on her shoulder.

"I don't know how to fix it," I confessed in a whisper. "I shouldn't have dragged everyone into my stand against Ralph. I should have known he'd retaliate."

She squeezed my shoulder. "You'll figure it out. I'm sure you'll find a way to get your army back." With that, she loaded her laundry basket and left the room.

I wandered to my room, still in a daze. Rochelle admired me. Rochelle with her put-together life thought I was doing something right. Which must mean there might not be something wrong with me after all.

I flopped onto my bed and stared at the ceiling. Why had the possibility of that Barnes and Noble job made me feel so empty inside?

If I was being honest with myself, the actual aspect of working at the bookstore was my least favorite part of my job. I may have come to enjoy reading, but sitting around while tourists browsed ancient classics wasn't interesting to me. I was only truly happy at the bookstore when the people I cared about were there, too. When Evelyn, Dahlia, Abigail, and Leena hung out at the bookstore, reading or working or talking. When I was hosting events, bringing people together for silliness, laughter, and conversation, and slowly but surely watching that group solidify into a community.

That's all I've ever liked doing: bringing people together. Being around people, period. The events at the bookstore. The Merrymakers. My regulars at Peet's. The bad movies club I'd founded in college, and then the online community I'd formed, a group of internet strangers who were invested in my silly Mary Kate and Ashley rewatch project.

When I thought about it like that, I could see it the way Rochelle did. I wasn't an aimless wanderer who gave in too easily to distraction. I was driven. I had purpose. It was just a purpose that didn't fit the mold of what people expected.

And there was nothing wrong with that, was there? What rule was there that required me to find purpose in—or even give a shit about—my job?

What happened tonight was a disaster, but it didn't mean *I* was. It didn't mean I couldn't fix it.

I turned my phone on. It slowly came to life, filling up with notifications. Missed calls, texts, emails, tweets. Malcolm trying to get ahold of me before he found me at Wok House. Rochelle asking where I'd gone. A written termination notice from Ralph. An email from Jim with *Thought you'd want to see this* in the subject line. I opened it.

Someone had posted my PDF of Louise's letters online, and now BookReport, a literary news site, had written about it, sharing snippets of the letters and noting that they would share more information as the story unfolded. I scrolled down to the comments, where some discussed the news and others debated the legitimacy of the letters.

Word was spreading.

I followed a link to a tweet that tagged the Bell Society and asked for their response. But Ralph hadn't said a word.

I went through as many tweets and comments as I could find. This small but chatty sliver of the internet devoted to literary gossip wanted answers. And Ralph was silent.

There had to be room for me to do something here, even if I wasn't sure what. I'd played the last card in my hand tonight, but there might be time to find another.

I got to my feet and grabbed my jacket on my way out the door.

CHAPTER THIRTY

I shifted my weight from one foot to the other while I waited for Malcolm to open the door. Our fight at Wok House still left me feeling raw, but he'd invested so much time in the Bell Society. He must want to rewrite the abrupt ending he'd been given today.

Malcolm opened the door slowly, just enough to stick his head through. "Come to get me evicted, too?"

"No. Would you like to invite me in?"

"No." There was no malice in his reluctance. He just looked at me like he was tired of not knowing what I'd do next.

"Okay. Then I'll tell you out here." I exhaled a puff of cold air and tried to gather my scattered thoughts. "You said you wanted to rise up the ranks and change the Bell Society. You never got to do it, and I know that's because of me. But if we put our heads together, maybe we can think of a way to tear down the Bell Society and make it something like what you always wanted it to be. Less rigid. More honest."

He'd opened the door more while I spoke, enough for me to see he was in his pajamas, a plain white T-shirt and plaid bottoms. He leaned against the door frame. "Do you have anything in mind?"

"No," I confessed. I thought about what he'd said at the restaurant, telling me I didn't think things through. Confirming that I didn't have a plan now felt like admitting he was right. But this was the best I could do. "But do you really want it to end like this?" I asked. "I started something tonight. I want you to help me finish it."

I could see my words rolling around in his head, like he was carefully weighing their meaning. And then, the corner of his mouth twitching in the trace of a smile, he held the door open and stood to the side.

"Let's get to work."

Minutes later, I sat across from Malcolm at the kitchen table, the same one where we'd eaten dinner together last week. But this time no spread of food sat between us, no Yvonne or Ellen to share embarrassing memories. Just a stark table and Malcolm's vacant expression.

"Do you know why Ralph hasn't said anything?" I asked.

He rested his elbows on the table and folded his arms. "I don't know if he knows how he's going to address it yet. Before he fired me, he was saying we shouldn't comment on it. He might be focusing on trying to salvage the deal with ByGone. He called them when we were walking back to the Bell Society. He was saying the letters were taken out of context."

I rolled my eyes. Nearly a century later and Louise was still being disrespected by a Bell man.

"So?" Malcolm said. "What do you want to do?"

I sighed, wishing I had an answer. "I want to stop him from getting away with it. He can't keep forcing people to worship Edward Bell and holding their businesses hostage. He needs to own up to his family's mistakes and give credit to Louise. If he's not talking right now, then maybe that's our opening. People have heard the news and they have questions. We'll talk."

Malcolm shrugged listlessly. "What else is there to say? Those letters are already making the rounds. Do you have anything else?"

I slumped forward and rested my chin on my arms. "No."

"Those letters have done damage, but they're not conclusive." Malcolm stroked his bottom lip with his thumb, looking thoughtful. "I've done a lot of research on Edward Bell over the years, looking for something I could use to convince Ralph to ease up. I've never found anything. Ralph controls his story too well. But we could try looking into Louise. If anything exists on her."

"It's worth a try," I said. I'd have tried anything Malcolm suggested. Anything to feel like I stood a chance.

He pushed his chair back and stood. "I'll get my laptop."

"We're starting now?"

Malcolm stopped, his hand on the back of his chair. "Unless you want to start tomorrow."

"No," I said. "Now is good." It was nearly midnight and my eyes were heavy, but my head was too busy for me to sleep anyway.

I'd really convinced him to go all in on this with me, then. We were both all in on this. I couldn't say exactly what that meant. There was more I wanted to be all in on with Malcolm. But since our argument in the restaurant, we'd fallen out of step, shifted backward to a hazy, in-between place I couldn't name. But this was a start.

We spent a while searching in circles. All we had was a first name, which wasn't enough to go off of. We tried combinations of Louise's name, various cities in Maryland, and the years she'd written on her letters. We added the word *writer* or *author* in case she'd written something else and gotten published, but nothing turned up.

I read back through the letters. Edward and Louise had fallen out in the autumn of 1935 when Louise wrote that a man named Thomas had proposed. In one letter, she shared the news of the proposal. Edward must not have taken it well because her tone in the next letter was frostier, writing, *You may be disappointed to know it is of no interest to me what you deign to allow.*

We tried searching *Louise Thomas 1935* in hopes of finding an engagement announcement, but that just taught us there was an abundance of Louise Thomases in the world. Malcolm and I sat side by side at the kitchen table wading through a sea of search results and brainstorming new possibilities. My back was starting to feel stiff after sitting in one place for so long.

"Maybe she didn't live in Maryland," Malcolm said when I got up to put on a pot of coffee. "We could try Virginia. Or DC."

"Okay."

He started typing. I sat down and continued scrolling through the PDF of letters on my phone, searching for some clue I'd missed.

"Wait," I said. I put a hand on his arm—then thought this might be a touch too familiar now. I retracted it and held up my phone. "She knew his wife, right?" I scrolled to the letter where Louise discovered Edward had submitted her stolen manuscript for publication. "'Josephine tells me a publisher has accepted one of your manuscripts, and the plot she described is remarkably familiar,'" I read. "She also sent that letter thanking Josephine and Edward for coming to her wedding."

"So they could be friends?"

"Or they're related," I said. "Maybe they have the same last name."

Malcolm lifted an eyebrow. "A relative having an affair with her husband? Sucks for Josephine."

"Good for us."

He gave a small laugh. It was subdued, but the sound gave me hope, like we were making our way back to normalcy. Within minutes, Malcolm found Josephine's maiden name—Wood—and was looking up her relatives on a genealogy site. She had just one sibling, a brother, but Malcolm scrolled to the side, checking her aunts' and uncles' lineage, and there she was: Louise Wood, daughter of Josephine's aunt Mabel.

"Cousins. Good thinking," Malcolm said. I turned to him, ready to bask in our victory, but he kept his eyes on the screen.

From there, we uncovered more of Louise's life. She lived in Arlington, and when she married Thomas, she changed her last name to Price. They had three children. Malcolm and I continued our way down the lineage. Their first child, Helene, had a son. A shiver ran down my spine when I saw his name: Vernon.

It couldn't be my Vernon. His last name was Newell, not Price. And yet...

A memory floated from somewhere in my brain: standing in the dim stairwell outside Vernon's apartment the night of the *Gatsby* event. Ralph had said he expected more from Vernon after everything Edward Bell had done for Vernon's family. And Vernon's response, hard and acidic: *You have no idea what he's done for my family.*

"It's our Vernon," I said.

A puzzled frown creased his brow. "There's more than one Vernon in the world."

I shook my head. "He's about the right age. Arlington's not too far from Bell River. They could have moved here at some point. He could have taken his father's last name. He said something once about some kind of history with Edward Bell." I turned to Malcolm. "It's Vernon. I'm right about this. We should talk to him."

He studied me. "You don't need me for that. You're closer with him than I've ever been."

I pursed my lips, feeling like I'd been caught in a lie. "But it's your long con. And it's my plan. We're joining forces."

"That doesn't mean we need to do everything together. You talk to Vernon, and I'll keep researching Louise's family in case Vernon isn't our guy."

"Okay." I watched Malcolm. His response made it clear that he wanted us to keep our distance, but I couldn't help myself. "Should I come over after I talk to Vernon?"

He hesitated. "Just text me."

"Right," I agreed quickly. "I will." I cleared my throat and pushed my chair back. "I'll let you know how it goes with Vernon."

Malcolm walked me to the door. My heart ached at how impersonal this was, him treating me like a guest. I allowed myself one brief glance at him, and then I slipped out the door without a word. I already knew there was nothing more he wanted to say to me.

CHAPTER THIRTY-ONE

As I approached Vernon's the next day, I couldn't help but glance at the bookstore just past it. It was open. Cynthia was probably in there, ready and waiting for customers. Ready to maintain the lie and tell the tale about the table where Edward Bell didn't write the book that wasn't his.

I averted my eyes and faced the door leading to Vernon's apartment. I'd never gone in this way, from this entrance here on the sidewalk. I'd always come through the door that connected the bookstore to his staircase. Coming through the street entrance was another reminder of all that had changed since yesterday.

I opened the door and stepped into the staircase passageway. This, at least, was familiar. I climbed the stairs and knocked.

After several long moments, Vernon opened the door. We stood there in silence until he said, "I told you not to."

"I know," I said. I bit my lip. I couldn't just casually ask him, standing here in the dark stairwell, if he was related to the woman Edward Bell stole his book from. "Can I come in?"

"If you must." He turned and walked into the kitchen. I

closed the door behind me, then stood awkwardly in the entryway while Vernon puttered around in the kitchen. The counter
was cluttered with the Tupperware of Abigail's scones, an empty
platter that had held Leena's deviled eggs, liquor bottles, and
other signs of last night.

"I'll help you clean up," I said.

"You'll sit down," he said, taking a head of lettuce out of
the fridge. "I'm making lunch. I only have so much egg salad,
so I don't have anything for you. I might have made more if I'd
known you were coming." The accusation in his eyes admonished
me for the inconvenience I was causing.

"That's okay," I said. "I'll sit." Two cats dozed on the
couch. I sidled past them to the love seat by the window and
sat down. There was the beginnings of a puzzle on the coffee
table, the border mostly filled in. I leaned forward to search
for an edge piece.

"I don't know what you're doing over there," Vernon said
from the kitchen. "I eat at the table."

I obediently moved to the dining table. I looked around for
some hint of Vernon's family—framed photographs, or a photo
album somewhere. All I could see was Catward Bell.

Vernon emerged from the kitchen holding a plate and a can
of seltzer. He set both in front of me. The plate held an egg salad
sandwich, neatly cut into two triangles, ruffles of lettuce peeking
from each half.

"You didn't have to do that," I marveled.

He just gave one of his trademark grunts and ventured back
to the kitchen, returning with another plate and can of seltzer
for himself. He took a seat in the spot opposite me. "And now,
because of you, I won't have any left over for tomorrow." He

picked up his sandwich and shot me a glare, but just before he took a bite, I noticed a flicker of affection in his eyes.

"I'm deeply sorry." I bit into my sandwich. I wasn't one for egg salad, but there was a certain appeal in a sandwich prepared for me by the town grump. The more I ate it, the more I liked it.

"Do you know if ByGone backed out of the deal?" I asked.

"Couldn't tell you."

I opened my seltzer and took a drink, letting the bubbles fizz on my tongue while I tried to think of the best way to broach the topic. "Those letters I sent around suggest that Edward Bell's novel was really written by a woman named Louise who lived in Arlington," I said.

Vernon was intently focused on a piece of egg that had fallen out of his sandwich. He picked it off his plate and tucked it back in.

"Louise had a few kids," I went on. "And one of her daughters, Helene, had a kid named Vernon."

Vernon took a swig of seltzer and went in for another bite. As he chewed, he slid a glance at me. "If you're trying to ask me something, go on and ask it."

My breath hitched. "Is Louise your grandmother?"

"What's it to you?" he asked, moving on to the other half of his sandwich.

"If Edward Bell stole her book and passed it off as his own, she deserves to have her story told," I said. "The letters I found aren't enough. People are asking questions, and Ralph's not saying anything. I need to find something that proves, without a doubt, that Edward Bell stole her book. It could change the Bell Society as we know it. Maybe Ralph will loosen his grip, and stop being so stubborn, and…hire back the people he fired. And Louise can finally get credit for her book." I watched Vernon expectantly.

"He didn't steal the whole book," he said. "The ending's different. She never sent him the last few chapters, so he had to make them up himself. Made for a weaker book, in my opinion." He wiped his mouth with a napkin and stopped when he saw me. "What's that look for?"

"So it's true? She's your grandmother?" He nodded, and I sat back in a daze. "Did she ever talk to you about it?"

"No. My mother did. When I was a kid, I found the manuscript in a steamer trunk in the closet over there."

I blinked. It was hard to imagine Vernon as a kid. "You grew up here?"

"More or less. My dad was a drunk and my mom left him when I was five or six. She stayed with her mom for a few months, but they didn't get along. My mom snooped around the house, found a pile of letters from Edward Bell, and pieced it together. She stole the letters, thinking she could blackmail Edward into giving her some money."

"Did she?"

"She didn't get a chance. Edward had heard through the family that she needed a place to stay. As soon as she got to town, he put her up here and gave her enough money to start a new life, no questions asked. Any time she needed anything, he was there."

I nodded, thinking. "I wonder if he supported her because he felt bad about what he did to Louise."

"Could be," he said dismissively.

"What happened when you found the letters?" I asked.

He sighed. "My mom got mad and told me I could never tell

anyone. She was worried coming out with the truth would lose us our home, our safety net. Everything. Even after he died, she wouldn't hear a word against him."

"Even though he stole her mom's book and got rich off it?"

Vernon shook his head. "I don't think she cared. The only Edward she knew was the one who supported her. She never told her mom that Edward housed and paid for us. And her mom never asked where her letters went. We're not big talkers," he explained.

I fought off a smile. "Shocking. But…why did you still keep quiet about it, all these years later? I know *you* don't feel the same way about Edward Bell as your mother did."

He shrugged. "I didn't see a point. I grew up, I moved out, this town wasn't my concern anymore. I only came back here to sort through my mother's things and get her affairs in order after she died. This was about twenty years back. I was grieving, I'd just lost my job, and I struck a deal with Ralph to rent this place until I decided what to do next. Time passed, I opened my lock shop, kept to myself. I was comfortable." He eyed me. "Then you came along."

I smiled. "Sorry about that." I watched him down the last of his seltzer. "Can I see the manuscript?" I asked.

He heaved a sigh. "Suppose so." He stood and reached for my plate, but I stopped him.

"I'll clean up. Thanks for lunch." I carried our dishes to the sink. When I returned, two bundles sat in front of my place, each tied together with twine. The first was a stack of envelopes, the second a pile of handwritten pages. I picked up the envelopes, seeing *Edward Bell* in the return address and *Louise Wood* in the address field. I touched the loose string of twine, then glanced

up at Vernon. He nodded in assent. I slowly pulled, watching the
string unravel. I pulled a piece of paper from the first envelope.

Dear Louise,

*I hope this letter finds you well. The weather has
been dreadful all week, but I am hopeful a spring
thaw will set in soon.*

*I had a marvelous time at your Aunt Gretel's
luncheon. It was such a pleasure to see you. I had no
idea Josephine had such a charming cousin! Would it be
too forward of me to plan a visit in a fortnight's time?*

Yours,
Edward

While Vernon left to settle on the couch, I kept reading.
Edward's letters grew less formal as he implored Louise to see
him again. In one letter he wrote, *I wouldn't worry about Josephine.
She is quite trusting.*

As their affair began, Edward opened up to Louise more.
He complained that he and Josephine had married too young,
declared Josephine too naive and childish, and praised Louise's
intelligence. In Edward's words, he and Louise shared *an understanding of the mind and heart, an intellectual and physical bond unlike
any love I have ever felt before.*

He wrote that the only time that he felt was his own was the time
he spent sitting at the table in the bookstore, writing letters to her.

I eventually came upon a letter that indicated Louise had
sent him the beginning of her novel.

Louise,

This is remarkable. You must keep writing. What do you imagine happens next?

Edward, after reading the typewritten pages Louise sent him, gave her suggestions for advancing the plot when she got stuck. Edward also shared his work with Louise, along with rejections he'd received from publishers, his frustration growing more evident with each one.

Then came a letter Edward must have written after learning of Louise's engagement to Thomas. *I will not allow you to marry this classless scoundrel*, he wrote.

At last, I reached the last page in the stack. Edward must have written this in response to Louise's note pointing out the similarities in their books.

No cause for concern. I have done a great deal of revising, rewriting, and improving upon the source, not to mention my contributions to the plot. I wrote the last several chapters completely on my own as well. In all, the book is entirely my own. I wouldn't think you'd have minded either way. You must be very busy with Thomas these days.

No need to make a fuss. I wouldn't want to upset Josephine.

Would you?

It was a simple question. It had all the appearance of innocence. But it held so much. The threat of revealing their affair to Louise's cousin lurked just beneath the surface of his words.

I moved on to the tall stack of papers and pulled the twine free.

The first page held the sentence that had now become so familiar to me: *When Hazel got fed up with the world, she liked to look out the window and imagine the passersby as her companions in misery.*

Unlike the page Louise had sent Edward, this one revealed the drafting process: she had crossed out a sentence in the first paragraph and scribbled a new one in its place. She misspelled the word *conscience*, crossed it out, and wrote the correct spelling above it. Her handwriting was looser, more hurried. The page she had sent Edward didn't have any of this—she must have copied it over from this one, showing only the final product in her neatest handwriting, no evidence of the errors or decisions she had made along the way.

The rest of the pages were similar: sentences, paragraphs, or sometimes whole pages crossed out. Questions she'd written to herself in the margins about whether to move a scene somewhere else, or why a character might behave a certain way. In comparison to the neatly handwritten (and then typewritten) pages she'd sent Edward, it would be clear to anyone—even Ralph—that this was the original.

I took a picture of the first page, then texted it to Malcolm. It's our Vernon. He even has the manuscript.

Malcolm replied with three exclamation points. I never thought I'd see the day.

See if he'll let you borrow it, he replied. Maybe we can set up a meeting with a reporter. I'll do some research.

T. J. Hull's pretty well connected in the book community,

I wrote back. I bet he knows someone you can ask. Here's his number. Tell him you know me.

Despite the weirdness between us, this revelation broke Malcolm's brain enough for him to respond with one of his typical freak-outs.

> Maggie what the fuck
> You can't just casually give me T. J. Hull's phone
> number.
> Idk what to say to him.

I smiled and turned my attention back to the manuscript while my phone continued to vibrate with Malcolm's panic. I flipped through pages, hunting for the last chapters where Edward's version of the novel was supposed to have deviated from Louise's.

I stopped when I came across a scene I didn't recognize: Hazel and her husband, Benjamin, fighting about the hours she was spending at the cheese shop. In the novel I'd read, Benjamin had been prickly about her opening the shop, jealous that she was making something of herself while his own dreams of running a pub went unfulfilled. But when their son fell ill and business at the shop took a turn for the worse, Benjamin swooped in to save the day, manning the shop while Hazel looked after their son. In the end, their son recovered, Benjamin converted the shop to a pub, and Hazel returned to being a homemaker, content that she had tried her hand at shopkeeping but finding that she would rather stay at home with her family.

In Louise's version, tensions between Hazel and Benjamin continued to mount. He would agree to watch their son, then wander off to a bar. He would volunteer to accept an early delivery, then forget and oversleep. During a heated argument, after Benjamin accused Hazel of letting her shop interfere with their lives, he insisted that she make a choice: him or her shop. Hazel chose her shop without a moment's pause, leaving Benjamin flabbergasted. He slunk off for good, returning every so often when he needed money. The novel ended on Hazel looking out the window of her shop, eager to share her passion with her next customer.

I flipped the last page over and straightened the stack. Unlike the first ending, I was left feeling inspired rather than baffled. Edward had wanted Benjamin to be Hazel's happy ending, but she didn't need him. She had herself.

I thought about the guy I'd talked to in the bookstore, who had insisted the ending to this book was feminist and raved about the genius of Edward Bell. I'd love to see the look on his face when he—and everyone—learned of the real ending. No shitty husbands to serve, just a woman and her cheese shop.

I checked my phone, scrolling through Malcolm's string of panicked texts to his last one, calmer in tone.

T.J. suggested Gabriela Reyes. She's a writer for the Baltimore Herald. He gave me her number. I played it very cool.

Proud of you, I replied. I just need to get Vernon on board first.

I joined Vernon in the living room and sat in the love seat, now partly occupied by a tabby that eyed me warily. Vernon, holding a puzzle piece and moving it around the border, finally found the spot he was looking for and snapped the piece into place.

"Can I borrow the manuscript?" I asked. "And the letters? I want to take them public. This is the proof we need."

Vernon glanced at me, then went back to sifting through puzzle pieces. "I don't know what you're expecting."

"Something. Anything. It's got to be better than sitting around waiting for Ralph to do god knows what. I'm sure he's plotting something." The first thing I'd done when I woke up that morning was check the Bell Society's website and social media to see if Ralph had issued a statement. He still hadn't. It only made me more uneasy, knowing he was up to something. For all I knew, he could have security camera footage of me trespassing and he might be at the police station right now filing charges against me. I wouldn't put anything past Ralph.

"Can I try?" I pressed. "I won't let anything happen to them."

He finally lifted his head, giving me a long, considering look. "Fine," he said. "But leave me out of it."

"Okay." Not being able to name my source might lessen my credibility, but there had to be enough, here in these pages, to prove Louise as the real author of Edward's novel.

I left Vernon to his puzzle, clutching the manuscript and letters tightly to my chest. This time, on my way out, I did pass the bookstore. I peered in through the window as I walked. Cynthia sat alone behind the counter, staring into nothing. She startled when she spotted me. I held her gaze until I passed the store. I couldn't get a read on her expression. I'd expected smugness, but I didn't see any. Just surprise, maybe curiosity.

I continued home with my chin high. She should be curious. Her time at the store might soon be up.

CHAPTER THIRTY-TWO

Gabriela Reyes agreed to meet Malcolm and me the next day. She offered to come to Bell River, mentioning that she was curious to visit the museum and see if any Bell Society employees would comment on the letter drama.

I expected she was in for a disappointment. The museum had gotten a slew of negative reviews in the last couple of days from people who were frustrated with the Bell Society's lack of response.

It wasn't just the museum, either. The café had gotten a negative review just that morning complaining that the apple cheddar biscuits had changed. Indeed, their picture showed that the biscuit was smaller, with no yellow flecks of cheddar and no visible pieces of diced apple. *It was flavorless*, they wrote. Abigail must not have shared her recipe with her coworkers.

Cracks were starting to show in the Bell Society's veneer. I hoped today's meeting with Gabriela would be the final push that sent the whole facade crumbling into ruin. Not too much ruin, I hoped, thinking of Rochelle, Abigail, Kat, and Malcolm. But just enough to convince Ralph to reinstate them and bring about some real change.

I gingerly placed Louise's manuscript and Edward's letters in my backpack. I zipped it up, then checked the time: half an hour until my meeting with Gabriela.

It only took ten minutes to walk to the Salty Skillet where we were meeting, but I slung the backpack over my shoulder and left early anyway. I couldn't keep refreshing the Bell Society's website waiting for word from Ralph.

The cold stung my cheeks, but I soldiered on. As I passed Wok House, I spotted a familiar figure sitting in a booth by the window, sipping tea with the same vacant stare I'd had when I sat there just a few days ago. I stopped in my tracks, watching him. Then I turned and went inside.

Ralph's brow furrowed when he saw me, but he didn't stop me from sliding into the seat across from him.

"What's brought you here?" he asked.

"I could ask the same of you."

"Just here for the lunch special." As if on cue, a server brought him a cup of soup and a spring roll. Ralph didn't make a move to touch either of them.

"You know, I came here earlier this week," I said. "When I was upset about getting my friends fired. You look sort of the way I did. Like you don't know what to do next."

Ralph lifted his gaze. I expected a denial, but he just picked up his spoon and started in on the soup. "I can't say I'm completely sure," he said.

My phone vibrated. I pulled it from my pocket, finding two texts from Malcolm.

I just got here.

Let me know when you arrive.

I checked the time. I still had ten minutes. I set my phone down and went back to watching Ralph. "Why?" I asked him.

"It's been my family's policy to…massage the details of Edward Bell's life," he said. "If they come across something that doesn't fit the vision they're selling, they burn it. Essays with racist viewpoints, burned. Evidence of his affairs, burned. By the time I came along, there wasn't anything left to burn. The archives were clean.

"But last year, when I was moving some things around in my study, I found those letters from Louise, hidden in a book. I knew I should burn them, but…" Ralph let his spoon drop in his soup and looked up with a sigh. "I couldn't. Burning a piece of history felt wrong. But I couldn't come forward, either. Two years ago, I sank everything I had into buying that B&B. My financial adviser told me not to, but…it seemed foolproof. I've turned every other business into a major tourist attraction. And I knew with that *First Dollar* movie adaptation coming out, a whole new surge of tourists would be coming to town. An Edward Bell–themed B&B, bigger and better than ever, would be a slam dunk. But then a producer backed out, and the whole thing fell apart." Ralph rubbed his forehead. "I've been trying to stay afloat ever since. I needed that deal with ByGone to keep us viable. Going public with those letters would ruin everything. So I locked them away and tried to forget about it. Until you found them," he said, cutting a glance at me.

"I've been going back and forth about what to do," he continued. "I don't want to deny it. But I don't see a way forward if I confirm it. No one's going to want to come to a museum about an author who stole the book he's famous for."

I ran my tongue along the underside of my teeth, the spark

of an idea coming to me. "They will if the museum's about who he stole it from."

"That wouldn't—"

"Louise's family could get some of the proceeds," I interrupted, speaking faster as the ideas came. "Imagine an exhibit dedicated to Louise and this scandal."

Ralph sighed and leaned back. "Who would come to see that? We'd be a laughingstock."

"Lots of people." I leaned forward, resting my elbows on the table. "You're sitting on one of the biggest literary scandals of the century. Look at how much uproar there's already been about this. People love drama."

Ralph tilted his head, thinking this through. "Even so," he said. "It's not practical. All I have are Louise's letters. I'm missing…everything else."

My phone vibrated. Malcolm again.

Gabriela's here. Where are you?

I glanced from my phone to Ralph, making a split-second decision. I moved his food to the side, then unzipped my backpack and placed its contents on the table with a heavy *thunk*.

"What is this?" Ralph said. His face went slack when he made out Edward Bell's name on the envelopes.

"It's everything else," I said. "Excuse me a minute." I called Malcolm. "Change of plans," I said when he answered. "Take Gabriela to the museum. Let her know we'll meet up with her after. Then come to Wok House. I'm here with Ralph. I've got a new plan."

"I—you—you're with *Ralph*?" Malcolm sputtered.

"I'll explain when you get here. Just trust me." I regretted the words as soon as I said them. I'd already held and broken Malcolm's trust once before. The pause at the other end of the line told me he was thinking the exact same thing. "Please," I added.

"Okay," Malcolm said quietly. "I'll be there soon."

I hung up, then stared at my phone. My pulse was racing. There was one more thing I needed to do.

"Do you have Vernon's number?" I asked Ralph.

Hardly taking his eyes off the manuscript, Ralph picked up his phone and scrolled through his contacts for Vernon, then handed it to me. I pressed the Call button and held it to my ear. Vernon struck me as the sort of person who didn't answer calls from unknown numbers. Though considering the low regard he had for Ralph, maybe it was a toss-up either way.

"Yes?" Vernon answered in a gruff voice.

"It's Maggie," I said. "I'm at Wok House with Ralph. I need you to meet us here now."

"You're involving me, aren't you?"

"Yes. But you'll like it. Probably."

Vernon hung up without giving a definitive answer. The equivalent of a door slam. I handed the phone back to Ralph, who was now eyeing me with suspicion. "What's going on?" he asked.

"We'll find out," I said, almost breathless. Ralph fixed me with a probing gaze, but he returned to examining the papers before him. And I, feeling like a solution was in sight, picked up his spring roll and took a bite. Now all there was left to do was wait.

CHAPTER THIRTY-THREE

Within ten minutes, we were all assembled. Vernon and I sat on one side of the booth, Ralph and Malcolm in the other. Ralph watched me curiously. Vernon was giving Ralph a surly snarl. Malcolm was eyeing the papers on the table.

"I really don't think these should be sitting on a restaurant table like this," Malcolm said, picking up the stacks. "That can't be good for them."

"You can put them in here." I handed him my backpack across the table. The bottom of the bag grazed my water glass, nearly toppling it over.

"See?!" Malcolm clutched the papers closer to his chest.

"Oh, it's fine," I said. Malcolm tucked them into my backpack, zipped it shut, and set it next to him. "Happy now?" I asked.

Malcolm patted the backpack. "Yes."

"Can you tell me now what this is all about?" Ralph said.

I tapped my fingers on the table, trying to think of where to begin. "Malcolm and I were going to meet with a reporter from the *Baltimore Herald* today," I said. "We were going to show her the manuscript and letters as proof that Edward Bell stole Louise's book. You weren't saying anything, so we were going to take matters into our own hands."

"Okay," Ralph said, giving Malcolm a sidelong glance. Malcolm pretended not to notice.

"But then I realized there might be another way." I took a drink of water, then looked around the table. "Ralph. Would you be willing to revamp the museum? Dedicate space to Louise and the truth about the novel she wrote? If we provided you with the manuscript and letters to display?"

"I suppose," he said slowly.

"Would you publish the original manuscript Louise wrote—in Louise's name—and make sure Louise's family gets the proceeds? Of not just book royalties, but anything the Bell Society does that has anything to do with *The First Dollar*?"

A measured pause. "Yes," Ralph said. "I'd also like to step down as director of the Bell Society."

I wavered, sure I must have misheard. "What?" I'd been building to asking Ralph if he would cede control, but I hadn't expected him to volunteer it. Even Malcolm and Vernon turned to Ralph in surprise.

"It's better for optics," he said, like it was obvious. "No one's going to support the Bell Society if it's run by the family that's been covering up for Edward Bell. If we get someone from Louise's family on board, people would flock to us. I would still be involved in some capacity, of course. I did expand the business into what it is today," he reminded me, his tone haughty. "But this would be a good move to maximize profits going forward."

I refrained from rolling my eyes. Of course for Ralph this comes back to money.

"Vernon," I said, leaning forward to catch his eye, "would you like to be the new director of the Bell Society?"

Ralph pulled back, looking back and forth between the two of us. "What does Vernon have to do with it?"

"He's Louise's grandson."

"*What*?" Ralph turned to Vernon, agape.

Vernon ignored him, watching me with a thoughtful expression. "I'll do it," he said. "As long as I don't have to do too much."

"I'm sure you and Ralph can work out the specifics of your role," I said. "But a few questions for you. In your capacity as director, will you hire back the people Ralph fired? Rochelle at the bookstore, Abigail at the Sunrise Café, Kat and her coworkers at the B&B, Malcolm at the main office? And send Cynthia back to the museum?"

"Done," he said. His gaze shifted to me for just a moment. "I'd want you at the bookstore, too. I've seen what you can do."

I smiled, but he was staring straight ahead. Understandable. Vernon couldn't possibly make eye contact when he complimented me. All the affection would make him implode.

Despite the compliment, I felt jumbled inside. I loved the idea of continuing the events, but the thought of working at the bookstore full-time—standing around day in and day out watching customers quietly browse, really just marking time between events—gave me that same hollow feeling I had at the thought of working at Barnes and Noble. People livened it up sometimes, like when Evelyn, Dahlia, and Abigail came around to read and work, but imagining the influx of literary tourists who would want to come and talk about books made my eyes glaze over.

"I don't know if I'd want to work at the bookstore full-time," I said. "I like doing the events, but the everyday stuff—"

Vernon waved a hand in the air. "Then you could work part-time at the bookstore running events, and the rest of the time you can be my liaison. Be me when I don't want to deal with people. Which is often."

"Really?" I ran a finger over my lip, thinking. "So I could work with the other Bell Society businesses?" I liked the sound of it the more it sat with me. "I could help them loosen Ralph's restrictions. They could come to me if they have any problems, and anything I couldn't solve, I could take to you." I sat up suddenly when another thought occurred to me. "And I could put on even bigger events—like a town-wide book festival, celebrating authors like Louise whose voices weren't heard. Authors who have been silenced, or whose books have been banned."

"I like that idea," Malcolm said, a smile curling his mouth.

"Great. I'll see if Riverside Dental's parking lot is free. Kidding," I added when his eyes widened. "But I'm serious about the festival. That could bring in a lot of tourists. And I throw an excellent holiday party," I slipped in.

Vernon chuckled. "Works for me." He tossed me a shrewd glance, and I realized he knew exactly what he was doing by appointing me liaison. Something like purpose ballooned in my chest.

"You can't just hire people willy-nilly," Ralph said, pressing a finger to his temple. "There's a budget."

"Liaison, deal with the budget," Vernon said.

"Roger that." I looked around the table. Ralph seemed resigned. Vernon was watching him with a satisfied smirk. Malcolm was lost in thought, staring out the window. "I think we have a deal," I said. "Everyone agreed?"

"Yes," Ralph said.

"Yes," Vernon said.

"No."

We all turned to Malcolm. He tore his gaze from the window. "I appreciate that you thought of me," he said. "But…I've been working here for ten years. I think I'm ready to move on. And I got what I wanted. The Bell Society will be taking a more critical look at Edward Bell and carrying books by more than old, dead white people, right?"

"We carry more than that," Ralph protested. "We have Frederick Douglass, and Harriet Jacobs, and—"

"Yes," Vernon interrupted, giving Malcolm a meaningful look. "No restrictions whatsoever in the bookstore. Or in any other business." Ralph grumbled but didn't disagree.

"Then I think it's time for me to move on to something else," Malcolm said. "Start a life of my own." He caught my eye across the table, his mouth pulling into a small smile.

A sliver of hope tentatively stirred in me as I recognized the words I'd said to him in this very restaurant just a few days ago. My tone had been heated then, accusatory enough to make him flare up and fire back. But now he just looked at me as if those same words had set him free.

"Hey," I said, turning to Vernon. "We're down an employee. I dealt with the budget."

Vernon gave me a thumbs-up. Ralph groaned.

Malcolm's phone rang. He answered it, then caught my eye. "Gabriela's done at the museum," he said. "What's happening? Are we meeting her here?"

I glanced at Ralph. "Are you ready to make a statement to a reporter from the *Baltimore Herald* about the changes the Bell Society is making?" Ralph nodded. I turned to Malcolm. "Tell her to come over."

In our crowded booth, Gabriela took copious notes and asked questions, most of them directed at Ralph. He got the hard-hitters about his family's dishonest past and his role in shaping Edward Bell's fabricated legacy. I got to answer questions about the Bell Society's plans for the future. I started off speaking with a tentative hopefulness, but as Gabriela nodded and kept writing, I spoke with more confidence, feeling like our new venture just might work.

By the time Gabriela left, it was late afternoon and we were all drained. Malcolm was leaning his head against the back of the booth, Ralph had taken off his glasses and was rubbing his eyes, and Vernon was staring longingly out the window like he could hardly remember a life outside the confines of this booth.

"I'll be going now," Vernon announced. He stood, then gave us an expectant look. "I'd like my grandmother's documents."

"They're going to the museum." Ralph finished cleaning his glasses with the bottom of his shirt and put them back on.

"The museum can have them once we've drawn up the paperwork. I don't want you running off and burning them. I know your family has a history of that."

Ralph glared at Vernon with an intensity that almost rivaled Vernon's scowls. Something occurred to me just then and I laughed. They both turned to me.

"You're related," I realized. "Your grandmothers were cousins. Which makes you..."

"First cousins...twice removed?" Malcolm said. "Don't quote me on that. But I was actually thinking something else. What are the odds that Vernon's a descendant of Edward Bell, too? Louise had her first kid the year after she and Edward cut things off.

What if Edward let Vernon's mother live above the bookstore rent-free because he thought she was his daughter?"

"As a rule, I don't think about that," Vernon huffed. "My papers." He held out an arm. Malcolm handed him my backpack, and Vernon turned for the exit. Ralph trailed after him, blathering about paperwork.

Left alone with Malcolm, I caught his eye across the table and he smiled just because. I relaxed into the booth, starting to feel like we might be finding our footing.

"Vernon stole my backpack," I said.

"I'm sure you'll see it again." He kept staring at me, half-smiling, not seeming to want to look away. "So you got your revolution," he said.

I beamed. "I did. You helped."

"Marginally."

"And you're starting a life of your own, huh? How does that feel?"

He laughed and ran a hand over his locs. "Bizarre. But in a good way. I think." He lifted his gaze to meet mine. "I was thinking of maybe moving to DC."

"Really?"

"There are plenty of government jobs there. I think I'd be good at something like that, where there's lots of rules and order. And, I don't know. A city might be a nice change of pace. I guess thanks to your assignments, I've seen a lot of what life outside Bell River has to offer."

"Imagine that," I said, pride and wonder touching my voice. "Hey, maybe you and Hal can be roomies. Hal and Mal. It could be a sitcom."

"Hal lives in Franklin," he corrected me. "But we are getting brunch this weekend," he mumbled.

"New city, new bestie, new you," I said. "And your grandma will be okay when you move out?"

"Yeah, she's been trying to get me to move out for years."

"So you admit it?"

He exhaled in a reluctant chuckle. "I still think she could use the help. But she's always telling me she's got other people she can rely on here. And I'd live close enough to visit. Her and you," he added. "Congrats on the new job."

"Thanks." It was still hard to believe that in an afternoon I'd gone from jobless with no prospects to getting a job that might actually work for me. A job where my duties primarily involved fun and people. "You should come to the next event," I told him.

"I wouldn't miss it." He smiled and shook his head, his eyes still on me.

"What?"

"I was just thinking about how none of this would have happened without you. And I'm sorry for what I said the last time we were here. I know you think things through."

"I often don't," I admitted.

"But you do in your own way. I think in straight lines, you know? You think in...I don't even know. Zigzags and diagonals. What you did today, changing the plan at the last minute and bringing us all together like this? I never could have done that."

His words reverberated through me, making me almost light-headed. "I'm sorry about what I said, too," I said. "And I'm proud of you for starting a life of your own."

"I know," he said. "Thank you." He lifted his water glass. "To the next chapter."

I lifted my own and clinked it against his. "To the next chapter."

Malcolm took a drink, then looked at me over the top of his glass. "Speaking of, you never read *The Grapes of Wrath*, did you? You still have to. I did the painting class and the pumpkin hockey. It's only fair."

"Bad news, unfortunately. Our club has been dissolved."

"I don't think that's something you can decide."

"I decided it with my zigzag thinking, which we've established is superior to yours, so..." I shrugged. "My hands are tied."

Malcolm rolled his eyes with a laugh. "What'll we do now that we don't have a club?"

"I guess we'll have to stop hiding behind the club and date each other for real."

He grinned. "I think that can be arranged. What do you say we zigzag to DC for dinner tonight? Celebrate your new job, my unemployment?"

I returned his smile, feeling warm and floaty all over. "It's a date."

CHAPTER THIRTY-FOUR

I'd thrown more elaborate holiday parties, but I was impressed with myself for putting this one together in three weeks.

The B&B's sitting room and lobby had been transformed. Garlands wrapped around the banister and framed the mantel above the roaring fireplace. About a third of the lights strung around the tree in the corner—a fake, pre-lit cast-off I'd found in Rochelle's garage—were dead, but I couldn't tell when I squinted. Past the plates of cookies and snacks, the eggnog and sodas, and the table where I acted as bartender, Bell Society employees stood talking and mingling while holiday music played softly in the background.

Abigail and Vernon stood talking by the staircase. She'd removed the more disgusting items Ralph had insisted upon putting on the café's menu—the apple cheddar biscuits, thankfully, still remained—but she was still working through the best way to add a literary bent to the remaining items since it was, after all, still a Bell Society business. Her latest idea involved adding menu items inspired by the authors themselves. I knew she'd been waiting for a chance to corner Vernon to ask about Louise's favorite foods. Watching them talk now, Abigail nodding and taking notes on her phone while Vernon spoke, I imagined she'd be busy testing recipes for the next few weeks.

"Hey, bartender." Rochelle approached the table, looking festive in a red sweater and dangly earrings.

"Hey, coworker." Just saying it brought a smile to my face. I still couldn't believe I was going to get to work with my best friend when she came back to the bookstore in the new year. "Can I get you anything?"

"No. The maple bourbon smash is living up to its name." She held up a clear plastic cup, still half-filled with orangish-brown liquid.

"Lightweight." I picked up my own drink, a cranberry gin thing I'd been experimenting with, and took a sip. I'd need to go lighter on the lemon juice next time.

"I haven't drank in a while!" she protested. She took a small sip. "It's good, though. Can you make this at the January event?"

I grinned and nodded. We'd talked about planning a bookstore event in late January. Cathy Larson put me in touch with a horror writer who was eager to put her own spin on *The Scarlet Letter*. We were still working out dates, but I was hopeful we'd have the event page up and running for registration soon. I couldn't wait to show Malcolm how much fun these events were. It was what I was proudest of doing in my time here. Although, I thought, looking around the room, this too—a gathering of Bell Society employees who I'd like to think were much happier with their jobs now that Ralph had ceded control—was something to be proud of.

I wouldn't have to put a cap on attendance anymore, either. When I'd mentioned that holding events at Vernon's apartment wasn't great for growth, Kat told me the B&B often rented out their great hall for functions—or they used to, until Ralph took over and ordered that the great hall serve as yet another Edward Bell shrine. But now we were free to do as we pleased, and that included holding a horror-themed *Scarlet Letter* event at the B&B. I was still planning to use the bookstore for smaller gatherings, like book clubs. But with the spacious B&B as our venue, we could expand our events to include other activities— book-themed dinner parties, literary trivia nights, bookish murder mystery games. Our events roster was shaping up to be busy but full of fun.

Kat joined me behind the makeshift bar, bumping me with her hip. "You're free. Go mingle."

"Thanks." I picked up my too-lemony cocktail and surveyed the room. "Have you seen my date?"

Rochelle pointed behind her. I looked over her shoulder and laughed when I saw him. Malcolm sat on a couch in the middle of the lobby, buried in a book. Some things never change.

I weaved through the room, pausing when I made eye contact with Cynthia. She smiled tentatively. I returned it with a nod and kept moving. Cynthia was helping out at the bookstore while I was occupied with my liaison duties, but she'd be going back to the museum when Rochelle returned in January. I had to admit that it wasn't bad having Cynthia around now that I didn't have to hide anything from her. Along with Rochelle, Malcolm, and Evelyn, Cynthia was helping me refine the list of books we were going to start carrying in the store. She'd also been updating me on the museum's efforts to rework their exhibits so that the centerpiece was Louise, her life, her influences, the book she wrote, and how Edward Bell stole it from her. Edward Bell's part of the museum would now be an afterthought: a thief, the book he stole, and then the books he didn't steal, none of which were nearly as popular or beloved as Louise's.

I passed Abigail, who was still cornering Vernon. Noticing the way his gaze was trained on the front door, I sidled up next to them.

"How are we doing over here?" I asked.

"Vernon says Louise loved pineapple upside-down cake," she said. "We're just trying to nail down a date when I can bring over some samples and do a tasting, but his schedule's pretty packed."

I glanced at Vernon. The plastic cup in his hand was empty, and only crumbs remained on his paper plate. I'd used the promise of good food to lure him here, but I'd also guaranteed an easy escape.

"I can set that up," I told Abigail. "Vernon, your meeting starts in ten minutes."

"Guess I'll be going." Vernon gave us a parting nod. I caught a twinkle in his eye just before he turned and headed for the door.

"He has a meeting at four forty-three on a Friday?" Abigail said dryly.

"Yep." I swirled my drink and took a sip. When I noticed Abigail's skeptical expression, I burst into laughter.

"I hate you both," she said.

"Just doing my job."

Vernon had, indeed, instructed me to get him out of any meetings or conversations that didn't interest him, by any means necessary. Last week, when a transition meeting in Ralph's office had gone long, I'd popped my head in the door and told Vernon he was needed at a fishing tournament in Australia. Vernon got up without a word, and I'd returned Ralph's frown with a polite smile. Finding absurd ways to get Vernon out of things was a definite highlight of my new job.

After setting a date for a cake tasting with Abigail, I entered it into my calendar app, then swiped ahead to next month, which was riddled with to-dos and reminders. The weeks leading up to the grand reopening of the revamped bookstore and museum in late January would be busy. I'd taken over the Bell Society's social media to build up hype for our changes, capitalizing on the interest we'd gotten since Gabriela's article published. We'd begun selling advance tickets online for people who wanted to be the first to see the new museum on opening day. If these ticket sales were any indication, there was more interest in Bell River now than ever before. Kat told me the B&B was booked solid in January and February. We wouldn't be able to afford those promised renovations anytime soon, but we were hiring two new staff at the B&B. A few more months like this and we might even afford to bring the B&B staff back to full capacity. Between my plans for the bookstore and this increase in tourism, I was starting to think we'd be just fine without ByGone.

I passed through a group of museum employees and plopped down on the couch next to Malcolm, who shut his book. "Hey," he said, throwing an arm around my shoulders. "Great party."

"That doesn't mean much coming from the person who's reading through it."

"This is a compliment. If I hated it, I would have left."

I laughed. "High praise."

"I wanted to give you something." He reached down and picked up a small plastic bag sitting at his feet. "I didn't wrap it, but I got you a Christmas present."

"Christmas isn't for another few days," I said.

Malcolm had already invited me to spend the holiday with him and his grandmother. When I'd told my parents, my mom had responded, Sounds serious, followed by a bride emoji. I might have taken issue with that suggestion a few months back—seen it as a reminder that I would never be on the path they wanted me to follow, that I'd always be miles behind everyone else, no clearly defined career, no husband, no kids. But this time I'd just rolled my eyes and laughed. I was going at my own pace. I liked my pace.

I took the bag from him, reading the text on it with disdain. "Barnes and Noble? You can't even support your girlfriend's independent bookstore?"

"Let me know when your new stock comes in and I'll support you all day long. Until then, yes, Barnes and Noble."

I laughed and reached into the bag. I pulled out a book with a bright yellow cover, showing two women eyeing one another suspiciously.

"I know Evelyn didn't write it, but it's pretty good," he said.

I looked up. "You read a rom-com on your own? And you're recommending it?" When he nodded, I asked, "Have I expanded your reading horizons?"

Malcolm tried for a straight face, but his eyes were glinting. "My horizons were fine before."

"But now they're bigger? Broader? More expansive?"

"They may be a little bigger," he said, breaking into a smile.

I set the book in my lap. "I got you something, too."

"You did?"

"Yeah. I don't have it on me, but it's another one of Evelyn's romances."

"Really?" Malcolm narrowed his eyes.

"It's set in the kitchen of a high-end restaurant that's struggling to stay open, and it gets bought out by a chain, who sends a woman there to make the restaurant appeal to a wider audience, which pisses off the snobby chef who works there, and obviously shenanigans ensue." I paused to take a breath and registered Malcolm's bewilderment.

"I just thought that since I got you a romance, maybe we were doing the thing where we picked a book to suit the other's tastes, maybe on account of our changing horizons," Malcolm said.

"We're not," I said. "My horizons have always been perfect." At this Malcolm fixed me with a pointed stare I couldn't help but laugh at.

"Can't wait to read it," he said, with only slight insincerity in his voice. He laced his fingers through mine. "Are you ready for tomorrow? Nine apartments, four cities? Last chance to reschedule."

Malcolm and I had agreed to help each other in our respective searches for an apartment—me in Bell River, him in a few cities within commuting distance of the admin job he'd managed to secure in DC. He'd taken me up on my ridiculous idea to schedule everything for the same day and get all the apartment hunting out of the way at once.

"No way. It'll be an adventure." The word struck a chord in me the moment I said it. I let it roll around in my head, considered the way it felt on my tongue.

Adventure, that's what it was. Not a plan. Plans were malleable, less certain. They were made with the understanding that nothing was definite.

But when I fill the bookstore with all the books we never

got to sell before, when Rochelle and I cohost our first event together next month, when I work with Abigail and Kat and the other Bell Society employees to implement their ideas, when I start planning the book festival, when Malcolm and I spend tomorrow racing around the DMV area touring apartments that held possibility and promise, it *will* be an adventure. One tailored to me instead of trying to squeeze myself into whatever situation would have me.

I wouldn't assign it a number, a letter, or anything that implied it was one of many. I would call it what it was. Something new. Something good. Something *me*.

Adventure.

READ ON
FOR AN EXCERPT OF

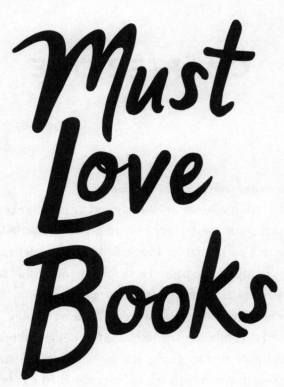

Must Love Books

BY SHAUNA ROBINSON

Meet Nora Hughes—the overworked, underpaid, last bookish assistant standing. At least for now.

CHAPTER ONE

Would you recommend this job to a friend?

The question echoed in Nora's mind as the silence ticked by. She glanced from the twenty-two-year-old girl across from her to the résumé on the table. Large, bold letters spelled out *Kelly Brown* at the top of the page. Nora folded and unfolded a corner of the paper as she tried to think of a response.

Recommend was a strong word. There were a lot of people Nora would recommend the job to. She thought about the man on her commute that morning, dozing with his legs spread wide enough to occupy two seats while Nora clutched a pole and practiced her resentful stare. She'd recommend the job to him any day. She'd recommend it like a curse.

But *friend*, that was the kicker. Nora lifted her eyes. Kelly's lips were curved in a trusting smile. She held her pen over her legal pad, ready to write down whatever tumbled out of Nora's mouth.

It was nonsense, frankly, that Nora was interviewing someone. This girl was interviewing for the same job title as Nora: Editorial Assistant of MBB. Meaningless Business Bullshit. Not the official title, but at this point Nora couldn't be bothered to remember the exact jargon. Either way, as a mere publishing peasant, Nora had no standing to interview a potential peer.

Nora did have seniority, she supposed, looking down at the résumé and seeing that Kelly graduated from college just this month, five years after Nora. That made five years of wisdom Nora had over Kelly, in theory—except Nora spent all five of those years here, as an editorial assistant, with no promotion in sight. There was nothing wise about that. Nothing to recommend there. Not without lying—and she wasn't sure she was okay with that.

Nora darted another glance Kelly's way. Kelly, by this point, was now politely looking around the room, taking interest in the blank walls, as if there was a greater chance of the beige paint answering her question before Nora did.

"Yes," Nora said slowly, stretching out the word as though it would precede a speech full of encouragement and experience. But now she'd kept her waiting, and it would be weird to end on her very long *yes*, so speech time it was.

"As long as you know what you're getting yourself into," Nora continued. "I mean, I've been here almost five years and I love it"—huh, so she *was* okay with lying, apparently—"but you have to be willing to adapt. Your responsibilities might change, or your title, or your boss. If you're okay with things changing on you, you should be fine. People are so friendly here," she added, wanting to end on a positive note.

Kelly nodded and wrote something down. Nora peered at the paper, imagining what the notes might say. *Took five minutes to answer one question. Shady as hell.*

When Kelly had no further questions to fluster Nora with, Nora escorted her to the next interviewer to continue the charade. On the walk to her desk, she replayed the interview in her head.

Whenever Nora mentioned anything to do with publishing—manuscripts, books, working with authors—there was a faraway look in Kelly's eyes, like she was on the verge of swooning.

And Nora didn't blame her. With an English degree and a love of books, she was just like Nora had been—just like everyone who came to work at Parsons Press. Even in Nora's interview five years ago, she remembered only half-listening to her interviewer as her mind played a montage of what it would be like to get paid to publish books.

It was a dream come true, wasn't it? Her childhood spent smuggling books and cracking covers everywhere she went—at the dinner table, in the lunch line, occasionally in the shower—felt like practice for a career in books. And when she spotted the listing for a publishing internship during her sophomore year of college, it was like a beacon pointing the way to her future. She'd clicked on it immediately, hope rising in her chest as she read the job responsibilities referencing authors and manuscripts. And the final line under the desired skills and qualifications section sealed her fate, three little words that curled around Nora's heart and told her she belonged in publishing: *Must love books*.

Three words was all it took for Nora to start spinning fantasies of her life in publishing. She imagined talking to the authors she'd admired as a kid, shyly asking Judy Blume to sign her tattered copy of *Just as Long as We're Together*. Talking through the changes Judy needed to make to her latest manuscript. Shaping books readers might cling to, the same way Nora clutched her own books like a lifeline. When it sometimes felt, growing up, that books were her only friends, the thought of being an editor and connecting books to those lonely and quiet readers like herself made Nora feel like she could be part of something magnificent.

Magnificent was another strong word. She didn't realize, then, how misguided her fantasies were. Not only was Nora laughably far from being an editor, but all her division published were business books that made her eyes glaze over.

Nora tried making it clear in the interview that Kelly could expect to work on only business books, but Kelly was too dazzled by the publishing fantasy to let the words sink in. And Nora, tired and drained and utterly dazzle-free against Kelly's faraway eyes, was once again reminded of two certainties: One, Parsons Press was no dream job. Two, she needed to get out.

Nora checked the time. Five minutes until Beth's goodbye party, and she hadn't even started setting up yet. She hurried to the office kitchenette and got to work, opening the cabinet, grabbing wine bottles by their necks, and hauling them to the board room. She noticed, rummaging through the cabinets, that they were out of plastic cups. Nora opened the first cabinet again, looked behind the stacks of shrink-wrapped paper plates and napkins. No cups.

Well, they could drink from the bottle.

She kept an eye on the boardroom's glass walls while wrestling the lid off the cheese platter. She spotted Beth—or, specifically, Beth's forehead and a hint of ruffled brown hair as someone leaned down to hug her. Beth was five feet tall, and Nora knew she hated hugs from tall people. Beth smoothed down her hair and got swept into another hug a few seconds later. It was no surprise she was so surrounded. People had been surrounding Beth for the last two weeks. Offering congratulations. Sharing memories. Wishing her well.

Nora swallowed her jealousy and carried the platter to the

boardroom. She edged closer to the conversation Beth was having with their IT administrator.

"Oh, I don't know anyone there," Beth said. "I haven't started yet."

"Well, if you run into a Bill Davis, tell him I said hi."

"Will do!"

Maybe that was why Beth got out and Nora didn't. Beth was so kind. And happy. People liked happy people. More importantly, people hired happy people. But Nora couldn't stop herself from thinking how silly it sounded, that Beth would run into Bill Davis at her new job one day and take the time to deliver a meaningless message on behalf of someone she'd likely never see again. She'd probably do it, too. Nora would have deleted the mental message immediately.

By this time, Joe and Beth had finished talking, giving Nora a chance to sidle up to her before anyone else could treat her like a carrier pigeon.

"I thought he hated me," Beth murmured once he was out of earshot.

Nora watched him cross the room to the wine table. "Maybe he forgot."

"That I got a computer virus from torrenting *Seinfeld* at work?"

Nora laughed. Beth grinned back at her, but Nora remembered when Beth came to her desk, wide-eyed and frantic. She remembered how they stood in Beth's cubicle, watching the pop-ups flash on her screen. It was almost cute how they'd worried, then, that she might get in trouble. They spent two hours deliberating the pros and cons of telling IT, but in the end, Joe just sighed and told Beth to drop off her laptop and pick up a loaner. That was their first inkling that maybe no one gave a shit.

That feeling only grew when executives at the Parsons Press headquarters in New York started dropping ominous hints about a restructuring plan "coming down the pipeline." During that hazy six-month period before the plan was revealed, everyone let loose a little. Nora took a later train to work, coming in at 9:15 instead of 8:55. Beth moved on to torrenting *Arrested Development*. They both started job hunting.

"You'll have to top that one," Beth said, evoking the future tense with impossible ease.

"Who will I tell?"

Beth blinked. "Me."

"Will I?"

She gave Nora a gentle, patient stare. "We'll still see each other. We'll still text. You're not getting rid of me."

"You're right," Nora said, knowing they could debate this forever, Beth with her optimism and Nora with her everything. She shoved a grape in her mouth to keep from casting any more gloom on the occasion.

It wasn't a big deal that Beth was leaving, she told herself. It wasn't even the first time Beth had set her sights on something new. Nora and Beth may have started out as editorial assistants together, but two years in, Beth ditched the editorial dream and forged a new path for herself.

Like Nora, Beth grew tired of the administrative work that came with editorial. Being an editorial assistant wasn't reading manuscripts and being captivated by prose like Nora had imagined. It was repeatedly reminding authors of deadlines, wrestling with Microsoft Word to format manuscripts, and forwarding those formatted manuscripts to her bosses. The actual interesting parts—reading projects, making suggestions for improvement, working alongside authors—Nora and Beth never had a hand in.

While Nora gritted her teeth and continued on, willing to pay any price to become an editor, Beth applied for a marketing coordinator job on their team. It gave Beth a new challenge, something else to explore and master. And now Beth and her roving eye had landed a sales job at an app development start-up.

Nora poured some of—whatever this was, from the bottle beside her—into her Parsons Press mug as Beth looked on.

"My mug is in my cubicle," Beth said, a touch of longing in her voice.

"Oh, you thought there would be cups?" Nora handed Beth her mug. "At a party?" She frowned a little to sell it.

Beth laughed and brought the mug to her lips. "Stupid, I know. I don't know what I was thinking."

Nora cracked a smile. "This way's probably better. Gives us more opportunities to *innovate*."

Beth made gagging noises at the buzzword and Nora laughed. Her smile faded as she surveyed the room. People stood in clusters holding plates and mugs, talking and laughing. All clusters she'd never been part of. Beth was her cluster.

"It'll be weird being here without you," Nora said.

"And with our anniversary coming up, too."

Nora nodded, staring into the mug Beth handed back to her. She and Beth had started on the same day, sharing embarrassed smiles about feeling overdressed that first morning, all blazers and dress pants in a sea of slouchy tops and jeans. Then Beth rolled her chair to Nora's desk ten minutes after their debrief with HR, navy blazer flung over her chair like an afterthought, asking how many allowances to claim on her W-4.

On the anniversary of their first year at Parsons, they each got a generic card from HR. Beth had peeked her head over the wall of Nora's cube and wished her a happy work friendiversary. The tradition had continued each year. Nora tried not to think about her five-year anniversary a few months away. There would be no one to celebrate with this time around.

"You okay?" Beth asked, peering closer at Nora.

Nora blinked her thoughts away. "Yeah." She forced a smile. "I'm excited for you."

"I'm excited for *you*," Beth insisted, making Nora's heart swell with appreciation. Only Beth could spend her own good-bye party hyping up someone else. "You've got that BookTap interview next week, right?"

"Yeah." Nora tried to mirror Beth's hopeful tone. She'd been thrilled to see the marketing specialist job listing for BookTap a few weeks ago. Parsons Press may have jaded her view of publishing, but she couldn't find it in herself to completely give up the chance to work with books. BookTap was another opportunity—a good one. Nora actually enjoyed using BookTap's app to rate and review books and see what others were reading. Beth, for instance, gave *Red Velvet Revenge* five stars yesterday (but Beth gave everything five stars).

Nora had made it through the phone screen and past the assessment assignment, which she still thought of with pride. In it, she'd managed to make steampunk sound interesting, which made her both brilliant and generous. Now all she had to do was make a good impression at the in-person interview next week.

But with Beth leaving, everything felt more urgent. Parsons was only bearable because of Beth. If she left—and if Nora didn't get the job at BookTap—Nora didn't want to think about where that would leave her.

Beth seemed to pick up on Nora's uncertainty, maybe from the way Nora plunked her head on Beth's shoulder. "It'll go great," she said.

Nora nodded, deciding not to disagree. Then someone else came to steal Beth, and Nora was left alone. She nibbled on a piece of not-sharp-enough cheddar and watched Beth laugh with someone from accounting.

Nora had known from her first day that Parsons Press wasn't what it used to be. This whale of a company had been around since the 1800s, since Dickens and Brontë and Poe—not that Parsons ever published anything that interesting. Parsons did publish Mark Twain's first novel, *The Gilded Age*, though no one Nora knew had ever read or heard of it. They hadn't published his other works, certainly nothing as beloved as *Adventures of Huckleberry Finn*. Which seemed like a bit of an oversight on the part of that particular acquisitions editor, Nora thought.

But still, Parsons was around during that time. She hadn't cared, at first, that Parsons only published nonfiction now, or that her division published business books teeming with snappy buzzwords: *synergy*, *leverage*, *disruptor*. Nora planned to use the position as a stepping-stone to the San Francisco office's more compelling divisions, like cooking, travel, or current events.

But the New York execs saw fit to cut these divisions before Nora could defect. The restructuring plan followed, aptly named the Disrupt, Innovate, and Change plan, or DIC for short. While Nora and Beth cheerfully referred to this as the DIC(k) plan, joking that it was Parsons's dickish alternative to a 401(k), the changes it wrought took a toll. Some employees were promoted into new roles, but others, like Nora's bosses, lost their jobs. What remained of Nora's team merged with another under-staffed division, and they were expected to publish the same number of business books with half the employees to maximize profits. Meanwhile, going-away parties like Beth's had become near-constant attractions in the Parsons boardroom.

After the party came to a close, Nora watched Beth empty her drawers in the eerie, quiet office and wondered when it would be her turn to leave Parsons behind. She accepted the cardboard box Beth handed her, and they each carried a box of Beth's belong-ings on their way to the elevator. As she walked, Nora peered into the box in her arms. She recognized the first Parsons book that mentioned Beth in the acknowledgments and birthday cards Nora remembered signing, but it was the pink hedgehog pencil holder that brought a rush of nostalgic joy. Beth threw away a lot of office tchotchkes tonight, but this present Nora gave her two years ago, now dotted with ink from Beth and her careless pens, had made the cut.

They sat side by side on BART, discussing books as the train hummed along. She listened to Beth rant about how Shirley Jackson's books didn't get the attention they deserved. When Beth asked Nora what she was reading, she pulled *Kindred* out of her purse, as if that answered the question. As Nora tucked the book into her bag, she caught the way Beth nodded a beat too long, knew Beth was too polite to ask why Nora had been stuck on the same book for over a month when she was used to Nora reading a book a week.

The dreaded moment came. The train sped away from 12th Street, giving them only seconds until Beth's stop at 19th. Beth stood and Nora followed suit, her head still buzzy with wine from the party as she tried to think of the perfect parting words. The well-wishes she wrote in others' goodbye cards sounded so superficial now.

Mind spinning, Nora gave a small half smile and said, "I love you."

She felt exposed, saying it. There was an implied distance in work friendships. But it was so plainly true that Nora couldn't *not* say it.

Beth didn't show any surprise, just said, "I love you too." Like it was fact. As the train slowed, Beth set her box down on her seat, Nora did the same, and Beth pulled her in for a hug.

Nora let her chin rest on Beth's shoulder. They stepped back when the doors opened. Beth picked up the two stacked boxes, grinned at Nora, and stepped off the train.

Passengers elbowed their way past Nora on their way in. She moved aside. The seats she and Beth had sat in less than a minute ago were already taken.

Nora braced herself against a pole, thinking of what tomorrow would bring. It was bad enough that an important author was coming to the office the next day. Worse that Nora would have to plaster a smile on her face to serve sandwiches at a meeting she wasn't invited to. But getting through it alone, without a friend to commiserate with, might be the worst part. The train sped onward as Nora stared mindlessly ahead, already dreading work tomorrow.

READING GROUP GUIDE

1. Maggie is passionate about things that have nothing to do with her work. What do you feel passionate about? Is it related to your career?

2. Outline the similarities and differences between Maggie and her best friend, Rochelle. Why do you think they get along so well?

3. Design your own silly bookish event. What book would you choose, and why?

4. Discuss all the ways Ralph's strict rules are so detrimental.

5. Maggie finds herself stuck between a rock and a hard place when she discovers Edward Bell's dark secret. Put yourself in her shoes: Would you reveal it, even though it could mean ruining Bell River?

6. Describe Malcolm. What motivates him?

7. Maggie and many people in her book club admit to not loving the classics, but they *do* love genre fiction. What's your favorite book? Do you consider it a classic?

8. Explain Vernon's involvement with the town's legacy in the past and moving forward.

9. Think about the pressure Maggie feels to follow the typical life plan (graduate from college, land a dream job, get married, etc.). Have you ever felt pressure to fulfill others' expectations?

10. What do you think is the most important lesson Maggie learns by the end of the book?

A CONVERSATION WITH THE AUTHOR

What inspired this story?

I love books set in bookstores. I also love chaos. I wanted to read a book about an unlikely bookstore employee—someone who doesn't enjoy reading and who gets into mischief when she starts skirting the absurd rules that make her job difficult.

Maggie simply doesn't feel passionate about any career path. Why did you decide to make this such an integral part of her character?

I grew up believing that whatever job I got would say something about who I was—my identity, my abilities, my interests. But the more time I spent in the working world, the more I realized that's often not the case. We might take a job because we have limited opportunities or because a job meets our needs even if it doesn't match our passions. I love that Maggie pushes back against the idea that we need to define ourselves by our jobs. I hope she makes anyone who feels lost or stuck realize that they are so much more than that thing they do to make rent and pay bills. It's okay to find fulfillment elsewhere.

Edward Bell is, frankly, a terrible guy. How did you dream him up?

I do love having at least one terrible person in my books. In the first draft, Edward Bell was actually Bell River's terrible, eccentric founder, but my editors smartly realized it would be more interesting if he were an author—especially because it would tie in so nicely with the bookstore setting. And they were right! I had fun diving into Edward Bell's character—mostly by thinking back on revered classic authors and imagining what dark secrets they might be hiding.

Maggie and Malcolm get drinks at Tome, an imaginary book-themed bar... Do you have any real-life recommendations for bookish destinations?

Novela is a bar in San Francisco where you can enjoy cocktails named after book characters. I attended a few happy hours there, where I'd stare at the glowing wall of colorful books and fantasize about touching one. (I did not, because I am not Maggie.)

Bell River, while a fictional town, is such an important part of the story. Why did you choose it as a setting?

A fictional author must hail from a fictional town, at least if I wanted to make my life a little bit easier! I loved creating the town of Bell River. I started writing this novel in the summer of 2020, which was a strange and uncertain time. It was pure escapism to dream up a small town whose biggest problem was having a bookstore stuck in the past.

This is your second book, the first being *Must Love Books*. Was your approach to writing this one different than your first?

Very different. For one, this was book two in a two-book deal, so there was none of that *this won't amount to anything* mindset that dominated the writing of my first novel. This book *had* to amount to something. A publisher had already bought it! And I was desperate not to disappoint! While *Must Love Books* was written in brief periods over the course of a few years, I wrote the first draft of this book in about two months, nearly a year before it was due. As with my first novel, there were moments when I felt like I had no idea what I was doing. I've been told that feeling doesn't go away, no matter how many books you write. Which is unfortunate.

This novel is almost an ode to the kinds of books people love but that don't get as much respect as classics (i.e. romance, horror, mysteries, science fiction, etc.). Why did you choose to explore this as a theme?

It reflects my own reading journey, in a way. I grew up reading a ton of middle grade and young adult novels. As I got older, I moved on to reading exclusively literary classics, because I was a Serious English Major and that's what Serious English Majors do. I'd been disappointed to reach adulthood and come to the (mistaken) realization that being an adult must mean I couldn't read YA anymore. It was thrilling to discover I could actually read whatever I wanted. I still love classics—they make me feel connected to all the booklovers throughout time who have read and loved these books that have been around for centuries. But it was freeing to expand my reading horizons and realize no book's genre or age category should be relegated to "guilty pleasure" if it's something that brings you joy.

Speaking of books we love—which books are on your To Be Read list right now?

How much time do we have? I've been eagerly awaiting *The Moment We Met* by Camille Baker for its mysterious dating app shenanigans, and Meredith Schorr's *As Seen on TV* looks like a fun twist on the small-town trope. I've also been excited to read *On Rotation* by Shirlene Obuobi, *The Fortunes of Jaded Women* by Carolyn Huynh, and *Long Past Summer* by Noué Kirwan.

Community is at the heart of this story. When did you realize this was so important to Maggie's journey?

Truth be told, I didn't! During the revision process, when I was still figuring out Maggie as a character, my editors were the ones who drew that connection for me. Up until that point, I knew Maggie was an extrovert with no career aspirations who loved bringing people together at her bookstore events—and that was about it. Then my editors pointed out that Maggie's love of the bookstore community could be just one thread in a greater desire to find and form community wherever she goes. After that, the rest of Maggie fit seamlessly into place. Characters don't typically come to me fully formed, and I'm grateful my editors could help me fill in the blanks of who Maggie is.

What's something you hope readers learn from *The Banned Bookshop of Maggie Banks*?

We spend a lot of time and energy trying to follow rules that don't exist. For some of us, these imaginary rules might dictate small things, like the types of books we think we're supposed to read. For others, these rules might govern bigger things, like milestones we think we need to reach by a certain age. But these rules aren't real. Taking a closer look at the rules we've set for ourselves—and deciding what to keep and what to discard—might, I hope, help each one of us forge a better, brighter path ahead.

ACKNOWLEDGMENTS

I'm grateful to Katelyn Detweiler for being unwaveringly enthusiastic when I told her about this book. I was so uncertain about it that I wrote it in secret, needing to see it on the page before I could know if it might amount to anything. Katelyn's excitement made me start to believe maybe this book could be a thing. Thank you also to the entire team at Jill Grinberg Literary, including but not limited to Sam Farkas, Sophia Seidner, and Denise Page. And thank you to Rukayat Giwa and the CAA team.

My editors, MJ Johnston and Jenna Jankowski, continue to be amazing partners in shaping my book. They sorted through my mess of an early draft and knew exactly which questions to ask and what suggestions to offer to completely transform this book for the better. Thank you as well to Jessica Thelander, Pam Jaffee, Margaret Coffee, Katie Stutz, Caitlin Lawler, and the rest of the Sourcebooks team for all that they do to make this book a reality.

This is stating the obvious, but: bookstores are really cool. Several years ago, I went to the Booksmith in San Francisco to attend Shipwreck, a monthly literary erotic fanfiction parody event. It was the weirdest and best thing I'd ever been to. Amy

Stephenson and Casey Childers did a wonderful thing in creating Shipwreck. These events brought so many people together and inspired me to write about the sense of community a bookstore can create. I'm grateful to Paloma Altamirano for going with me to my first event back in July 2013, and to Lily Miller for bringing me to so many more in the years that followed. While Shipwreck is currently no longer running, anyone curious can listen to the Shipwreck podcast (*Shipwreck SF*) or read the Shipwreck book, *Loose Lips*, for literary hilarity.

Thank you to my friends and family, whose support made this book possible. Thank you to the writing community for all your wisdom and support, especially the Lit Squad. And thank you Kate Reed and Bob Reed for being great.

My husband, Matt Hocker, was my sounding board throughout the drafting and revision process, listening to my ramblings, helping me brainstorm, and complying with my requests like an audience member at an improv show whenever I asked him for something out of the blue ("Give me a man's name," "Give me the name of a fictional restaurant," etc.). (For the record, the man's name Matt chose was Ralph, and the restaurant he named was the Salty Skillet.)

ABOUT THE AUTHOR

Photo © Rachel E.H. Photography

Shauna Robinson's love of books led her to try a career in publishing before deciding she'd rather write books instead. Originally from San Diego, she now lives in Virginia with her husband and their sleepy greyhound. Shauna is an introvert at heart—she spends most of her time reading, baking, and figuring out the politest way to avoid social interaction.